# Never Trust Home

An Exodus Novel

By Mister C.

1

# <u>*1*</u>

*Tulsa, Oklahoma - Sunday - 11:30 PM*
He was lost. He saw only what sat in front of him, everything else around him blurred and created a tunnel of light. Electronically locked doors barricaded him from seeing the most important person in his life. There were no windows carved into the doors, and nothing but a single agitated overnight clerk behind the counter standing in between him and his only refuge. His cellphone gave him nothing, the signal dead and scrambled by the hospital's radiation proof walls. The world around him swirled, collapsing in a vortex of possibilities. Anything was possible, and in the dull, white noise and commotion of the emergency room, nothing and everything made sense to him. The stress and strain of the situation justified answers that anyone else would find absolutely ridiculous.

It was driving him insane. He had to ground himself. He had to find the reality in the world around him. Something here had to hold him firmly in place. Something had to keep him from losing his mind.

The paper on the wall held his attention, telling him to watch for signs. He wasn't sure what signs he was supposed to watch for. He wasn't sure of anything anymore. Just that constant din around him, and the blinding lights overhead. *The signs; watch for signs. Call the number if you see the signs. 888-373-7888.* What signs was he supposed to search for? Why would he call the number? Who would answer the phone?

The letters on the sign refused to form words, until big bold letters across the top of the page informed him who was vulnerable, and how those people were lured in. *Lured in.* Manipulation, psychological abuse, physical abuse. He tried to read the smaller print, but his mind wandered, unfocused and fragile. The paper became a blur, wriggling in and out of focus like an old video camera. His eyes burned with a fire of exhaustion.

He was so lost.

He became conscious of the tension in the skin on his face. He tried to relax, his eyebrows dropping and releasing the tightness in his forehead, his jaw letting go of its intense bite on nothing but his own two rows of teeth.

He thought of that release, the one he needed to take the edge off. The one that could bring him back to the real world. *Release. Release. Strong, passionate release.* He glanced around, unsure how to get that here. He could take out his phone, sure, but he needed something else to come out. That wasn't acceptable in public. *Bathroom. Go to the bathroom. No one will think otherwise of you.*

"Mr. Langley?" A voice came from the counter. A long, Oklahoma drawl that sounded tired. He looked over, where that underpaid, overworked clerk behind the counter was waving him over. Mr. Langley; that was him. She was talking to him. It really was all real. He could come back to reality. He rose from his chair, unsure if she was really in a good enough mood to speak to him. "You can see him if you want."

Her attitude told him his assumption of her mood was correct, but who wouldn't be in a bad mood working this job at this time of night? Mr. Langley had seen the people coming and going. Alcoholics, drug addicts, and late night arrests. Two police escorts towing a prisoner around. He'd seen three of those so far. Not easy people to deal with at all, especially with little or no sleep.

He glanced at one of the outside windows to the parking lot, a younger man in boot cut jeans and a fitted t-shirt stared back at him in the reflection. Thick, dark brown hiking boots peeked out from the cuffs of those pants; comfortable and practical. Waving locks of brown dangled over his face, nearly connecting to his eyebrows, staring down at a healthy, muscular physique that stood out in a lobby full of obesity and sickness.

An athlete? No, athletes wore sneakers and held themselves up more confidently. A soldier? Of course not. Soldiers kept their hair buzzed and wore lighter colors. Coyote tans, olive greens, and camouflage as well as combat boots. Nothing about him matched.

Who was he? Even he wasn't sure right now. Nothing made sense.

*Blend in.* That was all he knew. It was the only thing in his head. The least he could do was try to blend in. *Go unnoticed; go unthreatened; go undetected. Fly under the radar. No one will even know you're there.*

"Room 113," the clerk told him as the double doors clicked loudly and opened to his left.

"Thank you." Soft, quiet, barely audible. Meek, mild, and distraught. Abnormal sounding to his own ears. Not matching with the strong body underneath his head. Not blending in.

*Get it together. Blend in.*

The doors almost closed before he was through. His motions dragged like he was walking through water. He shook his head to clear the brain fog, and continued walking down the hall. *Focus!*

Room 113. That was what he had to focus on: the numbers. That was all that mattered. Something real; something to ground himself in. 113.

This part of the hospital was eerily quiet. No people; no sounds. Not even the sound of his own breathing. Just his body; his existence. Just an empty shell, and room 113 at the end of the hall.

He saw the number on the door, almost looking like an apartment number. The placard, dull grey and perfectly square, told him he was in the right spot. The door handle turned slowly under the weight of his fingers, and the hinges turned on themselves without resistance, allowing him entry, quietly letting him in.

Quiet except for the monitors across the room. They were loud. Alarms blared at him constantly, ringing in his ears. Loud beeping, like a seat belt warning alarm, called for help. There were more numbers, too, things that he could see. Ridiculous numbers that made no sense. Numbers on an LCD screen that blinked red, warning of danger.

> *BP = 225/115*
> *BPM = 132*
> *BO = 90%*

Numbers that he couldn't reconcile. 113 made sense. First floor, thirteenth room. These numbers on the monitor didn't seem right. Blood pressure? 225/115? Resting heart rate of 132? Blood Oxygen Percentage of 90? It sounded impossible. Those numbers were fatal in medical textbooks.

Why did he know that? He'd never been to college. He hadn't even finished high school. What was the point of useless knowledge like that?

"I'm okay, kiddo." The wheezing, raspy voice came from the thing in the bed. The… man on the bed. Unrecognizable, looking like a monstrous blob that had tassels coming off of him. *IV lines. Electronic sensor wires. A ventilator tube, and a mask.* The mask hung off to the side of the head, exposing the face of his father.

"I'm twenty five. I'm not a kid."

"You are my kid," replied the man on the bed. "Get used to it."

"Charles Langley," said the younger man, more to himself than to the old man in the bed. He checked his watch. "It's eleven forty seven at night.

I'm in the emergency room of Ascension Saint John in Tulsa."

"You're grounded." The older man on the bed covered in hoses and wires chuckled at the double meaning. Charles had picked up the exercise from a psychology show, grounding himself in reality every so often like he was going insane. "You're not losing your mind."

"It doesn't seem real," said Charles. "It doesn't make sense."

"No," replied the old man. "It doesn't seem real, does it?"

The old man wasn't really that old. Forty five couldn't have been that old in the modern world. He was just out of shape. Very out of shape. He had been out of shape for as long as Charles could remember. There was a gap in that memory, a missing spot of emptiness that told him nothing of the old man. There was the image of him, dark headed, average sized, and baby faced, and now there was this. This was four hundred pounds of carbonation, sugars, and fats. This was a wrinkly bag covered in sparse grey patches of hair.

This was monstrous.

"Those numbers are bad," said Charles, almost unaware of what his father had said. He was still unable to peel his eyes from the screen.

"I'm having a heart attack, son," replied his father. "If the numbers were good, we wouldn't be here at the emergency room. Where's Abigail?"

"Home."

"Yours or hers?"

Charles smirked, and shook his head. "Her home is not my home. You know that."

A look of confusion crossed his father's face. "She wasn't with you tonight?"

"It's Sunday." Charles glanced away from the screen for a brief moment, but his eyes were inadvertently drawn back. "We both work in the morning."

"Damn," sighed the old man. "I forgot you have to be up tomorrow. I'm sorry."

"You didn't choose to have a heart attack."

The old man looked down at his body, so big it hung off the side of the bed.

"I'm probably pushing four hundred pounds," he said softly. "I pretty much did choose to have a heart attack." His eyes trailed up to his son again. "You're doing good taking care of yourself. You'll probably skip your workout tomorrow and still be fine."

"I can't do that," muttered Charles. "You know that."

"I do," replied the old man. "I don't know why you can't, but I know it."

Charles was silent, then, "me neither."

His thoughts told him otherwise. They pleaded to spill truths. He wouldn't let them. Not right now. The old man had too much going on right now. *So lost. So lost. Need to focus.*

The old man smiled again. "Did you even tell Abigail we were here?"

"She's sleeping," said Charles. "I don't want to disturb her."

The old man laughed, a cackle that turned into a viscous and mucousy cough. "She will be much more upset if you don't wake her up, than if you do."

Charles knew that, but something in him forced his hand. He was certain she would want to know, but even more so, he was certain he didn't want to wake her up with this. Something inside him told him she didn't care. She would rather be sleeping, and he knew it. It didn't make any sense to him, but he couldn't convince himself otherwise.

He was so lost.

"We aren't even together," he said out loud. "We're just friends."

"You grew up together," said the old man. "She's over at your house several times a week. I think that counts as more than just friends."

*More than friends involves intimacy. More than friends involves affection. She won't open up. She won't touch me.*

*Not now. He has too much going on. He doesn't need more.*

"I hadn't seen her in ten whole years," said Charles out loud. "That was before this last January. A lot happened, in those ten years, to both of us. It's only been a few months. We're still getting warmed up to each other."

Even to Charles, though, a few months felt like a long time to get warmed up. Especially for old friends. *Why won't she touch me? What's wrong with me?*

"You've grown, is what happened," said the old man. "I think you're better for it. Even through the struggle of everything you've been through. Look at you now."

"I'm an ex-convict working in a factory," said Charles. "She's done all of her training in the National Guard and is halfway through medical school to be a trauma surgeon. She's stooping to my level just associating with me."

"I see through all that on the surface," said the old man, waving his hand like he was casting a spell, "the woeful pity party you lead on. There's more to you than that. There always has been. You've never been who you pretend to be on the surface. You've never been much of an actor, either, and you've never been a good liar. Are you still doing your spy drills?"

Charles nodded. "Nothing else to do."

"It's a weird hobby."

Charles sat down in a chair against the wall and put his face in his hands. *More to the story.* There was always more to the story. So much going on in the world around him. He was so lost. *Not here; not now. He doesn't need the extra strain.*

"I have a lot going on," he said. "Work, Abigail, and now this. It's a lot to process."

"You do have a lot to process," said the old man, "and I know I'm part of the reason for it, even before now. I've always kind of been the cause of your trouble. I just worry that you won't process it before it processes you."

Charles rolled his eyes, and sat back in his chair. "What did the doctors tell you, wise old Buddha?"

The old man's eyes dropped. His whole face seemed to sag an inch or more. "They're going to keep me overnight to start with. I'm not in immediate danger, but they want to run tests in the morning. Calcium build up and plaque in my arteries kind of stuff. They want to assess my risk of another heart attack and advise how I should move forward with my health."

He looked down at his overweight figure again. "I'm guessing I'm not going to like what they tell me. Why don't you go home, Charles? Get some rest. You've done what you can, now let the doctors take care of the rest."

Charles Langley stared hard at the screen of high numbers, and decided that he had, in fact, done all he could for now. His body ached from lifting the old man from the couch and dragging him to the truck, and carrying him in and trying to get him checked in. That had been all he could do. He wasn't a doctor. All he could do now was wait, and it was better to wait at home in bed.

If he could sleep at all.

"Okay," he said with a sigh. "There's nothing I can do."

Saying it out loud always made it easier for him to understand. Nothing about this was easy to understand, but saying it out loud helped. It made it real.

# 2

*Tulsa, Oklahoma - Monday - 12:00 AM*
Walter Faucet walked through the sliding doors of the hospital, having to turn his body to avoid hitting the slowly creeping frames. He rushed to the counter, determined not to be passed off. His man was in the back, injured and alone. That man had been identified during the operation, and that put him in danger. Walter had to remedy that.

The lady behind the computer screen glared up at him as if she didn't want to accept his existence. Trying not to blame her for it, he maintained his composure, a natural part of his life now after years of practice at work, and pleaded with his eyes.

"Jimmy Limone," he said quietly. "He should be here. Checked in a few hours ago with a broken arm. I wanted to check on him."

The board of directors would be furious with this one. These kinds of things weren't supposed to happen on operations. There was always a plan in case something like this did happen, but that plan was simply to end the operation and tend to the injured. Bad guys would get away, and tonight they had.

Everything was supposed to go smoothly. Things like this cost money, and money was hard to come by in his world. In a split second, however, everything tonight had been shut down due to a broken arm. They hadn't even caught their man. The bad guys had gotten away. So many months of chasing them all down, and here they were defeated in the hospital.

"Mr. Limone is in room 114," said the woman behind the computer screen. "He should be ready for release very soon."

"Is it okay if I go see him?" asked Walter.

"As long as it's just you." She shrugged like she didn't want to argue, and reached under the desk. Walter heard a clicking sound. The big wooden doors beside him swung open silently, allowing him to push through into the long, empty hallway behind it.

"Thank you," he told her as he passed the open door to the office she was in. "I can't thank you enough."

"No one ever can."

Room 114. He had to get to Jimmy. He had to provide protection, and support. Not for Jimmy, though, Jimmy was fine, but for everyone around him. He had to keep Jimmy calm. Jimmy had been so close to catching this guy, and then…

The door opened at the end of the hallway, and a woman in a white doctor's coat rolled a big, burly man out of the room in a wheelchair. A beet red face stared backwards at the nurse, a thick neck twisted around to give the man a better angle of what he was yelling at.

Walter had just enough time to spot the door number as it swung out of view. 114.

"Goddammit!" squawked the man in the wheelchair, a thick New Jersey accent breaking the silence of the hallway. "It's my arm that's broken, not my leg. Let me walk."

"Hospital policy," mumbled the poor nurse behind him. Her face was scrunched, her eyes squinted and shining.

"She's just doing her job, Jimmy," Walter said as he approached. "I can take it from here, ma'am."

The nurse was all too happy to let the belligerent man she was pushing go into someone else's care, whether it was hospital policy or not. In fact, she vanished before Walter had finished speaking.

"Walt," said Jimmy, standing up from the rolling and unstable wheelchair. "Let's get out of here. We have work to do."

"You won't be doing anything," said Walter. "You're in a sling, and you've been ID'd as an undercover. Besides, what are we going to get done at midnight?"

"I have a description of the guy that broke my arm," said Jimmy. "We get him, and we can crack this whole thing open."

"You think we aren't already looking for him?" asked Walter. "We'll give the sketch artist something, but it'll be tough to pin him down without a name."

"We were so close," Jimmy muttered, rolling his eyes, and sighing. He grabbed on to

Walter with his good arm to balance himself as the wheelchair rolled away from him. "We had him. We were doing so good. I don't even know why he broke my arm. He just did it out of nowhere. Now we've lost our only lead to our guy, and we don't even have any names, or addresses, or anything. It got so out of hand so fast, and it was our first try."

He took a deep breath, trying to calm himself. "I bet the higher ups are pissed."

"I haven't been answering their calls," mumbled Walter. "It's amazing how fast word reaches old people in the dead of night like this, but I would imagine they are less than pleased with our current results."

"We don't have any good help," groaned Jimmy. "That's why it's all gone bad so far. It's hard to get my team into deep cover when three out of four of us are women, and one of us isn't even part of the investigation. Just like tonight, I end up doing most of the heavy lifting myself while the others sit with the recovery team. As a result, I'm the one that gets hurt, and now my team is out altogether."

"I know," muttered Walter. "I'm having trouble finding help. Times are not easy right now for anyone, so it's not easy to find volunteer contractors who want to risk their lives. What we do is more of a moral battle than a fiscal one."

"Thrill junkies," muttered Jimmy. "High risk, low reward. We're a bunch of idiots, aren't we?"

Walter couldn't help but smile. *We are, by definition, idiots.*

The door adjacent to them opened, room 113, and a young man exited the room. He nodded towards Jimmy and Walter, dropping his eyes to avoid eye contact before drifting around them so fast Walter barely got a look at him.

"Hey, buddy," Jimmy called after the young man, winking at Walter. "How old are you?"

The young man hesitated, and glanced back at them. A set of deep blue eyes stared back at them. "Mid twenties?"

"Damn," sighed Jimmy. "We can't take anyone under thirty. Sorry." Jimmy turned to Walter. "Just thought I'd start asking anyone, you know?"

The young man turned back to the exit, continued on for three long strides, and stopped in his tracks. Slowly, drawing the attention of Walter and Jimmy, the young man turned to face them. "Why thirty?"

Walter smiled. "He was kidding. We're just short on help right now and it's hard to find good people who will go through our recruiting process and stick with the job."

"What process, and job, is that?" asked the young man, stepping closer to them.

"Do you have any experience in undercover operations?" asked Jimmy, taking off with the process immediately. "We prefer ex-CIA, but any law enforcement experience is good."

The young man nodded as if Jimmy's remark about the CIA hadn't phased him. "Hence the age requirement. It gives the new recruit time to gather experience in the field. What kind of operations do you run?"

*No answer.* A tell tale sign of special operations and intelligence officers was that they didn't talk about what they did, even when asked about it.

Mid twenties didn't seem like an old enough age for that kind of job. Military right out of high school? College at Westpoint? Graduation into the CIA? Walter tried to do the math in his head. Two years of military training, four years of college, two years for Masters, and a couple of years in intelligence. It was possible. He'd have to be mid twenties just starting out in that line. Eighteen to twenty six just to get the spot.

Then what was he doing in the middle of Oklahoma?

"Listen," said Walter, reaching into his pocket and pulling out a small business card, "if you're seriously looking, call our recruiting office and see what you can contribute. Our business isn't exactly a lucrative one, and we really do have a tedious recruiting process. There's a lot of stress in doing this job. You might not like it, and you won't get rich doing it."

"Maybe I'm not looking to get rich," mumbled the young man, taking the card and reading it over. "The Red Sea Initiative?"

Walter had to shake his head. *What kind of person isn't looking to get rich?*

*People like us aren't.* How had Walter felt a decade ago when he'd been on the Mexico border staring into the eyes of the first predator he'd met in person. He'd felt like the floor had been swept out from under him. His world had turned upside down, and his sense of purpose? It had become a misty grey net that obscured his whole existence. The Red Sea Initiative had solved that for him.

The wooden doors at the end of the hallway opened again, and Walter saw two police officers, a man and a woman, leading a large man through the opening. The prisoner they were escorting was tall and bulky, the bodybuilder type, and covered in tattoos. He wore the prison orange jumpsuit, and had handcuffs with long chains on his wrists and ankles. He was bleeding from the nose and smiling. Not far down the hall, the prisoner locked eyes with Walter.

Then he went ballistic.

The prisoner thrusted himself sideways into the police officer closest to the wall, driving his head down into the side of the officer's head and knocking the officer unconscious. The female officer on his other side was dragged into the fray, helpless against the chains and cuffs that the prisoner began wrapping around her neck.

She squealed as the man squeezed the chains around her throat. Walter darted past the young man with a useless Jimmy in tow, racing for the end of the hallway before the police officers were seriously injured or killed. The female officer kicked the prisoner in the groin and spun out of his chains, but the man recovered before she could get away. His hands reached up to her throat, lifting her off the ground. He pushed her body against the wall and pressed upward, the demonic smile on his face reaching from ear to ear.

Walter was ten feet away now, watching as life seeped from the officer's eyes. Her face began to turn purple as he moved in. Three nurses came out of the office up front to help, but none of them were moving fast enough. That police officer's eyes were already rolling up into her head.

A flash of motion passed into view. The prisoner's left hand was twisted, and rotated internally. His left arm was pulled away from the officer's throat and stretched outward, forcing his other hand to drag her down with him as the arm under control was stretched out and driven downward onto the ground. Between two of Walter's running strides, three hundred pounds of violent convict came tumbling to the floor. Another scream pierced the air. The sound was unmanly and terrifying. It sounded like the female officer's squeals.

It was the prisoner, screaming in pain.

Walter skidded to a halt, along with the surrounding nurses. Standing at the end of that outstretched arm, holding the wrist in a bent and excruciating angle, was the young man from the other end of the hallway.

The young man held the prisoner's left hand in his grip, twisting with his bodyweight and using a foot against the prisoner's ribs as leverage to hold the man pressed on the ground. The criminal held on to the female police officer's throat with one hand as the young man tore the prisoner's other arm. Walter could hear the bones cracking in the prisoner's wrist, and see tendons and muscles shifting in his arms underneath his skin.

The young man's voice was low and soft, calm and collected. "Let her go, or lose your arm."

"Sir," called one of the nurses. Her face said the rest. Her wide eyes peered out of scrunched eyebrows, her mouth gaped with lips that peeled back to expose her teeth.

The prisoner's free hand slipped from the police officer's throat, and she scampered away. The nurses on the other side of the fray grabbed the woman and pulled her to safety, immediately checking her injuries. A red line and an irritated bruise colored her throat.

The young man restraining the prisoner didn't move.

Walter stepped over to the unconscious police officer by the wall and grabbed the man's taser, his fingers naturally going through the motions of releasing the weapon from its holster. He stood up and aimed the taser at the prisoner on the ground, signaling for the young man to release him.

The young man did not move.

"If I tase him while you're holding him," Walter said calmly, "you'll get zapped, too. He's going to go nuts when you let him go, so I'm probably going to have to tase him. I need you to let him go so you aren't affected."

Again, the young man did not move.

"Let me go!" groaned the man on the floor, whining at the flexion of his arm past its natural ability.

Walter slipped his finger into the trigger guard of the taser and took careful aim, waiting for the release.

The young man did not let go. Walter eyed the positioning of everything carefully, considering the speed and ferocity the young man had used to gain the upper hand.

*Training. Years of training. A lifetime of training.*

The young man's eyes burned a fiery blue, glowing in the hallway light, the eyelids relaxed and the nose barely pinched up. His jaw looked clenched, but the muscle flexion in his arms seemed non-existent. Walter was certain the young man was capable of ripping the prisoner's arm off of his shoulder.

He wasn't so sure the young man wasn't going to do it anyways.

Walter shifted his aim an inch, the prongs of the taser moving towards the young man. He felt moisture on his forehead. The nurses around him glanced at each other, all of them stiff and breathing heavily. He only had one shot, and there were two threats. He wasn't sure which one was more dangerous.

"Charles!" A voice shouted from the end of the hall behind Walter. He turned to look.

An older man in his late forties, a very overweight man hooked up to more cables than a breaker box, was standing in the doorframe of the room the young man had exited from moments earlier. Room 113. His peppered grey hair and nearly white beard reflected the hallway light, but it was his eyes that drew Walter's attention. Blue as the ocean. He could see it from down the hall.

"Charles," the older man repeated, calmer now that he had everyone's attention. "He let her go; he doesn't have to lose his arm."

It was over faster than it had begun. The prisoner's hand slipped from Charles's grip, and Charles used the foot on the man's ribs to push himself away, creating distance from the enemy. His foot came down in position, arms up, and palms facing forward with claw-like fingers.

*A fighting stance.*

Then his whole body relaxed. Walter recognized it immediately. He'd seen it several times in training and in different law enforcement and private investigator classes. He'd seen his own operators train in it many times.

*He's studied martial arts.* It looked like Aikido, or maybe Judo. Use of the weak points of the human body to control and manipulate. It looked professional. It looked expert. *Years and years of training.*

Who was this guy?

The prisoner laid still on the floor, his chains falling silent as his arm flopped to the ground. A soft groan of pain rose from the tile flooring. Walter kept his aim with the taser trained on the prisoner's back, his threat now decided. The female police officer stumbled up to her feet. Her body followed her hands over to her partner's body, where another nurse was checking his vitals. Her eyes darted to the prisoner on the ground, who spun his head to look up at Charles. Charles stared back at the prisoner, his expression neutral; his eyes calm.

*No fear.* Speed, efficiency, and brutality. The mixture of things that gave away a professional. Someone who had experience in fighting not just in competition, but out here in the wild. Walter looked at Charles's fingers and hands. They were steady. No shake; no tremble.

*Who is this guy?*

Mid-twenties, or not, Charles handled pressure better than Walter had ever seen anyone do before. How many people had gone through recruiting and failed, how many ex-cops and ex-special forces had cracked under pressure?

*Only professionals avoid talking about what they do, and Charles had avoided the question like the plague.*

The floor blurred. A swift motion distracted him from his thoughts. Movement in front of him. Someone scrambling to their feet. Someone growling; someone roaring. Someone huge, orange, and covered in inky pictures instead of pale skin.

His training kicked in, and he pulled the trigger on the taser.

# <u>3</u>

*Tulsa, Oklahoma - Monday - 5:30 AM*
*Watch for signs.* Walter's card told him the same thing the sign at the hospital had told him, except the card elaborated on the point. *Education. Awareness. Action.* A picture of a face. A little girl's face. She was a toddler; no older than three or four years old. Southeast Asian. She had a darker complexion, a smooth, shining face that reflected the rays of light edited into the picture. The person walking in front of her had been blurred, creating a dramatic action movie effect. At the bottom corner of the card was a small, square QR code that led to a website.

**Follow the link for details.**

Up, and down. Charles Langley's body flattened on the ground, then rose as if levitating. His arms pushed, and relaxed. *One hundred.* Go until failure. Go for the goal.

The Army Ranger workout plan on the Army's website contained mostly pushups and situps in massive sets of fifty reps, half mile sprints, and five mile runs. There were pull ups, and standard cardio sessions. A twelve mile march in full ruck; forty five to sixty pounds of gear not including weapons and ammunition.

He could see the details from where he was on the floor. The paper with the twelve week program of exercises to prepare for Ranger School was hung on the same poster board that he hung Walter's card on.

**The Red Sea Initiative**

The Army Ranger Training Program was his benchmark. He had to have one. A goal. A milestone. Something to push for. *A purpose.*

Now he was looking at the business card for the Red Sea Initiative. It was the same as the sign in the hospital. *Watch for signs.* Education. Awareness. Action.

Walter's voice reverberated in his head. *You don't get rich doing what we do. It's a very tedious recruiting process.*

Special operations, maybe? Undercover, for sure. That would explain the elimination process. Weed out the weak that aren't cut out for that kind of thing, and beef up the ones that could handle it. That kept everyone in the field safe with professionals that knew what they were doing.

Why did he know that? It wasn't part of his job to know things like that. He had just learned it while searching.

*Searching. A purpose.*

A jingle from behind him. Some sort of music. A piano nocturne. Deep bass notes climbing up and rolling down. The high pitched melody in a minor key sang a dark tone. He knew it; it was his ringtone on his phone. He only knew one person that would call him, especially at five in the morning. Besides, there were only two people he ever spoke with in general.

He stopped at the peak of his next pushup, brought up a toe underneath his body, and pushed himself back to his feet. Failure in exercise could wait when it came to her. He cared more about her, regardless of how she felt about him.

"Abby?" He asked after pressing the green icon on his phone screen. "It's a little early."

"Your father just texted me." It sounded like it had been said through clenched teeth. "Why didn't you call me?"

"I guess that means he's okay," said Charles.

"Why didn't you call me?"

He sighed. "You know why. I didn't want to wake you up in the middle of the night."

"I would have been fine getting that call," growled the female voice on the phone. "Instead, I get to hear it from the man in the hospital hours after it happened."

"Everyone says that they don't mind," said Charles, "in practice, it's better to let people sleep. You couldn't have done anything anyways."

He heard Abigail swear on the other end of the line. Then she took a deep breath. "Okay, you win this round. Is he at least okay?"

"He's okay enough to text you."

"That's not what I meant."

"They're running tests on him today," replied Charles. "They'll keep him for a little bit, and make sure he's stabilized. Then he'll have to go through some lifestyle changes and maybe a surgery or two."

"Oh my God," said Abigail. "Charles, I'm sorry."

"You have nothing to be sorry for," he replied. "It's not your fault. It would be nice to see you for dinner, though. What time do you get off tonight?"

"Before you do," she said. "You know that. That's the perk of not working in a factory. I'll come into town, pick something up, and meet you at your apartment at seven?"

"That works," said Charles. "I should be showered and dressed by then. What's for dinner?"

"Chinese," replied Abigail. "If I know anything about you, I know you love oriental food, or at least the American version. Hey, I've got to get ready for work. Anything else I should know?"

Charles glanced over at Walter's business card on the poster board. *Education. Awareness. Action.*

*Not yet. Too much else going on.*

"Not at the moment. I'll text you if I get any updates."

"Thank you."

*Education. Awareness. Action.* Three steps to take. The first was education.

His phone camera picked up the QR code instantly. The website appeared on his screen in a mere few seconds.

**The Red Sea Initiative**
**WE ENVISION A WORLD IN WHICH HUMANS ARE NEVER BOUGHT, SOLD, OR EXPLOITED.**

**Our Mission:** *We disrupt the darkness of modern-day slavery by partnering with law enforcement to fight human trafficking crime, equipping communities to protect the vulnerable, and empowering survivors as they walk into freedom.*

### <u>DONATE NOW</u>
### <u>FREE ONLINE TRAINING: LEARN TO FIGHT HUMAN TRAFFICKING IN FIFTEEN MINUTES.</u>

Links to give money, and links to learn more. *Education. Awareness. Action.* It was the first step and it only took fifteen minutes. He checked his watch. *Work in an hour and a half, twenty minutes of drive time, ten minutes to shower, another ten minutes to get everything else ready.* Fifteen minutes wasn't even pushing the limit.

He guessed he really could skip the rest of his workout for this. This was important.

Without reading further, Charles clicked the link, and opened the online training course.

# <u>*4*</u>

*Tulsa, Oklahoma - Monday - 8:00 AM*

Soft, smooth bed sheets laid beneath her. A huge improvement from yesterday's workplace. Weak rays of sunlight peered through the cracks in the curtains on the window. Dark reds and blues surrounded her, a moody glow from the linens and the walls.

The rustling of paper money came from in front of her, the door to the room allowing a sliver of light to shine in on her face. It would be the only warmth she felt.

She could count the bills without looking. Ten. Ten of those little *slip slip*'s of the money being counted. That could be ten dollars, it could be a thousand. She wasn't sure. It didn't matter. What came next was what really mattered.

"Thanks for your business." Joseph's voice from the door. "Enjoy."

*Joseph.* Her own internal voice spat the word in pure disgust like it was an insult. He enjoyed his chosen names that turned her insides over and left a bad taste in her mouth, but her mind and her thoughts still belonged to her. He couldn't take those away from her. Inside of her head, he was still Joseph.

*Olivia. My name is Olivia.* She had to remember who she was. It was all she had left. She was Olivia, and no one else could steal that from her. It helped her cope with the things she was about to do.

There was the sound of the door shutting. The soft, padded sound of footsteps on carpet. Soft breathing from in front of her.

A "friend" has come to visit.

A figure steps into the light. A black earpiece hangs from one of his ears. He wears a black suit coat, a white shirt, and black dress pants. A black neck tie hangs down the front of his body. The coat comes off as he steps to her left, and it falls onto the bed. A short, white beard points upward, making room as his hands remove the tie. Slicked back grey hair that starts in the middle to the top of his head, shakes as the man stretches his neck. Fingers fiddle with his wrists, the cuffs of his long sleeves popping open and making room for his arms to slip out.

The memory fades away as fast as it begins, the man and his actions tucking themselves away in the back of her mind. She hates what he does; her only option is to sweep it away and hide it. She has to keep her composure.

*Remember who you are. You are Olivia, not anyone else. You are still a person.*

But her day has only begun.

A middle aged man enters the room, his bright orange and yellow vest making him look like a crossing guard. He takes off a yellow helmet, and reaches across his body to his left hand. He removes a ring from the finger next to his pinkie. A smile crosses his face. He drops the ring into the chest pocket of the vest and runs his hands down the reflective yellow stripes on his sides like he's dusting himself off.

His image fades away as well, his fantasies bleeding over into her own as she's forced to portray a lost child separated from her family.

Except she doesn't have to pretend.

A very tall and thin man in a floral Hawaiian shirt approaches, his sunken cheeks sinking deeper as his lips pucker into a kiss. One button at a time, he undoes his shirt, and dead eyes peer down at her. It seems like only a few seconds until he is gone, the pain in between her legs forcing her to remain lying on her side.

A married couple, massive happy smiles crossing their faces, hold hands on either side of her, awaiting their own fantasies of having a loving relationship with the daughter they never had. Too loving, too physically affectionate, from the woman. Too rough, and too painful, from the man. They leave satisfied that they've done what they can to care for their "little girl."

A man in a white coat, a doctor with a stethoscope still hanging over his shoulders, leans over her with a disapproving grunt. His scowl grows larger as he bends forward, his face coming closer and closer to her hair. His nose touches her ear, and she hears him sniff, taking a deep breath and inhaling her smell. He exhales with a disgusting sigh, his eyes closing and his shoulders slumping.

A doctor that knows the human body; a doctor that likes to explore. A man with a sick mind that only thinks of its own pleasure.

A very old man in a black robe is next. He is barely visible in the dim light as he comes in and sits down in a chair next to the bed. He is balding; a very sweet faced man with a red stripe in between the ends of his robe. Some sort of sash, maybe?

He smiles, his hand reaching up to his neck to pull at the white collar tucked into the neck of his robe.

"I forgive you child," he says quietly, "let me purge you of your demons."

It doesn't feel like she's being purged. Instead, it feels as if he's purging himself, and she's being filled with his demons, demons that will haunt her nightmares for the rest of her life.

A nervous woman follows, large, heavy, and wringing her hands. All this woman wants is to love her daughter, the one that left home not too long ago. The woman is touchy with the little girl, feeling every inch of the girl's body and talking about how it compares to her daughter's. The woman comments on the little girl's developing body, telling her she's going to be a big girl one day. This woman is the only friend of the day that doesn't hurt the little girl, *Olivia,* but her prying fingers send chills all over the little girl's body.

The physical discomfort is just as bad as the pain.

Heavy footsteps fall again, a man in a tank top with a bulging chest and massive arms comes to the bed. He is covered in tattoos, and his long black hair is streaked with grease and gel. He rolls his shoulders like he's warming up to lift something heavy, his fingers tugging at his white basketball shorts. With an angry look on his face, his hands fly up to his neck and remove a gold necklace with a shark tooth attached to it. He lets out a deep breath, the rage and violence seeping out of him like an overfilled bathtub.

She feels that rage as he expresses it in the only way a man can with a girl half his size.

An olive green t-shirt, and light tan cargo pants. A silver chain around his neck with little tabs at the end that jingle like bells when he moves. He is almost bald, with just a single thin layer of hair growing at the top of his head. He is huge, a man with a lot of time on his hands to work out. A man that trains for any situation. A man so desperate for the affection of a female, that he finds it in this nine year old girl. He is not violent. He is loving and caring, but he is an older, fully grown man, and his fully grown man parts are still painful to her woefully underdeveloped body. He is a soldier with no one to gratify him; all he wants is love.

She is just too young and small to give it to him.

People come and go. All ages, from young men who go to college to old men that can barely stand on their own. Every color and shade of skin, short or tall, thin to fat, man or woman. There are people working all sorts of jobs, and coming from all reaches of life. She sees the toothless people that smell like skunk and alcohol. She sees the man in the suit sniffing white powder off of the smooth surface of her midriff. Each friend takes their time in taking what they want from the little girl. Some want to take the stress of a long day out on someone. Some want to be loved. Some just seek company.

She doesn't enjoy one single moment of it. She doesn't understand most of it. All she feels is pain, fear, and despair.

*Olivia. You are Olivia. You are human. You are still human. You are not just an object.*

As the mantra repeats in her head, the memories she has of lying still and taking it like she's told resurface, and she's reminded that sometimes she is just an object. To some people, she's not human.

Tears run down her cheeks as she stares at the curtains, seeing the pink sky behind dark grey clouds.

*Sunset.* It's all she can think of while trying to forget the things that were done to her that day. It is a never ending cycle of horrific memories, and haunting nightmares. She sniffs loudly, sobbing out choppy breaths, each strain of her breathing sending sharp pains from the bottom of her ribs down to the middle of her thighs.

The door opens. A man enters the room. It is the last person she wants to see.

"Let's go home, sweetie," says Joseph, holding the door open for the little girl, the child, *Olivia.* "We have a lot more work to do tomorrow."

He never uses her name. He never treats her like she means something to him. He treats her like an object.

Olivia sniffs again, pinching her eyes shut and wishing to wake up from this awful nightmare.

"Daddy," she begs, using the only name she is allowed to call him, "please don't make me do this again."

The response is cold, angry, and firm. "Let's go."

With no choice left, Olivia rises from the bed, limping over to the open door and trying to straighten out her back. She has to make appearances for the public. She's not allowed to raise suspicion. The pain in her abdomen is too much for her to handle, and she is forced to remain slumped over. Joseph takes her to the stairs, walking her out of the building in a way where no people will see them.

Those that do see them, never question anything about them. Society has taught them not to interfere.

# <u>5</u>

*Tulsa, Oklahoma - Monday - 12:00 PM*
It was a disaster. Clothes were strewn out of the side
of the open suitcase like it had vomited them up.
The sheets had been stripped and piled next to the
bed like a massacre. Two people stood at either end
of the carnage, squaring off with equally threatening
expressions.

"Kitsen, pick up your jammies."

"I don't want to," shouted the eight year old
girl with a violent thrust of her upper body. Her
arms remained crossed, and she kept her seat placed
firmly on the toppled suitcase.

Walter resisted the urge to roll his eyes,
almost causing him physical strain. Pedophiles and
human traffickers were no problem to handle, but
an enraged eight year old that wasn't getting what
she wanted was a whole different story. He stepped
carefully around the debris of the chaos at his feet,
moved closer to his daughter, and reached out. He
gripped her with a hand on each of her arms and
stared down at her.

"It's just a week," he said quietly, holding
fierce eye contact with the little demon. "Then we
can go home. Daddy has to go teach people how to

save the world, you don't have to go to school, and you get to learn a little bit of cool stuff, too."

Kitsen shook her head, wet, dark blonde hair flapping around her head like the arms of an octopus, and tried to shake her father's hands off of her. It was always obvious that, as a child, she didn't want to watch a bunch of people she didn't know run drills and sit in classes. He knew that. He knew it was hard to convince her to willingly go to the conference. He had tried six times now, and failed each time.

Thank God for Katie Swift.

Being a single father was never easy, but being a single father while running an international nonprofit at the same time was nearly impossible. He was lucky the conference was during the summer time, otherwise she would be in school. It was hard enough to find a babysitter here at the conference. Thank God for Katie Swift, and the fact that she had been there for him six times now. Where was she now, in the moment he needed her most?

Three knocks on the hotel door, and Walter sighed. Loud noises, and sounds of fighting had brought attention to his hotel room.

*Please be my team and not the police.*

It was both.

Katie Swift, thank God for her, entered the room with the air of a drama queen, making a scene of the situation and drawing the little girl's attention away from the rest of the people walking in behind her. Her brilliant, hip length blonde hair swirled about her in all directions as she twirled and danced across the battlefield of toys and clothes, never stepping on anything, to the other side of the room where the little demon, now turned into a perfect little smiling angel, jumped into her arms.

It always amazes Walter how much the two girls looked alike. Those little frocks of blonde, nearly identical bright teal eyes, and beautiful, *beautiful* smiles.

"Where's your watch, little girl?" Katie asked Kitsen. "You're supposed to have that thing on all the time. What happens if someone tries to steal you?"

"I hit the button," grunted Kitsen, "but that won't happen while you're here. Everyone will keep me safe."

"Yes, we will," laughed Rebecca Swift, trying to keep a straight face as she followed her younger sister into the room and over to the bed. "Everyone in this room is actually a ninja, and we'll fight off armies to protect you."

Rebecca was a stark contrast to the youthful image of her little blonde sister. The greeting smile and light blue eyes were the same, but her dark brown and grey hair and visible wrinkles at the corners of her eyes and lips gave her away as the older sibling. Even her clothes held contrast, her dark colored shirt and pants against Katie's flamboyant and loud colored dress.

After Rebecca followed Jimmy, still sporting his sling and smile from last night. He patted Walter on the arm and gave him a wink.

The police came in behind Jimmy.

Paul Edwards was a long time friend of Walter's, having worked the Red Sea Initiative's first handful of operations across the world a decade ago. Older and wiser now, he was the chief of the Tulsa Police Department. He was also leading Walter's current investigation here in the area.

The case that had simply crumbled to pieces in a single night.

The last person to walk in the room shared a short glance, and a smile, with Walter. Sharp, brown spears leered up at him from almond shaped eyes.

Walter put a hand up to halt the entry of his best operator, and leaned in close. The operator stared at him.

"I have a side job for you," Walter whispered. "Something outside of the Initiative."

His top operator glanced over at the others, and then leaned back in towards Walter with upturned eyes.

"Do I get to kill anyone this time?" she asked with a smile.

"No," Walter had to stifle a laugh. "Do you still do some investigative work on the side?"

The woman nodded.

"Good. I need you to find out everything you can about a guy named Charles Langley."

# <u>6</u>

*Tulsa, Oklahoma - Monday - 5:30 PM*
She always seemed to be there early. Too early. Maybe it was the military training, or maybe it was how she was raised. His guess was that he would never know. The only thing he did know for certain, obviously shown by her behavior, was that she wanted to be there. It was all she wanted, but she definitely wanted it.

*Why? She wants to be here, but she won't touch me. She won't...*

"Your timing is off," said Charles as he stepped out of his car. "It's five thirty."

"I got bored," she replied. "Figured I would get dinner knocked out while you shower."

*Bored? I thought she was at work.*

"It's take out," said Charles as they climbed the stairs to his apartment side by side. "It's already knocked out."

Side by side, yet there was so much distance between them. Up those wide stairs, what could have been hand in hand, but he had to remind himself. *Just friends. Just really good friends. That explains it all. Nothing else does.*

It was the absolute bare minimum. Six hundred square feet, one bedroom, one bathroom, a small laundry closet, a kitchen, and a living room. The only trace of a hallway was a four foot square space between the bedroom door, the bathroom door, and the laundry closet door, which all three met at a T-intersection. The kitchen and living room were separated by a small granite bar in between that led to the front door.

The living room, directly to the right of the front door, had a massive sliding glass door that led to a balcony, overlooking the community pool and the beautiful wooded area beyond. It was not a bad deal for $1100 each month. The only thing missing was furniture.

There was one couch along the wall, a very recent addition that Abigail had requested early. There was a wall mounted television across from the couch. There was a coffee table at the foot of the couch. There were no side tables or lamps. There was nothing on the walls.

The kitchen, as Charles exposed when prepping their plates for dinner, looked like a regular kitchen until the drawers and cabinets were opened up. Inside the dish cabinet were two plates, two bowls, and two cups. The silverware drawer consisted of two of each utensil. He had one pot and one pan in each size. He had just enough spatulas and ladles to accommodate those pots and pans. He had four cutting knives: Paring, Bread, Carving, and Santoku.

The absolute bare minimum. *Wash your dishes as you use them, and you'll never run out.*

Each room was stocked accordingly, with half of the contents of the apartment added in the last few months at Abigail's request. "I'm going to be here a lot, I need some accommodations." Said as a joke, but meant with sincerity.

The only thing she knew nothing about was the tall, slender safe in his walk-in closet. Five feet tall, and two and a half feet wide, the Gun Safe was only large enough for eight guns total.

"Why do you have that?" Abigail asked as Charles slipped sweatpants out of one of his dresser drawers, and a t-shirt that was rolled into a burrito out of another. His back was to the safe, but he knew that's what she was talking about. She always asked about it. "You don't even like guns."

"You can put other things in them besides guns," replied Charles. "Besides, I don't think I'm legally allowed to own guns given my past."

"You were a minor," said Abigail. "I can't imagine it applies to you now."

"I wouldn't know," said Charles, stepping into the bathroom. "I never tried. They aren't my thing. Like you said, I don't like them."

"Why do you have it?" she asked, stepping through the doorway, almost joining him. "It would be nice of you to tell me."

"Collectibles," he replied without hesitation.

"Charles." Her voice cracked. "I know you've had your troubles, but I need you to be a little more open with me. Think about where we're at. Think about Emily."

Charles froze in place, his eyes staring off into nothing. "I think about her every day."

"I know you do," said Abigail, stepping forward. "Just think about what she always tried to do for you when you were kids." She reached up and put a hand on his chest, the tender touch of her fingers sending tingles over his whole body. "Please."

*Touch.* Physical touch. Maybe not skin to skin, but the next best thing. The thing he wanted. *Just friends? Really?*

He turned to look into her eyes. They stared back at him, wet and shining. Green. Bright green. Wonderful orbs of emerald that captivated him and stole the breath out of his lungs. He was powerless against those eyes.

Then she turned away from him, and removed her hand. She stepped back and shut the bathroom door, allowing him the privacy she insisted on. He never understood why, but she always insisted on modesty. Always insisted on some sort of separation. Very little intimacy. He wanted more; there were times he felt that she wanted more, but she was always hesitant. She always pulled away at the last moment. *Just friends. Of course.*

He wanted to feel her touch again. He wanted that electric feeling. He needed it.

Then he was distracted by a word. Something Abigail had said to him. *Emily.*

# 7

*Kansas City, Missouri - Nineteen Years Ago*
"It'll be okay." Emily Langley reached out and touched her brother's hand as he cried on the couch.

*Touch.* His body lurched and he sniffled at the feeling. He was curled up into a ball and rolled into a thin blanket like a burrito. It was the only spare blanket they had. Emily had brought him one of hers from her room after her parents had gone to sleep, but he had refused.

"Momma is a good momma. She always is."

"She's not mine," cried sweet little Charles, her brother. His voice was muffled in the blanket. "She won't like me. Not like she likes you. She never tried to have me here before. Now she has to have me because the police told her to. That's the only reason I'm here."

"She is your momma, too," responded Emily, reaching up and peeling the blanket off of his face to reveal it. "They brought you here. They wouldn't do that if they didn't like you. They would have given you to someone else."

Charles shook his head and buried his face in the cushions. Emily knew he was having a hard time fitting into the family, but she couldn't understand why. His daddy was gone, to jail, probably, but momma had taken him in. Emily was excited to have her brother here all the time. It didn't matter if they had different daddies. Family was family, and Charles was no exception to that.

"You're our family," continued Emily. "There's nothing more to it. The only difference is that you live here now."

Emily couldn't understand why it was so hard for Charles to get that. He was still her family. Why wasn't he excited to be here? She was excited to have him here. His daddy was too drunk to take care of him, and her parents were asleep. That's why she was out here by the couch with him instead of in her bed.

She had heard him crying from her bedroom just outside the living room. She snuck out of her bed, made sure her parents weren't awake, and tip-toed out to see him.

"Charlie," she whispered, rubbing her hand up and down his arm. "I love you. You're my brother. If no one else loves you here, then I'll do it for them. I'll never leave you. If they send you away, I'll go with you. It'll be just the two of us. No matter what."

Charles looked up at her with bright blue shiny eyes that seemed to glimmer like the surface of a lake. "Do you mean that?"

"I sure do." Emily smiled. "I'm here with you instead of in bed. I can't let you be alone."

He wiped his eyes and sniffed. His face turned very serious. "Okay. Then I'll do the same for you. I'll never leave you. We'll always be together, and we'll always look out for each other."

"We're brother and sister," giggled Emily, "We have to stick together."

Little Charles smiled at her, and laid his head back down on his pillow. His eyes closed slowly, and he started to breathe slower. "Love you, sissy."

She smiled. *Sissy*. What a wonderful name. He'd never called her that before. She had to think of a good nickname for him, then. She leaned over and gave him a kiss on the forehead, and laid down on the living room floor next to the couch wrapped in her blanket.

"Goodnight, Emily." His voice almost sounded happy, like he had forgotten whatever was bothering him. His eyes opened for a moment to look at her. "Are you staying there all night?"

"All night," she responded, coming up with his new name. "Love you, bubba."

***

Miranda Langley, she was still a Langley unfortunately, stretched and sat up in bed. Her eyes adjusted to the light of the room, the morning sun peeking through the cracks in the blinds. Balled fists made their way to her face, stuffing her eye sockets and kneading the thin barrier that the lids created. She opened her eyes, stars sparkling in her vision and fading away from sight with every blink. Her eyes wandered to the open bedroom door, where she practiced her daily ritual of checking Emily's bedroom door. It was across the hall, the perfect angle from where Miranda could see the whole thing. Top to bottom, and side to side.

It was open, and Miranda could see straight to the empty bed.

In seven years, Emily never woke up before Miranda and her husband.

She climbed out of bed and slowly crept to her bedroom door. She peered down the hallway, towards the living room, and saw two miniature feet sticking out from around the corner of the couch. She covered her mouth to stifle a laugh. Emily still hadn't woken up before her parents. She had just not slept in her own bed last night.

She threw on a thin bathrobe to cover her pajamas, and made her way down the hall to the living room. There she saw her seven year old daughter, Emily Langley, lying on the floor in front of the couch, an arm extended upwards and fingers locked with the hand of Miranda's youngest child. Sweet little Charles Langley.

The call had come a week before. Arthur Langley, her ex-husband of two years, had been found passed out drunk in his front lawn again. It was their six year old son, Charles, that contacted the neighbors and got the police involved again. It was the third time in a month it had happened, and the final straw for the Missouri Department of Family Services. Charles Langley had finally gone into State custody. In less than a week, he was back with his mother, half sister, and soon to be stepfather.

The process wasn't easy or short, but he was here now. Their next step was to buy a larger house to get him a bedroom. She thanked her soon to be new husband for all that. He was the one making it happen. All she had done was take care of the boy. Her fiance was handling the rest.

Now Emily was trying to do her own part. Her life had always been about seeing and spending time with Charles, and Arthur had made that nearly impossible until now. Maybe it would be okay for little Charles Langley.

Charles Langley's life had been flipped upside down at six years old. He was lost, but Emily was going to bring him back to the light. *Amazing Grace. How sweet that sound.* She was sure of it.

As long as Emily was around, Charles would be okay.

# *8*

*Tulsa, Oklahoma - Present Day - Monday - 6:00 PM*

Charles could almost feel Emily's hand in his own. The cold sink counter couldn't distract him. The warmth of her touch overtook his thoughts like a flash flood. His mind fixated on the feeling of her fingers touching him. His fists clenched, pressing down on the bathroom counter and aching for the sensation of human contact. He had to find that security; that connection. Abigail refused to provide it.

Why? What was wrong with him?

What he needed, he realized when he opened his eyes and looked up in the mirror at his own bare skin, was a distraction from all that. There was no touch here in the real world, whether it be from Abigail or from Emily. No one cared enough to help him. He needed something to take his mind off of that itch; that need.

He'd had access to that help for years now. Ever since he'd gotten a phone, no, before that. He had computers and magazines in jail. He'd had access to it for an entire decade.

He reached for his phone and opened the Chrome Browser App. An incognito tab wouldn't help. No one looked at his phone. Not Abigail, not his father, and not his coworkers. He was safe from the prying eyes of those around him, and what Google knew didn't matter in the grand scheme of things.

He opened the bookmarks tab, revealing the link to a specific website and category that he preferred to watch. Over the years, he'd had the time to figure out the things he liked, and the things he didn't like. This one was easy. Four letters in all caps to click on and bring himself into hiding from the real world.

## MILF

His fingers slid up the screen over and over again, his eyes investigating the tabs for each video.

There was an older blonde woman with massive fake breasts standing over a young man on a couch. Her cleavage, contained only by the smallest shirt he had ever seen in his life, tied in the front by a knot that had to be held together by magic, hung over the young man's face like she was providing him shelter. She had no bra on, allowing the man to make eye contact with nipples big enough to be used as dinner plates.

Charles shook his head and moved on, too fake of a woman, the lips too puffy, the body too unproportionate.

Several other tabs all resembled the same image. Older women, huge fake body augmentations that made them look like dolls, all wearing blouses and skirts several sizes too small, and all hanging over a boy half their age who looked like he'd never seen a woman before.

Several of the women wore nothing at all. Blondes and brunettes; fit and meaty. The options were endless.

None of them interested him. They were all full of false promises, and no connection. They were all simply there for entertainment. They were nothing, and they meant nothing. He would mean nothing to them.

It felt strange. This category had never ceased to satisfy him. Starting this at the age of fifteen in jail, all the available women online had been significantly older than him, and that was what worked for him. Now? Ten years later? He'd followed them faithfully through the years, changing categories to find them here in the MILF section. He felt nothing for them.

They had betrayed him with those surgeries and injections to try to remain young. They should have just aged, and let him age with them. They could have grown old together. Instead, those women had broken the connection. They had lied with their bodies, to the world, and to themselves.

Most of all, they were trying to lie to him by convincing him that they were still worthy of love after turning themselves into a real life version of a doll. He would have loved them for who they were, but this?

They didn't care about him anymore.

*They never did. You just wanted them to. They betrayed you like everyone else does.*

They weren't real enough, he realized. Fake breasts, lip injections, bulging cheekbones, and stretched eyelids. It had to be that.

His index finger touched the *Categories* link, and he was brought back to the main categories page of the website. Each category had its own image next to its name that gave a visual display of what content it would contain. They were all listed alphabetically from Amateur and Asian to Vintage and Virtual Reality. The site had everything in between. Literally everything.

He scrolled up and down trying to read all the individual names. There were divisions in nationalities, skin color, hair color, and fetishes that ranged from Contemporary Church to Cartel Torture. The list felt endless. So much to choose from, and so little time to not be discovered by Abigail.

His eyes picked up on something, something he had never noticed before. There were words, no, numbers, in parenthesis next to the name of each category. Something every single thumbnail had in common on the site.

**18 +**

An age requirement. Legal girls on a sex work website. The disclaimer felt unnecessary, but Charles accepted it quickly. He knew all the girls on this site were the legal age of majority. It was the only way the site could operate legally.

There was nothing illegal about what he was doing. Immoral, maybe, but not illegal.

Boom. His eyes fixated again. This time they were trapped in the gaze of a young brunette girl in a slender sundress. The dress was a deep blue color, and hugged the girl's body to show every curve she had. Her green eyes sparkled at him, and pearly white teeth gleamed through a wide smile.

That got him. The curves, not too extreme in any direction, the lips normal and human, and the cheekbones not protruding from the skull like tumors.

He touched the link.

### Teen (18+)

The videos came up, and his heart jumped into his throat. His pulse quickened, the beats hammering away in his chest. Thin girls, thick girls, short girls, tall girls, busty girls, flat chested girls, blondes, brunettes, redheads, green eyes, blue eyes, brown eyes…

There was no limit in this category. His eyes widened, and a smile crept across his face. The girls were beautiful, and they looked like real girls. There were no body augmentations or fillers. It was unlike anything he'd ever seen in the last ten years. They all only had one thing in common.

*They're young. Too young for you. These are eighteen and nineteen year olds. That's six and seven years younger than you. That's not okay.*

Who was telling him that? That silent voice in his head was indistinguishable from male and female. Was it himself? Emily?

*Emily.* Escape. He had to have that escape. Now. He needed it now before it was too late.

His fingers were trembling above his screen. His lower body responded in kind to the stimulation it was receiving from his eyes, and he rushed to start the shower faucet.

When he returned to his phone, he selected a video with a tall, leggy blonde lying flat on a couch. The look she gave him set his insides on fire. Haunting eyes said "fuck me, fuck me please." A smile stared up at him. She wanted him. She cared. She hadn't betrayed him by filling her body with silicon and poison. She was just a normal girl looking for physical touch, just like he was. She was just a little younger than he was.

Then he decided to make a quick adjustment to his settings before getting started. His bookmarks tab opened, and he selected the drop box next to the folder containing his recent interests. He moved his finger over the screen, and touched the trash can icon, deleting the list. He returned to the site he was on, backed out of the video and back to the category page, and selected the star at the top of the screen.

A banner appeared at the top of the phone screen as he returned to his video and lowered his hands down to take hold of himself, firm and erect now.

**BOOKMARK ADDED**

# <u>*9*</u>

*Claremore, Oklahoma - Monday - 10:30 PM*
Olivia's stomach growled violently. Nothing today. Not a single bite. She looked down at her bare torso, ridges protruding for her sides like a ladder that led down her waist.

*Food.* It was the only word currently on her mind. *Solid food.*

*We have to keep you skinny,* Joseph would tell her. *Your friends like skinny little girls.*

She had been promised a bottle tomorrow morning to prepare her for work— working on an empty stomach never ended well for anyone— but the bottles didn't last long enough. They were just chunky milk that went right through her. An hour would pass, and she would be hungry again. They tasted like rotten eggs. She wanted something she could chew first, and then swallow. Sweet or salty, it didn't matter.

It would have made her mouth water, but it didn't. She was too thirsty for that.

Food and water. She took a deep, silent breath, and made her choice. She was probably going to die anyways, from starvation or from Joseph. At least she could die with a full stomach.

At least she could still choose. In her mind, her only safe space, she still had the power to choose.

The blanket came off of her. It had to be silent. She might be able to say she was going to the bathroom and get away with it, but she was supposed to hold it overnight. There were always consequences when she couldn't.

*Never leave bed. Never after dark. Stay still. Stay quiet. Silence is safety.*

She rolled over onto her side, the mattress below her uttering a long and low creak. She froze in place and listened. There was no answer to her bed's call. She moved again, and the mattress stayed silent with her. She threw her legs over the side of the bed and felt her toes touch the carpet. Silent and effective.

She raised herself to her feet, and the mattress groaned. This time, she listened while moving towards the door. No response.

Her hand reached out in the darkness, and she wrapped her fingers around the doorknob. It turned, and the door opened without making a noise.

She peeked through the open door and into the hallway. Darkness. No light, and no shadows. She took a very light step into the hallway, waiting for the floor to squeak. It didn't, so she took another step. Again, the floor stayed quiet. She continued, putting one foot in front of the other and trying not to make a sound.

Then her stomach growled again, so loud she thought she could hear an echo come from down the hallway. She couldn't help but freeze. She waited, and heard nothing again.

*Hurry.* She had to hurry. Every moment she spent out of bed put her at risk.

She tiptoed down the hallway, trying to keep as much of her weight out of her steps as she could and thinking the whole time about the consequences of her actions. What would Joseph do if he caught her?

What could he do that was worse than starving her? Something, anything, had to be better than this. Working in the yard, or meeting with friends, those never ended well on an empty stomach, so she never had one. Maybe it was worth working more. Maybe it was worth the pain.

Right now, it was worth dying over.

Before she knew it she was at the stairs, and then at the bottom of the stairs peering into the blackness of the kitchen. She struggled not to laugh. This was so much easier than she thought it would be. She might even be able to get away with this every night. She might never go hungry again. This was definitely worth the risk.

With a hand stretched out, she felt for the cabinet door that held the snacks. She knew where it was, but couldn't see anything in the dark kitchen. Stray beams of moonlight illuminated bits of the floor like white polka dots, but that was all she had.

Her fingers wrapped around something; a handle. She pulled, and the refrigerator door opened. She gasped, the light blasting into the kitchen like a lighthouse screaming for Joseph's attention. The crunch of the seals pulling apart sounded like an alarm, but before she could push it shut, she noticed something. Inside the fridge, staring at her through the crack of blinding light, was a bag of red grapes.

A tight inhale sniffed its way up her nostrils and took in the wafted scent of fresh fruit. She pulled on the fridge door and opened it wider, letting the light wash over her and bathe her in its wonder. *Grapes.* Sweet, sugary, red grapes. She reached out to grab them, and wrapped her fingers around the handle of the bag.

The plastic crinkled loudly in the quiet kitchen. Olivia didn't notice, blinded by hunger and overtaken by gluttony. She peeled open the top and reached in, picking the grapes from the stems and plopping them into her mouth. She bit down on two at the same time, the juices moistening her gums and lips, giving them new life.

*Fluids.* Sweet tasting fluids that had no trace of powder, and no clumps of milk. She closed her eyes and picked two more grapes. They tasted sweet, they tasted beautiful. They tasted like freedom.

She was going to do this every night. She would never go hungry again.

She sighed as she swallowed, the dry pain in her throat stinging momentarily as the icy juices poured into her and lubricated her very soul. Her eyes began to swim with tears as she grabbed another handful of grapes and dropped them in her mouth.

How many could she take in her mouth at once? Not friends that filled her throat with a nasty, salty taste that left her feeling disgusting. Not how many of their *things* could she have inside of her at one time, but how much goodness could she have in her? How much satisfaction? It was all she could do not to giggle with happiness.

The kitchen light behind her turned on, and her heart skipped a beat.

"What do you think you're doing?" cried the deep, bassy voice of Joseph from behind her. She scrambled away from the fridge, pushing the grapes back inside and slamming the door. What was left in her mouth poured out, and she screamed. She dropped to all fours and began crawling around the cabinets to get away.

*The front door!* She had to get to the front door. She could escape!

She felt fingers scratch her scalp as she moved forward. A palm slapped itself onto the top of her head, sending her face first into the tile. Something violent yanked her hair. Her head reeled back uncomfortably on her shoulders, pulling muscles in her neck beyond what they should have done, before her whole body was lifted from the floor. Hands and feet all left contact with the ground, and she went flying through the air.

An intense pain stabbed into her as she came to a hard landing at the base of the stairs. Three edges jabbed her, one at the neck, one in the middle of her back, and one at her hips.

*Consequences.*

"I'm sorry," she tried to squeal, but could barely get the words out through her gritted teeth.

Trying to sound scared, and not angry. Was she scared, or was she angry?

"Stealing food?" Joseph boomed, wasting no time in crossing the kitchen and bearing down on her. "In my house?"

*Escape.* It was the only word in her head, regardless of the emotion behind it. *Escape! Anywhere but here!* She turned over to crawl up the stairs. *Get away. Get away!* Even if she had to go out of a window, she had to get away.

Joseph's hands wrapped around her shoulders and picked her up again, dragging her body up the staircase and raking her along the corners of the steps on the way up. When the steps ceased to be a weapon, her body lifted from the floor again, and Joseph tossed her down the hallway. She crashed into a wall, feeling the drywall splinter on her back before sliding down to the floor. She rolled over and tried crawling away again.

"I'm…" She couldn't finish it. She was out of breath, a pain growing in her ribs, and her heart racing as Joseph appeared at the top of the stairs and began following her down the hallway.

*Escape! Escape out of the window!* It was her only chance.

"You think you can just sneak out of your bedroom anytime you want?" he screamed, his form growing larger as he came closer to her. "You think you can just help yourself to any of *my* food any time you want? I'll show you what you can and can't do. I'll show you what happens to kids who are bad. I'll show you what happens to kids who disobey."

"Joseph?" It was the woman only known to Olivia as the wife coming out of the bedroom in a bathrobe. Her voice was groggy and her words slurred together. Her hair was a mess, curly and frayed. Her eyes were wild with fear and her teeth were bared like an animal. It was so unlike the usual glare of hatred Olivia usually got. "What's going on?"

"I just caught this one sneaking food out of the fridge," laughed Joseph, turning to his wife.

Olivia took the chance. She turned and climbed to her feet, trying to make it to her bedroom before any more damage could be done. The window could be opened before Joseph got her. She could do it.

Hands grabbed her before she made it three steps, tossing her back to the floor. Her face smashed into the carpet, her nose bending to the side and going numb. She heard yelling, words that she couldn't understand. The world around her spun, stars inching their way into her field of vision. Her own cries and screams filled her ears as Joseph came down to the floor and put his weight on her. She felt a knee in her back, and hands holding her arms behind her. Her eyes filled with tears, different from the ones she'd had while eating the grapes.

Why had she gone to the kitchen in the first place? If only she could take it all back. She never would have thrown the blanket off of her in bed. She knew what she was feeling now. Fear, not anger. Pure fear, and pain from the way her arms bent behind her back, squeezed tightly in Joseph's grip.

Her body slid along the floor like she was being used as a sled. The hands shoved her, the knee in her back pressing her forward and running bare skin along the fabric beneath her. Her head slammed into the doorframe, bringing those stars into full view. Her shoulder hit shortly after that. She went flying into the air again, the weight from above her vanishing and the hands letting go. She hit a net of some sort, her body falling into what felt like a small box covered in some sort of scratchy canvas covering.

She could hear more yelling from all around her. "Bring it all in here! We'll get her straightened out."

A hand grabbed her wrist and forced it upward. She heard crunching, like the tearing of a velcro strap. She felt metal on her wrist, heard the velcro sound again, and felt pressure wrap around the joint of her wrist. She screamed at the pain in her hand, her attention on the sharp burning and cold stinging instead of the aching she felt everywhere else. The pressure of the metal cut deep into her flesh as she pulled at it. It wouldn't budge.

*Escape! Escape!* Impossible. She couldn't pull her hand free. Something had a hold of it, and wouldn't let go.

The light in the bedroom turned on, and she recognized where she was. A Pack 'n' Play as old as she was that had been stashed in the corner of her bedroom was now in use. She was in it, upside down and tumbling over to straighten up and face

Joseph. She looked at her hand. She was tied to the pack 'n' play by some sort of metal wrist lock. Police officers used these when they visited her for play time.

"How do you like those?" asked Joseph with a smile. "Let's see how you like being handcuffed to a box half your size all the time. See if you want to sneak out now! See if you want to steal from me, you little bitch!"

She tugged at the handcuff, the skin at her wrist breaking and drawing blood. She groaned, staring up at Joseph.

"What if I have to go to the bathroom?" she asked desperately.

Joseph didn't respond. He smiled down at her, reached behind his back, and pulled out a poofy white piece of fabric barely large enough for a baby. She screamed. *A diaper!*

"No!"

Another figure came into view in the hallway. Tall and slender, waving hair. It was sissy. Olivia wanted to cry out for help, but saw the look in her big sister's eyes. Green. Bright green eyes. Big, smoldering orbs that glowed in the light. Olivia could see it. The look on Sissy's face.

There was nothing that Sissy could do to help her. For other reasons, boy reasons, Sissy was in as much trouble as Olivia was.

And somehow, it was all Olivia's fault. It always was. It always had been. Even Sissy had admitted it.

No one was coming to help Olivia tonight.

# _10_

*Tulsa, Oklahoma - Tuesday - 8:30 AM*
Black. There was so much black in here. Uniforms, guns, utilities, equipment, keys, desks, cars, jail cells. In all seriousness, Walter was surprised the paper here wasn't black. The police were supposed to be a beacon of light and hope and safety. This was depressing. European police were covered in neon yellow, green, and white. Easily identifiable. Why was America so different?

*Why are we hiding?*

"You guys really went all out with the Dark Knight theme, huh?" he asked, walking into the conference room with his team behind him.

"We all like the color," replied Paul Edwards robotically, setting a manilla folder on the table and opening it up. "So we have no name for our main dealer. Jimmy, what do you have for us from that last guy?

"He said that this one brings in almost ten grand a week," said Jimmy. He says this guy sells his girl for a hundred and fifty each customer. That's gotta be a hundred customers a week."

Walter heard Rebecca groan from the end of the table. He was glad that Katie was staying at the hotel with Kitsen. Katie didn't like to hear these kinds of details. She was part of recovery, not rescue. She didn't really have the stomach for that kind of thing.

"We don't know for certain," sighed Paul. "We don't know much else. I mean, look at this board. We have a rough description and a sketch so bad that it doesn't even get us a match on facial recognition or local underground networks. We have a general area of where he's at, but only three days after he's been there. I don't see any patterns. I don't see a home base. I don't see a standard customer base. I don't see anything that makes sense. Whatever he's doing, he's hiding it well."

"They usually do," said Jimmy. "Everybody just thinks pedophiles and human traffickers are low class criminals, but they're not. These guys are hard to find. Just like everyone else, they don't want to get caught, and the suppliers are the worst. You can't lure them in, and you can't just walk up to them and ask for a hit. It's all done secretly, and usually with coded passphrases."

"What, exactly, do we know?" asked Walter.

Paul Edwards joined them in staring at the board. Aside from the rough sketch, there really was very little. A map of the city of Tulsa, with circles speckled across it. Each circle had a red X or a green checkmark next to it with a name of a man Jimmy had given them that might or might not be a real name. So far they only had first or last names, and nothing checked out on searches.

The red and green check marks either confirmed it as a location or made it a possible location. There were dates in each circle, some having more than one. It was supposed to be a history of the movements of the girl being trafficked in the city, but it made no sense. Paul was right. These general areas were wide ranged and scattered. Even the dates seemed to be random. There was nothing to it. Walter stared hard, and shook his head.

"How long have we been working on this?" he asked.

Paul glanced over at him. "A month."

"What's the longest it's taken us in the past to catch someone like this?"

"A week," sighed Paul, his eyes falling to the floor. "We've had our long operations, but those are large scale networks. This is one guy and one little girl. Does that mean we are getting old?"

"The traffickers are getting smarter," said Rebecca from the end of the table. "That's what we get for posting how to identify it and educating the public on social media. Adapt, and overcome. Plus, we're short handed right now. We're not firing on all cylinders. How do we even get a guy inside now that Jimmy's arm is in a sling. I can't really pretend I want to take up with a little girl."

"We've seen that kind of thing before," muttered Paul. "We need help, though. Walter, you can call one of your other teams and get someone in here, or I can dig into my narcotics team and see if they can spare a guy for us. Otherwise, we're picking someone up off the street."

"We could hire someone, Walt," said Jimmy. "There's lots of options."

Walter's eyes flashed at Jimmy, a moment of rage to tell him to shut the hell up.

The door to the conference room opened, and a voice echoed in the room. "Walt?"

Walter looked to see his top operator standing in the doorway.

"What is it?" he asked.

"That thing you asked me to do? It's done."

***

"You're confident after twenty four hours that you can give me a full report on this guy?" asked Walter.

"You're confident I can't?" she asked back, cocking an eyebrow. "I have to be honest, it didn't even take me this long. I've spent more time trying to make sense of it than I have actually finding information."

"So who is he?" asked Walter. "I saw him kick some ass like he was Liam Neeson. The real deal, not the pretend type. He said he was in his mid twenties, but even he sounded like he wasn't sure."

"He's twenty five," replied the woman, dropping a stack of paper on the hood of Walter's car. "Exactly mid twenties. Take a guess at his profession."

"Ex Army?" asked Walter. "Special forces? MMA fighter? I would guess the CIA, but he's too young, and too local to be that."

The woman just smiled at him, a smile that said he was wrong, so wrong.

"Alison, who is this guy?"

Alison picked up her report and glanced over it. "Charles Langley, twenty five years old.

Born and raised in Kansas City. He was a wrestler, State Champs for Missouri his freshman year. Had some trouble in life early on, alcoholic for a father that neglected to take care of him up until he was six. After that, he lived with his mother. Went to church, studied martial arts for discipline, and got decent grades. Never made it past his freshman year."

"What happened his freshman year?" asked Walter. Alison handed him the papers, and he glanced down at them. "Oh my."

"Life got flipped upside down," continued Alison. "Spent two and a half years in a Juvie lockup, got out at eighteen, and moved here to Tulsa, where his dad is also at. Been here ever since. I guess they've reconciled."

"Wait," said Walter. "What do you mean, he's been here ever since?"

"He's a normal guy," said Alison. "A little weird. No social media, just a work address, home address, and a phone number is all I could find. His name popped up on a social media search. Mostly posts from another page. His dad has been really active on social media in the last few years. Looks like he's turned his life around. Making good money and taking Charles on vacations. The name Charles Langley popped up on a social media post seven years ago at a dojo here in the city in a welcome post. My guess is he still trains there to this day."

"That explains the expertise," said Walter. "When did he start training?"

"No idea," said Alison. "He was young, though." She flipped the papers around in her hands. "HIPAA won't allow me access to medical records, so I have no idea what happened in the hospital, but I'm assuming that the old man was Charles's old man, Arthur. Based on what you told me about how he looked, my guess is heart attack."

She flipped through more papers. "Then there's just the miscellaneous OSINT stuff. Amazon account, Duolingo membership, Audible.com, that kind of stuff. He's been in the same apartment for seven years, basically the whole time he's lived here in Tulsa. Same truck for seven years. Same job for seven years. Just a normal kid in his twenties working a dead end job, I guess."

"Tell me he at least has some sort of law enforcement job," said Walter.

Alison pursed her lips and shook her head. "Look at the file. He was in Juvie, Walt. It takes a lot of connections to get into Law Enforcement with those kinds of charges. Right now he's a Maintenance Tech at Charter Nutrition. He works on the machinery. Augers and compressors and stuff."

Walter shook his head, staring at the paperwork in his hands. "Just a normal guy. Jail, and a factory job."

"Except he's in your crosshairs," said Alison.

"I'm telling you," said Walter. "The look in his eyes. The way he contorted that guy's arm. It was professional. I was expecting an Ex-CIA guy, not an Ex-convict/factory guy. You're sure there's no black site file on him? Some kind of deleted life that the CIA gave him?"

Alison laughed. "Nothing. I have access to the dark web. He doesn't even exist there. Want me to set up an interview? We are down a guy with Jimmy in a sling, and this guy really has you interested."

"He's only twenty five," said Walter. He stared down at the paperwork in his hand. A criminal record and court documents. He reached over and took the sheet of paper out of Alison's hand. On it were the numbers and street address for the man himself.

The young man that brought down someone twice his size and didn't feel an ounce of fear or regret. The one with burning eyes, and steady hands afterwards. The one that didn't hesitate, got the job done, and did it faster than anyone else. *Commitment. Pure and utter commitment. That's how he makes it work.*

And after all that, he was just a normal guy. Just like someone else he knew ten years ago. His top operator.

"I'll learn more tonight," Walter said, handing the papers back to Alison. "This evening, I think I want to have a chat with Mr. Langley."

# _11_

_Tulsa, Oklahoma - Tuesday - 5:00 PM_
To argue with a woman, or to not argue with a woman. That was the question. He didn't know why he was doing it. Her argument was perfectly sound, but he wanted her there with, and he couldn't stand that she wasn't. He needed her, and she just simply refused. He had so much to tell her. The research he'd done… _A purpose._

"I just don't have it in me tonight, Charles," she said over the phone. Her voice croaked like a frog, and wavered like she was sick. _Like she's been crying._ "I just need a quiet night here at the house. Is that too much to ask for?"

"Of course not," he said, trying to convince both himself and her that he meant it. "That doesn't mean I have to be terribly happy about it."

She snorted. "I wish I was there, but I just don't feel like I can leave the house right now."

He sighed, not wanting to beg. "I get it. I just don't like it. I like having you around."

She sniffed. "I want to be around, Charles. Can it wait a couple of days?" Her words sounded strained and forced.

She was crying.

"What happened, Abby?" he asked, a little more forcefully than he intended. *Like you're interrogating her. Stop that.*

"It's just a bad day at work." She sniffed again. "I'm sorry. I don't mean to be emotional. I'll be back over there in just a couple of days. I just need a resting day or two."

"You can talk about it with me," said Charles. "I'm always here for you."

"In a couple of days," responded Abigail. "In person. I promise. I want to see you. Just give me some time to recover."

He sighed, staring out of his balcony door. *Recover from what?* He wasn't able to respond. Somehow, he would find the wrong thing to say. He had something he wanted to say. The words were there, right on the top of his tongue, but it wouldn't be the right thing to say.

*Or would it?*

Three knocks at his front door.

"Was that your front door?" Abigail didn't seem to be crying anymore.

"It was," said Charles. "I'll call you tomorrow? Or you call me when you feel like it?"

"Who's there?"

"I have no idea," replied Charles. "I haven't answered it yet."

She sighed. "I'll call tomorrow, then. Just… be ready to answer. I want to see you just as much as you want to see me, and the same goes for talking."

He wasn't sure which one of them hung up. Then he opened the door.

A tall, muscular man stood in front of him. About six feet tall, eye to eye with Charles, black hair with thin streaks of grey trickling down the sides. Tired, brown eyes peeked through heavy eyelids that sat above purple and black bags. Wrinkles were beginning to make their way into his features, the sign of a rough life. Charles had guessed the man to be in his mid thirties based on the information from the internet.

Here in person, he looked much older than that.

"Walter?" *Mr. Faucet would have been better. Wrong thing to say again. You haven't even been properly introduced yet.*

"Mr. Langley," said Walter Faucet. "I'd like to ask you some questions. May I come in?"

*Never let the police through your front door without a warrant.*

Was Walter the police? Charles had thought he was just the head of the non profit organization, but the organization did work with the police. Charles hadn't done anything wrong, except for hurting the prisoner at the hospital, so why would the anti trafficking activist be visiting him?

*Teen (18+).* Hadn't he done something wrong? *No. It's not illegal. You're fine.*

Charles stepped to the side of the door and allowed Walter to walk inside the apartment. Walter entered, hesitated at the sight of the simple design of the interior, and then moved into the living room.

"Make yourself at home," said Charles, moving to the balcony door. "I'm sure the balcony would be more comfortable. Believe it or not, there's more seating out there."

"You keep things simple here," said Walter. "I like it. It's efficient."

"It's my girlfriend," said Charles. "Before her, I hardly had any of this stuff."

Charles opened the glass door to the balcony, and the two of them stepped out onto the concrete pad. A cool summer evening breeze met them on the other side, tingling the little hairs on their arms and necks. There were two large and plush rocking chairs, where the two men placed themselves.

Charles watched Walter stare off into the scenery around them, so deep in thought he looked drugged.

"What is it you'd like to ask, Mr. Faucet?" asked Charles.

Walter never moved from his position. "Who are you?"

The question stunned Charles. Walter looked over, his gaze met with the distorted face of confusion.

"I saw you take that guy out in the hospital like you were some professional fighter," continued Walter. "Not just an MMA fighter, but a legit street fighter. Like something out of a movie. Suddenly I'm interested. That joke of a job for you becomes a little bit more realistic. I start thinking that maybe, if the qualifications are enough, we can actually consider you for a position. We are really short handed right now, and if you're good enough, I could make an exception."

Walter sucked in a breath, and cast an awkward glance at Charles. "Try not to be upset at this next part, but I did some digging on you and found out that you're just a regular guy. Typical American job, typical American truck, typical American apartment, albeit the lack of typical American decorations. The math doesn't line up, but we are shorthanded. So, I'm here to find out more. Tell me who you are."

Charles looked out over the apartment complex on the other side of the railing. The pool; the woods; the buildings. He took it all in, the same surroundings he'd had for seven years. Seven long years of the same old, same old. Just staying steady, drifting along the surface of the sea and going wherever the breeze took him.

There was only one answer that he could think of. It was the only answer that made sense to him.

"I don't know." His gaze returned to Walter.

"You don't know?" Walter asked.

"No," said Charles. "I was a star wrestler in school. I was a prized student at a martial arts dojo at home. Then everything kind of just went to hell, and I've not been sure about it since."

"I read about that," mumbled Walter. "You had a good clean record inside, though, and you've been living a nice life ever since."

"Nice?" Charles had to chuckle a little bit. "I live alone in a one bedroom apartment in my mid twenties. My dad just had a heart attack two days ago, and…"

He trailed off, thinking about Abigail. She was being distant, but she just needed a couple of days. There was no need to complain about her. She just needed space. He would know why in a couple of days. The timing was off, that was all. No need to complain.

"You ran a background check on me?" Charles asked. "Is that the first step in the hiring process?"

*Also technically illegal without consent.*

Walter shrugged. "I was curious, and it still didn't tell me anything. Besides, it wasn't a formal background check. Just some basic Open Source stuff."

Charles nodded. "Stuff that's easy to find."

"Do you have any debt?" asked Walter.

Charles shook his head. The truck was paid off, and he didn't own a home.

"Savings?"

Charles nodded.

"Retirement savings?"

Charles nodded again.

"Then you're better off than half of the American population," said Walter. "Do you have any hobbies?"

Charles hesitated for a moment, thinking about the dojo. He thought about the things he knew, and why he knew them. No one else knew those things about him, those secrets. No one had any idea, not Abigail, not his coworkers, and not his father.

Then he realized who he was talking to. The Founder of an anti human trafficking organization that dealt in undercover operations. The one that had jokingly offered him a job, and came back to take it more seriously.

Charles sighed. *One chance. Take it.*

"I listen to a lot of podcasts," he started, "read a lot of books, and read a lot of articles about spycraft and what's usually referred to as the 'grey man principle'."

He waited a moment, anticipating the question. It never came.

"I spend most of my time just trying to blend in and go unnoticed," he continued. "I'm trying to be grey, trying to live that life."

Then came the question. "Why?"

Charles hesitated. "I'm not sure. Maybe it gives me something to shoot for, like another job."

Walter sat straight up. "So, you're really taking an interest in the industry?"

"Not many people will hire an ex-convict," said Charles with a shrug. "Even one like me. I was thinking about doing private investigation. Maybe starting my own side deal."

Charles hesitated. "Can I tell you something without you thinking I'm really weird."

"We're already past that, my friend." Walter leaned forward, his elbows on his knees.

"I use a lot of OSINT tools online to do research sometimes," continued Charles. "I run a lot of situational awareness drills and practice a lot of tradecraft stuff I've picked up from the intelligence community."

"Why?" asked Walter.

"Because it gives me something to do," said Charles. "Something to focus on and something to keep my mind busy. Besides, I'm not happy doing what I'm doing. I just want to do something more meaningful than working in a factory. Law enforcement is kind of out of the question. Maybe being a PI would be better. I could help people."

Walter leaned back in his chair and let out a sigh. "So that's it. You want to help people?"

Charles nodded. "We all want to be the hero. It would be nice to make a difference in the world. That's part of why I was so interested at the hospital."

Walter nodded slowly. "Okay. Now, my next question: Who do you want to be?"

*The interview has started. He's already testing me.*

"Who do I want to be?" asked Charles, his face scrunching up. "What does that mean?"

"We're short handed right now. I can take a look at your life and tell you some things about yourself. You're dedicated. You're not afraid of commitment, and you aren't satisfied with how your life is going. You want a big change."

Charles shrugged. "I like the structure, but it does get a little boring sometimes."

"Here's my offer," sighed Walter. "I told you the recruiting process was tedious, because I need to see what you're capable of. I need to see how dedicated you will be. I have to see your temperament. I'm willing to skip all that because we're getting nowhere fast in our current case. It's supposed to be a simple one, but it's turned out to be a nightmare. I have someone that can run you through some simple drills here and there, and I have a board full of evidence that my team can't figure anything out on. We typically require law enforcement experience, and the age requirement, but you sound like you're doing the right thing with your hobbies. I want to see what you've got, Jimmy from the other night wanted to see what you've got, and now my top operator wants to see what you've got. Are you off on the weekend?"

Charles glanced away for a moment. "Another statement that might make you think I'm weird."

Walter laughed. "Weird doesn't even scratch the surface."

"Your nonprofit organization," said Charles. "It's hosting a training conference here in Tulsa. Down at the Grand River View Resort Hotel. I did a bunch of research overnight after running into you at the hospital. My job requires forty eight hours notice, so, first thing yesterday morning, I requested the rest of the week off so I could try to get into that conference."

Walter laughed again, a deep belly laugh. "And how did you expect to get in? It's not an open to the public kind of thing."

Charles shrugged. "Like I said. I train to be grey. Getting by people without being noticed is the whole point of that. When you want something bad enough, you make it happen. Besides, I had three more days to get in."

He sat back in his chair and stared out into the distance. "When I saw the testimonies of children on your site, I tried to imagine what it would feel like to be the reason that those children can live a normal life. When I did that, my whole brain just fixated on that. I'm in, Walter, regardless of whatever training I have to do to prove myself. You say dedication? I show you dedication. I'll do whatever I have to do."

He laughed. "Walter, I don't even know what your Omega Operators do when they're out in the field, and I'm already diving in head first."

"Well," Walter shook his head. "We definitely aren't Liam Neeson. What I need you to understand, first and foremost, is that this isn't a hobby. This is serious business. Lives are at stake. One mistake can cause serious damage to people around you."

Charles nodded. "Understood."

"Most people think about undercover operatives in human trafficking networks and think of the movie, *Taken,* right?"

Charles chuckled under his breath. "We all wanted to be Liam Neeson in school. We didn't want to have to waste a lifetime of training to get the skills, though."

"That's not how things are actually done," continued Walter. "We do things differently. What you see in the movies isn't rescue. It's slaughter. Some people believe in that kind of thing as a punishment for pedophiles, but those people don't ever really put in any effort to help. No, Rescue in real life is a long, boring, and uneventful process."

Walter sat up in his chair, resting on his elbows, fingers interlocked in front of him. "We don't believe in reckless rescue. We believe in using a well thought out and careful response. We don't go into a place without connections with both law enforcement and some form of aftercare facility that we vet and we know we can trust. Once we have those two things, we need to coordinate with law enforcement and justice systems to capture and convict the traffickers, and then create an environment for victims to feel safe. Then they can start the recovery and transition process."

Walter took a deep breath. "Rescues should be quiet and safe. We don't go on armed rampages to kill traffickers. All we do is go undercover to gather intelligence and incriminating evidence against traffickers, and hand it over to the authorities for them to handle the arrests. We help get the children the help they need, and get them to a recovery facility."

"I keep trying to think of a good comparison," muttered Charles. "Nothing comes up that doesn't end in extreme violence."

"What we do doesn't sell in the world of entertainment," laughed Walter. "Like with my man, Jimmy, and his broken arm. Although some things can get out of hand, we still tend to keep things under as much control as possible. Everything was going smoothly until that guy broke Jimmy's arm, and then we shut the whole thing down to get Jimmy to the hospital."

Charles shook his head. "Why did they break his arm?"

Walter shrugged. "No idea. The attack came out of nowhere."

"That doesn't make any sense."

"No it doesn't," said Walter. "That's what I'm saying. We need help on this case, and I'm willing to roll the dice on you. Our operators do a lot of training and are seriously vetted before being put into the field, but we'll have to do things differently with you."

"You're just going to throw me to the wolves right off the bat?" asked Charles with a smile.

"You seem pretty efficient already," said Walter. "Calm, collected, and well thought out under extreme pressure. Also, while we do have a case, we're not making any progress. So I think we have time to put you through the wringer."

Charles stared at the floor for several moments. "How does it work? The whole rescue thing?"

"There's two stages to rescue," said Walter. "The first is the physical rescue, and the second is the reintegration into normalcy. The physical rescue is what you're looking to be a part of. It's what the Red Sea Initiative does. No weapons or anything. It's too dangerous to carry around knives or guns. Our only weapon is our courage."

"That's fine," sighed Charles. "I don't like guns, anyways."

"In our current case," continued Walter, "we're sending our UC, which is just Jimmy, undercover to try and buy the services of the little girl. That way we can get tangible evidence for a conviction. Once Jimmy is with the girl, the police will roll in, arrest everyone. That includes Jimmy to protect his identity. Twenty years or more is what we look for, all the way to a possible life sentence."

"I can't just jump into a sting operation," laughed Charles. "I've studied this craft, but I have no field experience, or even actual training. There's no telling how I would actually handle myself under that kind of pressure. We all have a special hatred for pedophiles."

"According to what my research could find on you," said Walter, "you handle pressure pretty well. You already have the awareness to know your limits for your age, although you did attack a guy twice your size in the hospital."

Charles scoffed and shook his head. "That was easy. I had the advantage of leverage and the element of surprise. It was calculated and meticulous. I still need real, hands-on training in this particular industry."

"You're off of work the rest of the week?"

Charles nodded.

"Can you be at the police station at eight o'clock tomorrow?"

Charles checked his watch. "Eight o'clock tomorrow? I could be there right now."

# *12*

*Claremore, Oklahoma - Tuesday - 8:00 PM*
*He didn't even say goodbye.* Charles had just hung up on her. A knock at his door, and a quick, "Are you calling, or am I?" Then nothing. She hadn't made him that upset, had she? He wasn't happy that she wouldn't come over, but that wouldn't justify this. Not to him. He was better than that. He always had been.

At least, he had been the last time she had known him.

She couldn't tell him what happened. She never lied to him. She couldn't do that, but she couldn't tell him the truth. It was too dangerous for both of them. She could get hurt, or he could get hurt. Worse yet, she could lose him entirely. He could leave.

Her best plan was always honesty. She was always as honest as possible, and avoided questions she couldn't answer. It had been a rough twenty four hours for Abigail, and she really didn't think she could have left the house today. She felt sick. She felt tired.

She felt like she needed to be with Charles.

But Charles would ask what happened, and she couldn't tell him that. He could never know.

She wanted to scream, but she couldn't. It wouldn't end well for her.

*He hadn't even said goodbye.* Who was at his door? Who was making house calls at nine at night? Charles didn't have any friends, and his father was in the hospital. Why was he so quick to just hang up after needing to see her so badly?

He was all she had left. She couldn't lose him. Now someone else was in his apartment with him. Who could it be?

*It's another woman. It has to be.*

She picked up her phone, and dialed his number again.

It rang once.

It rang twice.

It rang a third time, and she squeezed her eyes shut.

"Abby?" She jumped and gasped, her eyes flinging open as she sat up in bed.

"Who was it at your door?" That was not how she wanted to start the conversation, but it just blurted out before she could think.

*Way to scream the fact that you don't trust him right to his face…*

"I have to be honest, Abby," he replied. "It's kind of a long story."

"I have all night." Again, the words were out of her mouth before she thought about them.

*You sound anxious and distrustful. Tone it down, girl.*

"We both have things going on in the morning," he said. "Is that what's bothering you? Someone being at my door?"

"We didn't end things on the best terms when you hung up," she said.

*Wrong again. You sound crazy.*

She heard him sigh. "I know. I'm sorry, I didn't mean to be rash. I've just got a lot going on right now. I'm a little distracted."

"I know you didn't mean it," she said, trying to be a little more tender toned, "and I know you have a lot going on. I'm not trying to be crazy or anything. It just made me feel a little strange about it all. Can you at least tell me who was at your door until you can tell me the whole story?"

"I'm not sure you would believe me," said Charles, sounding a little strained.

"Try me." It was quick and excitable. She wanted to sound chipper, like she really wanted to know for the right reasons, not the real reason. She hoped it came off the right way.

"I think I got a job offer." Again, he sounded a little confused. "A job offer that I'm really interested in."

"What is it?" asked Abigail. "Or is it a long story?"

"Um." He was definitely confused at this point. "It's a long story. I'll tell you over dinner. When do you think you can come over?"

"I'll come over right now if you'll tell me." He was silent on the other end.

*You sound absolutely insane now. What is wrong with you?*

"Tomorrow?" he asked. He sounded a little more confident now. "I'll probably be home early if you want to come by at five or something like that.

I'll cook something really nice for you. I'll stop by the store on the way home and get steaks. Maybe steak and eggs. How does that sound?"

"Oh my," she said with more than a little genuine surprise in her voice. "You've never made steaks before."

"Will you come for steaks?"

"I'll be there at five," she giggled. "Wait, why will you be home early?"

"I have the day off for this new job thing," he replied. "I'm kind of doing a… some type of interview in the morning."

"Goodness," she sighed. "That's quick."

"They're in need of help. Goodnight, Abby, I'll see you at dinner tomorrow."

"Goodnight."

*I love you.* Her stomach did somersaults just thinking the words, and she squeezed her eyes shut and scrunched up her nose until she heard the call end.

It was still too early for that.

She set her phone down and rolled over, closing her eyes and trying to rest. She smiled. Everything was okay. Charles was looking into a better job opportunity, something he was really excited about. He was making big progress in his life. He was moving forward, and he was still considering her to be a part of things. That was good.

Then the smile flipped over. *He has tomorrow off.* Attendance at work was his biggest pet peeve. Seven years, and he'd only had to call in a handful of times. That meant he had requested the time off, and it had gotten approved. His job required forty eight hours of notice to approve time off. In order to get a Wednesday off, he'd have to have requested the time off on Monday morning. First thing on Monday morning. That meant he had decided on it Sunday night overnight.

Charles had known about this new job for over two days.

# <u>*13*</u>

*Tulsa, Oklahoma - Wednesday - 8:30 AM*
"Thirty reports across Tulsa over the last month. We have locations circled on the map, but we only usually know the locations of his operations about two or three days after he's been there. We've had Jimmy out in the field talking to suspected customers, and trying to pinpoint a location. No one will talk. He's trying to establish relationships, but our guy has his customer base locked down. He's being super careful about his operation. Unfortunately, though, that all ended a couple of days ago when Jimmy was attacked."

"What happened?" asked Charles. "Can I get a list of events on how Jimmy got attacked?"

"I'd let Jimmy tell the story himself," said Walter. "Of what actually happened that night, but leading up to the operation, we had Jimmy talking to a specific customer, trying to get an encounter and set things up, and he finally got a meeting with the big man himself to work out the details."

"So he just met with the guy, and the guy broke his arm?" asked Charles.

"The guy never showed up," replied Walter. "The customer broke Jimmy's arm. We're trying to track him down, but we never got a good name. These people use pseudonyms."

"It's all random," said Charles, squinting up at the board with the circles on it. "There's no real pattern in the way he's moving around."

"That's the conclusion that we've come to," said Walter. "He's picking places pretty much at random to sell her. We're not sure why he picks the places he does, either. The green checkmarks means the location has been confirmed by someone, the red X means that it's just a suspected location, and it hasn't been confirmed."

"Who's giving you these locations?"

"Jimmy. He was getting them from that customer before the guy vanished. Again, only a couple of days after the guy had been there, so it's not really much use to us."

*Everything is of use. Always.*

Charles stared hard at the map on the wall. Something felt familiar about the circles on the board. They did have some sort of pattern to them. He was sure of it, he just couldn't place what that pattern was. Seven years in Tulsa, and he still wasn't sure what was where.

"The circles," he started. "How does Jimmy get them? Are they addresses?"

"City blocks," said Walter. "All done in code. Jimmy was working to get exact locations, but all we have is about a half mile radius."

The glass doors squealed open behind them, and they both turned. Four people entered the room with strange looks on their faces.

"Holy shit, Walt," cried the man with the broken arm, who Charles was guessing was the one Walter called Jimmy. "You really got him. I never thought I was going to see him again."

"I thought you would bring in another team," said an old man in slacks and a tucked in button up shirt. He was a chubby old man, very grey all over, even in the eyes. He stood up tall with a round face, and a relaxed stare that reminded Charles of a circus clown.

"I'm taking a chance," said Walter. "This one reminds me of the early days."

The chubby man widened his eyes at Charles. "In that case, I'm Paul Edwards, Mr. Langley. I'm the Chief of Police here in Tulsa. I'm the one officially leading this investigation."

"Officially?" asked Charles.

Paul nodded towards Walter. "Walter and I go way back, so I know how effective he is in this game. I technically hold the reins here, but I let him do all the work. He's better, and younger."

"Jimmy Limone," said Jimmy, coming forward with his good hand stretched out. Charles took it, the unnatural handshake feeling weird coming from the left hand. The shake was firm, however, and Jimmy made hard eye contact as he moved in. "We met the other night at the hospital. Can I say that was the most impressive takedown I've ever seen?"

"You haven't seen very many takedowns, then," replied Charles with a smile. "You should try watching some MMA, you'll see some more impressive stuff."

"That dude had to weigh twice what you do," laughed Jimmy. "It was nuts. No MMA fight would ever have something like that."

Charles shrugged, glancing over at one of the two women coming forward into the room and extending her own hand. He grasped it, somewhat shocked at the grip she had.

"Rebecca Swift," she introduced herself with a confident smile. She spoke with a proud voice that filled the room. Her teal eyes burned into his face like laser beams. Rebecca shook locks of brown and grey hair out of her eyes and looked him up and down. "Are you old enough to be a part of this team?"

"Are you?" asked Charles. "I thought the age requirement was thirty."

She leaned back with a hand on her chest, her eyes wide. "Oh my, what a great liar you are. You'll do well undercover."

She turned away from him, and his attention settled on the last person in the room.

"I'm Alison," she said, not even approaching him. She nodded in his direction, hazel eyes analyzing him like he was a threat.

He nodded in return, and tried to focus on the task at hand. Perhaps the comment to Rebecca had been a little too much.

Alison, however, would not make it easy for him to concentrate. A black haired and slim figured woman he figured to be about mid thirties, her arms bulged in the slightly undersized black short sleeve shirt. That shirt hugged her torso, bulging at the chest and sinking back down at the stomach. Her waist was trim and maintained a perfect hourglass figure, her hips and legs filling the denim jeans she had on.

Something about her face, the structure of it, the bubbly cheekbones and pronounced jawline told him she was foreign. Her accent was American English, but her body told him otherwise. The build of the face. Slavic. That's what came to mind.

*She was the only one that didn't give a last name. Jimmy Limone. Paul Edwards. Rebecca Swift. Alison.*

"What do you make of our board?" asked Jimmy. "Did you figure anything out?"

"He's choosing his locations at random," replied Charles, forcing his eyes back up to the board. "No addresses, only areas. For now, that's all I can make out of it."

"So we're not looking for a pattern?" asked Paul Edwards.

"Everyone sets a pattern eventually," replied Charles. "No one can be truly random. He'll go back to the places he likes, or where makes more money."

"So what's our next step?" asked Walter, drawing the attention of everyone in the room to Charles.

"Figure out why he's choosing those locations," he replied with a nervous glance around the room. "I mean, if we can figure out why he picks where he sets up, we might be able to predict where his next location would be. I know that takes time, but it's really all we have to go on."

"So let's take a look at the locations," said Paul, stepping closer to the board. "Why these locations?"

The room fell silent. Charles looked at everyone, noticing Alison was still staring at him. He returned his attention to the board, focusing on the circles up there instead of the ones attached to Alison's chest. He could still see that pattern. What was so familiar about them? Something in his mind, and image, reminded him of the way the circles were outlined on the wall.

Seven circles across the top of the city, almost all right along I-244. Two more along highway eleven north of 244. There were ten bunched up together going south along highway sixty four, two towards downtown. Four along the Arkansas River. Two on the south end of town on the highway leading south: Seventy five. The ones along the Arkansas River were marked two or three times. Whatever was there, he was attracted to the waterfront.

"How many people have we had actually in these locations?" asked Charles. "Physically, I mean."

"Just me," said Jimmy. "I've been in each of these places once."

Charles raised his phone and took a picture of the map with his camera. "I'm going to check them out myself. Care to come with me, Jimmy?"

"You stay out of this, Jimmy," said Alison, putting a hand on the man's shoulder. "You're in a sling, plus now they know what you look like, and will associate you with the police. I'll go with him. Is that good, Walt?"

Walter glanced between Charles and Alison. "Just promise you won't hurt him."

# *14*

*Tulsa, Oklahoma - Wednesday - 11:00 AM*
They drove both sides of the interstate, and Charles hadn't noticed anything. They were downtown, driving up and down highway sixty five and staring around them. Charles could not figure it out, so Alison decided to take him up along the Arkansas River and see what he could spot there.

The waterfront. Something about the waterfront made this guy come back more than once. It was silent in the car, neither one of them knowing what to say. She would glance at him as they closed in somewhere, and he would shake his head. Nothing jumped out at him.

*Focus. Do your exercises. Look at your surroundings. Something easy.* He checked the door mirror of the car, noticing an old model Toyota sedan following close behind them. He watched the car, trying to identify the details of the vehicle and driver as well as he could from his angle. White male, possibly late forties, thinning hair. Red Toyota sedan, hatchback, license plate RT2-N3T. He tried to save it in his brain. Memorization was key here.

"What are the makes and models of all the vehicles behind us right now?" asked Alison. "Quick without making it obvious."

"I can only see one in the door mirror," said Charles. He glanced up in the rearview and saw a silver Cadillac to the left behind them, then nothing in the driver's side mirror. Those were always at weird angles to the passengers. "Silver Cadillac and a red Toyota."

"Makes and models."

"I don't know the models," said Charles with a scoff. "Toyota sedan hatchback, looks like a nineties model, which is probably a Corolla, and I don't know the Cadillac lineup."

"The Caddy is an early two thousands model sedan," began Alison, "likely a mid decade model Deville. You're probably right about the Toyota. I figured you'd be better at that one. Walter said you practice awareness drills, and I noticed you glanced into the mirror. I wondered if that was what you were doing. Anyways, it's easier when you're driving. You'll see more in the mirrors because they're set up for you to see everything. Again, you'll learn the looks of the designs of vehicles as you practice. You'll learn how each manufacturer built and designed their vehicles in each decade."

"Why is this important?" asked Charles.

"It leads to better situational awareness all around," said Alison. "It helps us be able to naturally get details without thinking about it for identification purposes. The more we do it, then the faster we can do it. That helps in high stress situations. Plus, it's the same with people. The more you try to identify details about people, the more accurate you'll be in the long run."

"Is it weird?" asked Charles, checking the mirrors again. The Cadillac was gone, but the Toyota was still on their tail. "Walter picking me up pretty much from the streets for this? I feel a little out of place there, even as excited as I am to be a part of this. It just feels like I shouldn't be there."

Alison sighed. "For this operation, I think you're fine. As careful as this guy is, it's still a small operation in a relatively small town. Bigger picture, you still have a long way to go, which is fine because we have the time to train you for now. Usually, the Initiative doesn't take on recruits under thirty. You and I are the exception because we showed the right amount of potential at an early age. Passion and dedication are huge as well. If Walter sees it in you enough for him to make that call, the same way he did with me, then I trust his judgment. Jimmy was the one that suggested we pick you up, and the way Rebecca displays herself to you tells me she's happy to have someone around that she thinks is attractive, and thinks that she's attractive."

"Yeah," sighed Charles. "Not sure I should have said that out loud, but she didn't seem like she hears that kind of thing a lot."

"She doesn't," replied Alison. "She's almost always got a pretty dark attitude. This job makes her very morose."

Charles shrugged. "At least they don't all hate me."

"I also wanted to reach out," she added, looking over at him. "I thought it was strange that you displayed so much aptitude for this with so little background. I was very interested. I read your court records and everything. You are a very interesting person."

The Toyota seemed to refuse to back off through each turn, riding right on the tail of Alison's car.

"Why over thirty?" asked Charles. "I asked Walter at the hospital, but he avoided my question. Obviously, I hadn't impressed him that much yet."

"Pedophiles are generally older men," said Alison with a smile. "Very, very patriarchal. Older men really tend to like younger boys and girls. Sometimes, older women go for young boys, but it's mostly men. Since we're almost always posing as customers of human traffickers inside of our sting operations, it's important to play the role."

"So how do you fit in?" asked Charles. "You're neither old, nor a man."

"I'm usually part of the recovery team," replied Alison. "Although lately, I've been helping Jimmy on ops and posing as a customer of children as well. We're short on men on our team."

"Jimmy must have to carry a lot of the work with only women on his team," said Charles as the car pulled along the side of the river. Up ahead there was the massive thirty story building, the hotel and resort where the anti human trafficking conference was being held.

*The Hotel.*

"Officially, he's the team lead," said Alison, "but everyone kind of just does what I tell them to. I... can be a little intimidating."

"You don't scare me," chuckled Charles.

Alison glanced at him with a smile. "You barely know me. Once you get to know me better, you smarten up."

Charles glanced off to the right, seeing a Long Night's Inn sitting there. *A hotel.* He sat up in his seat. Waterfront. Tourism. Attraction. Suddenly, it all fit.

"Pull over."

"Where?"

"Find a spot. I think I've figured it out."

She pulled off the highway at an intersection close to the Hotel and Resort for the conference. It was a small strip mall that contained two shopping marts and a sushi store.

Charles was out of the car before it had come to a complete stop, his phone in his hand and his map open. He remembered the pattern he'd noticed on the map. A search on his phone from seven years ago when he'd moved to Tulsa. When all he'd wanted to do was escape home and didn't have the time to find an apartment.

He had googled hotels, and the pins had laid themselves across the town of Tulsa like the circles on the map.

Alison struggled to follow him, throwing the car in park and forgetting to shut the vehicle off. "What do you think you have?"

"These circles are general areas of where our guy is reported to be, right?" he asked, and she nodded in confirmation. "We're right here." He stepped closer to her with his phone in his hand, pointing to the spot in the picture he had taken. "Where are the circles closest to us?"

She leaned in to look at the phone screen, then glanced around, spotting what Charles had spotted. The two signs. Grand River View, and Long Night's Inn. The two circles were closest to the hotels.

"He's using hotels as bases of operations," she mumbled, turning to face him, her face mere inches from his. She was tall, eye to eye with him, same as Walter, the brown eyes peering into his own.

He had to force himself to step back. "That's what all of them have to be. If he could make thousands of dollars each day, then a few hundred bucks in hotel rooms isn't anything from his bottom line. It keeps him on the move and away from home. It keeps him out of our crosshairs. That's why there's no home base. He hasn't shown it to us, because he hasn't used it for business. He can bounce around in different hotels under different names at random. There's no shortage of hotels around here."

Alison laughed. "It makes sense. Let's run the route again, and make a list of the hotels inside the circles. Boy, the others will be upset when they find out you cracked the code. They've been working on this forever."

She was laughing when she got back in the car. Charles reached for his door, only to find it still open. He climbed in, and instinctively checked his door mirror when it slammed shut behind him.

There was the red Toyota sedan at the end of the parking lot, with the man inside of it paying keen attention to Charles and Alison.

***

The range was extreme, but Charles had hit the nail on the head. Every circle had a hotel in it. From two stars to four stars, every location was the square block of a hotel, or a small pack of hotels. Charles filled a notepad with details. Average room prices, hotel conditions, and even makes and models of vehicles in the parking lot.

"You can tell a lot about a person by what they drive and what condition it's in," Alison pointed out. "Don't go peeking through people's windows, but take a look at the paint, look for dents, or even how much bird shit is on it."

The circuit got made again in reverse, circling the map on Charles's phone. The dates on the map still looked random, but Charles knew there would be a pattern to them. Higher priced rooms meant higher priced time with the girl, which attracted a higher class customer than something cheap.

The police station rolled into their view, drawing Charles back into the real world for a moment.

"Keep driving," said Charles, as they pulled up to the entrance. "Don't turn into the parking lot."

He checked his mirror again, watching the red Toyota Sedan hug their rear bumper.

"Good catch," Alison smiled again, continuing down the road. "I was wondering if you'd see it. What do you want to do about it?"

*Bag him up and bring him in.* It was Charles's first thought. Even if it wasn't connected to their case, at least they would know who it was and why he was following them.

It was a he. Charles could see him through the windows. He could see unkempt stubble on the man's face, a short buzz cut, and knobby knuckles.

"Pull over down the road," said Charles. "Somewhere where he'll follow us into. I don't imagine he'll willingly go into the police station."

"Where?" asked Alison.

Charles pointed at a sign in the distance. "That fast food joint down the street."

She donned a look of confusion for several moments, but, as naturally as she could make it look, Alison pulled into the parking lot and parked across from the building.

Charles raised a finger. "Wait here."

"What are you doing?" asked Alison with a tight squinting of her eyes.

Charles smiled at her as he unbuckled his seatbelt and opened the car door. "Buying lunch. You want a cheeseburger and fries?"

A blank expression stared back at him as he exited the car and made his way into the fast food store, double checking to make sure the Toyota pulled into the parking lot as well. The driver pulled into a spot close to the door of the restaurant, watching Charles closely. Charles made sure to keep his eyes forward, using only his peripheral vision to watch the Toyota. The man didn't exit the vehicle, or shut the engine off. He only watched Charles.

Charles pushed the glass doors open, walked into the store, and approached the counter. The woman behind the counter smiled at him and asked him what he wanted in a pleasant tone that he wasn't used to hearing from fast food employees.

"I just need a couple of burgers and small french fries," he said.

"How many of each?" asked the girl behind the counter, her smile unusually bright.

Charles looked back out the window at the man in the car, not quite making eye contact with the driver. "I'll need three of each, please."

# <u>15</u>

*Tulsa, Oklahoma - Wednesday - 11:30 AM*
Artificial thunder rolled as the feet of Jimmy
Limone stomped back and forth at the end of the
conference table, where his stocky frame caused
him to rumble on the floor. The other three people
in the room stared at him, watching the smoke pour
from his ears.

"Jimmy, take it easy," said Walter, "You've
been ID'd by the bad guys, and your arm is in a
sling. We can't exactly have you doing a whole lot
with this case anymore."

"Are you kidding me?" Jimmy cried out in
the small room. "Your solution is to take me off the
case entirely and put me full time at the
conference?"

"You'll have Katie and Rebecca as well,"
said Walter. "Paul's wife, Jamie, is going to take
care of Kitsen so I can be there as well."

"When I said to hire this new guy," growled
Jimmy, "I didn't mean replace me with him."

"I'm not," said Walter. "You can't be out on
operations. Your cover has been blown, so I need a
new face in the field. I also need the conference
taken care of. I'll be there on and off like I have so
far..."

"So I get to deal with the wrath of the board, not you?" Jimmy was bracing himself against the wall. "I get to explain why we're not getting the job done and you get to escape all responsibility?"

"I'll handle the board," said Walter. "I need you and the Swift sisters handling the training and PR stuff. At some point, I'll have Charles there, too. He needs to see how these things work as well."

"So we have to deal with these trainee ding dongs while you go on an adventure in our backyard with Alison and the new guy?" asked Jimmy.

"I will be there in and out," said Walter. "Paul can handle most of the investigation. I need Alison training the new guy. That puts us at the conference. Just keep things steady when I'm not there and distract the board from our mishappenings with this case until I can get a hold of them."

Jimmy groaned. "Not the board. I hate dealing with those idiots. They have no idea what people like us go through out in the field."

"I know," muttered Walter. "Deal with them for now, and I'll be up there to smooth it out later on. If everything goes well, the board will be happy we have extra help and can move forward easier in the future."

"What if it doesn't go well?" asked Jimmy. Rebecca and Paul looked up at Walter with matching expressions, waiting for the response.

All of them knew what would happen if things didn't go well. Walter had already been warned several times for taking unnecessary risks, and had skated by the skin of his teeth because he'd been successful. The board of directors would be furious if he made the same mistakes, and failed. He was already on thin ice for taking too long with this case, not to mention Jimmy's medical bills. If he brought in a new guy and everything went haywire, Walter was at the mercy of the board.

"I'll handle it." Walter's voice came out through clenched teeth.

"Walter said we needed a new male team member," said Rebecca from the chair at the end of the table. She looked over at Jimmy with canted eyebrows. "He said having just one is hurting which operations we can be a part of. It's really hard to get three women into the mix when most pedophiles are men. The Initiative is losing operators to the lack of funding we're getting right now. People are really struggling to remember why we do what we do. This new guy could be exactly what we need right now. We need to take advantage of it. We need to be out in the public eye getting our fundraising back underneath us before we lose more crew members, and there's only a few of us that can do that. Katie has the personality, I have the experience, and you are injured. We all need to be where we're needed."

Jimmy rested his good hand on the table, and sighed deeply. "Okay." It was a growl, not a regular human voice. "I'll do my part, but this new guy better prove to work out." His eyes raised to meet Walter's. "If he can't get the job done, or if I get shafted by the board without your support, or if you keep shoving us around like this without any consideration, I might be the next one out the door."

***

Charles nudged open the restaurant door and stared at Alison through the windshield of her car. From the look on her face, she had no idea what he was doing, and that was what he wanted. That meant that she was too far away to interfere with his plan, and the man that was following them was too close to get away. The windows in the Toyota were rolled down, so even though the engine was running, there was no chance of escape.

Charles gave Alison one quick smile, and turned to the Toyota. The man in the Toyota, looking down, noticed Charles's movements out of the corner of his eyes. He looked up, made eye contact with Charles, and went berserk.

He reached around for the gear shift, the phone in his hand clattering to the center console. He couldn't seem to find the handle. Then he found it, but couldn't get it to move. Then, it was too late.

Charles reached in the window and pulled the interior door handle, opening the door from the inside before dropping himself in the passenger seat.

"I've seen you following us all morning," he said calmly, raising up the paper bag. "I haven't seen you eat. I got you—"

Before Charles knew what was happening, everything descended into chaos.

The man reached out and threw a punch at Charles, missing and hitting the bag of food right in the center of the logo. The man's arm caught on the gear shift as he drew back, sending the gear shift all the way down into drive as the bag of food was thrown through the open window. The car lurched forward, bumping into the parking bumper and sending both Charles and the driver into the dashboard. Charles hit the gear shift forward, knocking the vehicle into reverse instead of park and sending the car rolling backwards through the parking lot.

The man threw another punch, swinging a wide back fist in Charles's direction that Charles expertly blocked with a forearm, leaning towards the driver to dampen some of the force behind the swing. Charles grabbed the forearm in both hands, pulled the arm against his chest to hold control of it, and pulled the man towards him and out of the driver's seat. The man's fingers locked into the door handle behind Charles and opened the car door.

Charles felt himself lean backwards as his only support fell away, and both of them tumbled out of the door and onto the concrete. The car continued on an unmitigated warpath towards the opposite side of the parking lot.

Gripping the man's arm tightly, he threw up a leg to go for an armbar, but the man was able to shift his weight away from Charles and wrench his arm free. Charles heard a woman yell his name followed by a string of expletives. He rolled to face his opponent, who was actually crawling away from him and towards the unmanned red car.

The car came to a halt by itself halfway across the parking lot as the owner of the car gathered his feet under him and made a break for the driver's side door. He reached the door and grabbed the handle, only to have the door flung open in his face and be knocked to the ground holding his nose. Alison stepped out of the car, which stayed put like it was afraid of what she would do to it if it moved, and stood over the man.

Charles scrambled to his feet and joined her side, being wary of any incoming punches from either his attacker or his infuriated trainer.

"Who sent you?" He'd always wanted to ask that. It didn't come out sounding like Liam Neeson had said it. More like Don Knotts.

Alison glared at Charles, pointing a finger in his face before returning her attention to the man on the ground. "Answer the question."

The man did not answer the question.

Alison glanced around the parking lot, looking for spectators, before she took one step, landing the sole of what had to be a size fourteen combat boot in the man's neck.

"Who, what, when, where, why, how, and now."

The man grunted and choked, but was ultimately more afraid of Alison than whatever else scared a man like this. "Solomon. My name is Solomon. I'm supposed to follow you around and report what you're doing and where you're staying to a friend."

"Which friend?" asked Alison. The man didn't speak, earning him extra pressure against his throat. He still didn't speak. What he did was more of a squeal.

"My car!" he tried to scream.

"Your car is fine," said Alison. "I saved it from any damage. What should you do for me in return?"

"I'll talk," groaned the man. "I swear, I'll talk. Just let me breathe."

Three whole seconds passed before Alison stepped off the man's neck, and she reached down and grabbed the man by the collar.

"Get in the trunk." She dragged the man over to her car, popped the trunk with the keys, and threw the man towards the open back.

The man looked up at her. "Seriously?"

"I don't have a way to restrain you in the back seat," said Alison. "So you get to ride in the trunk. I'll park your car over here and have the impound guys come get it."

"Oh come on," groaned the man. "Don't do that. I'll cooperate, I swear."

"Get in the trunk. Your car being impounded depends on what you give the guys downtown."

The man climbed into the trunk of the car, and Alison slammed the door down on top of him. Then she shot out a hand and grabbed the shoulder of his shirt. "Let's go."

Charles had never been dragged across a parking lot by anyone in his life. Being dragged by a woman, however, was a lot more embarrassing than he thought it would be. Having the door to the back seat opened for him, and then practically being thrown in the back seat by said woman, was downright humiliating.

She was in the car and driving before he had fully recovered from that humiliation. She was back on the highway and speeding down to the police station before he was able to speak.

"That didn't go as planned."

# <u>*16*</u>

*Tulsa, Oklahoma - Wednesday - 1:00 PM*
Never in his life had he seen anything so amazing,
and he was completely unsure how to feel about it.
Part of him was terrified at the six foot tall woman
dragging the man named Solomon by the ear
through the glass entrance of the police station. The
other part of him wanted to sleep with her. His first
thought was his phone, the bookmark on his tab,
and a growing sensation in his jeans. He had to
shake his head. *Focus on work. Take care of that
later.*

Never in his life had he been so impressed
by the power of a woman like this. Every woman he
had ever met had been meek and mild. Even
Abigail, a military combat medic, strayed away
from most things like physical contact and
confrontation. Alison carried the aura of an
Amazonian Goddess around her. When she walked
into the room, all the attention was immediately on
her.

It was magnificent to behold.

"Stalking, assault, battery, theft, whatever
you want," she boomed, her voice like a siren,
beautiful and confident. "Make up something if you
have to."

Solomon vanished when two police officers hauled him away, and the conference room to their right cleared out with a calamity of sound and motion. Jimmy stormed through the lobby, charging past Charles with a hard shoulder check that sent the young man flying into a nearby chair.

*What was that about?*

Jimmy was out the door before anyone could say something to him. Charles looked up at Alison, who turned her attention to Paul and Walter without concern.

"The guy stalked us all around town, then attacked Charles in a restaurant parking lot," she told the two of them. "I got him to admit someone hired him to follow us. Sweat him about who hired him, and use his car as leverage. He seems to be really worried about it."

"He attacked Charles in the parking lot?" asked Walter. "Why?"

"I'm not sure," replied Alison. "Charles went in to get us lunch, and the guy ambushed him when he came out."

*She covered for me.* Thought Charles. That was weird considering how upset she was. *Why?*

A hand reached out and grabbed Charles under the arm, lifting him out of the chair and dusting him off. It was Rebecca, staring up into his eyes with green mirrors that reminded him of Abigail.

"Excuse Jimmy," she muttered. "He's not very happy right now."

"Was it me?" asked Charles, trying to put some distance between himself and Rebecca.

"Kind of," she said under her breath. "Walter pulled him from the case because he's injured, and is putting him full time at the conference. He's not happy you're replacing him."

"I guess I don't blame him," said Charles. "As much as I'm excited to be on the case."

"I do," Rebecca chirped, pointing a finger in his face. "You're all we've got. Walter's right, Jimmy's hurt and borderline useless. You're the one man on the team we have available. I believe in you, and I stood up for you, so don't mess this up."

"Thanks for the vote of confidence," he told her.

"I have to go with Jimmy," she said, placing a hand on his chest again, this time not dissimilar to how Abigail had a few nights ago. "Good luck, we're all counting on you."

"Charles," Alison called, waving him over to where she and Paul were standing with Walter. "Get over here. We've got some bad news."

Charles approached, watching Alison closely and still expecting a sucker punch as punishment.

"It looks like it's just us for this investigation," she continued. "Walter and the others have to take on the conference."

"We can't be at the conference?" asked Charles.

"You're too new," replied Alison, "and I don't like being there."

"I thought the conference was for new people," said Charles. "Am I not included in that? Don't I need the training?"

"I'll train you out here in the field," said Alison. "I really hate those conferences."

Charles laughed. "So what's next?"

Paul nodded towards the back. "You want to sit in on the interview of this guy? I'll handle the questions, and you guys can watch through the windows?"

Alison looked at Charles, who shrugged. "Why not?"

***

There were no windows in Interrogation here in Tulsa. The rooms were just tiny little squares with a table in the middle for interviews. Charles and Alison were given the option to watch on the cameras. Charles chose to be in the room with everyone. He wanted to watch the man's body language when he was interviewed.

*Training exercises. Always learning.*

Paul sat at the table, and Alison stood on the other side of the room behind the man. Charles remained by the door, within sight of Solomon and watching closely. Charles glanced up at Alison, who was watching Charles instead of Solomon. Her eyes seemed to pierce his soul, watching his every move.

*Maybe she's just making sure I'm doing it all right.*

"Mr. Solomon," said Paul, taking out a notepad and a pen. "My name is Paul Edwards, I'm the chief of police here in Tulsa. I'm going to ask you some questions, the first one being has anyone read you your rights?"

Solomon shook his head.

"Well, then," sighed Paul, "It's my job to inform you that you don't have to answer these questions, what you say in this room can and will be held against you if it comes down to a court case, and that you do have a right to have a lawyer present if you feel the need."

Solomon remained silent, staring up at Charles. Paul turned to look between Charles and Solomon.

"Do you know the man standing behind me, Mr. Solomon?" asked Paul.

Solomon shook his head.

"Do you know the woman he was with earlier?"

Solomon glanced over his shoulder, shivered, and shook his head.

"Would you like to tell me why you were following them around town?"

Solomon shook his head again.

"According to them, you told them you were hired to keep an eye on them by a friend. Any idea who that friend was?"

Solomon's face changed, sinking an inch or two. It was like he'd lost his luster for holding out on the police. His gaze dropped to the table, and he gave a slight nod. Barely noticeable. Charles recognized it.

*Concession.*

Then Solomon's eyes rose to meet with Charles again. "You're Langley, right?"

"You do know who I am," replied Charles. "I'm assuming that means it was me you were following?"

Solomon nodded his head. "You really caught me off guard jumping into my car like that. I just kind of panicked."

Paul turned and looked at Charles with that face that silently said, "seriously?", and shook his head. He returned to his notes, and Alison grinned from across the room.

Something felt wrong. The scared man of a few moments ago was gone, and had been replaced by this new guy. He almost treated this like he and Charles were old buddies.

Like he was comfortable.

"How did you know who to follow?" asked Charles. "Did you get a picture and a name?"

Solomon nodded again, this time not saying anything. His eyes fell to the table, his eyelids drooping. His hands were down in his lap, but Charles could see the man's forearms flexing rapidly, as if he were wringing his hands. There was the scared man again.

*He still doesn't want to admit who it was. He is afraid of whoever it is. Very afraid.*

"So who hired you to follow me?" asked Charles, leaning forward away from the wall. "I don't recognize you, so it wasn't just you on your own. I wasn't aware I had any enemies trying to keep tabs on me."

"Not an enemy," sighed Solomon. He wouldn't look up now, and his lips pursed. "Someone close. Someone worried about what you're doing and who you're with."

"You're going to have to be more specific," said Charles. "It might help if you dropped a name."

*Who else could it be? You have no friends.*

Solomon glanced around the room, his lips tight and his eyes squinting. His nose scrunched up, and he blasted air out of his lungs in a deep sigh. He shook his head, and raised his eyes again to look at Charles.

"You really want to know?"

A pit dropped in Charles's stomach. There were only two people in his life. Only one was capable of sending someone to follow him. Only one would be insecure about what he was doing, and who he was with. Slowly, he nodded.

Solomon smiled. "Abigail Smith."

# <u>17</u>

*Tulsa, Oklahoma - Wednesday - 4:00 PM*
Canceled. First she hired someone to keep tabs on him, and now she was telling him she couldn't make it to dinner that night. She had been so adamant about finding out who was at his door, and this had been her only way to find out. Now she was very adamant that she couldn't come over.

"She's afraid because you caught her spying on you." Alison stepped over to her car and looked out over the view of the city around the hospital. A wide open sky faced them, a stark contrast to the tall buildings to their left. A modern day Wild West, with shades of tan coloring everything around them. "How's your father?"

"He's dying," replied Charles. "They'll get the tests back later this week to find out if he needs surgery or not."

Alison sighed. "That can't be easy to deal with for either of you."

"It is what it is," Charles said with a shrug. "He's set me up if he does die. I get his house, and a Life Insurance policy worth half a million dollars."

"You make it sound like such a good thing," said Alison. "Don't deflect, it only hurts you in the long run."

Charles didn't respond. He stared up to the left, a grand city towering over him.

"You know, for a single guy, you really do have it made. Apartment all to yourself, a good job, and a girlfriend that hires someone to babysit you."

"Everyone keeps saying that," said Charles. "I know my life isn't horrible, but come on. I live in a one bedroom apartment at, like, six hundred square feet. I make great money, but…"

He trailed off, not entirely sure where he was going with his monologue. Alison was right. He really did have it made. So why wasn't he happy with it?

"Talk to me about it," said Alison, spinning around and leaning backwards on her car. "How much money do you make?"

"Hell," laughed Charles. "I get a raise every year. I'm up to thirty two bucks an hour."

"So just over sixty five each year," she said, nodding. "Let's say you join The Initiative. We're contract based, but not paid. It's all volunteer stuff. Your operations would be funded through donations and fundraising. Walter works for most of our funding, but our operations are very different from the life you have here."

"Try me."

"We stay in cheap hotels," continued Alison. "Usually about twenty bucks a night. One star joints that make the cheapest hotels in the cheapest cities look fancy. On the off chance we get big funding for a large operation, say we need to look like high rollers to get into an organization, we get a good place."

"A couple pairs of clothes, a phone, and a hotel room." Charles had to smile. It reminded him of his life before he met Abigail. "Actually I kind of like that."

Alison laughed. "You really are a strange man, Charles Langley."

"What about you?" asked Charles. "How strange are you?"

Alison pursed her lips and crossed her arms over her chest. "Should I tell you my story? You never told me yours."

"I won't make you tell," said Charles. "You're technically the boss. Besides, you know my story. You wrote up a report on me for Walter."

She smiled at him. "I know what the report says. You and I both know how notorious those things are for leaving out important details. That's for you to tell me. If we're going to work together in this industry, we have to be able to trust each other. That means being honest about our pasts."

"Are you going to make me build up a report on you?" asked Charles. "For practice?"

Alison smiled at him, a predatory smile. "There's nothing out there for you to find." She thought for a moment, staring off into the distance over his shoulder. "Okay. Let's train a little bit. If you had to guess where I was born, where would you guess?"

Charles took a moment to look the woman up and down. She was tall, strong, and confident like a Viking. She had that foreign look to her. She had no accent, but that could have been practiced. She was older. Those almond shaped eyes, and that chiseled jawline. She had thick cheekbones that sat closer to her eyes than her chin. He settled on Slavic roots, based on her facial structure.

"Russia?"

She smiled at him. "California. My parents were Russian and vacationing here in the States. Dimitri and Anastasia Rotskoya. They had me out there in Los Angeles, and in less than a few weeks of being here, they fled back to Russia."

Charles would have known Russia for certain if he'd have known her last name. *Alison Rotskoya.*

"So you grew up in Russia?" he asked.

Alison shook her head. "*They* fled. Not *we* fled."

Charles leaned forward off of the side of his truck. "No way."

Alison nodded slowly, pursing her lips. "They surrendered me at an orphanage in LA, and went home to Russia without me."

"Why?"

"I wouldn't know. They never came back. They never spoke to me or had any kind of contact with me. I looked them up shortly after I joined the Initiative, but they never responded to me."

Charles rocked back and forth uncomfortably. "I can't imagine…"

And then he thought of his mother.

"So how did you come about the Red Sea Initiative?" he asked her, trying to shake that thought out of his own head.

"I grew up living like this," responded Alison. "Sneaking around the foster houses, and the orphanage. Sneaking around the city at night. I was always avoiding someone. When I was fourteen I was taken in by a middle aged man who said he could provide me with a life and work. Take a guess what that work was."

Charles's eyes widened. "Prostitution?"

Alison shook her head. "Prostitutes get paid. What I did was sex slavery. Six years, until I was twenty."

"You were trafficked out of the Foster Care Program?" asked Charles.

She sighed, her shoulders slumping and bringing her size down several inches in all directions. "The justice system estimates that over sixty percent of child trafficking cases in the US have had past experiences with the child welfare system."

Charles sat back. "I had no idea."

"No one knows because the government isn't going to just openly admit that it sucks," sighed Alison. "The government doesn't take care of children. It sure never took care of me. Even when my trafficker was caught, all they did was tell me I had to move on. I was too old and not American enough for their help, even though I was born in America. I spoke English, I could read, and I could write, but it just wasn't enough for them. That's when Walter and his early team came and got me. I saw what they did, and I wanted in on it, just like you do. Walter saw what I was capable of, took me under his wing, and gave me a second chance at life. He became my new family because I have none. That's what he's trying to do for you."

"I thought you didn't know all the details of my life," said Charles. "How do you know about my family?"

"It doesn't take a genius," replied Alison. "I know your father is in the hospital because Walter and Jimmy told me. It isn't difficult to infer that he was having a heart attack. A middle aged obese man is in the hospital, it's safe to say the cause is probably America's number one killer. Then there's your mother. She's not currently in the picture. Bad relations, or no relations?"

Charles's eyes dropped. "Bad relations."

"Thanks for being honest."

He had to look up at her to make sure it was her speaking. Her voice changed. It was soft, caring, and delicate. It didn't dominate. It didn't sound like her.

Except when he saw her this time, it did fit. Suddenly, physically, she seemed more like a girl than a woman. Her face had softened, her eyes shined, and her body looked slimmer and less developed. She looked less muscular, and she didn't carry that power and intimidation.

Charles hesitated for a moment before saying anything. "This is part of that trust building, isn't it?"

Alison nodded again.

"I come from Kansas City," he started, standing closer to her. "My father was an alcoholic, and lost custody of me when I was about six. Then I went to live with my mother. Turns out she couldn't handle me, either, though. I was never an easy child to deal with. I had a lot of… emotional trouble."

Alison nodded, her eyes locked on him, her head tilted slightly to the side.

"Early on she put me through martial arts and wrestling to help me cope with the harder things that I was struggling with. She tried church, but it never stuck. The wrestling didn't do much, either. It just taught me how to hurt people. Krav Maga is what saved me. The lifestyle aspect of it gave me something to focus on. It gave me a sense of discipline. I don't know where I'd be without it. I wouldn't have it made, that's for sure."

Alison remained silent, waiting for him to continue. She tried to hold eye contact, giving him her undivided attention, but his face dropped to the floor. She straightened up and put a hand on his shoulder.

"You don't have to say anything until you're ready." She turned to open her car door, and slumped inside. She hesitated.

"Goodnight, Charles."

He stepped back into his own truck. "Goodnight."

She stared up at him from the small sedan, mesmerizing him. His eyes met hers. Her eyes glowed in the dusk light, big and brown, beaming at him.

"You struggle with trust?" she asked.

Charles nodded, his mind struggling to remain in the present. "I've only ever been able to trust one person in my whole life."

Her eyes glistened, a shimmering layer of tears forming in them. "Tell me about her. Tell me about your sister. It's okay."

It was okay. For some reason, Alison didn't feel like a stranger. He had met her twelve hours ago, and here he was sharing his life story with her. She had come from a hard background, not so different from his own. She was relatable. She understood.

"Okay."

# *<u>18</u>*

*Kansas City, Missouri - Eleven Years Ago*
"What does the Bible tell us about the Prodigal Son?" asked the Sunday School teacher as she held up the children's book to show the pictures to the others. On the cover was a hand drawn picture of two men, one with a grey beard, and the other with a black beard. One was thick and old, and the other thin and young. One was clothed in a nice robe and headwrap, and the other wore a simple and torn up brown cloak. They were surrounded by farm animals, they were embracing, and they were smiling.

Charles Langley had never heard the story of the Prodigal son. In fact, he had never been to Church before moving in with his mother. He wasn't exactly sure he liked Church. Something about it made the hair on his arms and the back of his neck stand up. He couldn't place what it was. That, and the fact that everyone in the building always seemed like they were judging him.

It was the eyes. The eyes always told the truth. Everyone's faces spoke kindness, but their eyes felt hurtful. Everything about this place felt like a lie.

He had no choice, though, since his mother was religious. The family made it early to service every Sunday and gave their tithes. They took their religion very seriously, so Charles was here in Sunday School sitting next to Emily and listening to the teacher talk about the Prodigal Son.

On the surface, it was simple. The father of the family gave his two sons each half of everything he had, and the younger son went away and spent all the money. He became poor, starving, and homeless before working for a pig farmer. Supposedly, back in Bible days, this was the lowest of working conditions that anyone could have.

Then he realized that even his old father's servants had better working and living conditions than he did, and went back home. He felt shame for squandering his part of the family fortune, and didn't consider himself a part of the family anymore. He offered his father a deal to work as a servant instead of coming home as a son. He felt it was a good way of paying penance for his sins as a failure. The father wouldn't let his son be a servant. He accepted his son back into his home, celebrating that his son had returned to be with the family.

The moral of the story, the teacher explained, or the complicated part, as Charles saw it, was that God's unconditional love for everyone does not depend on faithfulness. All that was required was to repent of sin, and God would hand out forgiveness.

"'Father!'" quoted the teacher, turning at a strange angle to read from the open book while the children looked at the pictures. "'I have sinned against heaven and before you. I am no longer worthy to be called your son. But the father said to his servants to quickly bring the best clothes, the freshest food, and the most comfortable shoes. Let us celebrate, for I thought my son was dead, and he is alive again. He was lost, but now he is found.'"

The older brother was upset about this, understandably, but the father explained his rationale to him. 'Son, you are always with me, and all that is mine is yours. It was fitting to celebrate and be glad, for this your brother was dead, and is alive; he was lost, and is found.'

Charles wasn't sure what was so important about this story. To him it sounded like it was okay to do anything as long as you repented in the end. That didn't fit with what everyone around him was saying. It was confusing, like what the Bible said was different from what people told him.

"A parent's love should be like God's love," continued the teacher. "That's the point of the story. We try our best to be like God with unconditional love. For our children, our family, and our friends."

Something burned inside of Charles's chest when she said this. He felt it deep behind his ribs like he was boiling. His cheeks felt warm, and he just couldn't help but tighten his face into a knotted expression.

"God forgives us for our sins no matter how far gone we are," continued the teacher. "Just like a parent will always love and forgive us."

His breathing quickened, and his eyes flooded with tears. His face felt hot. His body shook violently.

"Always remember," said the teacher. "It's always okay to come back to God, just like it's okay to come back to Mommy and Daddy."

*Daddy.* The world collapsed around him at the sound of the word.

"He doesn't love me!" The words were out of his mouth before they crossed his mind. "Daddy doesn't love me! God doesn't love me!"

It was a scream of rage and distress. Countless pairs of wide eyes stared at him as everyone in the room turned to face him. Faced with a horde of pale and frightened faces, he scrambled backwards to get away. He needed to get away. He needed space to breathe. He couldn't catch his breath. Why was everyone so scared of him? Why didn't anyone love him?

His heart raced. He couldn't control his breathing. No matter how deep he breathed, he couldn't get enough air. The world around him spun. The classroom faded from existence around him. He tried to focus on the faces, but everything quickly became an unrecognizable blur of color. Mashed sounds of voices and movement echoed in his head like he was in a cave.

His chest and head were on fire now. His hands shook, his teeth chattered, and his arms and legs pushed in all directions hopelessly at nothing. He was lost; lost in a torrent of swirling colors and shapes that his brain couldn't seem to bring into focus.

"Bubba?" The voice reverberated in his head. He wasn't sure if he'd heard it or thought it. It came again. "Bubba?"

He looked around the room, searching for the source of the voice. He recognized the sound of it, but his brain couldn't think of a name.

"Hey."

A form appeared in front of him. A shape, pink and colorful. The sound was audible, but quiet and muffled like he had cotton in his ears. It sounded soft and sweet. He took a deep breath, and felt like he could breathe again. The burning sensation started to ebb away. Why?

"Hey. It's okay." That voice again. It was louder and clearer. He recognized it. Who was it? A girl's voice. She called him Bubba.

*Emily.*

He looked back at the form in front of him. It was coming together clearly now. It was the form of a young girl his age. Blonde hair, green eyes, and a pale, soft smile. *Emily.*

"It's okay," she said as she knelt down in front of him. Her eyes looked sympathetic and sorrowful. She looked like she was worried about him. "It's okay, Bubba."

One of her hands reached out to touch him, and he reached back out to grab it in his trembling fingers. The touch of her skin on his sent chills up his arm that skittered through his whole body. Every muscle released the tension. His chest felt lighter. His breathing felt easier. He felt calmer; better. All of his breath purged itself of his body and expelled into the room around him. His head cleared.

"S-sissy?" he whimpered quietly, taking in another breath. This one seemed to do the trick, filling his lungs and clearing his vision.

Emily nodded at him with a smile on her face.

"I'm here, Bubba," she replied. "I promised I'd never leave you. I never will. We're in this together. Always. I love you, even if no one else does."

He smiled. He had come back from the darkness. He had been lost, but Emily had found him. He leapt forward and wrapped his arms around her, and she returned the favor. He would never be lost again.

Not as long as she was alive.

# *19*

*Tulsa, Oklahoma - Present Day - Wednesday - 7:00 PM*

The numbers on the monitor made sense this time. There were no alarms, and less wires. Daylight even crept through the window of the room, landing right on Arthur Langley's face and warming the room up. Charles didn't even feel the need to ground himself.

His father still looked pale, and his eyes still sat deeper into their sockets than normal, and rings of dark colors surrounded the eyes, but life had returned to his face. His smile looked genuine, and his face didn't look pained.

"The test results will come back sometime on Friday," groaned Arthur, trying to adjust his position in the hospital bed. "The one in particular they're concerned about is the Coronary Calcium Exam. It's supposed to tell them how much plaque build up I have in my heart, and whether or not I'm going to need heart surgery."

"I guess this means we won't be taking a family vacation next year?" asked Charles.

Arthur laughed, and then coughed. "We might have to split the cost."

Charles's concern was the lack of family able to go on vacation with, but he kept his mouth shut. "Maybe next time, I'll just finance the whole trip. Pay you back for all the years we've gone on your wallet."

"I'm the parent," sighed Arthur. "It's my job to give you the experience. Besides, I have a lot of making up to do."

Charles pictured his father lying in the front yard, unconscious and covered in vomit. An image from almost twenty years ago, and an image he should not have remembered. Memories from childhood only resurfaced like that when they were bad, and this one was a clear image burned into his mind.

Alcoholism was just too much for the old man to handle.

Another image leapt into his mind. The image of himself in the bathroom of his apartment, videos of naked women doing the things he wanted them to do, when a woman he cared for, genuinely cared for, was in the next room. Did he have a problem? If he cared, wouldn't he be able to wait until Abigail was okay with it? Couldn't it have waited until she was at least out of the apartment?

Was pornography more than he could handle?

*Stop it! Focus!*

"I just feel like a mooch," he said out loud. "I just leech off of you every year."

"You pay for everything on your own," replied Arthur. "In accordance with your own life. Most parents my age with kids your age still have to pay for their children's bills. A close friend of mine is still paying her children's groceries every month, and her daughter has a husband and three babies. I'd say you can afford to leech off of me one week out of every year."

Charles was shaking his head. He stared out of the window, a sour look on his face.

"I don't understand," said Arthur, his voice cracking. "You work a decent job, you make decent money, have your own place, pay all of your own bills, have savings, and even a retirement plan. You're in a good, growing industry in the modern world. You make amazing money for your age. You have a wonderful girl in your life that seems to be getting serious."

Charles considered Abigail hiring someone to watch him, unable to trust what he was doing and who he was with. That did seem serious, but not in a good way. It had come out of the blue, too. They'd had one bad night, not even really much of an argument or a fight, and she had been worried enough to hire a stalker.

It didn't feel right, that was for certain.

"You are doing great," continued Arthur, "considering where you've come from. From having to deal with me, to… Emily. You even took a prison sentence and didn't turn it into an excuse to fail. You don't drink, you don't do drugs, yet here you are worried that you're mooching too much off of your old man because he takes you on a vacation every year."

"What's it all for?" asked Charles. "To just work on machinery in a factory, and pay my bills? What's so important about it?"

"Mechanical work is the future, son," chuckled Arthur. "Everything is heading towards automation, and someone is going to have to maintain and repair all of that equipment. The robots are going to take our jobs, but it'll create jobs for maintenance guys like you. You've already got a foot in the door there. You're set for the rest of your life. Then, once you're too old to work, you can be an instructor. You'll never have to worry about not having a job. Plus, knowing you and money, you'll never have to worry about retirement, either. Just you and the new family you're going to make. You, Abigail, and maybe a couple of little ones."

Charles made a fake gagging noise at the thought, and Arthur laughed. The laugh turned into another phlegm filled cough.

"You'd make a great husband and father. I believe that despite what you had to grow up with."

"How does all that make a difference?" asked Charles. "In the world around us? Just working on machinery? What impact does it make in the bigger picture?"

"It keeps the economy running," said Arthur. "You sound like you're trying to get into political activism."

Charles groaned, and rolled his eyes. "Don't start the political stuff with me. This has nothing to do with politics."

Arthur hesitated a moment, then nodded. "Tell me what it has to do with, then."

*Activism. Purpose.*

Charles sighed, sitting back into the big reclining chair next to the hospital bed. His father could be dead in a few days. He could be dead in a few minutes. There was no point in keeping things secret. He had to tell someone, just to get it off of his chest. There were only two people to tell.

"Those two guys that were with me the other night at the hospital? They're what you would call activists, I guess. They're a part of a non profit organization that fights human trafficking."

"Volunteer work?"

"Pretty much," replied Charles. "It's private investigation and undercover operations. They do fundraising to fund their operations, and they go deep into these organizations posing as buyers of children to gather information to hand over to the police."

Arthur's eyes widened. "That sounds very risky."

"It sounds life threatening," laughed Charles, "but there's children out there in danger. Children. Kids as young as infants, and even teenagers and adults are being sold."

"Like prostitutes?"

"Yeah," said Charles, "but not the kind you like. These girls, and boys, don't get to keep any money. They're abused constantly, physically and psychologically. Some of them are born into it. Imagine growing up and thinking the world around you is nothing but one constant and horrifying nightmare."

"You could always donate to those guys," said Arthur. "Help them get the funds they need to manage their operations. You are pretty badass, but you're no Liam Neeson."

"No one is Liam Neeson," said Charles. "Not even these guys. They're just normal people striving to help children in captivity. Besides, they're not just short on funds. They're short on manpower. I've been doing all these 'grey man' things and studying all of this intelligence stuff for years now, and what has that all come to? It's just a glorified hobby to make me feel like I'm some secret agent living a double life. The reality is I'm stuck at a dead end job in a factory, living in a one bedroom apartment alone with a woman that literally hired a stalker to watch me. I'm tired of this life, and it's time for me to do something about it."

Arthur stared at Charles for a very long time in silence. "Abigail sent someone to follow you?"

Charles shook his head. "Apparently she's worried I'm cheating on her, or whatever. I wasn't even sure we were really dating, but come on. Like I have any luck with women."

"You would if you would talk to them," replied Arthur, still staring.

"I don't want to talk to women," said Charles, feeling his chest tighten. "Women have always caused me problems. The only woman that ever stuck by me was Emily, and how did that go? You know what I want? I want to do something with my life that means something. I want to be able to make a difference in the world. I want to make a difference in people's lives. I want to fight the forces of evil, and I want to have someone by my side that trusts me, understands me, and can support me."

"Son."

"What?"

"Take a breath. There's no need to yell."

Charles sucked in air, completely unaware that he was out of breath. His chest ached with a deep burning sensation. He tried to recall the last few moments, trying to listen to his own tone of voice. Had he been yelling? Yes, he had been yelling. He looked around.

He was standing on the opposite side of the room from the chair he'd been sitting in, halfway through pacing across the room. He hadn't even noticed he'd gotten up out of the chair. He took another deep breath, resting his hands on his hips and continuing his restless walk back and forth from one end of the room to the other.

"I didn't realize I was getting out of control," said Charles. "My name is Charles Langley, I'm back in a hospital room at Ascension Saint John in Tulsa, Oklahoma. It's sometime in the afternoon on a Wednesday, and I'm ready to take my life in a different direction."

His voice had risen again by the time those last words exited his mouth.

"Charles." Arthur raised his hands to get his son's attention. "There's only one person that can take your life in a different direction. Just make sure you do it right. Do what you do. Plan, prepare, and perform."

Charles looked over at his father. "I have a plan."

"You do?"

Charles nodded. "I've had it for a long time, I just haven't told anyone about it because I didn't have an opportunity."

Arthur's face stretched as he opened up with a toothy smile. "No you have one. What are you going to do about it?"

## <u>*20*</u>

*Tulsa, Oklahoma - Thursday - 11:30 AM*
"She hired someone to follow me." It was all he could think about. "Then she canceled dinner. She was terrified that someone strange was at my door, and now she won't come talk about it. What in the world is going on in my relationship?"

"Some women have trust issues, Charles," said Alison. "It comes from a tormented past. From what you've said, you don't really know too much about it. All you know is that she joined the National Guard. Sometimes people hire PI's in order to find out more information. Some people, particularly lower class people, just get a friend to do it or do it themselves. If you've been distant at all, she might just have asked someone to follow you for the day and learn more about you."

Charles picked up his drink, contemplated it, and set it back down. He couldn't help wondering what had gone wrong with Abigail. He hadn't been distant. She had been distant. She had been the one to deny all affection. She had...

She had asked about that safe, and he had avoided the question.

All she wanted was to know more.

"She's always been a little skittish and distant," he said, "but to hire a stalker? To cancel dinner after having our first argument? To avoid all contact? Has been driven insane with jealousy? What did I do wrong?"

"Tell me what happened," said Alison. "How exactly did your conversation go?"

So Charles told her, and according to his version of the story, even he thought his attitude had been less than acceptable on their phone call before Walter had shown up. The thing was, he felt like he'd more than made up for it in their last call.

"You never answered her question," said Alison. "You didn't even try. She begged you to tell her what was going on, and you just said, I got a job offer. Wouldn't that scare you if it was the other way around? If she called you out of nowhere being distant and standoffish, and told you she was considering a career change with no details on where or what it was going to be, wouldn't you be a little nervous? Isn't that why she questioned you? Isn't that why she sent someone? Because she's scared of losing you."

"Then why did she cancel dinner?" asked Charles. "She was practically begging to know the answer, so much so that she willingly offered to stay up all night on the phone to find out. Then, less than twenty four hours later, instead of finding out, she blows it off."

"Sounds to me like she'd had a bad day, and you made it worse," said Alison. "From a woman's point of view, it sounds like you're manipulating her in order to get her to come over and see you."

Then Charles understood. He grabbed his phone and dialed Abigail's number, watching Alison try not to smile at his panic. Five rings, and a voicemail box.

*She's gone. You've lost her.*

He shook his head. No reason to blow her phone up, just a message to let her know.

"I'll just text her and let her know I'm willing to talk."

Alison nodded like she was giving her approval. He avoided eye contact with her.

**Whatever's going on, I want to talk about it. We need to have a serious discussion, please.**

"There," he said out loud. "Not too combative. Get her attention, get her here, and get her talking. I really do want things to work out with her."

His phone gave off a loud ding. A text message notification. Abigail's name appeared on his phone screen.

Alison laughed. "That was fast. Straight to voicemail on the phone, and an immediate text within seconds? She's pissed."

*She's crazy.* Charles thought as he looked down at his phone.

**My family wants to meet you. Please come to dinner tonight. I want to see you. I love you.**

"What?" He was stunned. He showed the phone screen to Alison, who burst out laughing. "She went from giving me the cold shoulder, all the way to I love you and please come meet my parents, in less than thirty seconds. What is going on with my relationship?"

Alison couldn't help herself. "Doesn't sound crazy at all."

Then it hit him. *Love.* She used that word. That word that he wasn't sure he had said to anyone in ten years. Did he feel the same way for her? He wanted to say yes, but his mind thought about the last person he'd said that to. What had happened to her?

*You can't let that stop you.* He tried to tell himself. *No more excuses. You want this, too. Make it happen.*

*I want to make a change in my life.* His own words echoed in his head.

The answer echoed back, the voice of his father, Arthur Langley.

*You're the only one that can make that happen. You have the opportunity. What are you going to do with it?*

His fingers found his response before his brain could second guess it.

**Okay. Dinner tonight at your place. I'll be there.**

He looked back up at Alison. "Okay. I'll deal with that later. What's next on the list of exercises?"

"Are you sure you can handle it with your current situation?" asked Alison.

Charles nodded. "Anything to get my mind off of it. Please."

"Do you have a targeted conversation?" Alison asked, still trying to calm herself down.

Charles nodded, trying to focus on a man's voice behind him. He was speaking, but Charles couldn't hear any responses. *A phone call.* It had to be.

"Now draw a clock on your notepad and try to pinpoint on the clock face where your target is at. Then write down how far away you think he is."

Charles made a quick guess, drawing a line to the six on his clock, and writing ten feet. That sounded good enough. He'd never done this drill, and didn't even know where to begin. He looked back up at Alison, who looked over his shoulder.

"Turn around and see," she said. "Who were you listening to?"

Charles turned and looked for the man who he had been hearing. It was a short and thin man, sitting at a small round table by himself, and talking on the phone. Charles turned back to Alison and pointed him out to her.

"He's at four o'clock, and about fifteen feet away," she said. "How close were you?"

Charles showed her his clock, and she shrugged.

"That's not bad considering how new you are to this one. It takes practice to actually succeed at these exercises. Don't compare yourself to me, yet, either. I've been doing this for most of my life, so I have a lot more practice than you do."

Charles shook his head with pursed lips. He tried to remember what the man's voice had sounded like and why it had felt like six o'clock and ten feet. He tried to memorize the memory of the sound and the numbers, then he gave up. Too much work too soon. Too much distraction coming from Abigail.

*I love you.*

"Lunchtime is the wrong time to start this," said Charles. "There's too much going on for me to pick it up as a beginner."

"The fault of man is not that he can't do something," started Alison, taking a sip of her drink. "But that he makes excuses for his failures."

"Wise words, Confucius," chuckled Charles, his eyes darting around behind Alison. "How good are you? Let's see what you're capable of." He spotted a young girl at a table behind Alison, a girl talking to an older woman. "What about the two ladies behind you? Can you hear their conversation?"

Alison stared at him for a moment, then reached out and took Charles's notebook. She scribbled on the paper and tossed it to him. He glanced down, seeing the clock and the number of feet. He looked back up at the girls. When he faced the clock from Alison's point of view, she was spot on. He couldn't tell the distance, but her angle was perfect. He went ahead and assumed the distance was within a foot or two of being right as well.

"I told you," she sighed. "I've been doing this my whole life."

Charles wasn't listening. He caught himself staring at the young girl. Her silky brown hair, her bright eyes, her enchanting smile. He noticed the color of her skin, a glowing and radiant pink. She was beautiful, albeit young. He was reminded of his new favorite category on the website he'd found a few days ago. The category that he'd visited every night since then while alone at his apartment.

"Mother and daughter," Alison said out loud, although not loud enough for the women to hear. "They're having a conversation about school."

Charles barely noticed. His eyes drifted down the girl's neck and shoulders, her thin arms crossed in front of her and pressing together a well developed chest. Something inside him ached. He recognized it immediately. It was the feeling he got when he opened up his bookmarked tab on his phone. Every day since he was released from jail. Sometimes two or three times a day. Regardless of the category throughout the years, that was the feeling he felt now. Sexual desire. His mind wandered to what he wanted to do with the girl.

"Her boyfriend just broke up with her," said Alison. "Her classmates didn't like him, and are happy about it. She's a softball player, a volleyball player, and a dancer. They spoke about all three."

Charles's chest burned. He barely knew Alison was even speaking. That girl was beautiful. He felt the need to feel her skin against his. He wanted to kiss and caress her. He wanted to please her. His hand nearly moved to his lap, the growth there becoming uncomfortably hard and bent at a strange angle. It needed to be adjusted. It needed to be touched.

His mind forgot Abigail, and wandered to this young girl.

"You know, typical teenage girl stuff." The comment yanked Charles from his trance.

"Teenage girl stuff?" he asked, blinking hard.

"Yeah," said Alison. "You didn't hear her say she was in the eighth grade?"

Charles's stomach turned. He'd been staring at, and thinking about, a fourteen year old girl. She was still beautiful, and he still burned, but he felt disgusted. He felt wrong. He felt like a pedophile. He thought about the category on the website. *Teen (18+).* This girl was too young to even be in that category. Way too young.

Yet here he was, burning for her.

*What is going on with me?* He thought of Alison speaking about a man adopting her and making her sleep with other men. He thought about the young girl they were looking for and all the older men she would be forced to see. Was he one of those men now? Was he going to start touching himself to thoughts of someone below the legal age of consent? Was he just as bad as all those other pedophiles?

No, he wasn't there. He hadn't wanted to hurt the girl. He wanted to love her, to make love, and now that he knew her age, he was disgusted with himself. He didn't want her at all now that he knew. All he wanted now was his videos, and some alone time.That would fix his problem. That didn't make him the bad guy. There was a difference, wasn't there?

"Are you okay?" asked Alison. "You look a little off."

"Let's do another exercise," said Charles, trying to focus on his task at hand now. He couldn't seem to shake that hunger. The same hunger he'd felt for Abigail. *Go to the bathroom. It won't take that long. Take care of it real quick. Fix the problem.*

He couldn't shake the disgust. He needed a distraction from the girl, and the lump in his jeans. He needed something to make the lump go away. The distraction he wanted was on his phone, unavailable to him in public. *Go to the bathroom. It'll only take a minute.*

"What's another good one?" he asked shakily.

Alison stared at him, those hazel hawk eyes analyzing every detail. His voice, and his body language. She had to know something was up. He needed to get himself under control. Neutral countenance, and calm expression. He had to get back to that.

He kept repeating to himself over and over again. *I didn't want to hurt the girl. I just wanted to love her. I didn't know her age, so that doesn't make me a pedophile. It doesn't make me a bad person. I feel disgusted with myself, so I'm not the bad guy. I'm just a little riled up right now. I've just been doing these boring exercises with no progress on the actual case, and it's bothering me. With this case, and training, and the deal with Abigail, I'm just stressed. That's all. I just need a fix. I'm not anything like one of these human traffickers. Traffickers want to hurt children. I just wanted to be nice and gentle with her, and I don't want to anymore because I know she's too young. I would never hurt her, and a trafficker would. A trafficker wouldn't care about her age, and I do. There is a difference between myself and traffickers.*

# *21*

*Claremore, Oklahoma - Thursday - 7:00 PM*
Dinner with the inlaws. It was the only way he could think about it. Just a small single family house in a small, midwestern town. She loved him, so why couldn't it be a good thing? He had known her mother previously, but this was different. So much time had passed in the last ten or fifteen years. So much had changed. It was meeting new people all over again.

To the outside eye, nothing was wrong with the home. To Charles, it seemed like everything was wrong. It was somehow different here, in what seemed like enemy territory. He'd been within arms reach of a violent criminal at the hospital, and he'd been in hand to hand combat with Solomon, all without hesitation or fear. His girlfriend's parents' house, on the other hand, now that he knew for sure she really was his girlfriend, now that she loved him and wanted to commit to him, made the hair on his neck and arms stand up.

What was the difference? There was danger elsewhere, but not here. He felt comfort elsewhere, but not here. He wasn't a hardened killing machine, and he didn't think he was an adrenaline junkie.

Why was this so much worse than a fight with a man twice his size?

*The suddenness of it all.* It was just too much all at once, and completely out of nowhere.

*I really should have taken care of myself before I came here.* A small itch still burned in him, and a strange, salty taste had entered his mouth. He was salivating and thinking about the bookmark on his phone. *I could really use an orgasm right now.*

Three vehicles in the driveway kept him parked on the curb and distant from the house. That gave him time to prepare himself and take in the details around him. It gave him time to ground himself in the moment. Abigail's Nissan Sedan, a Toyota Rav4, and an old square body Chevy pickup.

*What model was Abigail's car?* Alison's voice started asking him questions in his head. A Nissan Sentra. The pickup? Probably a Silverado. Red with a gold stripe down the side. He tried to think of which years they might be from. What colors were they?

Abigail had a dark blue Nissan Sentra, mid two thousand tens model. There was the white Toyota Rav4, probably from the early two thousands or late nineties, and the old school red Chevy pickup with the gold stripe down the side of it. Square body. That's how those were described. He wasn't sure about the years those were made, but he knew they were old. Pre millennium.

Exiting his own vehicle, trying to distract himself from internet videos, and making his way up the driveway, he tried to make mental notes of the house. He glanced around the neighborhood and looked for landmarks. He looked for things that felt out of place. Nothing seemed weird. A typical Midwest American household in a typical Midwest American neighborhood in a typical Midwest American city. Alison would be proud of him.

The front door opened, and a woman rushed down the driveway towards him. She was tall, slender, sporting a skin tight spandex shirt that accentuated her shape. Her trim waist, small, perky breasts, and thin, well defined arms begged for his attention. A black, high waisted mini skirt did nothing to hide the majority of her legs.

"Abby," he started, only to be cut off by her lips. Instead of interrupting him with words, though, she planted those lips onto his. Her arms flung up over his shoulders, wrapped around his neck in a very serious vice grip, and pulled him in. This was nothing like the shrewd girl he'd been with a few nights ago.

She wasn't wearing any lipstick, and Charles thanked God for that. His mouth was still wet, but there would be no stains on him tonight. There was very little makeup at all on her face, but he didn't mind. Her skin glowed, and her eyes hypnotized him. Even her teeth seemed to be extra white. She didn't need the makeup. She was beautiful.

"Thank you for coming," she said. "I owe you an explanation."

Charles wasn't sure he could have said anything, even if he wanted to. She did owe him an explanation, but he really didn't care anymore.

"When you called saying you got a job offer," she continued, cupping his face in her hands.

"I thought I was going to have a panic attack. That was the moment I realized that I wanted to be with you. Really be with you. I wasn't sure how to approach it because we haven't been super serious so far, so I asked my parents what to do, and they said they had to meet you first. Obviously, you know my mom, but it's been a long time so she wanted to get reacquainted. My step dad really just wanted to make an impression and see who you are. You know how dads are with their kids. Anyways, I'm sorry I couldn't tell you earlier. This didn't seem like something a text message could do any justice. Plus, I really wanted to kiss you. I've wanted that since we were kids. You know I've always had a crush on you, but now it's like a raging fire. Am I talking too much? I'm talking too much. I'll stop."

She headbutted him, or at least that's what it looked like she was doing. He would have been less surprised if she had. Their lips met again, a powerful sigh expelling from both sets of their lungs. His chest caught fire, all thoughts of internet videos vanished from his mind, and his hands reached up to grab her waist. He pulled her closer, pressing her body against his. His fingers squeezed her sides, feeling around to the tense muscle at her lower back. He inhaled the smell of lavender and vanilla, recognizing the perfume she'd only worn once: on their first date.

That touch was everything he imagined it would be. It sent ripples through his body that tingled along the surface of his skin. He felt electrified.

She pulled back, giggling. "Oh my god, we're making out in my parents' driveway." Her laugh sounded insane, a mixture of emotions from lust to excitement and anxiety. "Like we're high schoolers again." Her hand found his face. "I don't mean to be like this, but I just want more." She peeked down at their bodies, or at least the parts that were touching. "I can tell you do, too."

He felt his face warm up, and avoided telling her it had been like that for most of the day.

She stepped away from him and dusted herself off. "I'm sorry."

"Don't be." His voice cracked, and he was unsure if the words were even articulate. The taste of her lips hung on his tongue and made him numb like poison. The sight of her in that skin tight shirt, the flowing skirt waving around her hips. He'd never felt like this about anyone. "I want more, too."

She smiled, and put a hand on his chest. It gripped his shirt, the urge to pull him in trying to take over her. "Later. We'll have plenty of time for that once I'm moved in. Come on, my parents are inside."

"Moved in?" The words caught in his throat. She looked at him.

"Did I not mention that?" She asked. "All that blabbering, and I never mentioned that I wanted to move in?" She hesitated. "I guess I should ask if you still want me to. That thought never crossed my mind. I guess it should have."

He stared at her. Four months of hesitation and shyness, broken in a single moment. All the barriers of the past few days; gone. The stalking, the argument, the teasing. None of it mattered anymore. She loved him, and he loved her back. There was no question about that. They could iron out the kinks later on.

"I want you with me," he told her. "Throughout whatever we go through."

She smiled, and caressed his face again. "Good. Let's go inside before my parents get suspicious."

She took him by the arm, hooking her wrist on the inside of his elbow like an escort and leading him towards the front door. Charles followed blindly, trying to decide if what was going on around him was real.

*I am Charles Langley.* He thought to himself. *It is seven PM on a Wednesday, I'm at my girlfriend's parents' house in Claremore, and things are getting very serious very quickly.*

Grounding himself didn't seem to help. It still felt weird. The beautiful woman on his arm, too tall to rest her head on his shoulder, and the new career in his future that could lead him to travel a good amount of time. How was it all going to work? She barely trusted him when he was here.

They would iron out the kinks later.

The front door opened as they approached, and a pudgy older woman came into view. It had been a long time since he'd last seen her, and the woman had not aged well. She was a very meaty woman with dark brown hair that was greying slightly. She wasn't as tall as Abigail, but she was still taller than average, making her a very large woman indeed. She stared at him through slitted eyelids that squinted through thick lensed glasses. The thin lipped smile greeted him warmly, welcoming him back from a lifetime away.

"Mrs. Tyler." He nodded. "It's been awhile."

"So long that you haven't heard the name change," said Abigail's mother. "It's Smith now, but just call me Mindy. I have to tell you, Charles, I'm so happy Abigail found you again. I couldn't pick a better man for her. You two were always so close as kids. You guys and…"

She hesitated, and Charles knew why. People always did when mentioning Emily.

"I agree," chirped Abigail. Her voice was cheery and girlish. "Come on, you can meet my step dad and…" Her voice trailed off again. Her face turned pale. Her smile vanished.

Charles chuckled. "And who?"

"I…" Abigail hesitated. "I'm sorry. I'm still so flustered that I got ahead of myself. I was about to say 'and my mom'." She giggled again, this one sounding forced. "Come on. Meet the family."

Charles was led inside the house, glancing down the hallway and counting three doors before the back door at the end of the house. The right side of the front door had a living room, but Abigail turned immediately left and facing a wide open kitchen. On one side of the kitchen sat the cabinets and utilities, and the other wall opened up to a staircase leading to a second floor.

Charles assumed the second floor was where the bedrooms were at. Probably three bedrooms. He pictured the layout of the house. Front door. Living room on the right. Kitchen and dining on the left. Hallway in front leading to the back door. Three doors down that hall, likely a bathroom, a closet, and a laundry room. Upstairs, second floor, likely three bedrooms and another bathroom. A big house for a family of three. Expensive for just the two parents. Maybe Abigail helped with the bills. Maybe they were downsizing after she moved out?

He had to resist shaking his head. No sense in thinking like this. Work mode: off. Boyfriend mode: on. Simple as that. Meet the family, and get Abigail moved into his apartment. After that, questions could be asked and answered; kinks could be worked out. For now, baby steps. Alison could be proud of him another time. This time was for Abigail.

There was a large oak table in the middle of the kitchen, set up right at the base of the stairs in its own little dining half of the room. Decorative and beautiful, it showed signs of age and wear and… were those scratch marks on the wooden legs? Did the Smiths have a dog?

"You're Langley, right?" A gruff voice, a smoker's voice, coming from the end of the table. It was almost an echo of Solomon's interview from the day before. "Charles Langley? The man stealing my daughter away from me?"

He was heavyset, particularly in the belly. Dark haired with a high hairline and a thinning top. He wore a grey mustache attached to a thinning grey beard. He had a dull countenance, right down to the green-grey eyes hidden behind heavy eyelids. His smile was wide and forced, too many teeth showing to be a natural reaction. The teeth were stained a faded yellow. *Smoker's teeth.* The hand that reached out to greet Charles was thick and wide, like an inflated rubber glove. Charles took it, the padding reminding him of a boxing glove with fingers.

"Welcome to our home," said the man Charles assumed was Abigail's stepfather. "Although it sounds like we'll be short one here pretty quickly. Abigail tells me you have a place of your own in Tulsa?"

His face, his eyes, said something different than the rest of his face. *The eyes never lie.* The age old rule of body language. What was different about this man's eyes? It was hair raising.

"It's not great, but it's a good start. It's small, and I'm not much of a decorator, but Abby has helped me really fill the place in over the last few months."

Abigail's stepfather was not letting go of Charles's hand.

"Of course," said the big man. "It's always good to start small and grow together. You two are young, and ambitious, though, so you'll do just fine. I hear you make good money, and Abby here will once she's a doctor."

Charles wasn't sure, but he thought he saw Abigail shiver when her stepfather called her Abby. It was strange; she never did that when he called her that.

"Please, sit down. My wonderful wife, Mindy, has made us a delicious cajun pasta dish she learned when she was down south. I forget what it's called."

Mindy smiled, moving around the table and taking a seat next to Joseph. "It's just called a One Pot Creamy Cajun Pasta. Nothing fancy. I have to say, Charles, it's so good to see you doing so well after all these years," she said. "I'm so happy you haven't let your past weigh you down."

Charles pulled out the two seats on the side of the table that put the staircase on his right, allowing Abigail to sit in between himself and her stepfather. Something about that man didn't sit right, and he wanted distance between the two of them. Nothing said that he was putting Abigail in harm's way, but if it came down to it, Charles wanted the extra few moments to react.

*Why do I feel like that?*

"I've done what I can over the last seven years living out west," he said as he sat down next to Abigail. "I've tried to set aside as much money as I can and pay everything off. You know? The Dave Ramsay way. I wasn't sure what kind of a future I was investing in until tonight."

He shot a wayward glance at Abigail and thought, *Until about two minutes ago.*

Mindy reached up and began taking plates from the table. She served each plate with a large ladle out of the huge pot full of cajun pasta. The pot sat in the middle of the table, steam rising from the uncovered top. Abigail and her stepfather exchanged a strange glance. Abigail looked worried, and her stepfather looked… contemptuous?

*Stop it! Work mode: off!* Trying to distract himself, Charles took in the scenery.

The kitchen cabinets were light wooden colored and sported brass handles; the countertops were a dark marble color. There seemed to be no end to the amount of storage in this kitchen, a stark contrast to Charles's meager apartment. He felt moisture on his forehead.

Would Abigail really be content with what he had to offer after living like this for so long? From a large, multi-bedroom house to a one bedroom apartment?

"Our girl tells us a lot about you, Mr. Langley," continued Abigail's stepfather. "Maintenance tech at the factory up there making good money, living on your own, debt free, state champion wrestler in school, current karate black belt…"

"It's actually Krav Maga," Charles interrupted. "It's Israeli, and draws from several different martial arts for a more practical style of self defense. But yes, I trained when I was a kid, so picking up where I left off out here to obtain my black belt wasn't terribly difficult."

"When did you start?" asked Mindy. "I forget."

"I was eight," replied Charles. "My mother put Emily and I into…" He stopped at the mention of Emily. He glanced left, and saw a cynical smile on Abigail's stepfather's face. It vanished as Charles looked, exchanging itself out for a look of concern. For a moment however, Charles had seen it. Has this man been enjoying Charles's discomfort?

"Wow," sighed the man sitting at the end of the table. "Almost twenty years. A literal lifetime. That'll come in handy. Maybe you and Abigail can learn some things from each other. You with your Krav Maga, and her with her Army Combatives. It's good to know she'll always be safe. Not that I don't trust you to protect her with your own ninja skills, but I feel better knowing she can handle her own if she's ever caught alone or off guard."

The microwave on the counter next to the large refrigerator caught Charles's attention. Actually, he was fixated on what sat on top of the microwave. Of all the feeding utensils he'd expected to find, he never would have guessed he'd see a baby's bottle. Standard sized and colorless, it nearly blended in with the white backsplash of the kitchen wall. A baby's bottle in this house? They didn't have a baby. It could have been leftover from Abigail's childhood, or maybe preparing for a future family. Whatever it was, it didn't belong here.

*Making Alison proud.* Details were important. Make a mental note, and remember. *Stop it! Work mode: off. Boyfriend mode: on.*

He looked back at Abigail, struggling to keep his eyes above her waist. That skirt, and that top. The hunger. The burning. The growing in his pants.

*Eyes up!* If he got caught looking down, his first impression on the step parents would go downhill very fast.

"Well, I believe I've forgotten my manners," laughed the big man at the end of the table, drawing Charles's attention back up. "I never actually introduced myself. I'm Abigail's stepfather. Most kids your age call me Mr. Smith out of respect. You're family, though, right? You can go ahead and call me Joseph."

# <u>22</u>

*Claremore, Oklahoma - Thursday - 7:30 PM*
"You said it was Israeli?" asked Mindy, as the four of them dug into their dinners "Your martial art? What did you call it? I'll butcher the name if I try."

Charles chuckled. "Krav Maga originated when some Hungarian guy who ended up becoming an Israeli citizen created this art of self defense based on all of his experience in street fights over the years."

"So it's not originally Israeli?" asked Joseph with his eyebrows scrunched up.

"It is," replied Charles. "It was designed for the IDF, the Israeli military, and draws from karate, boxing, aikido, judo, and wrestling. The main focus is on real world situations, and it's more of a lifestyle than anything else. The best part about it is that nothing is set in stone. Everything is adaptable to each situation, giving the learner full freedom to choose what works for him."

"Do you compete?" asked Mindy.

"There's not really a competition," said Charles. "The IDF hosts a sort of competition every year, but it's in Israel, and it's almost exclusively for members of the IDF."

Joseph leaned forward. "Is it popular? The art, I mean?"

Charles shrugged."Not particularly. My mother just happened to stumble in on it when she was trying to put us in martial arts. I was… having trouble adjusting to the change in scenery."

"Abigail told us," said Joseph, turning back to his dinner. "It's amazing what you've accomplished considering your past."

Charles shrugged. "I think my mother just wanted to find a fighting sport that taught its users to avoid confrontation. Little did she know that if confrontation isn't avoidable, then the first act is to act quickly and efficiently. That means extreme violence early on. It means attacking weak points on the body, even if it causes severe injury."

"Or even death?" asked Joseph with a side glance to Charles.

"That's why we train so much," said Charles. "Ours is three nights a week here in Tulsa. Like Liam Neeson. You have the ability and knowledge to take a life, it's knowing when to pull the trigger that really makes a man with something."

"Do they teach you when to pull the trigger?" asked Joseph. "Like, actual weapons training? You use firearms and what not?"

Charles shrugged again. "There isn't a whole lot of live fire training, but there is a lot of disarming and hand to weapon combat stuff in there. Like I said, it's a very realistic style, so more of a public setting than an open dojo."

"Tell them about the bus," said Abigail with a slap of Charles's thigh.

Charles smiled. "There's one where everyone is on a bus, and a man enters with a pistol. The pistol is usually airsoft or simunition, so everyone is also wearing protective gear. Anyways, it's up to someone to step in and properly and safely disarm the attacker."

"How did you score on that one?" asked Joseph.

"The same as he scores on everything," replied Abigail. "At the top of his class."

"Do they teach you to shoot?" asked Mindy.

"A couple of times a year everyone goes out and tests with a pistol," replied Charles. "Most of the rest of the time is force on force training."

"So what do they tell you is the right time to pull the trigger, Mr. Langley?" asked Joseph. His eyes looked up from behind canted eyebrows, making him look angry.

"Everyone says to pull when your life is threatened," replied Charles. "I think that's way too broad. Nobody really knows what that means."

"You do." Joseph stared at Charles, making hard eye contact with the young man. Charles felt the words deep in his chest. They felt like a challenge. When his eyes met with Joseph's, he felt like a mad dog standing off with someone on his turf.

"I do."

"What about your Army Combatives?" asked Mindy, looking over at Abigail. "Is that anything like Krav Maga?"

"No," laughed Abigail.

Charles let his eyes remain locked with Joseph's eyes, refusing to break the contact.

"Army combatives are less about striking and more about creating distance in order to get to your weapon. The Army doesn't like a whole lot of hand to hand stuff. They train us to shoot our opponents when we get the chance."

"Actually, it's a lot like Krav Maga," said Charles. "A mix of disciplines designed to be effective in combat. It's one of the few that draws from multiple arts to create a better fighting style."

"I've done level one and two combatives so far," said Abigail. "Level one is basic weapon retention and defensive wrestling. Stuff you see in law enforcement, too. Level two involves a little more focus on weapon training."

"How many levels are there?" asked Mindy.

"Four," replied Abigail. "I plan on taking all of them."

"Look at that," laughed Joseph, breaking the staring contest and putting a hand on Abigail's shoulder. "Nobody can hurt my little girl. Not even me."

Joseph's smile hogged the attention of the room, but Charles paid extra attention to the details. He saw Abigail's eyes drop to the table in front of her. She did not smile. *Why would he say that, and why would Abigail not take it as a joke?*

"I wouldn't let anything happen to her," said Charles, flashing her his own smile directly at her and ignoring anything incoming from Joseph.

It was a direct challenge to Joseph's authority, one that put the man aside entirely and focused solely on Abigail. It gave a complete disregard to Joseph, and any protection, or danger, he could have posed. Abigail smiled back at him. Her hand leapt onto the table and grabbed his tightly. Her eyes said something that didn't make sense.

*Don't provoke him.*

"Tell me something, son," started Joseph. "Do you drink?"

"I do not," replied Charles, breaking away from Abigail's gaze and returning his focus to Joseph.. "I saw what it did to my father, and I want no part of that."

"What about a cigar?"

Charles settled back into his chair. "My father and I smoke them together occasionally. Usually on vacation."

"Would you smoke one with me?" Joseph's eyes pleaded. The pitiful tone of his voice sounded fake.

Charles shot Joseph his own smile. "The only good advice my father gave me was never turn down the chance to smoke a good cigar."

His hand throbbed, the fingers of Abigail's hand giving it two solid squeezes like she was trying to tell him something. That gaze she had given him repeated itself.

*Do not provoke him.*

***

The light of the cigar flared. The butane lighter hissed softly, and the glow illuminated the palm of Charles's hand. The sun was setting over the horizon, darkness engulfing himself and Joseph. The only light between them glowed from a few inches in front of their faces as they puffed on the fat cigars.

The taste of the cigar made Charles's stomach turn over. He kept his face from scrunching up, but he struggled to continue through the cigar. The taste reminded him of sour milk that had been brought to a boil. At least, that's what he thought that would taste like.

*God forbid I ever have to find that out for sure.*

"You know," Joseph wheezed, apparently doing his own best to make it past the horrific flavor of the cigar. "Abigail told me you're trying to get out of the maintenance gig?"

Charles sighed, holding back a cough. "It gets old after a while. I've been doing the same thing for seven years. Maybe I'm just getting burnt out. I just feel like I'm not contributing anything to the world around me."

"You're maintaining the machinery at an animal feed manufacturing plant," said Joseph. "Right? Abigail told me you're down there at Nutrien?"

Charles nodded his head. "That's what everyone keeps telling me. The world stops when the machinery stops, and it's guys like me that keep it running." He alternated to shaking his head. "It just doesn't feel fulfilling. I don't get to see the impact I have on the overall industry, and I guess that kind of bothers me."

"So what are you looking into?" asked Joseph. "Any specific industries? There aren't many options for a man with your past."

"Hasn't Abigail told you?" asked Charles.

"You haven't told her," returned Joseph. "According to her. It kept getting avoided in conversations."

Charles thought about it for a moment, trying to remember the conversation he and Abigail had on the phone the other night. *It's a long story; I'll tell you at dinner.* She had canceled dinner, and tonight was supposed to make up for that. He really hadn't told her.

"I guess I didn't," he mumbled. "It's kind of a long story. I met someone in the hospital when my dad was having a heart attack. Two police officers brought in some big guy, who decided to fight the police. The guy I met got to see a display of my martial arts skills and offered me a job."

"Is it police work?" asked Joseph.

*Hell of a guess.* "Not exactly."

"Does it have to do with the woman you were with the other day?"

Charles turned to look at Joseph, who smiled. "Abigail told me. She said she sent Solomon to follow you, and found you with some other woman. I have to be honest, I'm not sure I would want to move in with you after that, but Abigail seems hooked on you. My question is, was that woman from the new job, or are you seeing someone else?"

"She is from the new job," replied Charles. "She's sort of my trainer. I never got to talk to

Abigail about sending that guy to follow me, nor did I tell her that he attacked me, and we had to take him down to the police station."

"You did what?" Each word came out of Joseph's mouth as slowly and pronounced as humanly possible. Charles saw the dim light of Joseph's cigar fall to the ground, the older man's mouth gaping open. "He got questioned?"

"Yeah," said Charles. "How do you think we found out Abigail sent him?"

"Did…" Joseph hesitated. "Did he say anything else?"

"He knew me," replied Charles. "He said she gave him a picture of me and told him to follow me around for the day and report back to her what I had done and who I was with. Paid him five hundred dollars for it." He shrugged, trying to lighten the mood. "At least I know I'm worth some money to her."

Joseph let out a quiet sigh. "And what about Abigail? Is anything going to happen to her?"

"Other than a serious conversation about how we're going to move forward with our relationship?" chuckled Charles, "and maybe why we do the things we do? I don't see anything legally happening to her. I'm the only one that can really press charges. Maybe Alison, but I don't think that'll go anywhere."

"Alison…" mumbled Joseph. "The trainer lady."

Charles nodded. "Yeah, that's her name."
"What about Solomon?"

Charles shrugged. "I didn't press charges for stalking, and he didn't really give me much of a fight in the Mcdonald's parking lot, so they cut him loose."

"Good," sighed Joseph, coughing. "I don't want anything to come of this. It was a mistake for both of them, and I'd hate to see them pay the price."

There was silence, and Charles, who was strategically facing his cigar down to let it burn without him puffing on it, took a drag for show. Joseph reached down and picked his cigar up, having to relight the end of it. As he took a deep drag of the freshly lit cigar, Charles heard him sigh and saw him shake his head. A hand ran over his forehead, as if the man was relieved.

"Are you working with the police?" Joseph asked after a long and smoky breath.

Charles hesitated. The tone of the question, loud and confident, unsettled him. It didn't sound like a curious man conversing with his daughter's boyfriend. That question sounded like an aggressive accusation. The statement from earlier about harming Abigail, and Abigail's response. Nothing about this moment felt okay.

*When in doubt, a half truth can easily mislead a target in the right direction.*

"The truth is," started Charles. "The new job is contract work for an NGO. It's a non profit organization that tries to spread awareness for crimes against children."

"Crimes against children?" asked Joseph. He sounded surprised, but in a very dramatic sense.

That fake sounding tone of voice made its return. "Like what?"

"Human trafficking," replied Charles.

"So it is police work?"

"More like activism."

"So do you get to know anything about current cases?" asked Joseph. "Like the people they're looking for and what crimes are being investigated."

Charles hesitated. It was a normal question to ask, but it didn't feel right. Again, it felt more like a probe than a conversation.

"No," he lied. "I just have to read up and educate myself on the subject for now. There's actually a conference going on right now, where the organization is doing training for law enforcement on how to recognize trafficking and running drills on how to operate in the field."

"Where is this at?" asked Joseph.

"Grand River View in Tulsa," replied Charles. "I haven't been yet. They've been putting me through my own sense of training and getting a feel of where I'm at for the job."

"What job is that?" asked Joseph. It sounded like another accusation. Joseph's questions were becoming short and sharp. They felt like jabs of a knife, where Joseph could chop away at Charles's defenses until he had what he wanted.

Charles remembered every spy movie he'd ever seen. Those people didn't give away all their secrets. They told half truths to misguide their targets. Maybe his future father in law wasn't the best start, but the whole conversation just felt wrong. Charles was beginning to feel like he'd already said too much.

"Fundraising. I'll travel around a little bit, spit out some facts about the underground criminal world, and beg for money to help our guys fight it."

Joseph seemed to take a step back towards the door. "Fight it how?" Now he sounded worried. Joseph wasn't just accusatory, he was downright frightened. *Why?*

"Funding law enforcement training," replied Charles. "It starts with education, and translates into awareness. It's up to us to protect our children. If we don't do it, no one else will."

"That's right." It was a whisper, and Charles heard the cigar hit the deck, and a foot crushed it. Charles followed suit as the glass back door slid open, and Joseph stepped inside. "So you're going to keep Abigail safe, too?"

Why did he sound so terrified? Why was he interrogating Charles like this? It all felt wrong. It felt like he was getting off on the wrong foot with his future in-laws. *Lighten the mood.*

Charles let out a short laugh. "I think Abigail is going to keep Abigail safe, but any time she needs help, I'll be there to back her up."

Charles stepped through the door, and took a moment's hesitation to think about the conversation. Why was Joseph so hell bent on keeping Abigail safe? She was in her twenties, and trying to live her life? It was a dangerous world, but it wasn't that dangerous. That comment earlier about himself not being able to harm Abigail, and Abigail's big green eyes staring down at the table.

*Who does he think I'm going to have to protect her from?*

***

"It was so nice meeting you again, Charles." Mindy reached out to shake Charles's hand, and he took it. She smiled at him, a smile that looked painful and hard to put on. *The eyes never lie.* Her eyebrows furrowed just the slightest, her eyelids remained slitted. He noticed the discoloration around her cheekbones, like bags under the eyes, or bruises. They were faded, concealed by makeup or old and healing. Black eyes and swollen cheekbones would explain the slits for eyelids. The comment about hurting Abigail, and Abigail's stare into the table.

He turned away, unsure if it was right to bring it up. Joseph was standing off to the side, but stepped forward in between Charles and Mindy with his hand out, as if blocking the woman from view.

"Son," he barked loudly in the small entryway, "it was good to meet you. I can't say how proud I am that Abigail was able to find such a good one. Take care."

Joseph squeezed Charles's hand, the muscles in his arm flexing with the power. Charles recognized it, and flexed his own hand to protect the bones, using the muscle of his palm to push out on Joseph's grip. Joseph's eyes flickered down to their hands for a split second. *The eyes never lie.* Joseph's squeeze was intentional, and Charles's counter had taken him by surprise.

*Minor details give everything away. Good investigators notice those things.*

Alison would be proud.

"It was good to finally meet you two," Charles replied, confidently winking at Joseph. "I'm so happy that Abigail and I are able to move forward without any secrets. It feels good to really begin to move forward in our relationship, and be able to take things up a notch. I'm glad we have finally reached that level of trust."

He noticed it again. Joseph's eyes almost jumped to Abigail. It was just the smallest motion in the world, but anyone paying attention to that kind of thing could pick it up easy enough. *The eyes never lie.* The word secrets and trust had set off the glance. So there was a secret the Smiths were keeping from him.

Alison really would be proud.

A noise came across the house from behind Joseph and Mindy. Charles's ears perked up like a dog's. His neck extended upward. He saw Joseph's eyes widen momentarily, and felt the flinch squeeze his hand. More importantly, Charles saw Joseph's gaze flicker to the right, towards the staircase leading to the second floor.

Charles was sure he'd heard a cough from the back of the house, and even Joseph hadn't been able to resist the urge to glance. *The eyes never lie. There is someone else in this house.*

The larger sized house, and the thought of three bedrooms for a family of three. It all fit together. The bottle on top of the microwave. He got it. The secret that the Smith's were hiding from him. A baby.

But why would they hide that?

"What was that?" he asked before anyone could change the subject. He risked a look over Joseph's shoulder, trying to peek at the top of the staircase. Joseph stepped in the way.

"What was what?" Joseph tilted his head and furrowed his eyebrows. That fake voice, back again.

Alison's voice in the back of Charles's head. *Too strong, back off a bit.*

Charles shook his head. "I thought I heard something."

Joseph did not laugh his usual chipper laugh. His voice was stern and serious. "It's an old house. It makes a lot of noise."

Charles turned to the two women, who looked away from him. Alison's voice again. *Too weak. Turn it up a little.*

"It sounded like someone coughed upstairs."

In his mind, Alison slapped him with a hand the size of a dinner plate. *WAY too strong.*

Joseph did not smile. "A lot of noises sound like that. The compressors in the AC and the refrigerator make that sound when they start up."

Charles couldn't help but glance to the nearest AC register on the ceiling above. He didn't feel a breeze. Was it pointed at him? He glanced back at Joseph, who was still gripping his hand tightly in a handshake that was taking too long to finish.

Alison spoke to him silently. *Some secrets are dangerous. You are vulnerable and on enemy territory. Back off for now. Retreat, and regroup.*

"Okay," said Charles, nodding and dropping his eyes. "That makes sense. It was just a little weird. Makes me think there's someone there when there isn't. I don't want to believe in ghosts or anything, but it had me going."

Joseph snorted a laugh without smiling, and released Charles's hand. Charles took a step back, and felt a soft, small hand on his shoulder.

"I have an idea," said Abigail, stepping around in front of him. "Why don't I…" She glanced at her mother, then at Joseph. "Go stay at Charles's house for the night? That way we can get a feel of what living together is going to be like."

Maybe Charles had seen too many movies, but people that spoke like that were making a suggestion to distract the conversation. Abigail looked at Joseph, who gave her a stern look, with a hint of thankfulness in his eyes. He nodded his approval, and Charles was certain his theory was right.

*There is someone else in this house. All three of them know about it, and none of them want me to know about it.*

"You're a grown woman, Abigail," Joseph muttered. "You can make your own decisions. We'll see you back here tomorrow to get your stuff packed."

Abigail turned to Charles, pushing on his shoulder and trying to turn him out of the door. Mindy opened the door, giving him that painful smile again. He stepped out onto the driveway with Abigail hanging on his arm. She had one of her arms hooked in his elbow again, using her shoulder to push him down the driveway. He let her, wondering if she was excited to get him home and continue their earlier conversation, or if she just wanted to get him out of that house.

"Abigail?"

She shushed him violently without looking away from the area in front of them. "Just keep walking. Let's go home."

Maybe Charles had seen too many movies, but an old saying crept into his mind.

*Abusers can't hide who they are for very long. It's too powerful of a force to keep bottled up.*

# <u>*23*</u>

*Tulsa, Oklahoma - Thursday - 9:00 PM*

"You mean to tell me that we've been looking at that map for a month with nothing, and he figures it out in a half an hour?" Jimmy Limone threw his sling onto the bed, halted, and gripped his arm with a tight grimace on his face.

"He's local," said Alison. "He has a perspective and an advantage that we don't. He knew what was in those circles because at one point he had seen it on his own map."

"Isn't that a good thing?" asked Walter. "Doesn't that make him an asset? A good find? One that you found, Jimmy?"

"I should get a bonus," grumbled Jimmy, reaching for the sling to put it back over his shoulder and reset his arm.

"Jimmy," whined Katie, holding a terrified Kitsen in her arms. Kitsen fumbled with her watch, wringing it around her wrist. "You have got to take it easy. We aren't the only ones in the hotel, and the walls and floors are not that thick."

Jimmy sighed as he put his sling back on. He glanced down at the little girl, who shied away from him. "Sorry, Katie Kat. Sorry, Kitty Kat." He took a deep breath, and turned to Walter. "So, what exactly do we know that we didn't before?"

Walter shook his head. "Not a whole lot more than we did. The advantage of knowing the locations he's selling the girl at, and when, is now we can figure out a pattern. What hotels is he using on certain days? Is he moving partially throughout the day? What kind of hotels attract a certain type of customer base?"

"Can we check the records for names?" asked Jimmy. "Hotels require ID to reserve a room. We can find the guy if he's using the same ID over and over again."

"Unless he has a fake ID." Alison slowly moved out of the shadows of the dimly lit room. "They only run a couple of hundred dollars for a good one, as long as they don't need to be scanned, in this part of the country. If he was making good money, he could have several IDs."

"You know that for a fact?" asked Jimmy. "About the IDs?" He shook his head. "Nevermind. Of course you do."

"We can't check names of occupants without a warrant," said Walter, moving over to the bed where Kitsen and Katie were sitting. "It's hard to get a warrant without something solid. All we have right now is a map with circles around hotels and some dates from some undercover operators."

"That's not enough?" asked Rebecca.

"In this day and age," sighed Alison, "you would be amazed at what accounts for not enough. Probable cause has become proven beyond all deniability."

"You would think people would be a little more sensitive to this kind of crime," grumbled Jimmy.

Walter sat down on the bed, taking his young daughter in his arms. The little girl curled up with her head lying in her father's lap, her eyes fluttering shut. He glanced at the clock, feeling horrible for keeping her up this far past her bedtime.

"The system has to be fair to everyone," said Alison softly. "If the government is allowed access to things simply because it's a certain type of crime, it opens doors to add crimes to that list. Privacy should still be taken seriously. The government will always take advantage of power like that."

"You and your anti-government antics," said Jimmy with a wave of his hand. "So what's the next step?"

"The conference," sighed Walter. "It's drill day. I'll need all hands on deck for training."

"Everyone except for Katie?" asked Alison. Walter nodded.

"It is kind of my job to watch Kitsen," Katie muttered.

"No, it's not, Katie," said Walter. "But you do it anyway. I cannot tell you, from the bottom of my heart, how much I appreciate you always being here for Kitsen."

"Maybe I should get the bonus," grinned Katie, as everyone watched a grin stretch across Kitsen's pretending to sleep face. "Besides, Kitty and I love hanging out and being girls. Plus, you've given me a lot of opportunities in the last ten years I've been with The Initiative that I didn't deserve. I'd do anything for you…" She glanced around nervously, her own cheeks turning a bright and beautiful shade of pink. "And everyone else, of course. Even the new guy. We're a team. This is what we do."

Walter couldn't help but notice a smile cross Alison and Jimmy's face as they exchanged the sideways glances they usually did when he and Katie got awkward. He also noticed the scowl that always came from the older sister, Rebecca.

"Where is our newbie?" asked Rebecca, obviously desperate to change the subject. "Shouldn't he be here with us?"

"Dinner with the inlaws," chuckled Alison. "His girlfriend's parents invited him over for dinner. I guess they have been struggling for a few months, so I gave him some time to work things out for the night."

"He told me he wasn't even sure they were really together," said Walter. "Now he's having dinner with her parents?"

"You know how boys can be," said Alison, rolling her eyes.

"You checked him out," chuckled Jimmy. "You've been spending the most time with him. Are you jealous he's got a girl his age."

Alison's eyes shot pins at Jimmy. "He's young, Jimmy. He's green, but he's smart. He's been studying this craft for a long time. I like him, but I need him to focus."

"I'll bet you do," chuckled Jimmy, and the Swift sisters giggled. Alison's face did not change color.

"Do you think he's going to work out?" asked Katie through stifled laughter. Walter didn't say anything, but he felt Kitsen's head adjust slightly to hear the conversation better. He glanced down to see her eyes still closed like she was sleeping.

*Faker.*

Alison paused, giving the thought some time. "He's a little strange, and I don't like what he did with the guy that was following us." She took a moment to consider, then nodded. "He's got the knowledge, and he's picking up on the drills quickly. I was worried at first he was just looking for a way to escape the day-to-day life, but with a little work he could turn out to be something."

"Okay," sighed Walter. "Jimmy, can you handle seminars alone, or do you need a Swift to back you up?"

Jimmy nodded. "I'll do what I have to to get back out in the field. No one will let me in on the actual drills because of my arm."

Walter nodded. "Then do it. I'll have the others running drills with me, but I want Charles with someone at all times. He needs supervision."

"I'll take him," Rebecca chirped without hesitating, almost girlishly. Walter saw fire flash from Alison's eyes. The two women exchanged predatory glances, and Walter wasn't sure which one he would choose to win a battle. Alison had size and spunk, but Rebecca was a true pistol.

"I'm his trainer," Alison growled. "I have been in the Initiative longer than any of the four of you except Walt, and I've dedicated my life to this craft. I know the ropes, and I did the research on him. I've taken the time to build rapport with him. For now, he's mine. He's coming with me."

"Damn," laughed Rebecca, throwing her hands up in surrender. "I just thought I could get to know him a little. He is one of my team members as well."

"You'll get to know him," said Alison. "As time goes on he'll sit in here with us, and be more active with the team. Right, Walt?"

Walter shrugged, and looked over at Alison. "That's assuming he survives being around you."

Even Kitsen couldn't help letting out a giggle at that one.

# <u>24</u>

*Tulsa, Oklahoma - Thursday - 9:30 PM*
Breath. Long, drawn in, held, and released. Pressure dissipated. Sagging shoulders dropping several inches as the tension left. Her head hung back. Her eyes closed. Her mind cleared. Here she was. New home. Pressure gone.

*Freedom.*

Abigail Smith felt her whole body shrink with the sigh. She felt tight muscles in her neck and shoulders relax for what felt like the first time she could remember. She was safe, at least for now. She was always safe here at Charles's apartment. No one could find her here. No one could hurt her here. She had Charles to protect her.

Except Charles seemed distant tonight. He wasn't acting like the man he'd been for four months now. He wasn't speaking as much, even for the quiet man he was. Tonight had been close; too close for comfort. She had gotten him out of there in time, but he was still suspicious. He knew they were keeping something from him, he had to know. He'd be stupid not to suspect something with everything that had gone on. She just had to direct him another way long enough to make things permanent. Once she was free, none of this would matter.

It had been a rough week, and tonight had been no exception. She wanted it to be a happy night. He would get to meet her parents, and she would get to move in. Everything had gone wrong, and they had all underestimated his observation skills.

At least she was here. She had that to be thankful for. She was here with Charles, and that was what she wanted. Everything from here on out could be handled as long as she was here.

Men were too easy to distract to worry too much about it.

"I love you," she whispered to herself. She had finally told him that tonight. She meant it, and had felt it since the very beginning. More importantly, it had allowed her success in moving out. She was almost free. "Just one more step."

"What changed?" Charles's voice came from behind her. She never heard him walk out onto the balcony with her. *Sneaky paws.*

"These last few months I've not been sure what I want," she said, feeling the truth come from her for the first time in days. "Tonight, or even yesterday, I made up my mind. You being aloof really spooked me. It got me thinking about how I've been as a girlfriend. I haven't been, really. I've been more of just a friend."

Charles didn't reply. She couldn't even hear him breathing. She turned to face him, watching the look of suspicion slowly disappear from his face. *Too easy.*

"I realized that we all need companionship," she continued, moving forward and placing both hands on his chest. He was solid underneath that shirt, the muscle trained and strong. It made her heart skip a beat. "When it was just the two of us, I never really thought about it much. Everything just felt like it was the way it was, and I didn't have to put in much effort. When I felt like I could have lost you, though…"

She hesitated for a split second, and leaned in to kiss him. He accepted her without a fight, his hands finding their way around the small of her back and pulling her closer. She inhaled, taking him in as his body pressed against hers, moving her arms out of the way so she could feel his chest against hers.

*Thank God he's not a boob man.*

She wrapped her arms around his neck and held him against her. She slipped her tongue in his mouth, and he answered with a tightening of his grip on her back. One hand slid down to her backside, the fingers digging into what she had to offer. It sent a tingle up her spine.

*Hopefully he's not a booty guy, either.*

She couldn't help that she was a flat girl. She was six feet tall, and weighed just over one hundred and twenty five pounds. It was hard for anyone to have any meat on their bones with those numbers. She had worried greatly about the size of her breasts, and her butt. Every man liked a girl that had one, the other, or both. She had neither.

*I'll start doing squats, or hip thrusts, or something. My tits will get bigger if I get pregnant.*

But it didn't seem to matter what she had. The way he touched her. Firm, but tender. Full of love and full of lust. He was hungry for her body, and he wanted to share the intimacy with her. She felt every move he made, his other hand sliding up in between her shoulder blades and sending shivers through her body. Had she ever been touched like this?

He backed off first, and she stared at him through half closed eyes, her mouth still hanging open just a bit, and her top lip curled up. She wanted more.

His face was almost unchanged. Those wondering eyes, the suspicious expression. They were still there. *Too easy?*

"So that's why you sent someone to follow me around?" he asked.

She flinched, thinking about her answer. Her philosophy was always the truth, but this time was different. This was the truth that would end any attempt she had at a future with this man. The one she was trying to run from. The truth that would destroy her future. Charles could never know that truth.

So she lied with another deep, pressure relieving breath. "Yeah, that was me."

***

*Men are too easy to distract.* Thirty five seconds. He'd lasted thirty five seconds the first round. She counted them, starting from the time she took him into herself to the moment he climaxed. Thirty five seconds with no warning and a belly full of warm fluids. The thing she wanted, and didn't want. The thing that came with consequences on all fronts. The thing that could set her free.

Embarrassed, Charles asked for forgiveness before Abigail shushed him, laid him on his back, and gave him the experience of his lifetime.

It was his first time. He'd never had any partners before her. She'd had more partners than the number of seconds he'd lasted the first round. He'd saved himself for something special; something like this.

She'd been spoiled years ago.

She was his first. A special occasion and a special place she would always hold in the heart of the man she loved. Would there be others after her? If the second round ended the same as the first, there wouldn't. He would be all hers for the rest of their lives. *Freedom.*

And the second round ended as the first had. They both roared with ecstasy as she rolled back onto him, pushing him deeper inside of her to consume everything he had to give.

The third time around, Charles had taken control. Her efforts to build his confidence had paid off. His shoulders broadened out, his movements felt more confident, and his voice boomed in her ear. He filled her a third time, sealing the bond she had striven to create with him. It was like nothing she had ever experienced before.

She had never experienced love.

No sleep. They had gone all night. Again and again, taking out the built up tension and frustration of the last four months, maybe even ten or fifteen years as Abigail remembered it. She could not remember when the first time she'd thought about this was. All she knew was she could not have been more pleased with the results.

It was worth every second of the wait. She had never been treated like this; never been taken care of like this. Even with his bulky weight pressing down on her, her hips and knees aching with the strain of locking him to her, and the muscles of her arms weak with overuse, so much attention was paid to her pleasure. So much care was taken to her needs and wants. So much emotion expressed in honor of her. It was…

There wasn't a word for it.

By the end of it all, the sun had risen on a mess of stained bedsheets and shining bodies. They laid there, naked and unashamed of each other, sharing their souls with each other.

Then an alarm blared from a watch on the bedside table. Their lips separated, and their grip on each other slackened. Charles smiled at her, kissed her, and pulled her tight.

"I have to go," he said, climbing out of bed. "Thank you for that. No one has ever done anything like that for me."

*No one has ever done that for me.* She thought. *No one has ever loved me.*

"Charles." Abigail reached up and put a hand on his shoulder, the top sheet slipping down off of her bare torso and exposing her. For the first time in a long time, she didn't feel the need to cover back up. "Can I stay here for the day? I don't want to go back home, even to pack, and I'm not sure I can make it to work after all that."

*He's going to wonder how I still have a job.* She couldn't help but think that. *I've only worked one day this week.*

Charles turned to her, dressed and ready for the day already. He leaned in and kissed her. If he had any suspicions, he didn't voice them.

"You stay here as long as you like," he whispered. "This is your home now. Packed or not. There's always time to go get your things later on."

"You can't stay with me?" She asked him, placing a hand on his face. It was her new favorite thing to do.

"Not today," he replied. "We're doing actual work today. Looks like they're going to hit me hard in the next day or two and really vet me."

"What kind of work are you doing?" asked Abigail.

Charles sighed. "Yeah, I came to the realization last night that I still hadn't told you what this is."

"Do we have time for a long story?" asked Abigail with a malicious smile.

He nodded. "We do."

Abigail wasn't sure how to feel at the end of Charles's story. She wasn't sure how long it had taken to tell her. The culmination of the last five days of miscommunication and separation was enough to send shivers up and down her back, and for more than one reason.

She never knew Charles was out and about with some other woman. She never knew he'd been in a fight, and barely knew that Arthur had a heart attack. He was working hand in hand with the police to catch a local man selling a young girl. No names, and no descriptions. Nothing. They knew he was using hotels, and when he had used them in the past. He spared her no detail, even going into how Solomon had confessed to being hired and how this Alison woman had been training him.

In a flash she was up out of bed and putting clothes on, trying to ignore the soreness between her legs. She took a deep breath, and shook her head. "I'm glad you haven't gotten hurt. I hear these human traffickers can be really dangerous."

"Where did you hear that?" asked Charles.

She shrugged. "The Internet?"

Charles snickered. "Not like everyone thinks they are, I'm guessing. I don't really have much experience in this world, but according to Walter and Alison, this isn't like the movies. They aren't trained assassins and killing machines."

"Who's Walter?" asked Abigail, then her voice dropped very low. "Who's Alison?"

"They're the team I'm working with," replied Charles. "Walter's technically the CEO of the Red Sea Initiative. Alison is on the team I'll be put on. There's Jimmy, and he's the real team leader. Then there's Katie and Rebecca. They're sisters."

"That's a lot of women," Abigail said quietly. "This doesn't seem like a women's world."

"The ladies say they're usually on the recovery teams," said Charles. "Alison poses as a supplier. She's a larger woman, about as tall as you, and a lot heavier."

"Is she pretty?" Abigail asked.

This question was always a test from every woman. Charles knew that, and thought very carefully about his answer.

"She's a lot older than me, and she's a human trafficking victim. She poses no threat to you, I promise."

Abigail wasn't convinced. "Is she pretty?"

"After enough alcohol, she would be."

He chuckled, but his face told her that he knew that was not the right answer.

Charles sighed. "She's pretty. She's kind of mean to me. She likes to drag me around like I'm a wagon. It's not that fun. Usually after I mess something up, too, so it's even more embarrassing."

"You mess things up?" asked Abigail.

"That's why I'm in training," he said. "When I'm a lot more experienced, I'll be untouchable."

"No one is untouchable," said Abigail. "There's always a threat coming from every angle in that world."

There was so much she didn't know, and that was just the past week. What about the past few months? What about the past several years? What else had she missed out on? She glanced over at the tall gun safe in his closet, barely visible through the closet door. *He doesn't even like guns. Why does he have that?*

"Why'd you go to jail?" she asked out of the blue.

He sat back, visibly shocked at her question. "You mean you never read the news articles. No one ever talked about it?"

"They did," she answered with a shake of her head. "What I meant was what exactly happened that night? News and gossip doesn't tell the whole story. I want your side."

He froze in place, his face turning pale. His eyes never moved, but she could see the sickness in his face. She'd made a mistake. *Too far, too soon.*

"I'm sorry," she said. "I shouldn't have brought it up, but with all this stuff I didn't know, it has me thinking about the other things I don't know. We obviously need to work on communication. I was just curious what really happened that night. I think about it every time I see that safe in your closet. The gun safe that can't possibly have any guns in it. I just wonder what's in it."

"I gave a statement about that night. It was in the police report, and on the news website."

"I know." She nodded. "I wanted to get your personal side of the story. I want to hear you tell it. I want the things that get omitted from police reports. I want it all."

*If only I could give you my all.* She thought. *If only I could tell you. It would cost us everything we have.*

Charles stared across the room, looking out the window with a gaze of hypnosis. Shaking his head, he gave her a small smile, leaned in to kiss her, and reached over to pat her on the rear.

"We don't have time for that long of a story," he said quietly. "I'll be back."

He stood to leave, clearing the bedroom door with what looked like as much speed as he could muster. She leaned up to watch him start to disappear down the open apartment to the front door. He froze, and turned his attention to her clothing. His eyes sized her up, taking notice of the fact that she had put on one of his T-shirts instead of her own.

"You're dressed," he said. "What are you going to do for the rest of the day?"

Abigail smiled. "I thought I'd get lunch. Will you be back for a lunch break?"

Charles nodded. "I can be."

"Chinese?" The two of them ate a lot of Chinese food. Lunch and dinner both; it didn't seem to matter. Any time they ate out, it felt like it was Chinese food. This was the second time this week, and as she thought about it, they were consistently eating it twice a week, every week. She wondered if China One could have stayed in business only on herself and Charles.

"We should do Mexican food next time," he told her, obviously having the same thoughts that she had.

"The only one close to your apartment is Taco Bell," replied Abigail. "Hard pass for me.

"You got dressed just to get lunch?"

"I'm going to do the only thing I have left to do this week."

"What's that?" asked Charles.

She approached him, and ran a hand up and down his arm. Her eyes locked with his, that hungry smile overtaking her face. Her fingers found his, and soon enough, their hands were weaved together.

"While you're out being a hero, I'm going to go see your father."

# <u>25</u>

*Tulsa, Oklahoma - Friday - 10:00 AM*
Arthur Langley's stats were still not healthy. As a combat medic, it had taken no time at all to judge that. Abigail's stomach turned at the sight of the EKG screen, where his blood pressure, heart rate, blood oxygen, respiration, and body temperature. All of those numbers were abnormal. Normal blood pressure was 110/70. Arthur's was 145/92; Stage 2 Hypertension. Normal resting heart rate for a man in his mid forties was between seventy and seventy five. Arthur's was ninety five. Normal blood oxygen levels were above ninety five percent. Arthur was at ninety. Normal respiration was between ten and twenty breaths per minute. Arthur was almost at thirty. Body temperature should have been ninety eight degrees. Arthur was well over one hundred.

"They can't get the numbers to come down?" she asked, sitting down in the chair next to the bed. "Even almost a week later?"

Arthur laughed. "Believe it or not, the numbers are down."

"You're still in hypertension," said Abigail. "Blood oxygen is low, which is really bad because your breathing is high. You're feverish and your pulse is racing just sitting there on the bed doing nothing."

Arthur looked down at his large body. "My blood has a lot of distance to travel. Heart has to work harder to get it to where it needs to be. Don't worry about me. What about you? How are you?"

Abigail sighed. "I moved in with Charles."

Arthur nearly choked. "You mean to tell me that you actually like him enough to live with him? You are a trooper, and braver than any woman I've ever met in my life."

Abigail dropped her eyes. *If only he knew.* "I know it kind of happened fast, but it just felt right."

"Five months is fast?" asked Arthur. "In the modern world, five months isn't fast."

"The modern world also has the highest breakup and divorce rates of all history," said Abigail.

Arthur sighed. "It was a different world back then. Women weren't taken care of back then. They weren't allowed to leave if they were being abused or hurt regularly. No one cared about them, or supported them. They were condemned for being divorced for being a bad wife, even if it wasn't her fault. It was always, 'you should have been a better wife'. Back then, it was better for a woman to stay."

Abigail thought about her mother, an older woman that grew up in that generation. *Back then, it was better to stay.* She thought about herself, attaching to Charles as a means of escape. She thought about a little girl, the one that had no choice. The one that couldn't escape.

"Fear is a powerful motivator," she whispered.

"What are you afraid of?" asked Arthur. "Tell me, Abigail."

Abigail giggled, trying to hold back tears. "What are you? My dad?"

"If things go well, I might be, legally speaking."

She smiled, shutting her eyes before the tears could escape. "I don't want to lose him."

"Why do you think you would lose him?" asked Arthur.

Abigail shook her head. "If you guys knew, even you would want me gone. I can't. Charles can never know why. You can never know why. I wish I didn't know why."

Tears squeezed through her clasped eyelids, wetting her cheeks. She sniffed. "Arthur, I don't know what to do. All I want is to be with him, but I don't know if I can."

"Why can't you?" asked Arthur, his face turning sour.

Abigail shook her head. "You can't know."

Arthur sighed. "I go in for surgery tomorrow afternoon," he said. "It might be a good idea to tell me before then."

Abigail's heart leapt into her throat. If Arthur was going in for heart surgery in less than twenty four hours, then he couldn't know the truth. The truth would only make it more stressful on his heart. The truth might literally kill him. He needed the rest, and the strength, to make it through the next week or so. That meant she couldn't tell him.

For his sake, and for Charles's sake. She'd already said too much.

She smiled. "I'll tell you when you've recovered. It'll be a little easier on your heart."

Arthur looked up at his EKG monitor. "Doesn't look like anything is easy for my heart, kiddo. It probably never will be."

She reached over and patted his hand. "Then we'll wait until it recovers. We'll have that conversation over dinner at your house."

Arthur smiled. "If I'm still around by then."

"You will be," said Abigail. "And the three of us can sit down and discuss it. If *I'm* still around by then."

"Why wouldn't you be around?" asked Arthur.

Abigail sighed. "I could really see it this morning," she said. "He doesn't trust me. I know I have my secrets, but I just can't tell him yet. It could ruin everything we've fought for over the last five months."

"He's a good man," mumbled Arthur, nodding his head. "A smart man. He'll take whatever secrets you have, and he'll work through them logically. If you're scared, he'll understand why. He can see things from other perspectives. He loves you. You just have to tell him. The two of you will make it through whatever else hits you, but you have to establish that trust. He's finicky when it comes to that. He's skittish and weary about the people around him. That's why it's so important that he has you. That's why it's so important that you're honest with him. You're someone he trusts. He hasn't had a lot of reasons to trust people, especially women."

*Emily gave him plenty of reason to trust women.*

Be that as it may, Abigail nodded, thinking of Charles's mother. When had he last spoken to her?

"I guess you're right."

"Just have an open conversation with him," suggested Arthur. "I promise, he will make things work with you. If he doesn't, send him to me and I'll set him straight." He pointed a finger at her, and his face became stern. "That means take care of this before tomorrow afternoon when I go into surgery."

***

"I just want to have an open conversation about this," said Abigail, dropping down onto the couch with a styrofoam box full of street tacos. "I'm sorry if it's cold. There's not a Mexican restaurant close to your place except the Taco Bell, and I told you that was a no go."

"It's fine," laughed Charles. "I just figured we eat Chinese so much, we ought to change it up every now and then."

"Your dad says he's going into surgery tomorrow afternoon," said Abigail. "Open heart surgery. It's risky business."

"What kind of risks?" asked Charles.

"It's not emergency surgery," continued Abigail. "So they have time to really plan the surgery out and get the details sorted, but he's extremely obese. That means a deeper cut, and higher chances of hitting an artery or getting an infection afterwards. There's all sorts of risks, from heart attacks and strokes, to kidney problems and arrhythmias."

Charles shook his head. "He's paying for the rough life he lived."

She settled into the couch, and dug into her food. *Wrong thing to say again.*

"How about you?" she asked. "How was your morning?"

"More training," sighed Charles, rolling his eyes. "Writing after action reports, situational awareness drills. Really boring stuff. Even the team meeting in Walter's hotel room was dull."

"You guys meet in a hotel room?" asked Abigail.

"Yeah," grumbled Charles. "All the way on the twelfth floor. We didn't even discuss anything interesting. More team introductions, and some stuff about this afternoon is all."

"What kind of stuff?" asked Abigail.

"The conference at Grand River View," replied Charles. "That's where everything is at. We'll be running police drills and learning the public relations side of things. I kind of wish I had Katie's job. All she does is sit in Walter's room with his little girl and babysit for him. In the team meeting, she told us all how she was going to take Kitsen out to the pool and play Mermaids all afternoon."

"Walter must be the boss to get such a high room," mumbled Abigail. "Katie must be good at doing some certain things to have that kind of freedom."

Charles nodded. "Yeah, it does have a pretty good view, but he's a relatively humble kind of boss. Nothing fishy about the guy, though. I think Katie and him are secretly in love, and are just using this as an excuse. He needs someone to watch Kitsen while he's out working. Plus he's giving me a chance that no one else would. I'm just some guy he's known for less than a week, and he had me in the room number where his six year old daughter is at."

"I'm happy for you," she said. "It's like a contracting job?"

"Kind of." Charles shrugged. "It's a case by case kind of thing, so yeah, kind of a contract based thing. It's almost a private investigation thing. I don't know how to describe it. I'd never heard of anything like it before, but I've grown to love it."

"More than you love your current job?" asked Abigail. "It's intelligence work, like secret agent stuff."

Charles laughed. "I wish it were that cool. Instead, the seven of us are packed into a two bed hotel room trying to figure out what to do next, and yes, I do love it more than my current job. Here I'm making an impact in the world around me by changing children's lives for the better. At my current job, I just make the machines do what they're supposed to do."

"So what are you going to do next?" asked Abigail.

Charles shook his head again. "We're not sure. We've figured out where he's operating at, and why. Our main goal is to get an inside man for a sting operation, or get one of his customers to cop to the whole thing. Other than that, we're kind of stuck."

Abigail hesitated for a moment, thinking about the customers that could tell, or the other people close that could ruin him. She could do it right now. She could end it all. All she had to do was tell Charles what was going on at home, and the police would take care of the rest. She would be free, and she and Charles could move on and continue their life together.

"Do you think it's just little girls that get trafficked?"

"According to Alison and Walter," started Charles. "Anyone at any age can be trafficked. Boys and girls, from infants to elderly. It's just whoever can be taken advantage of at the time."

Abigail looked out of the glass balcony door. Money for college. She remembered it just as easily as she had ten years ago. The face of her new step father, and the offer he had made.

*You'll need money for college.* He had told the sixteen year old Abigail one day, sitting at that large kitchen table. *If you want, I can help you get it.*

He had earned money from her efforts, but she had never seen a single penny. Instead, she joined the National Guard to get away for periods of time. It wasn't long before her little step sister was old enough to earn money as well, and could take Abigail's spot. What a wonderful day for Abigail, and the end of Olivia's perfect childhood. Eighteen years old, and shipping off to basic training at Fort

Benning, where Abigail's teammates there would harass her.

How many times had she woken up in the middle of the night to hands creeping up under her clothes? How many new and old members of her unit had violated her? Was it worth reporting? Was it worth the effort? She'd looked it up, and decided not.

Just over five percent of all women in the military experienced unwanted sexual contact during their time. Less than a quarter of those women ever reported it, and two thirds of those that reported it faced retaliation of some sort afterwards. Over half of those were assaulted by people of a higher rank.

So what was the point of reporting anything? Might as well make the money. Those high ranking officials could afford it, and she could skim what she wanted off of the profits before handing what was left back to Joseph. He would never know the difference, and every penny she had got her closer to freedom.

But would it stop there? How many men in general throughout her life had forced themselves on her? How many had she let torment her body for money that went to her step father?

Only one had been easy on her. Only one ever cared.

"Are you okay?" He was caring now, his face curling up in concern, his voice soft and soothing. "Abby?"

"Charles," she mumbled, setting her food on the table next to her. She couldn't tell him, not yet, and yet she had to tell him. It burned in her throat. The only man that was ever nice. The only man that ever cared, but he wouldn't care anymore if he knew how polluted and adulterated she really was.

She had been able to take him in for the experience of a lifetime because she had a lifetime of experience. He would never touch her again if he knew that he was really too good for her.

She already had everything she needed from him for today. She knew all the details, so her job was finished. She was free for the night. No more holding back. Five months of waiting. Five months of this game of wondering if it was going to work out. It was. It had to. She would make it happen. She knew what he wanted. She'd known all along.

Men are just so easy to distract.

She leapt forward, pushing his food to the side and landing it on the table. Her arms wrapped around his neck, and her lips attached to his. She couldn't. It was too much for him. He wouldn't be able to handle it. She shoved her tongue in his mouth, grabbing his face with her hands and throwing a leg over him. She didn't want to talk anymore. Talking led to suspicion. Talking led to pain, and remembering. This was simple, and it satisfied them both. He got the feeling of being inside her, and she got to be loved.

He wouldn't ask her any more questions. He would be too distracted. It was just too easy.

His hands pulled at the back of his T-shirt, pulling it up and over her head and exposing her naked torso. His fingers explored her, finding every nerve and stimulating her senses. It was tantalizing.

It was like nothing she'd ever experienced before. No one ever just touched her. No one wanted to explore her body. They all wanted to use it.

Charles was different, and he had to think she wasn't like this. He had to believe she was all his. She had to keep him busy, and this was the only way she knew how.

He was a man, and men were easy to distract.

# <u>26</u>

*Claremore, Oklahoma - Friday - 2:00 PM*
Joseph moved out of the living room and shut the door behind him, shuffling down the hallway, and into the kitchen. Mindy was at the sink, scrubbing dishes from last night.

"What happened?" she asked. "Did Abby call?"

"They're onto me," muttered Joseph, nodding with a gloomy look on his face. "Charles, and the police. They don't know it's me, yet, but they're close. They've already gotten hotels, and days of the week. I was right about that guy. He was a cop. Jimmy. The one where Jackie broke his arm."

"Assaulting an officer is a federal crime," said Mindy. "Jackie can go away for a long time."

"He's in hiding," said Joseph with a wave of his hand. "If he hadn't broken that guy's arm, he'd be sitting in a jail cell telling stories about us."

"Where is he?"

"The less you know, the better. Just worry about keeping house, and don't ask questions. Just take what money you get from this."

Mindy nodded. "What do you mean, if he hadn't broken that guy's arm, he'd be in jail?"

"They're closing in on me," replied Joseph. "They were going to take him that night. The thing is, if you hurt one of their guys, the first thing the police have to do is render aid to one of their own. It shuts down the whole operation. So, Jackie breaks this guy's arm, the cops focus on that, Olivia and I get away, and so does Jackie. Everyone wins except the good guys."

"Does that mean we are the bad guys?" asked Mindy.

Joseph laughed. "Who cares? We're bringing in upwards of ten thousand dollars a week just in profits."

"Yeah," sighed Mindy, "but are we the bad guys?"

"Are the Waltons the bad guys for pushing small businesses out of town with Walmart and Sam's Club?" asked Joseph. "It's no secret those guys do it on purpose. How about Bezos and Amazon? They've taken over most of the online shopping. It's just part of getting rich. Sometimes, you have to do bad things. It doesn't make you a bad person, though."

"Right," said Mindy, going back to her dishes. "Just getting rich."

"In a couple of years," continued Joseph. "All the debt will be paid off, and we'll be set to retire long before the government supports us with Social Security. We just have to keep things running smoothly until then."

Mindy nodded. "Okay, so what are we going to do about Charles and the police?"

"They've been pushing and pushing up on me," said Joseph. "I think it's time to push back."

"Pushing back doesn't sound like it'll keep things running smoothly."

Joseph agreed. It sounded like the words of an insane man. Make them scramble. Make them shit their pants. Make them scatter like cockroaches and be unable to function together."

"And how do we do that?"

Joseph smiled. "Charles told Abigail exactly where everyone is going to be this afternoon. Now you tell me: What father can think clearly when his daughter is missing?"

# <u>27</u>

*Tulsa, Oklahoma - 4:00 PM*

"Five million hotel rooms in America. I looked it up last night." Alison led Charles into the hotel lobby. "Traffickers use them because of the amount of people coming and going. It's a good way to hide their business. Hotels are also one of the top five venues for trafficking, mostly dealing with forced labor. I was amazed to see how much of the cleaning staff in hotels weren't legally employed. Not to mention the obvious. Where else would you meet a prostitute?"

*Not here. It would be too expensive for me.*

"How do you think this looks on the balance sheet?" Charles muttered over to Alison as they made their way to the check in desk. Two women in T-shirts stamped with The Red Sea Initiative's logo on their fronts checked them in and sent them in a different direction than this morning. The sign with the arrow pointing in that direction said, *Training.*

"Higher end clientele," replied Alison. "Prices go up for an encounter, and customers prefer a place like this because it's cleaner and nicer. Dingy hotels attract a lower class clientele that pays a discounted price for the cheap conditions and low income affordability. People pay for cleanliness and convenience.”

“That’s smart,” mumbled Charles.

“It’s run like a business,” said Alison. “I told you. Some operations get so big they can hire accountants and money launderers.”

“Do you think this guy has an accountant?” asked Charles.

“I doubt it,” replied Alison. “Our intel only reports one girl with a large price range. Some guys report paying as little as one hundred fifty dollars, and some guys report paying upwards of five hundred dollars. Usually smaller operations like this just go with cash payments to keep things simple. No having to wash the money, or try to keep the books. One man, one child operations are simple and easy to run, and still have the potential to earn thousands each week.”

“Higher prices for higher costs,” said Charles. “Simple accounting for simple transactions. Cash for the paper trail, and low income to avoid laundering. It all makes sense.” He stopped in his tracks. “Hold on a minute.”

“What?” she asked, turning back to face him. He pulled out his phone, opening his photos folder and looking at the map from the conference room in the police station.

“The dates,” said Charles. “Certain days of the week. He’s in different hotels on different days of the week to avoid setting a pattern, but he would have a clientele that knows where he’s at, right?”

Alison nodded. "That would mean he has certain customers that buy on certain days of the week."

"Which means he has a marketing network," said Charles. "Probably coded, but he has a way to connect with his clientele and let them know where he's at on a specific day."

"That would mean he has a way to communicate what his price is every day, too," said Alison. "That way everyone brings enough cash. Or he had one in the beginning, and his customers just know what they are now."

"Hotel prices change, though," said Charles. "At least once every year, he'll have to jack up his price, just like anyone else does in the economy."

"Inflation," muttered Alison. "He has to have more income to pay for his own personal things, so he raises his prices to make up for it." She nodded, and led him towards the large conference hall. "We'll have to see what Walter and Jimmy make of that. We might be able to do a social media search."

"Phone records?" asked Charles as Alison approached the clerk.

She shook her head. "Not without warrants, and phone companies hate dealing with the police."

*Who doesn't?* Charles thought.

Walter came into view, the man gathering up his team and standing in front of a room full of plain clothed police officers. Charles waved as they approached.

"Walter, you'll never guess what we just came up with."

Walter patted him on the shoulder. "Later. Right now, we have to get this training done. Have you ever cleared a building before?"

***

Guns. He hated guns. Brutal, unforgiving weapons that caused absolute devastation. He'd seen the destruction; he hated it. What these things were capable of haunted his nightmares and stole nights of sleep away from him, and yet here was Charles Langley, holding a practice Glock 17 in his hands, and moving forward towards the door where the others were staged.

Rebecca, Alison, and two police officers were waiting for him, two on each side of the door and prepped for entry. They were staring at him, waiting impatiently for him to quit being a whiny baby and pick up the weapon. It was part of training; it was part of the job.

Realistically, Walter had told him, the likelihood he was ever going to be performing actual police drills in the field was zero. Charles, being undercover, was more likely going to be inside the raid already, getting arrested as a trafficker. The job required Charles, however, to be present at these training seminars to demonstrate and train with police officers to help their efficiency. This way, everyone knew how to communicate, and Charles would be less likely to get hurt if something did happen.

Alison nodded over for him to join her and Rebecca, letting the two police officers handle their sectors. Charles wasn't sure what his job was, but being at the back of the line gave him the advantage of being able to, and having time to, figure it out without asking anyone. He stepped up to Alison and Rebecca, the two powerful and imposing women ready to go, and signaled to the police officers to breach.

A police officer stepped out and in front of the door, launching a foot out and landing a front kick directly next to the doorknob of the door. The door flung open, crashing into itself with a crunch of splintering wood. Rebecca moved fast, slipping through the open frame and moving in the opposite direction from the direction the door had swung. She went inside, and straight to the right, hugging the wall on the inside. Without hesitating, the second police officer moved in, mirroring Rebecca on the left side of the door. Alison was third, going in and moving straight into the room down the middle. In a single split second, three people had entered the door with weapons drawn, covering every angle in the room.

Charles glanced at the first police officer, who nodded at him to move in. Without knowing exactly what to do, Charles ducked into the room with his weapon up and against his chest, taking a guess at the pattern and following Rebecca's path along the right wall. Right, left center, right, and left. That made sense. He glanced back to see the first police officer coming in and moving to the left with his partner, with Alison continuing down the middle.

Rebecca looked back at him, and shook her head, pointed two fingers at his eyes, and then one finger towards the back of the room over his shoulder. "Diamond Formation."

Charles looked at the others, trying to figure out what she meant. It didn't take Sherlock Holmes to see the big picture here.

Alison was in front, facing forward towards the back of the room. Rebecca and the first police officer faced forward as well, standing a step or two behind Alison and keeping their weapons in what was known as the "low ready" position. The second police officer had moved behind them, forming a short little diamond shape, where three were facing forward and the fourth watched side to side. Obviously, there was only one place left to take.

Charles stepped into formation, spinning around to face the entrance and keeping his field of view behind the team. As the back of the diamond, he would be in charge of watching the rear and making sure no one was able to ambush from behind. That made perfect sense to him.

"Halt." Rebecca's voice came from behind him now. He froze, and instinctively dropped to one knee. He wasn't sure why, but he'd seen it in movies, and it did make him a smaller target. He felt a hand on his shoulder, soft and small. Rebecca.

"Charles, as the point man in back, I want you to assess the outside. Usually a driveway or a parking lot. I know there's nothing out there right now, but try to picture the hotel parking lot. Think about the types of vehicles out there, and see if anything sticks out. It'll help you keep an active mind about who's in and out of the building."

"Assessing the threat means taking in all available data and working out possible outliers that give away enemy positions and plans," Alison spoke up from the front of the pack. "Anything that looks out of place could be a possible ambush, or booby trap."

Charles turned to Rebecca, and she nodded at him.

"Just a mental exercise," she said, patting him on the shoulder. "It'll come in handy someday."

Charles nodded, and the hand pulled on his shoulder. He turned his head and started to follow the group again, crossing another door frame into a hallway. He tried to think of the parking lot that morning as he'd entered the hotel. Did anything stick out to him? Mostly huge Chevy Suburbans and Ford Escapes of all colors, figuring in with the law enforcement presence. There were the occasional personal vehicles that stood out. A red Toyota Corolla, reminding him of the man Abigail had sent to follow him. *Solomon.* Details were important. A black Chevy Equinox. Mid two thousands model? Like the one his mother had when he was a teenager. The first vehicle he had ever driven.

That sent shivers up his spine.

One vehicle stood out in his mind. Something that didn't belong, or match anything around it. Something that couldn't blend in at a place like this, or any other place for that matter. Something familiar; something he'd seen before.

An old square body chevy pickup, probably a Silverado. Red, with a gold stripe down the side.

# <u>28</u>

*Tulsa, Oklahoma - Friday - 4:15 PM*
Kitsen Faucet, what a terrible name. She hated it. Why did her daddy have to name her Kitsen? He was so mean to her for no reason at all. Her daddy brought her to these boring places, her daddy left for days at a time to "save the world", and her daddy named her Kitsen Faucet. She hated her daddy for all that. "Save the world". What about her? Wasn't she supposed to be his world? What time did she get? One day out of a couple of weeks, like that was enough? What was she supposed to do stuck in these rooms all day? Thank god for Katie. Without a momma to take care of her, where would Kitsen be without Katie.

Katie taught Kitsen how to braid her hair. Katie taught Kitsen how to paint her nails. Katie taught Kitsen how to put on makeup. Katie was teaching Kitsen how to be a girl, not a prisoner, and not a thing to set aside like a book. Katie showed Kitsen that not all of life was about bad things happening to kids and police officers running through fake buildings. Katie was the best thing in Kitsen's life. She kept asking her daddy why Katie couldn't be her new momma, but her daddy always shrugged the question away. He never cared.

Maybe she would just call Katie momma, and see what happened. Maybe Katie would like it.

"Kitty!" Now that was a good name. Thank God for Katie, who's voice rang from her sunbathing chair like a beautiful songbird. "I've got it all finished! Ready to see the difference?"

Katie was supposed to be putting on half of a face of makeup and a half of a face without makeup to show Kitsen how different a girl could make her own face look. Kitsen was excited to see the results. She didn't know there was such a difference between the same person and two different faces. Just the thought of half of one face and half of another on the same person made her giggle.

Kitsen had been busy playing in the pool while waiting for Katie to finish, and began climbing out to join her only true friend. The door to the back of the hotel opened, and a large man came out and joined them. He wasn't in a bathing suit. He was in jeans, a t-shirt, and boots. Kitsen didn't think that was a very smart idea for getting in the pool.

Katie glanced up at Kitsen like she was keeping a secret. She really did look like two different people at once. Half her face covered in freckles, and the other stark white with shaded eyes.

She smiled over at Kitsen as Kitsen came closer. "Maybe I can scare them off with this face. What do you think?"

She turned around to face the oncoming man, who's face had somehow changed color from white to black, and the man leapt into action. He dove at Katie, tackling her and sending her tumbling out of her chair with a tremendous crash. The force knocked Katie clean off her feet, the small body of the girl toppling down under the weight of a massive black shadow. Kitsen screamed, the shadow reaching back with a huge arm and slamming a huge fist down onto Katie's face. Katie's arms flopped to the ground beside her, and the shadow rose to its feet.

His face hadn't changed color. The man was wearing a bank robber mask. Kitsen screamed again, and the person launched towards her. She was up off of the sidewalk in a split second, her arms and legs flailing out to hurt the person as he came closer. Fingers dug into her ribs, and giant palms squeezed her from either side of her body.

"Stay still." It was a man's voice, almost a growl. "Quit moving."

She did not quit moving. Did he really think she would? She thrashed, her feet hitting the concrete. The man wrapped his fingers around her arm. Her mind raced, her thoughts on escape and help. *The watch! The emergency button!* It would call her daddy. She had practiced all the time, and she knew it would text his phone and tell her she was in trouble.

*What if someone tries to steal you?* She looked around the pool area, noticing her naked wrist. The watch was on the side table next to Katie's chair.

She turned to the man and kicked hard where her daddy had shown her to kick, in between the legs. He dropped down to the ground, his hand slipping from her arm with a big groan of pain. She pulled her arm away and jumped forward, stepping over Katie's limp body and coming down on top of the glass. She grabbed her watch from the table, tapping her finger on the screen to wake it up. The man in the mask stumbled back to his feet, but it was too late. She had the screen pulled up, the SOS button round and red. She pressed it and clenched the watch tightly in her hand.

*Send the text, send the location. Do not lose the watch, or I can't find you.*

The man never hesitated. His arm curled up behind his head like a snake, then shot forward in a strike that landed flush on her face. The watch went flying out of her hand, and her arm was gripped again. She reached for the watch, but the man yanked her away from the table and to the door to the hotel. She screamed, earning her another punch to the side of the head.

"Shut the fuck up, kid," growled the man yanking her arm so hard it send pain up into her shoulder. "You're coming with me."

***

"Coming through the door," said Walter loud enough for the room to hear. "Move from one side of the hallway or room to the other, treating the other side of the door like a pie. This allows you a clearer view of what's on the other side of the door, and gives you a better picture of what you're up against before you move into the unknown area."

Walter moved through the door, the weapon in his hand pulling back against his chest as he moved left to right.

"I bring my weapon close to my body," he continued. "This keeps any potential attackers on the other side of the door from taking my weapon whether I know they're there or not."

He backed through the door, and extended his gun. He moved through the door again, this time with his gun at arm's length. A hand shot out and pushed the gun aside, a woman stepping into view and throwing fake punches at him.

"See?" asked Walter. "If I come through with my arms extended, Alison can take my weapon a lot easier."

He repeated the motion again, this time with his weapon against his chest. Alison reached out and reached for the gun, and he pushed out with the weapon, striking her in the chest and pushing her back. "This way, I have more control. I can use the weight of my body to aim the pistol, and take a shot if necessary."

Walter's phone gave off a loud ding, and he rolled his eyes. "I'm sorry, I have to check that. That's my daughter's text tone."

The room laughed, and a man came forward to take the pistol from Walter. Charles watched Alison, who winked at him and waved him over. Charles crossed the training room and joined the two of them by the door.

"I would have had him either way in reality," laughed Alison, as Walter pulled his phone out of his pocket.

Charles shrugged. "I'm not convinced."

Walter stared down at his phone screen, and glanced back up to Charles. Walter had wide eyes and a trembling lower lip.

"What is it?" Charles asked.

Walter's face turned pale. "My daughter's emergency SOS signal."

He was gone before anyone else knew what was happening. Charles started after him, stopped, and remembered what Katie had said. *Play in the pool all afternoon.*

Alison barked a loud order for someone to watch the exits. Walter hit the elevator button, calling a ride, and Charles ran for the pool door.

"Walter!" he shouted. "They're out at the pool."

Walter turned to look at Charles. "Right!"

Charles spun around, smashing his body through the door leading to the pool, and out into the open.

***

A few feet in front of the door lay Katie Swift, her face half covered in makeup, and half red from what had to be some sort of impact. Someone had hit her.

"Kitsen!" Walter barged into the empty pool area and checked everything. Under the chairs, in the pool, and in the toy boxes. She was nowhere to be found.

He dropped to his knees next to Katie, who groaned and opened one eye. Charles knelt down next to them, and they were both brought to attention by the fence gate outside slamming shut.

The eye on the red side of the face below them barely opened, the tissue around it starting to swell.

"Walter?"

"What happened, Katie?"

"I'm not sure." Her voice was barely audible, just a mumble. "I turned around, and then I was on the ground. I think someone hit me."

"Kitsen?" It was Charles asking now, confident and aware. His eyes locked onto that gate.

Katie shook her head. "I don't know."

Walter pulled his phone out, ready to dial 911.

"Someone took her." Charles again, standing up to his feet. "That gate was closing. They're in the parking lot."

"Let's go," said Walter.

"Call the police, and stay with her." It was the same voice from the hospital. It sounded dangerous. "I've got this."

"Don't kill anyone." But Charles Langley was gone before he could finish his sentence.

***

The grand escape. Moving through a packed parking lot full of law enforcement. That was difficult for anyone, let alone a middle aged man dragging an uncooperative young child. At least he wasn't going down the stairs.

The girl didn't scream, but she wasn't being quiet, either. She was groaning and squealing. It was the thrashing around and fighting that was slowing him down. Every few paces he had to stop and yank on her arm. She would squeal, and follow him.

He wrenched open the truck door, and threw the girl in. His key went into the ignition and turned. The engine fired up. He smiled.

*Home free.*

Something grabbed his arm from behind, squeezing with enough force to numb his hand. He felt a hard impact on the side of his face. Something pulled him, and he went sliding out of the truck.

When he hit the pavement, he rolled, and used a nearby Cadillac Escalade to regain his feet. A flash of motion passed before him, and a second impact caught him in the right side of his abdomen. The breath left him, and refused to come back. He doubled over, clutching his stomach, only to catch one more impact to the face from below. It felt like a bowling ball landing on his forehead.

His head smacked against the window of the Escalade as he straightened, and someone grabbed his arm and pulled. Joseph Smith felt his body come into contact with something, another body, and then went soaring over it. He landed hard on the ground, his arm locked up underneath his opponent's arm. He threw a hand up to cover his face, feeling fingers dig into his scalp.

Then his mask came off of his head.

***

The takedown had been easy. Disable the hand to loosen the grip on the truck, then palm strike to the head to discombobulate the man. Meet him when he regained his feet, left hook to the liver, knee to the face, then a backdrop to put him on the ground.

Charles Langley had the man's arm tied up under his own arm, hooking over it and squeezing it under his armpit for control. The man raised a hand to protect his face, anticipating the punch that Charles so desperately wanted to throw. Walter's voice in the back of his head.

*That's not how things are actually done. We aren't vigilantes. This isn't the movies.*

His hand shot forward, and his fingers gripped the crown of the ski mask on the man's face. Charles pulled, revealing the face of Abigail's step father, Joseph Smith.

"Holy shit!" In a second of hesitation, his grip loosened on the locked arm, and Joseph ripped his arm free of Charles's grip. The hand protecting the face shot out, clapping on the underside of Charles's chin and knocking Charles off of his feet. Charles rolled back into the truck, finding Joseph regaining his feet.

"You should have just stayed out of it." Joseph leapt forward, a boot flying towards Charles's face. Charles slipped to the side, hearing a steel toe hit the sidewalk of the truck with a magnificent *bong*. Charles rolled to the side and regained his footing, climbing back to his feet, only to see that red Chevy Square Body Silverado with the gold stripe pull away with terrible screeching tires.

*Gone!*

"No!" He cried at the distant truck, and then felt a missile impact his lower body. He glanced down, wrapping his own arms around whatever had hit him.

Kitsen was sobbing, her face buried into his stomach, her arms tightly gripping his waist.

# <u>29</u>

*Tulsa, Oklahoma - Friday - 5:00 PM*
He'd always wanted to sit on the check in counter of a hotel. Sitting there, swinging his legs like a child, and watching the police wander the building left and right.

"Hey." A police officer stopped in front of him and stuck a finger in Charles's direction. "Get down from there."

With a tired sigh, Charles hopped down from the desk and leaned back against it, propping his elbows on it to support himself. He watched in the distance as Walter walked around in circles, holding Kitsen tightly.

"Ten years, I've been with the Initiative. I've never seen him upset like this." Alison stepped up to the counter, and jumped up to sit on it like Charles had. The police officer pointed the finger in her direction.

"Get down from there."

She stuck her tongue out at him. "Make me."

The police officer trailed his eyes up and down Alison from head to toe, and decided it wasn't worth the trouble. Charles turned to Alison.

"I saw his face," he said. "Our guy."

"Do you know him?"

"Oddly enough, I do."

She stared down at him. "Who is it?"

"Abigail's stepfather."

"Your girlfriend's stepdad?" asked Alison. Charles nodded.

"Do you think he's our trafficker?"

Charles nodded, thinking about the cough in the house, and the way they had shuttled him out the front door so quickly. The baby's bottle on the microwave, and the extra sized house for a family of three. It all made sense now.

"Yes, I do. They told me the other night that they didn't have an extra kid. I don't know who the little girl is."

"Daughter, or niece," said Alison. "Almost half of all trafficking happens with family members or close family friends."

"She was in the house that night for dinner," said Charles. "She was hidden, but she was there. I heard a cough, or something, from the back of the house. They all made me think I was crazy."

Alison nodded her head. "Daughter, then. That's unfortunate."

"Why?" asked Charles.

"Familial trafficking can be challenging to identify because it's hidden within the confines of the family," said Alison. "On top of that, most authorities don't have training in familial trafficking. We deal mostly with actual trafficking rings that come in from other places. As a result, familial trafficking usually get misidentified as child sexual abuse, which has fewer consequences than child trafficking. Prosecuting traffickers is especially difficult because the survivors of familial trafficking find it hard to testify against family members out of loyalty or fear. They feel ashamed of how disgusting society sees them, and purposely avoid telling others about what's going on. They worry that the family will be torn apart, and they wear that when they tell authorities, it might lead to something worse than their current situation."

"Why do they think that?" asked Charles.

"That's what they're made to think," replied Alison. "It's all mental abuse and manipulation."

"So if we get him, does that mean we might not get the prosecution?" Charles asked.

"When there is a conviction in a familial trafficking case and the trafficker is sent to jail, many survivors end up reunited with their families. Unfortunately, because the trafficker is a family member, over half of survivors of familial trafficking will have to see the person who abused them once they are released. As long as someone else saw him, though, this should be easy. Kidnapping charges is a ten year minimum in most places. If no one else saw him, then it makes it a lot harder."

"Why?"

Alison shrugged. "No real proof that it was him. Kitsen won't say anything about the truck or the guy. Everyone says it's easy enough to get a warrant and send police to search his house, but the reality is the time it takes, especially with a network like this guy has, gives him the time to hide and clean things up. Then it becomes your word versus his. A judge could make it look like you were just mad at him for something and wanted him out of the way of your girlfriend. Especially if he cleans up and we find nothing at his house."

"That's assuming he's keeping her at the house." Charles thought of the night he'd had dinner at the Smiths' house, and hearing the cough. Everyone had made him think he was crazy. *Everyone.* And yet there was the girl he was searching for, within fifty feet of him.

"Where do you get all these weird things you keep talking about?" asked Alison. "Where do you think he's keeping her? You keep on like these guys are evil masterminds. He's moving her to hotels during the day, and taking her home at night. That's how they operate. It's too difficult and expensive to do it any other way. He can't keep her at a storage facility. It costs too much."

"What do you mean?" asked Charles.

"Think of it like a business," said Alison. "If he sells her for one fifty, and sells her ten times a day, he's got fifteen hundred dollars every day. Take out costs of fuel and hotel, which rotate between a hundred for a room and three or four hundred for a room, and you have to make a profit. Otherwise, there's no incentive to sell her. It's all about making money. The evil is in the lack of care for the child's safety, not in the sadistic pleasure of torture. These people see the profit as better than working a job."

Charles glanced over, watching Walter's hand drop down to Katie's face, caressing her uninjured side with his palm and stroking her cheek with his thumb.

"Is Katie the kid's mother?" asked Charles.

Alison shook her head. "Kitsen's mother left when she was young. She stuck around for the beginning of the Initiative, but it was so stressful for them that she just packed up and left. Left Kitsen with Walter and never even tried to get back in contact. It must have driven her insane because I can't imagine abandoning your family like that."

Charles could. He knew what that was like.

"Walter was a mess," continued Alison, "and Katie stepped up to help. She's technically one of our team members, but she spends most of her time watching Kitsen. I think Walter has a crush on her."

Charles watched Walter's eyes stare down into Katie's, the emotion behind them a mixture of rage and love. "I'd say you're right."

"He hurt Katie." Alison's voice was low, almost a whisper. Underneath that whisper, Charles could hear the throaty growl. "He hurt Kitsen."

*He knew where to find them.* He didn't say it out loud, and he didn't feel like he had to. He just hoped Alison didn't connect the dots.

"I would like to know how he knew about everything," growled Walter, turning his attention back to his daughter, pacing back and forth in the lobby with her in his arms. Charles glanced at Katie, whose face was still cut in half, one beautifully covered in makeup, and the other already bruising. Her eyes remained glued to Walter, a look of desperate longing covering both halves of her face. Charles's eyes moved over to

Alison, who stared back at him with furrowed eyebrows.

She had to know. She was good enough to make the connection. He turned back to Walter, who couldn't stop pacing, and couldn't put his daughter down.

Charles sighed, his eyes falling to the ground. "Because I told Abigail."

The lobby fell silent. No one moved, police or otherwise, staring at Charles. Walter froze in place, and Alison's legs ceased kicking back and forth. He saw her head lower, but her eyes searched the area, watching the people in the room instead of him for once. He could feel Walter's gaze piercing him.

"What do you mean you told Abigail?" asked Walter. "Abigail who?"

"My…" Charles hesitated, unsure what to call Abigail at this point. "Girlfriend."

He thought about the cough at Joseph's house again, and the baby's bottle. He thought about Abigail's aloofness, and her rush to get him out of that house. The way things had happened, and the way everything had worked out.

*It was all a setup.* He thought about the conversations they'd had, and the information she'd asked for. He shook his head. *Joseph used her.*

"She was just my girlfriend," he mumbled, hearing footsteps approaching on the padded floor. "It was just a conversation. I saw who the trafficker was today in the stairwell. It's her stepdad. I had no idea until ten minutes ago."

"And you told her these things?" Walter's voice was close, coming closer, angry, and becoming angrier.

"He didn't know." Alison flung herself off the counter, leaping to her feet in between Charles and Walter.

Charles slumped to the ground, elbows on his knees.

"He's just supposed to know that his girlfriend's dad is the guy we're looking for?" Alison continued, straightening up and facing Walter.

"What if he knew the whole time?" asked Walter. "If he's been undermining us this whole time?"

"We weren't making any progress until he joined this case." Alison was almost yelling. "He's been a part of every discovery since he joined."

"It's awfully strange how easy it was for him to figure it out." Walter yelled back, and Charles could see Alison shrink an inch. He thought about what she'd said a few nights ago. Trafficked for six years? Abused? Of course she wouldn't take the yelling very well. "Maybe he knew those things in advance as a part of getting inside our organization. Maybe he's been a plant from the beginning."

Alison took a step forward, trying to stay firm under Walter's pressure. Charles looked up to see the little girl in Walter's arms wiping tears from her face.

Fear. Kitsen and Alison were afraid. He looked over to Katie, finding a look of concern on her face. *A father's rage. Uncontrolled.*

"He's…" Alison hesitated, the first time she'd done so since Charles met her. "He's green, Walter. We're still training him. There was no way he could have known."

"So green he almost got my daughter killed?" Walter was yelling, and all three women flinched. Alison, Kitsen, and even Katie from across the lobby. Three fearful women.

*Fearful women. Emily.* An instinct in Charles rose up, an anger that stemmed back from somewhere he wasn't sure. He'd had enough from Walter.

Charles rose to his feet. "So green I saved your daughter's life."

Again, the attention of the room was on him. Alison turned to face him, and he stepped around her, throwing an arm out to push her behind him. She moved out of the way easily enough, and he was sure she had let him do that. He squared up with Walter, giving the man plenty of space in front of him.

*Never let your enemy get too close.*

"Put that child down," Charles told Walter.

"What?"

"Put your child down," continued Charles. "You want to yell at me because you're upset about this, that's fine, but you do it to me. You leave Alison, Katie, and your daughter out of this. This is not their fault."

Walter froze again. His eyes widened, his lips pressing together with the force of hydraulic pistons. Slowly, carefully, he set Kitsen on the ground, and let her run away. The little girl, without hesitation, ran to Katie and jumped on her. Charles felt a hand on the left side of his ribs, the fingers pressing slightly, as if Alison was trying to get him out of the way.

He stood firm, unmoving. He was not going to let her take the brunt of the force for him. Even if she was technically responsible for him in some weird bureaucratic way, and was even possibly larger than him in some ways, he deserved this, and he could take it.

No woman deserved that kind of abuse.

Walter stepped forward, inches from Charles face, the two men staring eye to eye. "Tell me the truth."

Alarm bells rang in Charles's head. *Enemy too close! Enemy too close!*

*Talk. Words can be just as effective.*

"I've known Abigail for two decades," started Charles, keeping the confidence in his voice and standing firm. Alison's fingers pressed deeper into his side. "We were childhood friends that lost connection when I went to jail. Five months ago we reconnected and started hanging out as friends again, trying to become more serious. When I came across you guys and started the transition into your organization, she freaked out and thought I was leaving her. She's the one that sent someone to follow me because she was worried about what I was doing and who I was with." He turned to Alison, who stepped away and removed her hand.

He took a deep breath. "I went to dinner at her parents' house, and she asked to move in with me. She's been home with me ever since, and we talk, like romantic partners should talk. I didn't realize that her stepfather was the trafficker until ten minutes ago when I pulled his mask off of his head while saving your daughter's life, and then avoided taking a steel toe boot to the skull in order to save my own life. Now, it's your turn. Let me have it."

Walter took a deep breath, sucking in air through clenched teeth. "I want to."

"Do it," Charles stepped closer to Walter. "Get it off of your chest, Walter. I am a big boy. I can take it."

Walter let out the deepest breath Charles had ever heard. The hand on his back returned, resting on his shoulder and pushing, but he resisted.

"You gave sensitive information to a person that had no right to know," started Walter. "This is not an open book industry. We put our lives on the line to protect children, we go deep undercover with some of the most dangerous organizations in the world. You can't just tell anyone you want about what you're doing. It's a danger to you, and to everyone around you."

Walter was yelling now, the whole attention of everyone in the hotel now focused on the two men.

"What you did almost cost me my daughter," Walter continued. "It almost cost her and Katie their lives. I was right at the hospital. You are too young and too inexperienced to be on this team. You are not good enough to be a part of the Red Sea Initiative."

Walter stepped back, sucking in another labored breath, trying to exhale it slowly. "I never should have brought you into this." Walter turned to the nearest police officer and pointed at him. "Has Charles given his statement?"

Unfazed, the police officer nodded his head. Walter turned back to Charles. "Get out of here."

Charles hesitated, feeling Alison's grip on his shoulder tighten. Walter flung a hand towards the lobby door, pointing a stiff finger out of the building. "Get out!"

Charles took a step, Alison's hand falling off of his shoulder and letting him go. He took another step, his eyes floating over to Katie and Kitsen as he shuffled around Walter and moved to the entrance. Their eyes looked away. Again and again, his feet dragged him towards the door, the entire population of the hotel watching him make the walk of shame.

He was a big boy. He could take it. *What did I just do to myself?*

The doors opened, letting him through and opening up a new world for him. It was a world of monotony, a world of unfulfillment, and a world without a future. His father had told him that machinery maintenance was the future, and it looked like Charles was never getting out of it.

# <u>30</u>

*Claremore, Oklahoma - Friday - 5:30 PM*
Abigail marked the box with the word, CLOTHES, and stepped back. Almost everything she owned now sat in boxes, and most of those were already in her car. This was it, the last box.

*A new home.* A wonderful thought that echoed loudly in her ears. *Freedom. Almost there.*

*Escape.* The memories this room held, the filth and degradation that the sheets on the bed represented. The room that barely belonged to her anyways. A room where "friends", customers of Joseph's operation made to sound nice and friendly, came to experience the young girl known as Abby.

The name still made her cringe every time Charles said it. The name still meant nothing but pain to her, and she had no way to tell him. He liked the name, and he meant nothing by it. She might as well let it happen.

She remembered all the things she let happen. She remembered the fights she had put up on this bed, and the submissions she'd been forced into. It had driven her to desperation. She had run to the National Guard. She had run to Charles. She had run for her life.

Her bedroom door opened without warning, and a form entered her vision that made her skin crawl. A large, round man that called himself her father. Joseph.

"Hey Abby," he mumbled softly, his tone taking the form of a parent speaking to an upset toddler. "Are you upset about Charles?"

"Charles?" she managed to ask. Shivers crawled down her spine like spiders at the mention of her pet name. *Don't believe what he says.* She told herself. *It's not true. Charles wouldn't do anything to hurt you.*

"You don't know?" asked Joseph. "He didn't tell you about the other woman?"

*Alison.* Charles had mentioned her. A new work partner. A pretty woman, he had said. He had finally admitted it. Older, and abused, but wasn't that his type? Abigail was only a year older, but she was older, and she was abused.

He had admitted Alison was pretty.

"No," she whispered, trying to maintain a sense of ignorance.

"I was having suspicions about him," continued Joseph, "so I went to Tulsa to check on him today and make sure he wasn't going to hurt you, and I found him with another woman."

"Who?" she asked, trying not to roll her eyes.

"A big woman," said Joseph. "Tall, and built. Like an athlete."

*Alison.* How could Joseph have known what she looked like unless he'd seen her?

*They work together. They have to be around each other. Don't get ahead of yourself.*

"What were they doing?"

"Having lunch." Joseph shrugged. "Laughing and giggling like a high school couple. I followed them around town. They moved fast, but I kept up. I'm putting in the extra effort to look out for you, babe. Hell, I even took a day away from Olivia to help you out. It's my job to make sure Charles is good enough for you."

Abigail swallowed hard. *Not true.* She repeated it in her head. *Charles would never.*

Then the question anchored itself in her mind. *Olivia was here at the house. I was here at the house. Joseph was gone.*

Abigail had missed her opportunity to get Olivia out of danger.

"Is he?" It was all she could think to ask, and she knew what he would say. "Is he good enough for me?"

Joseph shook his head. "He's not. He really loves this new girl."

The words rang out in her head. Charles had been distant since he met Alison. Charles had been hesitant to move forward with Abigail since then. Charles had all but quit his job to hang around Alison.

*Stop it! Don't let him get inside your head.*

"What's Charles address?" asked Joseph. "Tell me where he lives and I'll drive by and see if she's there."

*Freedom. A new home.* Under no circumstances could Joseph find out where Charles lived. She needed the place to escape. She needed to be able to hide. Once she was away, she could run farther. Now, she just needed to get away.

"It's fine," she said. "I'm heading over there tonight, anyways, so I'll just check for myself."

"Are you sure?" asked Joseph. "I'm just looking out for you."

Abigail shook her head. "I'll handle it."

"I can even give him a little scare if you want," chuckled Joseph. "No one hurts my little girl."

*Except you.* Abigail thought about Charles. His distance; her reluctance. He admitted he thought Alison was pretty, and Abigail had not been the best romantic interest until the last day or two. Men had needs; even Charles wouldn't be able to hold out forever. Had Alison gotten to him first? Was he just using Abigail until he had things locked up with Alison?

Joseph twisted his face up, and shook his head in response. "Did you tell him anything about us?"

Abigail's body turned to stone. "What?"

"Did you tell him about Olivia, or yourself, or anything?"

Abigail shook her head. "No. I would never. Why?"

"I just want to make sure," mumbled Joseph, almost under his breath. "You don't know who you can really trust anymore."

The image of Charles leaving the apartment in a rush without telling her his secret blazed in her mind. She saw it clear as day. He hurried to leave

Abigail to go see Alison. Abigail wasn't trustworthy. He had to know that. She didn't deserve his trust. She didn't deserve his love. He knew all of those things.

Maybe he was stepping into another relationship with someone else. Wasn't it called "monkey barring"? Hanging onto the last one until a firm grip was held on the next. Why wouldn't he? He'd dealt with a ridiculous Abigail for so long, why wouldn't he get tired of it? Why wouldn't he trade Abigail in for a sexy, tall, lady spy? Anyone else would.

Did Abigail really want to risk seeing them together at his apartment tonight? Could she handle that? Charles knew she was coming back, but he wouldn't know when. If she showed up without warning…

"I'm not feeling well," she muttered. "Maybe I'll stay here one more night before going back over there."

"That's fine." Joseph moved his hand to the top of her head and ruffled her hair. "Listen, if you get scared or lonely, come get me. I'm always willing to stay with you to keep you protected. I'll even sleep in bed with you if you want."

Abigail shivered. She couldn't help it. She knew what thoughts were behind that comment. Her stomach wound up in knots tight enough to hold a boat to a dock.

"Thanks, Joseph," she whispered, "but I'll be okay."

Joseph grabbed Abigail's hand and squeezed lightly, the sign he used to give her before work in the mornings many years ago. The same squeeze he gave Olivia every morning. "Abby, we're long past that name. Please, call me Daddy."

*Vomit.* It took everything she had to avoid actually throwing up. All she could do was nod at him and turn away. Her bedroom light flickered off, the late evening sun glaring through the window and turning the room a deep orange.

"You don't need Charles," said Joseph, as her door creaked shut. "You need a good guy, like old Tom Leonard. Do you remember how much fun you had with him?"

The fun they'd had together? With Tom Leonard? She did remember. The man that showed her the reality of the world around her. The man that displayed her step fathers true colors. Tom Leonard: Abigail's first… *friend.*

# <u>*31*</u>

*Claremore, Oklahoma - Ten Years Ago*
Abigail always wanted a puppy. Her family never made a livable wage, or had always found some other excuse to avoid bringing one home.

This puppy, however, a beautiful red golden retriever newborn that did nothing but attack her with its tongue, was real. The soft, delicate fur, the sweet lavender smell of dog shampoo, and the sloppy wet puppy kisses made her heart leap out of her chest. She couldn't stop giggling. Sixteen years old, and she was rolling on the ground with a tiny baby puppy like she was six.

Then the puppy vanished, and the face of her smiling stepfather hovered over her. He was laughing, too. A wonderful, deep, belly laugh that brought a smile to her face. This man rescued Abigail and her mother from poverty. At a time when Abigail was ready to join the Army for a signing bonus and decent money, Joseph Smith had come along and saved her family.

Better yet, Joseph Smith had gotten her the puppy she always wanted.

"You look like you're having a blast," laughed Joseph as the puppy turned its wonderful affection on him. "I'm glad you like this dog. I knew you wanted one, but I wasn't sure he'd be right for you."

"I love him!" She squealed like a child. "He's perfect. I can't thank you enough."

"I think you can," said Joseph. "I have an idea. Real quick, can you help me out with something?"

Joseph stroked the dog, stepping back into the doorway and allowing another man to come through. Abigail recognized him at once.

"Tom!" She screamed. "I didn't know you were coming over." She leapt up from the bed and wrapped her arms around him. He chuckled, his hands stroking her back, moving down to her hips. Steadily, one hand slipped down and gripped one side of her rear. She leaned back and looked up at him, furrowing her eyebrows. "What's going on?"

"This is how you can thank me," laughed Joseph. "I got you the puppy you've always wanted, and he's just plain adorable, but he's not you. Tom here, he's not into dogs. He's into you."

Abigail's heart pounded. Tom was into her? She glanced at the man's bulging biceps.

"Tom here has something he needs you to do," continued Joseph. "He's even offered to pay. Think about how easy it would be to pay for college if you do this kind of thing. Anyways, when the two of you are done, I'll give you the puppy back and the two of you can play to your heart's desire. Deal?"

Abigail's eyes widened. Police chief Tom Leonard wanted her? All she had to do for that dog was sleep with him? Every sixteen year old girl's dream was to be with a man that looked like this.

*Sixteen year old girl. Man like this.* Something should have set an alarm off, but it didn't. She was all about this man.

"Deal." She said sharply and with fierce eyes.

Joseph laughed. "I'll be downstairs, keeping your best friend busy. Have fun."

Joseph vanished into the hallway, shutting the door behind him. Abigail tried to move her arms to Tom's neck, but he pushed her to arm's length, waving his finger in a circle with a mischievous face.

"Turn around and put your hands behind your back," he growled. She giggled, and did what she was told. Cop foreplay. What a cliche. Oh well, it was every sixteen year old girl's dream, wasn't it?

*Sixteen year old girl.* How old was Tom Leonard? Those alarms remained silent. She just had to jump at the opportunity. Her friends at school weren't going to believe this.

Then, staring at the wall, she asked herself: *why is my stepfather pawning me off to a family friend, like some piece of meat. Wasn't he supposed to protect me from this kind of thing?*

Cold hard steel clamped her wrists like pincers, cutting into her flesh. She winced, and whined. "That hurts."

A palm touched her back, warm breath filling her ear. "You're under arrest. Don't resist."

*Why did Tom Leonard agree to have sex with a sixteen year old girl? Why was he paying for it?*

The hand shoved hard into her back, and she flopped face first onto the bed. This wasn't a sixteen year old's dream. What did she do wrong? Did Joseph set her up? Was she really under arrest?

Fingers dug into the waistband of the polyester running shorts she was wearing and pulled, ripping the fabric and tearing the shorts nearly in half. The same happened to her underwear, long fingernails digging into the flesh around her hips and thighs and cutting her legs on the way down. She squealed.

"Stop. What are you doing?"

"Don't resist." His voice shivered like… like he was… *Oh my God.*

She heard a belt buckle jingle. "Don't you dare resist, you bitch. I'll beat the shit out of you. No jury in the world will convict me because I'm Tom Leonard. You want this because I'm Tom Leonard."

Tom wouldn't speak to her like that. He was at the high school all the time, high fiving the girls and fist bumping the boys, and… staring. *Why did Tom Leonard want to have sex with me?*

*Because I'm a sixteen year old girl.*

Her breath caught as hands pushed her legs apart and hairy skin touched the inside of her thighs. She squirmed, and a palm smacked her in the face. She felt fingers in her hair, gripping tightly and pulling right at the roots. Searing pain shot through her scalp.

"Tom," she whimpered, "what are you doing?"

The hand at the back of her head pushed, smothering her face in sheets and blankets. She tried to inhale, desperately coughing through the fabric like a thick mask.

"Shut up," he growled again. "I'm doing what I want. I'm doing what I want because I'm Tom Leonard. You have the right to remain silent. Just lay there and take it like a good girl."

***

It was over, she knew that as she lay crumpled up in the corner and wrapped in nothing but a blanket. Her aching jaw and throbbing head hung low between scuffed up knees, and bruised arms held her legs close to her chest.

True to his word, the man calling himself her stepfather opened the bedroom door, and let the beautiful new puppy barrel into the chaotic bedroom, finding its target and freezing in place. Barely recognizing its beloved playmate, the puppy let out a pathetic whine. Almost as if it could sense her distress, the dog slowly crept over to Abigail. A wet nose pressed into her thigh; warm, moist breath coated her skin. Her eyes, surrounded by colorful patches of black, yellow, and purple, caught sight of the animal. The two of them stared hard at each other; the new pet sensed the distress, the worry, and the anxiety. The nose, along with a long head, slipped from the thigh to the crook of her hips.

Warmth. Love. Affection. The Puppy. Abigail's arms, aching with a deep soreness that she could feel in her bones, reached down and wrapped around the animal. A wagging tail and a lapping tongue went into full gear to try and make her feel better. A beautiful creature whose only purpose now was to lighten the life of its only friend, the little red dog licked Abigail's neck. She pushed the face away, pointing it over her shoulder and hugging the dog. The puppy whined, and Abigail sobbed.

Her neck was already wet, with saliva and other bodily fluids of the first man to deface her. In her bed, in her bedroom, in the safety of her own house. A man she trusted. A man she saw around other girls her age. A man in uniform. A man that was supposed to take care of her.

The puppy was no longer allowed to lick her. She couldn't stand to have another tongue touch her skin.

# <u>32</u>

*Claremore, Oklahoma - Present Day -*
*Friday - 7:00 PM*

A low noise echoed in the quiet kitchen, sounding like a cornered bobcat. The little girl at the head of the table wrapped her arms around her tummy, and scrunched up her face. The man to her right widened his eyes, exchanging a glance with the woman on the little girl's left. When he looked back down at the little girl, he seemed to display a sorrowful look, pitiful and sympathetic.

"Are you hungry?"

The little girl stared up at him with wide eyes and tightly closed lips. Why did he even ask? He had to know. Every night he shut and locked the door behind her, chaining her to that pack n play. Every night he threw her onto the floor and sealed her off from the freedom of… well, everything other than her bedroom. Every night he either gave her the bottle, or he didn't. A reward for working hard, or a punishment for being lazy. He knew.

She couldn't say anything out loud. Speaking out of turn never ended well for her.

The wife glared over at Olivia sternly. Olivia tried to avoid looking at the woman. She kept her eyes on the man speaking and tried her best to keep her head tilted forward submissively. Men liked submissive little girls. Carefully, barely breathing, she nodded in answer to the question. She said nothing and made no noise. Silence kept her safe.

He slid a paper wrapper with a Burger King cheeseburger in it over to her. Her eyes brightened, and her posture straightened. The bobcat in her stomach roared again. She reached out to grab it, but the man snatched it back quickly before she could get her fingers on it. Her expression changed again, her eyes raised up from the cheeseburger, and she furrowed her eyebrows.

"Hold on there just a second," he said, fondling the cheeseburger in his hands. "Not so fast. Before you can have this, you have to promise me something."

Olivia glanced back and forth between Joseph and the cheeseburger on the table eagerly. Silence kept her safe, so she nodded again without words or noise.

"You have to promise me that you'll do whatever I tell you from here on out," continued Joseph. "If you don't, you'll have to face the belt again. You won't get any more food, not even a bottle of milk. You might even have to go back to working in the yard. You don't want to do that, do you?"

The little girl shook her head with eyes so wide the lids barely held them in place.

Joseph smiled. "Good. Now say you promise to do exactly as you're told from this point on. Go ahead and say it out loud."

*Speak when spoken to.* "I promise."

"To?" Joseph slid the cheeseburger closer with a sly smile.

She leaned forward towards the food, mirroring the incoming feast and feeling her dry mouth begin to moisten. "To do as I'm told from here on out."

He pulled the food back away from her, his eyelids narrowing. "Now say it all together."

The little girl sighed, and leaned forward more, following the retreating food with pained desperation. Her eyes remained focused on the logo plastered onto the wrapper. *Burger King. Have it your way. Have it your way, Joseph.* "I promise to do what I'm told all the time."

"Thank you, Olivia." He slid the cheeseburger over to her, and she devoured it quickly. Delicious didn't do the taste justice. Nothing did. The taste made her brain misfire and her body shiver. Her tongue tingled just at the touch of the meat. That dry mouth became an oasis of sticky saliva, fast food grease, and slimy melted cheese.

The wife did not break her glare the whole time. Olivia didn't care. Those slitted eyes, so dark they didn't even look green, pierced Olivia like daggers. Olivia accepted the glare with as much bravery as she could. At least she wasn't alone in her room. There were people around her, and that was all that mattered.

Joseph smiled down at Olivia as she ate, making sure the little girl was making eye contact with him before speaking. "You can be a good girl."

Olivia smiled. She couldn't help it. She was a good girl. She wanted nothing more than to be a good girl. She tried not to giggle despiste herself, knowing what consequences that would bring. No matter how emotional she was, she knew one thing: She did not want the belt, and she did not want to go back to the yard. She never acted out of turn while Joseph was watching.

Three taps echoed from the front door in the other room, and Joseph stood up to answer it without hesitation. Olivia focused on her food, trying not to shake and dance with joy. Wonderful. Life changing. The taste; nothing compared to it. She glanced up at the wife, still watching in Joseph's place, ready to rat Olivia out if need be, ready to... Those eyes. They had changed. The wife's eyes looked softer now. Different; something other than that hatred. Something Olivia recognized from earlier days, from the other girl. Sissy. The look that came from big green eyes that looked like the brighter version of the wife's eyes. Shining; like a puppy. The emotion behind those eyes; Pity? Sadness?

Olivia could hear Joseph in the front room speaking to whoever was visiting. The conversation involved laughter, and some rustling of paper. Everything in the other room sounded fun. After a few moments, Joseph came back into the room with another man. One look, and Olivia made up her mind about him. The new man peered hungrily into her with dull black eyes that traced the edges of her body with every movement she made. His greasy hair sagged down the sides of his head, but his forehead had little hair at all. His pale skin made him look like a ghost, and his crooked nose reminded her of an evil witch. His smiling, open eyed, furrowed brow expression; the look of a predator. She leaned back in her chair and pushed away the remnants of the food as the two men came into the room. In a fit of emotion she let out a fearful squeal, shrinking back away from them.

"You have a friend here to see you," said Joseph.

*A friend?* Friends were for work. This was home, and she never worked at home. She used to dig in the yard before actually going somewhere else to work, but she didn't have to do that anymore. Work happened at the workplaces, not here. She shook her head, her skin crawling at the thought of being alone with the man in her own bedroom. Joseph clicked his tongue, his face softening.

"I thought you were a good girl," he sighed, his eyes moistening, his head shaking, and his mouth hanging open. His voice cracked and sounded low and distressed. "Besides, you promised. You wouldn't break a promise, would you, Olivia? Especially not to your daddy."

The little girl's eyes widened. She didn't care much for her father, but she still wanted to be a good kid. Working, seeing her friends, did not feel good, but a good kid would not break a promise, and Olivia had made a promise. She needed to be a good kid. It was all she had left. Plus, she had done good for him so far, and he was starting to use her name. He was starting to take care of her. He protected her from the police, even when Sissy tried to turn her in.

Maybe she could do a little extra here at home for him.

Slowly and hesitantly, Olivia climbed out of her chair and approached the new man. The new man smiled down at her with a nearly toothless smile that made her want to throw up. He was not a friend. She willed her skin to crawl off and make her ugly, but it refused and stayed attached. She looked back over her shoulder at Joseph, who was already sitting at the table and setting paper money into stacks. One directly in front of him, and the other in front of the wife.

As Olivia's gaze rose to the face of the wife, the wife's eyes locked with Olivia's in a stealthy side glance, where Olivia saw it again. Pity. It had to be the look of pity. If no amount of hate could justify this to the wife, then why could Joseph do it? Did that mean she wasn't good? *You made a promise.* She needed to keep that promise. She had to be a good kid.

The new man held out his hand, and Olivia reached out and felt the rough, scratchy flesh. He squeezed her hand, the rough surface of his palm stabbing her. The wife returned her stare to the money in front of her now. No help; no hope. It disgusted her to think about this man and what he wanted, but Olivia had promised to do as she was told. Good kids kept their promises.

*Olivia. You are Olivia. Even Joseph calls you that now.*

# <u>*33*</u>

*Tulsa, Oklahoma - Friday - 6:00 PM*
He was lost. Over and over again; just when he thought he was found, he was lost again. There was no getting out anymore. He was stuck. Even Abigail had turned on him. Stuck at home; alone. Stuck at work; alone. Back to square one. At least his father would be there to support him again.

*If he makes it through surgery. Might be back to square zero.*

Always lost. Never found. A father having open heart surgery, a lover that betrayed him, and a career path gone forever. No belonging anywhere. No being a part of something more than just himself. Just a dead end job fixing broken or malfunctioning machinery in a factory.

Charles Langley stared at the bottle of whiskey sitting on the railing of his balcony with a tumbler full of ice sitting next to it. He'd never taken a drink of alcohol in his life. It had ruined his father's life, and, in a way, his own. Everything had gone to shit the moment he'd gone to live with his mother. Again, and again, Charles came back to that one moment, that one image. His father, unconscious on the lawn.

Nothing good ever came from getting drunk, but it seemed like the only answer to his problem right now. The only way out; the only solution at the end of a stressful week.

*An escape.*

Those websites, those videos, were itching at him. He wanted to avoid those. Those young girls online reminded him too much of the girl in the restaurant. *Fourteen years old.* So young, and he had wanted her. *He had wanted her.*

A weekend wouldn't normally be so bad if he had work to look forward to on Monday, but he'd requested all his PTO anticipating landing at the Red Sea Initiative. He could have gone in anyways, maybe canceled his PTO, but his mind kept telling him to sit and sulk. The weekend wouldn't be so bad if he could have laid his stresses on his father, who was currently going into open heart surgery. It might have been easier if a romantic partner was there to listen, and give support. Abigail was not there, and she wouldn't be coming back any time soon. He couldn't stand to have her around. He wasn't even sure if he could be nice if she was.

No. Sunday was ending badly, like the rest of the week had, and Charles Langley was ending the day staring at the bottle of whiskey. He thought about his father in the hospital; he thought about the DNA the two of them shared. He thought about the girls on the websites; he thought about the girl at the restaurant.

*From the MILF category, to fourteen years old. Younger and younger I go. Joseph, here I come.*

*With enough time, I'll be on your client list. Maybe then I could at least have the chance to get her out of that hell.*

Knocking at the door, his apartment door, so loud, yet barely audible over the sounds of the Midwestern evening. Insects and frogs buzzed their mating calls, all trying their hardest to do the one thing Charles was certain he could never allow himself to do again.

Or was it even his choice anymore?

The knock came again, louder this time. Someone trying to get his attention at the door. *Abigail.* It had to be Abigail. His phone had been off for the majority of the day, with only a few hours being on this evening to speak to his father about surgery. Abigail would have been trying to get ahold of him, wondering if he was safe. There's no telling what Joseph would have told her when he got home.

It didn't matter. The result would be the same. *Send her away.*

Charles stood from the chair and approached the door. He reached for the door knob, interrupted by four of the most furious knocks on his door he'd ever heard in his life. He hesitated for a moment. That did not sound womanly. *Joseph?* Abigail could have told Joseph where Charles lived. Joseph could be here to get revenge for the beating he'd received earlier.

Charles turned the door handle, half expecting it to burst open in an ambush. The door didn't budge. No force from the outside sent it towards him, with a hunking giant plowing through to kill him. He pulled it open an inch; the door still didn't burst open. He opened it enough to see through the crack to the other side. A woman flung her hands out in frustration.

"Did you forget to charge your phone?" cried Alison Rotskoya. "I've been calling for an hour."

"I turned it off," muttered Charles, opening the door all the way. "I didn't want to hear from anyone. I was going to turn it back on in a little bit to wait for my father's call."

"Turn it back on now," growled Alison. "You're going to need it."

"Why?"

"Because you and I are going to see this through," Alison commanded. There was no mistake; it was not a request. "We're going to your girlfriend's house and we're going to finish this job."

Charles shook his head. "What do you mean?"

"Walter's a mess right now," Alison continued. "Katie's injured, and Jimmy's got a broken arm. Rebecca can handle the conference and the team, but this isn't over. There's still a little girl out there being raped and abused, and we still have to rescue her."

Charles shrugged. "I believe I've been fired."

"Walter can't fire you; you were never hired."

"Thanks for the vote of confidence."

"I'm hiring you right now," said Alison. "Behind his back. Behind everyone's back. He'll be pissed, but he can deal with it. Right now, you're my only way into this, and whether I can either trust you to help me, or I can leverage your spot with the police to force your hand."

"You don't trust me either?" chuckled Charles, making his way back out to the balcony and picking up the bottle of whisky. *Time to hit it hard.*

"I'm not one hundred percent," replied Alison, following him out. "I don't think you've been in on his scheme the whole time. That doesn't make any sense. You couldn't have known Walter and Jimmy would be at the hospital, even if your stepfather in law told you that's where they were headed. I do believe you and Walter running into each other was a hell of a coincidence, but the evidence points in that direction. I don't know where you're at now, although I firmly believe you want to be a part of the team."

Her eyes watched as he filled the whiskey tumbler and set the bottle back down. "I thought you didn't drink."

He shrugged. "I figured it was a good weekend to start."

"Have you started?"

He lifted the tumbler as if to toast. "First one in my life."

An impact to his hand sent the glass flying and deep brown liquor splashing everywhere. The glass tumbler crashed into his sliding door, thunking loudly like a glass bird smacking a window and shattering on the ground. A palm landed square in the center of his chest, thrusting him backwards against the outside wall. Alison's fingers dug into his chest and shirt, squeezing a handful of fabric and paralyzing the young man with fear.

"That's bullshit!" she yelled in his face, bringing herself within inches of him. "Listen to me: That's the same excuse your father told himself all those years ago. Do you know why? He gave up. He gave up on all the hard stuff that he had to do. He gave up on you. You're not giving up. You're not giving up on that little girl. You're going to fight this."

"Walter doesn't want me in this anymore."

"Walter doesn't want anything but his daughter right now," said Alison. "Can you blame him? He hasn't been at the conference all day. He's been sitting at the hospital making sure Katie's okay. Kitsen never leaves his side. Again, can you blame him? She almost got taken. Now he's frazzled, and that is exactly what this trafficker wants. He wants a divided and distracted force. We can't let that happen, and you and I are the only ones left to get the job done. I've got Paul Edwards going with us to Claremore. He has connections with the police and the judges out there. Rebecca will stay here with Jimmy to help him handle the conference well. Walter will come to his senses soon enough, especially if we catch this guy. Got it?"

Charles didn't move. "You… you want me back in?"

"I'm putting you back in," said Alison. "You're our only way in on this investigation, so I'm giving you the option to prove yourself to me. From there, we'll get Walter to follow through."

*A chance.* He didn't smile. He wouldn't dare. *A second chance.*

*An escape.*

"What's the plan?" he asked.

Alison released him and stepped back, grabbing the bottle of whiskey from the railing and taking it inside. "The plan is to go to Claremore and take care of this."

Charles followed her in, all the way to the sink where he watched her pour thirty dollars down the sink drain. *Don't waste your money, and it won't go to waste.* "Do you have anything more specific?"

"You tell me," said Alison, tossing the empty bottle into his trash can and resting her palms on the counter. "You know the family. What's next?"

Charles shook his head, taking a moment. What was next? What would he do if he was the trafficker?

*No.* He was not a trafficker. What would Joseph do?

"Joseph is going to clean the house," said Charles. "He probably already has. He'll empty the place and make it look like the little girl was never there."

Alison was nodding her head, squinting her eyes at him.

"He'll hide the girl for a few days or so," he continued. "Take the loss on the business side of things in order to protect the long term money making aspect of things."

"So what are we looking for?" asked Alison. "A long time, loyal customer that can be trusted?"

"Someone he not only trusts to keep the secret," continued Charles, "but to take care of the girl. He'll get a free pass for the week, whatever he wants as long as there's no damage to the product, right?"

Alison was nodding. "Incentive to keep her, within bounds, and in one piece."

"As the heat dies down," said Charles. "He'll pull her back into the house and continue the business."

"So what do we do, Charles?" asked Alison. "We can't pick this back up in a week when things settle. We need results. We need this little girl out of danger."

Charles glanced up at Alison. "We do the only thing we have left to do," he said. "We flip his closest allies. That'll give us locations and customer names to start with, and give us a solid conviction down the road."

Alison smiled at him. "Who do we start with?"

# <u>*34*</u>

*Claremore, Oklahoma - 7:00 PM*
The one and only Abigail Smith. The girl in the center of the room surrounded by the people she trusted the least. She didn't hate her mother, or Olivia, but she couldn't trust either one. Tell either of them anything, and they would be forced to squeal to Joseph out of fear. Tell her mother, and her mother might even go to Joseph out of greed. She really liked the money. As a consequence, Abigail had no one.

*I have Charles.* She had the love of her life. She had him, and she had to see him tonight. No word from him since he'd left from lunch this morning, but so much had happened since then. Almost twelve hours, and it felt like a lifetime had passed. It was terrifying. She needed to get out of here. Her things were packed. Her car was loaded. All that was left was to escape.

But she just couldn't get away.

"Charles Langley," sighed Joseph, his spare belt twirling through the air like a baton. "How come I've never heard of him before last week?"

Abigail looked over at her mother. Mindy looked away and let her daughter handle her own conflict. *Fear and greed. Great motivators.* Abigail took in a deep breath, and stood her ground.

"He's been gone a long time," she started confidently. "I grew up with his sister, Emily, but I always had a crush on him. He went to jail for a long time, and he's just been living around here since then."

"And we just so happen to end up in the same area as him for you two to be together?" asked Joseph, not looking at Abigail. He seemed lost in thought.

"Yes," she sighed. "Six months ago I found out he was in Tulsa, and jumped on the opportunity to reconnect."

"Six months?" cried Joseph. "You've been seeing him for six months, and I just heard about it last week?"

"I hid him until I was sure he was right for this family," said Abigail. "That's where I've been. I quit my job and lived off of my National Guard income so I could go see him."

"You did all that, knowing what it would cost you if I found out?"

"I love him."

"You love him?" groaned Joseph, rolling his eyes. "I caught him with another woman, and you still love him?"

*It wasn't true,* thought Abigail. *Nothing he says is ever true. I just have to get to Charles. We'll sort this out. I just have to get away.*

"I do," said Abigail. "I'll make it work."

Olivia flinched with every swing of the belt, cowering in a rocking chair. The belt rocked back and forth like a pendulum.

Joseph sighed. "Tell me about him."

"He's a year younger than I am." Abigail's voice trembled. Her confidence shook. "Born and raised in Kansas City with his mother. His dad was a drunk. He was a martial artist and a wrestler in school. Never played any sports other than that. Went to church on Sundays."

The belt snapped, landing in Joseph's other hand and stretching out like a snake. It stopped Abigail dead in her tracks. Her eyes widened. Her fingers shook. *Level one combatives, don't fail me now.*

"Love is a good thing," Joseph muttered quietly. "You're outgrowing this house anyways. I knew it would happen eventually. Actually, you should be starting a family soon enough, right? You're already moving in. Soon enough you'll be married and carrying babies."

He glanced over at Abigail, and held out the belt to her. "I'm willing to let the secrets go, if you can show me you can discipline your children."

Abigail's eyes flickered to the belt, then to Joseph's face. "What do you mean?"

"You want to see Charles?" asked Joseph. "You want to leave the nest and begin your own family? You have to show me you're capable of taking care of what needs to be taken care of." He stepped forward, forcing the belt into Abigail's hands.

She took it, her whole hands trembling now.

Joseph smiled. "Would you like to know the situation?"

Abigail swallowed hard, holding back tears and trying not to close her eyes. "What situation?"

"Olivia, here," Joseph yelled loudly, turning and waving his hands towards the little girl. "She bit her friend tonight. He was treating her as nice as he could, and paying her a wonderful sum of money, and she bit him for it. Is that what we do to friends?"

The realization hit Abigail like a truck. She blinked tears away, a lump forming in her throat the size of a bowling ball. She swallowed, remembering the lesson she'd been taught many years ago. A lesson taught with the same belt that she now held in her hands.

"No, that's not how we treat our friends." It was choked, and strained, but she got the words out.

"So how should we handle that?" asked Joseph, his voice booming through the room. "Olivia doesn't want to go back to picking up rocks in the yard, so we have one option left. We have to make sure she doesn't bite another friend."

"I'm sorry." Olivia's voice cracked and squeaked with fear as she cowered deeper into the rocking chair. Abigail stepped forward. Olivia would be safe if she could just get to Charles. She could tell him everything and he could help get them all free. She had to be able to see Charles. Olivia's eyes flooded, the little girl quivering. "Abby, no."

"Make sure she learns her lesson," said Joseph, stepping behind Abigail. "Show me you have what it takes to raise your own children correctly, and you and Charles can live happily ever after."

*It's not true. He's lying. You'll never be free. You have to escape!*

The belt felt wet in her hands. She gripped it tightly, unsure if it would stay. She shook violently. A tear fell from one of her eyes as she took another step towards Olivia. She had to see Charles tonight, she just had to. He would make things better.

"You don't treat friends like that," whispered Abigail shakily. *One more time. Then I can save you.* Silent words fell on deaf ears.

The little girl squirmed to get away. Abigail could almost feel Joseph's breath on the back of her neck as she leaned forward and grabbed Olivia by one of her arms to keep the little girl from getting away. *One more time. We'll escape, I swear.* Convey it with her eyes, that's all she could do.

"Sissy," Olivia cried out, pulling at her arm to get away. "Please, don't." The little girl was in tears, her whole body squirming to get away from Abigail. Abigail raised the belt over her shoulder. "Sissy, please, not you, too."

"Show me you have what it takes." Joseph was right in her ear, whispering and breathing down her neck. "We don't treat friends like that, do we?"

Abigail choked back a sob and held her breath. She knew the rules. It was Olivia, or Abigail, and Abigail had to get out. She could come back with help. She knew it. It was the only way. *One more time.*

"No we don't."

*Level one combatives don't fail me now.*

She reached back with the belt, and used the force of her swing to spin around and slap Joseph in the face with the long, leather strap. The big man recoiled, throwing up his hands as Abigail came around for a second strike. Both Mindy and Olivia screamed, and Joseph let out a primal roar. He shoved himself forward, tumbling into Abigail with the force of a freight train and bringing her to the ground.

With Joseph's weight now crushing her, Abigail curled herself up into a ball, spread her legs, and attempted to wrap them around Joseph's neck. He reached up to grab her, and she wrapped an arm around his wrist and immobilized him. Pulling tight, she launched both legs above his shoulders, and slipped them around his head. His face dipped down into her crotch as she squeezed, putting him right where he'd loved to be so many years ago. Too bad she didn't know how to perform a triangle choke before.

Joseph's body curled up on the floor. His knees pushed him upwards, and he used his spare arm to support himself as he rose to his feet. He was losing consciousness quickly, but Abigail felt her body come off of the ground. She was up in the air before she knew it, and just when Joseph's face turned purple, he dropped her back on the ground.

The impact knocked the wind out of her, and she sprawled out, releasing him back onto the floor and giving him distance and time to recover. She scrambled off to the side, trying to escape, but his hand gripped her ankle and held her back. She leaned back, reared up her free leg like a horse, and kicked him in the face as hard as she could. She felt something squishy underneath the sole of her boot, like the pop of a giant bug, and stared down at the obliterated nose that had once been on the front of Joseph's face.

The hand released her ankle, and she climbed to her feet and dashed for the door. *Olivia! Can't leave without Olivia!*

Abigail turned back to the others, but Mindy already had her arms around Olivia, lifting her from the ground and moving towards the door. Olivia had her eyes squeezed shut, a desperate cry escaping her throat.

Then Mindy collapsed, dropping herself and everything else onto the ground. Joseph climbed on top of her, his mangled face twisted in a rage so absolute, that Abigail lost all concern for everything other than herself.

*Escape!*

Without a moment of hesitation, she turned to the front door, and dashed into the front yard. The darkness surrounding her turned her brain into survival mode. *Must have light. Must have a car. Must get away.*

She turned back to her car and got in the driver's seat before anyone could follow her out of the house. She reached in her pocket for her keys, fumbling with everything inside with sweaty and trembling fingers that slipped on everything. Her keys and her phone went tumbling into the cupholder next to her. Abigail shook violently as she gripped the steering wheel and started the car with keys that jingled in her spasmodic hands. She had to see Charles. She had to see him now. There was no time to waste.

The car screeched out of the driveway, and Abigail let out a deep scream. Everyone in that house would be dead. Everyone except the man that would be coming to kill her.

Charles would protect her.

Miles away, coming to a stop at a stoplight, Abigail looked down at her phone in the cup holder, where it had fallen with her keys, and saw a text from the most recent phone number she had saved in her phone. She choked out a sob as she looked at the name, and read the message.

**Come home. I need you here.**

She almost smiled. He needed her. He wanted her. He still loved her.

Everything was going to be okay, at least for Abigail.

# <u>35</u>

*Tulsa, Oklahoma - Friday - 10:00 PM*
The door opened. Abigail simply turned the handle and opened it. *Unlocked.* That word echoed in her head like a skipping CD track. Charles left the door unlocked for her. He never left the door unlocked for any reason whatsoever. There was too much risk involved. *He was expecting me, wasn't he?*

But she hadn't texted him back. He had no confirmation that she was coming. *Then why is his door unlocked?*

The darkness in his apartment overtook her like a blanket over her head. The silence stopped her like a brick wall. Nothing. Absolutely nothing. The sounds of the insects and animals outside just cut off like she'd hit the power button. Moonlight crept through the glass balcony door, a sliver in the curtains open just large enough for the man standing in between them to be silhouetted in the glow. He stared out the glass, motionless and quiet.

"Charles?" Abigail stepped into the room. *What in the hell is going on? This is not like him.*

"I turned my phone back on." A mumble, slow and very articulate. "My father was supposed to be coming out of surgery, so I turned it back on to get the call."

Abigail closed the door behind her and stepped into the black void of the living room. "Did they call?"

She saw his head nod, a faint motion that barely caught her eye. "They did. That's why I texted you."

*What is this? Why is he being so strange?* Abigail stopped in the middle of the room, worried something was wrong. "Charles?"

The man was silent. Several seconds passed by with no response. She was almost starting to wonder if he had heard her. *This is so unlike him. Door unlocked, back to the door, staring off into the distance, speaking low and articulate. What is this?*

"He's dead."

"What?" Abigail felt a chill run over her body, numbing her fingertips. A burning sensation filled her chest like her lungs were full of glass shards.

"He went into surgery, and died on the table." Charles's voice was nearly inaudible. "They tried three times to bring him back." His head turned in her direction just the slightest bit. "I got the call ten minutes ago."

"You should have texted me about that," she whispered. "I would have driven faster. I would do anything if you needed me to."

He was silent again, for so long she started to worry.

*He just said he got the call ten minutes ago. He texted me almost a half an hour ago. He said that was why he texted me. Is he lying to me?*

"Would you tell me the truth?"

Abigail swallowed hard. *He doesn't know the truth. He just knows there's something you're not telling him.*

"Of course." Her voice was shaky and weak. She sounded hysterical. "The truth about what?"

Charles shook his head. "Don't do this. Don't play that game with me. Just tell me."

"I do," she replied. "I do trust you. It's just…" *You can't trust me.* She couldn't bring herself to say it. "Charles, the other morning I asked you about Emily, and… that day. You never told me. It's like we don't trust each other, but that changes now. We're going to agree to tell the truth from here on out."

"I agree," mumbled Charles. "You start first. Was I crazy at dinner for hearing a cough in the back of your house?"

*He doesn't know the truth. Keep him distracted.*

But he did know. He had to know. That's why he attacked her so strongly as his opening question. He didn't, couldn't, know about Olivia, but he knew the noise was a cough. He knew someone was in the house, and he was looking for a trafficker.

If he didn't know, he had to be suspicious.

*I promised to be honest.*

"I didn't hear a cough," she immediately broke her promise. "It's an old house, though, it makes a lot of noise. I'm probably just used to the noises and didn't notice."

Charles was still silent. She could almost hear the gears in his head running. He was trying to put the puzzle together. *Keep him distracted.*

"Charles, please, I don't want to see you hurting like this. You just lost your dad. Let me at least hold you and just be here to comfort you. That's all I want to do right now. Just let me be here for you."

"Tell me about Joseph."

She gulped again, hoping he didn't hear her in the silence. *He can't possibly know, but he does. Somehow he does. What happened?*

"What about him? He's my stepdad."

"Did he ever do anything to hurt you?"

"Hurt me?" *How would he know?* "What do you mean hurt me?" The words blurted out in an insane mixture of laughter and crying all at once. "Charles, your father is dead. Let's just be together and grieve. Please. You need to grieve."

"Answer the question." His voice was a growl. "Don't dance around it like we're kids. Did he ever hurt you?"

*He won't love me anymore if I tell him the truth.* If Charles knew, she would be nothing but tainted meat to him. She couldn't tell him. "Charlie."

"Do not call me that." He sounded angry. He sounded like Joseph.

"No. He doesn't hurt me." *Liar!* Was that Joseph's voice in her head, or her own? *You lying bitch! I thought you loved him!*

"So he's just hurting other girls?"

*Does he know?* He couldn't know. She hadn't told him. He hadn't come close to catching Joseph.

*Or had he?*

"Other girls? What are you talking about?" She sounded desperate. She sounded insane.

"Walter's little girl," said Charles, "and the little girl he's trafficking around here. Joseph is the trafficker we're after."

*He knows. How?*

"What are you talking about? What little girl?" What had Joseph gotten himself into?"

"I probably wouldn't even be asking," Charles started, "if I hadn't stopped your step dad from kidnapping Walter's daughter today. Ran him down in the parking lot, and barely got Kitsen out of the truck before he took off. I probably wouldn't be sure, but I saw his face."

*He knows. He doesn't love you anymore. Game over.*

"I wouldn't even have you here," Charles continued without waiting for a response, "except I've realized something."

"What?" Abigail whispered shakily. Her hands began to tremble, and she wrung them to calm herself.

"The only way Joseph could have known where the little girl was." Charles turned around and faced her, eyebrows slanted inwards and his eyelids slitted on his dimly lit face. His lips were pursed and his nose scrunched up. "I told you where she was."

Abigail shook her head. "Charles, listen to me."

"Why?" asked Charles before she could continue. "Why would I listen if all you're going to do is lie."

"I'm scared," she whimpered, her fear taking over her whole body. *He doesn't love you anymore. Make him love you again. Tell him the truth. You have no other option.*

"I don't want to lose you." She stepped forward. "I don't want you to think horribly of me because of all of this. You don't understand what he's like. You don't know him."

"I will if you tell me about him."

"Then please listen to me."

"We will." Abigail's heart stopped, hearing the woman's voice come from behind her. She turned, seeing a shadowy figure come around the corner of the hallway. A massive silhouette, taller than Abigail and wider in stature. Broad shoulders and wide hips came into view, and a thick, muscular arm reached out to the light switch.

The overhead light brightened the room, momentarily blinding Abigail. The flash dimmed, her vision returned, and she saw the woman standing at the edge of the living room. The woman Charles was training with, and the one Joseph had warned her about.

The woman that had been alone with Charles before Abigail had arrived. *Alone together.*

Alison Rotskoya stood ten feet away, staring hard at Abigail. Her broad shoulders reached out to the side. Her thin waist curved inward before stretching out over wide hips and bulging, muscular thighs. Alison Rotskoya brought three words to the forefront of Abigail's thoughts. *Magnificent. Beautiful. Terrifying.*

Then another word. *Competition.*

*They were alone together.*

"No more lies, Abigail," said Charles. *Abigail.* He didn't call her that. She was Abby to him. That horrible nickname never felt so right, all of a sudden. Her real name, coming from the man she loved, was so much worse.

"We're listening."

Her vision blurred as her eyes filled with tears. A massive lump crawled into her throat. *He knows, and he doesn't love you anymore. You're a monster, and you're getting what you deserve.*

*You should have just stayed home and beat your little sister.*

"He gave me the puppy I always wanted," she let out a disgusting sob. "In return, I had to sleep with one of his friends, who beat me and raped me."

She tried to remain standing, but her legs refused to hold her weight. She stumbled and collapsed onto the couch.

"I went through that for years, even after I joined the Guard. The guys on base did it to me, too." She sniffed and shrugged. "At least on base I could keep some of the money."

She looked up at Charles who stared intently down at her. No sympathy, and no pity. It was Joseph's voice in her head, now. *He doesn't love you anymore, you little traitor. You just can't help but betray him and me. Time for your punishment.*

"Olivia was born a year after this all started," she continued slowly, trying to keep her brain and mouth in sync. She sniffed again and squinted her eyes shut. *I can't look at him. I can't look at anyone. It hurts too much.*

"She didn't start seeing friends until she was six. Joseph groomed her early, though. Basically from the day she was born he kept telling her things. She wasn't human. She was an object for pleasure and money, just like her older sister."

She leaned back into the couch and pulled her legs up to her chest. "It's been all her for three years now. I've been given a break from work, but I'm not free." She looked up at Charles. "He wasn't going to let me come here. He was going to make me beat her with a belt in order to see you again, but I knew it was a lie. He was never going to let me out of there. He got into my head earlier tonight so I wouldn't move out. He's threatened me if I don't help him. He's hurt me before."

She took a deep breath. "So I used that belt on him tonight. I kicked him in the face, and got out. My mom tried to get Olivia out, too, but they got held up. I just ran."

She glanced up at Charles, thinking about him telling her Joseph fought him in the parking lot. "Didn't you think he was going to hurt you?"

Charles didn't move. *He's an experienced martial artist. He probably wasn't scared at all. It must be so easy being a man.*

Abigail shut her eyes again. "Okay. She's in the spare bedroom upstairs at the house. Joseph keeps her handcuffed to a little pack n play. Up the stairs, to the left, first door on the right. To the right of the staircase are my bedroom and theirs. Mine is the first one. Theirs is at the end of the hall."

"And what are we supposed to do with that information?" asked Alison.

Abigail squinted the tears back again. "I don't know. I don't know anything anymore." She looked up at Charles. "I'm just telling you everything I know. However it helps get this whole thing over with, I don't know, but I promised the truth. You believe me, right?"

By the look on his face, Charles didn't believe a word she was saying.

***

He did believe her. Every word, even if it wasn't true. His only thought at the moment was to put his arms around her and hold her; to console her with sweet nothings whispered in her ear; to love her. He was glad she had shut her eyes, otherwise, he might not have been able to maintain his composure.

*Hard ball. We have to play hard ball. Do not let your emotions get in the way.*

"Does he have a set schedule of what hotels he uses?" He asked Abigail. *Abby.* He wanted to call her the sweet name; he wanted to touch her and comfort her, but he had to play hard ball. Names meant something to people. Alison had told him that. To use her full name after all the months of calling her Abby was the most devastating part of it all.

Abigail's face scrunched, her eyebrows furrowing. "I don't think so. Nicer hotels on the weekend for the classy friends that have more to spend and work during the week. Cheaper hotels during the week to cut costs. I know that."

"Do you have any names?" asked Charles.

Abigail shook her head.

"Miss Smith," Alison chimed in. "I'm afraid I have to tell you that there are consequences to your actions over the last week, months, and years. Do you understand the scope of that?"

Abigail nodded, her face cringing and her eyes draining of all fluids.

"You do have options, however," continued Alison. "Options that we are willing to consider. I came from a background not so different from yours. I was abandoned and sold into trafficking until the guys at The Initiative rescued me. There is a way out for you, too. We can provide that way out if you want it. Do you want to hear my offer?"

Abigail shook her head. "I deserve this."

Charles glanced up at Alison, who nodded at him. He let out a sigh, relief causing his chest and shoulders to sink several inches. Alison had given her good cop portion, it was time for Charles to finish it off.

Flies with honey.

"Abby," he finally said, "it's really hard to have you living here if you're in jail."

Abigail looked up at Charles with wide eyes. The tears subsided, and she straightened out. "What?"

"I can't have you here with me if you're not here with me."

Abigail looked over at Alison, who didn't budge. Alison had become the statue in place of Charles. Abigail turned back to Charles. "You still want me here?"

"If you can prove to me that you can move past this," he said. "If you can show me you want to live here away from the life you've been forced to live so far, I will get you out."

Abigail leapt to her feet, only to be stopped by a hand coming up into the air. Charles stuck out his palm to her.

"Listen to me," he said. "This is not going to be easy, and you're going to have to be in danger, but we can do this together."

Abigail sat back on the couch, staring into the wall. She seemed to consider his words, and nodded her head.

"I told you everything," she said softly. "Now it's your turn. Tell me the truth."

Charles winced at the words. His face wouldn't let him resist. She caught him off guard. "What do you mean by that?"

Abigail looked back up at him, a determined look on her face. "I told you about my past, everything you wanted to know. Now you tell me yours. You never told me what really happened to Emily. You just said you would. Do you trust me enough to tell me that?"

He shouldn't have, but he did. Charles looked up at Alison, who cocked an eyebrow. He remembered their own conversation about becoming a team. *Trust.* Alison wanted to hear it just as much as Abigail did, and for the same reason. Trust. If he could trust them with his story, they could work as a team and finish this. That would be the only way, and he was the only one that hadn't shared. Alison had told him, and Abigail had told them both.

The story of the night that changed his life.

Charles let out another deep sigh, shaking his head, and switching his glances between the only two women in his life. He pursed his lips tightly. "Well, I guess I have to live up to my word."

Alison smiled, and Abigail turned to face him. "Trust me, please. I know you trust her."

"He hasn't told me, either," said Alison, holding eye contact with Charles.

Abigail turned to face Alison, nodded, and turned back to Charles with the most resolute face he'd ever seen. "Then trust us."

*I'm not getting out of this one.* Charles focused on Alison, the more trustworthy of the two, and decided it would be easier to just get it over with. He stared into her glowing hazel eyes. "You already know that I had a sister named Emily?"

Alison tilted her head like a dog. "Had?"

Charles nodded, watching Abigail mimic his movements in agreement. "Yeah. Had."

# <u>36</u>

*Kansas City, Missouri - Ten Years Ago*
All four tires below him wailed in pain at the stress they were under. His body crashed into the window on his left, the force of his mother's sliding Chevrolet Equinox flinging him into the driver's side door.

*You should have put on your seatbelt.* His mother's voice in his head screamed at him. *What is wrong with you?*

*My sister is in trouble.* His own internal voice responded. *I promised to always protect her, and I will.*

A phone call to the police wouldn't do anything to help. The police never responded on time. How long had he sat in his father's front yard waiting for them to come, wondering if his father was even still alive? Police weren't exactly worthless, but they certainly weren't the best option.

That's why he was here, and his parents were at home. So distracted with their own perfect solution that they had never seen him take the keys, much less heard him roar off in their car. They relied on the police to solve their problems, but

Emily was relying on her little brother, Charles Langley.

He was her only hope.

The Equinox, moving forward much faster than he really wanted it to, pulled into the thin alley, where Charles Langley spotted his target. The small blue pickup truck with only two passengers. A man in his mid thirties, and a fifteen year old girl named Emily.

*I will protect her.*

The truck moved slowly, brake lights illuminating the alley around him in the darkness. His own headlights flashed the surrounding walls. Charles stomped his foot onto the gas pedal as hard as he could, feeling the pedal dig itself into the carpeted flooring. With less than a foot of clearance on each side of the vehicle, Charles's Equinox sped down the alleyway. The lights on the back of the blue truck became brighter, and the tailgate grew bigger. Closer. *Closer.*

Brake lights flashed again in front of him, and changed angles. The truck swerved out of the way, and an open street came into Charles's view. Cross traffic filled his windshield, and he wrenched the steering wheel to his right again to follow the truck. The car skidded again, swinging the tail end of the vehicle out into the other lane. A huge Ram pickup clipped the tail end of his Equinox as it entered opposite traffic, fortunately sending him sliding back into his own lane. He spotted the blue truck ahead again, and gave it everything. Honking horns came from all directions as he sped through traffic, and an enraged truck driver leapt from the

Ram to scream at the insane driver of the runaway Chevy.

Out in the open street, Charles used the light of traffic and street lights to keep his target close. He swerved in between cars passing all obstacles in between himself and the truck. His headlights shined, and he watched shadows of two figures in the cab struggling physically with each other. Emily fought her kidnapper with a violent effort, trying to escape. The blue truck came closer, the driver distracted by his uncooperative victim.

*Crunch.* Plastic on plastic. The front end of Charles's Chevy pressed into the tail end of the truck. Charles was launched into the steering wheel, plopping back into his seat when his foot came off of the gas pedal. He turned the wheel left, swerving around the back of the truck to hit it, spin it out, and bring it to a stop, only to overcorrect and go flying into oncoming traffic.

*Small adjustments,* he kept telling himself as cars sped towards him. *That's all it takes to move a little. Breathe, and stay calm. Freak out, and you die. You're no good to Emily if you die. Stay cool; stay methodical. A level head is the greatest weapon we can have.*

Easier said than done.

No matter which direction he turned the wheels, the oncoming car seemed to go in the same direction. It was a game of wills on this side of the road, seeing who did and didn't trust their insurance coverage. He spotted enough space to hop into the correct lane again, but a minivan was speeding towards him and closing that gap quickly. Charles spun the steering wheel again, his vehicle making a sharp right turn directly in the path of the minivan. He resisted the urge to shut his eyes, watching that space between himself and the front end of that minivan shrink.

He missed the front end of the charging minivan by a few inches.

Then the blue truck was in front of him again, the tail lights just ahead, crossing an intersection and hurdling around a corner down another side street. Charles focused solely on the blue truck. The truck with his target in it. *Emily.*

A hybrid moved into his field of vision, blocking his view and pulling through the intersection just before he did. As a result, Charles and his Chevy made a devastating T with the hybrid, sending both cars flying across the intersection. Charles tumbled across the cab of the vehicle, and an explosion like a gunshot filled the car. Glass scattered through the inside, and Charles felt a collision on the front half of his body with the hardest pillow in existence. The Chevy slid to a halt, rocking up on two wheels momentarily before coming to a standstill by the sidewalk.

Charles shook his head to clear it; another bad decision. His world went in circles, wobbling side to side like the skin of a shaking dog. A bolt of pain tore through his skull like lightning. He glared at the steering column across the car. A white bag slowly deflated, protruding from the spot where the horn used to be. Another bag slowly released pressure on the right side of his body, giving him room to move in the cab.

He reached back and grabbed the door handle, pulling it towards himself and pushing off the opposite side of the car with a leg. The door creaked open slowly, and resisted the push to move. Charles slid out onto the concrete, his world spinning in circles, voices surrounding him. In the distance he spotted those same tail lights, a blue vehicle turning down the alley and making a run for it. It was upside down in his vision, although he could feel his feet on the street below him.

*Emily.* He scrambled to his feet, pushing past onlookers and moving towards the alley with the truck. He ignored the voices, the shouts, and screams from behind him. His arms flailed around him like pinwheels, his legs almost unable to support him. The world in front of him spun rapidly, throwing his balance off and bringing him to his knees. He rose again, remembering not to shake his head to clear it before taking off again. Someone asked if he was okay, and he didn't answer. His life, his safety, didn't matter. Only Emily mattered.

His shoulder connected with the brick corner of a building, his world flipped over again, and everything came back into focus. He braced himself against the corner of the building. Where was he? His eyes picked up the back of the truck again, right side up now, turning left at the very next intersection and disappearing under an overpass. The spinning world slowed down, his balance returned, and his legs burned with a fiery determination to move forward. He took a step, then another. His target was the stoplight in the intersection, the only point of the world that remained motionless. He could make it to the stoplight, and from there he could find the truck. He could find Emily. He just had to move fast. Faster than he'd ever moved before.

His mind cleared, his vision sharpened, and his legs moved swiftly as he came into the intersection. He rounded the corner to the left and followed the path of the truck. Street lights lined both sides of the road on the other side of the overpass. The illuminated road shone brightly in the darkness of the night. He spotted the target. One hundred yards away, parked halfway on the sidewalk, and holding down the end of long black tire streaks on the road. The lights of the truck were off, and the cab was empty. To the right of the truck sat a huge park, filled with trees and concrete walking paths. The police were not coming, or they would not get here in time.

Charles had no other options. He promised to protect Emily at all costs, and he intended to keep that promise.

Good kids kept their promises.

The darkness enveloped him, blinding him and hiding his surroundings. His feet thumped in the soft grass. His eyes adjusted to the moonlight, the vague shadows of trees around him building a map in his head. He listened, the wind howling through the leaves and branches, and the distant sounds of traffic filling the voids. No sirens, no police. They would not get here in time to help.

A squeal, muffled and strained, came from his right, and instinct snapped his head in that direction. No thinking, only moving. Only one thought in his head. *Emily. Move. Keep your promise.*

Silhouettes appeared in between the trees, illuminated by the light of the moon as the two forms wrestled in the grass. Charles's legs propelled him forward, fueled by a deep burning rage. Another squeal, the soft sound of a 'help' escaping the lips of a young girl underneath a full grown man.

A primal scream escaped Charles, and the larger silhouette on top turned to face him. A streak of moonlight revealed the man's face, fear and anger mixed together in his expression. The body turned, a flash in the light of the moon reflected off of a metal surface in the man's hand. An arm raised to point at Charles, a black hole staring into Charles's forehead.

*Gun!* Charles threw his hands up and pushed on the arm. The arm sailed upwards, a flash of light and another explosion popping inches from his face. A wave of heat passed over the top of his head, air pressure pulling at his hair. He leaned forward into the man, pushing off to the side and taking the man to the ground.

"Emily! Run!" He squeezed hard on the arm, digging his fingers into the flesh of the forearm and putting his weight over it. *Control the weapon. Maintain control or you're dead.*

The second silhouette rose from the ground and vanished into the darkness.

*Neutralize the threat.*

Charles picked the arm up off the ground and pushed hard, driving the weapon back to the ground. The hand held onto the gun, and Charles repeated his move. The arm landed on the ground, and Charles heard the clatter of metal in the grass. With the weapon free and clear, Charles let go of the arm to attack the man on the ground. *Wrong choice.* The larger man shifted his weight, tossing Charles off to the side. Charles dropped down onto his back, attempting to wrap his legs around the man's torso to keep some form of control.

A fist landed on his jaw. Pain shot through his head again, and his vision filled with stars. Another punch to the head, this one harder than the last. He felt his legs release the man's torso, and the weight on top of him left his body. His arms fell to the side, and something shifted above him, rolling him over on his side. He glanced up to see the shadow of the man follow Emily into the black, disappearing into the trees. Charles looked to his left, his eyes drawn to a glimmer in the grass. Metal.

He reached over and wrapped his fingers around wood and steel, his brain building the image of a revolver. Something he'd learned about many times in class. Small frame, small caliber. Five bullets in the cylinder. Four left in this one.

For the first time in his life, Charles Langley picked up a live and loaded firearm. *Finger off the trigger, watch where the muzzle is pointed, and be aware of your target and what is behind it. Watch the hammer on this one, if it's pulled back, the trigger will be very touchy.*

He rose to his feet, his thoughts and equilibrium still scattered. Consciously, he put his 'trigger finger' up onto the frame of the gun, ran his thumb over the back to make sure the hammer was dropped and not half cocked, and ran in the direction the two shadows had gone.

Blinded from the flash of the gunshot, Charles collided with a small tree with his left shoulder, sending him spiraling off to the side and onto the ground. His training kicked in, and he adeptly rolled over and jumped back to his feet. High pitched ringing filled his ears, every other noise around him sounding like he had water in his ears. His own footsteps thudded in his head like a speedy heartbeat.

He could hear breathing. Wheezing, high toned breathing of a teenage girl on the run. A shape exited the trees and out into a nearby clearing, the moon lighting up the face of the young girl a couple of years older than Charles. In the clearing she turned to face him, Charles closing in on the edge of the trees, running to her, backing her up, neutralizing the threat. Miniature street lights lit up a nearby path, illuminating the beautiful face of his sister. Her eyes widened, her mouth opened, and her voice echoed in the open area.

"Charlie! Look out!"

Her warning came too late. The man appeared from behind the closest tree at the edge of the yard, grabbing the gun in Charles's hand and pushing him down as he came into the open clearing. The two of them went tumbling to the ground, and the revolver went flying out of Charles's hand. The gun clattered to the side, and the man scrambled for it on all fours. Charles reached up and grabbed the man's leg, pulling it back towards himself. The man kicked at Charles, missing the boy's face by inches before wrapping his own fingers around the grip of the gun. Charles dug the toe of his shoes into the dirt behind him and pushed, leaping for the weapon as the man swung it in his direction. Charles threw out his arm at a forty five degree angle and caught the incoming arm at the bicep with a vice grip. The man's arm bent savagely at the elbow, slinging the hand with the gun towards Charles's face. Charles ducked his head down and pushed up with his defending arm.

A clap. Another blinding flash. A wave of burning heat flying up the back of his forearm like a furnace blower. More muffled ringing. A bullet that passed within an inch of his arm and flew wide of the rest of him. With his other hand, Charles smashed downward with a palm strike, aiming for what he thought was the man's face.

His palm connected with the dirt and grass to the man's left, and Charles felt a fist dig deep into his ribs. The strike drove him over as he grabbed for the gun to control it. *Maintain control of the weapon.* He dropped his weight on the hand, pinning the weapon to the ground underneath him. He tucked the weaponized hand under his arm and squeezed it tight to his body, trapping and controlling the threat. Charles dropped onto his side from that strike to his ribs, trying to crush the gun out of the hand. The man rolled over to climb on top of Charles, but Charles used his non grounded shoulder to dig upward into the man's throat. The momentum of both bodies moving in opposite directions drove the man back onto the ground. Charles rolled over the man, bringing the arm with the gun with him and trying to tie the man up in his own limbs. The man yanked his arm free from Charles's hold, dragging the sights and jagged parts of the gun across Charles's ribs and bicep. The gun moved up in between the two fighters, the barrel pointed square into Charles's nose. The finger on the trigger pulled back.

A foot planted itself in the side of the gun, sending it flying to the side, another shot ringing out in the park. The weapon swung to Charles's right just as the shot went off, blinding and deafening him a third time. The weight of the man beneath him rolled to the right, and more weight toppled down on top of him, pulling him free of the scuffle. Soft hands grabbed tightly at his neck and face, and he felt a warm breath on his flesh.

*Emily.*

"Go," he hoped he said out loud. "I'm fine. Run."

He felt her weight lift from him as his vision returned, still hearing nothing but a tinny ring. He felt grass across his back, laying his head down in the dirt and trying to breath. The shape of the man above him pulled Emily up off the ground and threw her to the side. Charles calculated the position of the man and kicked up with both of his feet, judging the placement of the man's legs correctly. At least one foot landed in the man's crotch. The man's form doubled over forward, and Charles leaned up and swung a right hook to knock the man over. He rolled to his left with the falling man, reaching and grabbing for any hold he could get for leverage.

*Take the back and get the choke.* He felt hips and shoulders digging into his front, and pushed on the man's back to lay him flat. Easy pickings. He reached up to wrap his arm around the man's neck, only to feel an elbow dig into his ribs again. sending him back to the ground and out of physical contact. Charles and the man rose simultaneously, charging each other and grappling fiercely like grizzly bears. The man's arms locked underneath Charles' armpits, and the man lifted Charles from the ground and tossed him like a shot put.

Charles rolled in the dirt, seeing a blur of darkness above him as something passed over him. A small humanoid shape that attacked the man with a trained violence learned only in martial arts.

*Emily.*

Arms spread in all directions, hugging each other. The two forms tangled and crashed to the ground together like an avalanche, the smaller form crushed beneath the bigger form.

Charles rolled onto his back, feeling a sharp rock underneath him. He reached behind himself to grab it, deciding he needed the advantage after all and watching the two struggling opponents fight on the ground. The man dropped a hammer fist onto Emily, smashing her face. Emily clawed and scratched upward. The bodies shifted directions in front of him.

*Use any weapon available. Win at all costs.* His fingers grabbed the rock underneath him.

It wasn't a rock. It was metal.

*The gun!*

A mad chimpanzee rained heavy hammer fists down on the young girl, clobbering her again and again. She cried out in pain and terror and he grunted and groaned with what sounded like pleasure. Charles pulled the gun out from underneath himself, the weapon backwards in his hand. He quickly flipped it around, gripping it tightly and slipping his finger into the trigger guard.

The man growled and pushed down with both hands. His back was to Charles, Emily was underneath him. Charles stood up and faced the two, pointing the gun at the man's back and placing his feet shoulder width apart. He raised his support hand and steadied the gun, pulling the hammer back and trying to line up the sights on the man.

*How many shots have been fired?*

He stared down at the man's back, lining up the barrel with it. The man leaned forward, crushing Emily's throat. Emily's hands reached up to the man's face and grabbed his eye sockets, unable to press hard enough. One arm fell to the side. No sound came from her.

Charles squeezed the trigger.

The force of the weapon threw him backwards and tossed him onto the ground. The flash blinded him again, and his already blown out hearing only picked up a muffled thud. He landed on his back, his hands coming apart but the gun staying in his hand. He quickly scrambled back to his feet, trying to maintain his aim at the man's back.

*Once the threat is not moving anymore, maintain aim at the target in case it's not completely neutralized. Do not pull your attention away until you have confirmation. Keep a peripheral view of threats around you in case it's not over. Remember, attacks can come from all sides.*

Charles wasn't sure how to do that now. He could barely see the shapes on the ground. He couldn't hear anything. He couldn't breathe. He could barely stand up. His whole body shook. The gun trembled in his hands.

Slowly, his eyesight came back into focus, the ringing began to subside, and he saw the mass on the ground reflected in the light of the moon. The man, unmoving and still, dark and shrouded in the night. The man on top of Emily.

*Emily!*

The gun fell to the ground–he'd forgotten to clear the weapon when releasing it in case someone else gains control of it– he dashed over to the mass of bodies and grabbed the man by his shirt. He tried to tell Emily to push, but words would not come out of his mouth. He couldn't hear it, anyway, just like he wouldn't hear her response. His tongue felt dry. His strength felt depleted. All he could do was pull.

The body moved. Charles pulled again, dropping his weight backwards to get leverage. The man's body slid off to the side, and Charles climbed back over it to get to the only thing that mattered in his life. The one thing he cared about. The girl under the man. The girl that fought for her life. The girl with her eyes closed. The girl with a bloodstained shirt. The girl with a black hole in the center of her chest.

*Be aware of your target and what is behind it.*

"No." He couldn't hear himself, but he muttered it under his breath. He couldn't help himself. He grabbed Emily, a much lighter lift than the man, and held her up in his arms. "Emily."

She felt limp. Her head sagged backwards as her body came off the ground. Her arm drooped lifelessly to her side, bouncing as he tried to get her up into his arms. She needed his support. She needed him. He had promised. At all costs. He tucked an elbow underneath the back of her head to keep her from hurting her neck.

"Emily." Her head lulled in his arms. She didn't move. Fluid pumped out of the hole in her chest as she was jostled around. "No. No. No. No." He cradled her head, trying to feel for a pulse, or breathing, or something to say she was alive. He couldn't find anything.

Sirens in the distance. He could hear them now. Faint and far away, or close and muffled. The police were showing up just in time to be useless, to not help, to shift blame for what had happened. Just as he'd suspected. Here they came for him. He didn't care. Nothing mattered anymore. The only thing that mattered to him was in his arms, and void of life. He looked down into her face, barely visible in the dark and motionless. It was his fault that she was dead. *Be aware of your target and what's behind it.* The bullet had passed through the man on top of her, and into her chest. Only one person could have made the decision to shoot. The boy with the gun. His vision blurred with tears now. He whined, placing his face as close to Emily's ear as he could. She was dead because of him.

"I'm sorry, Emily," he wheezed through a deep sob. "I didn't mean to."

***

"Has the jury come to a decision?" asked the judge. Gold framed spectacles hung from the end of his nose as he switched his gaze from the orange clad young man across the room from him and over to the twelve people in the large box.

A thin and frail woman stood from the bench at the end of the box, reading from a small note in her hands through thick eyeglasses. "We have, your honor."

The judge nodded. "Proceed."

The woman glanced down at the paper in her hands. "We, the jury, find Charles Langley, on the first count of reckless driving and endangerment, guilty. On both accounts of leaving the scene of a motor accident, we also find Charles Langley guilty. On the first account of murder in the first degree, we, the jury, find Charles Langley guilty."

The woman hesitated for a moment, as if trying to justify her next words. She pushed her glasses higher up on the bridge of her nose, and took a deep breath. "After deliberation on the second account, we have found Charles Langley, on the second count of murder of an underage person in the third degree, also guilty."

The judge let out a sigh, not of relief, but of disappointment.

"Thank you, jury," he said, his eyes low. "Mr. Langley, you have been found guilty of all of these charges, and I have no choice but to give you the maximum sentence, which, given your current age, will be no more than three years in juvenile detention, wherein you will be released on your eighteenth birthday in accordance with juvenile detention law. As a minor being tried, you will not be sentenced past that date which you achieve majority."

The rest of the judge's speech was drowned out as Charles turned away from the judge to find his mother in the crowd. She was there, alright. She was rising from her seat, he prayed, to forgive him and fight for him. To say something, to beg for him, to plead in his case.

She never even looked at him. Taken into her new husband's arms, his mother turned away, slid to the center aisle, and made her way to the exit as fast as she could. Her hand wiped her face as she left.

Someone pulled him to his feet. They gave him a nudge towards the door by the jury, again no one making eye contact with him as he passed. He stumbled, and an onlooker from the crowd turned to look at him. He tried to make eye contact, but the man simply shifted his gaze away. The corrections officer holding Charles yanked him back up a little more aggressively, and pushed him through the door.

He was silent and still the whole way to the jail. Two corrections officers led him from the small patrol car and into the jail, ran him through his check-in process, where his pictures and fingerprints were taken, and led him down the hall to his jail cell. The door opened in front of him, and he walked in willingly, turning around for the officers to take his cuffs from his wrists through the little slot in the door after it was closed. The doors locked behind him, the small window in the door closed, and he was left alone in the room.

He glanced to each side, the walls of the tiny cell already feeling like they were closing in on him. He turned to the bed, leaned forward, and collapsed on the bed. He shuffled around, turning over and sitting erect and stiff with his knees hanging over the edge. He couldn't move. He wasn't even sure if he was breathing. He looked to his left to see the blanket and pillow left for him, nasty and stained from the last person to use them. Probably not even the last person in this cell. *When was the last time they were washed?*

It didn't matter. They were all he had left.

He laid down in the bed, dropped his head on the pillow, and pulled the blanket over himself. It was scratchy and old. It smelled like body odor and some sort of musty mildew. He sniffed anyway, not because he wanted to smell, but because he needed to breathe. When he exhaled, it was chopped and weeping. He whined like a dog, wheezing and sobbing into the fabric. It was all he had to hold on to.

He was lost, and Emily was gone. She wasn't ever going to be there to find him again. He was trapped in a cell and surrounded by criminals; by animals. *You are where you belong!* He had nothing left, and no purpose. His trainer, Dan Thomas, would never let him back into the dojo, his mother would never take him back into her home, and his father… Where was his father?

It didn't matter. Nothing mattered. Only good kids got to go back to their lives, not animals. The fact of the matter was he had made a promise to keep Emily safe, no matter the cost, and he had failed at that promise.

The fact of the matter was only good kids kept their promises.

# <u>*37*</u>

*Tulsa, Oklahoma - Present Day - Friday - 11:30 PM*

"Holy Mary, mother of all God's children, Alison!" Jimmy Limone fumed as he paced rapidly back and forth from one end of the hotel room to the next. "What did I do to make you hate me so much?"

"I don't hate you, Jimmy," came Alison's voice from the other end of the phone. "I need the team strategically placed. You and Rebecca are perfectly capable of handling the board of directors without confrontation. Tell me that's the case with anyone else on the team right now."

Jimmy looked over at the middle aged man cradling his daughter, and the younger woman with the bruised face lying on the bed. His eyes flickered up to Rebecca, who stared furiously down at her injured younger sister.

"I guess you're right," he sighed, a little quieter. "If not me, then who?"

*Who had said that? Shakespeare? Jesus?* He hesitated in his pacing for a split second, but resumed a moment later.

Alison was right. The board of directors didn't like her, and likely wouldn't even ask where she was. Walter was dangerously unstable with the attempted kidnapping of his daughter, and Katie was on bed rest for several more days. Just the sight of her face might scare the board silly, which Jimmy wouldn't mind seeing. Rebecca was more upset over the attack on her sister than anything. Compared to the rest of the team, Jimmy had it easy.

"If you keep pacing like that," said Katie in her soft and soothing voice, "you'll agitate the people below us." She gave Jimmy a weak, exhausted smile with her eyes still closed. "Do you know how much noise just walking around generates on these floors?"

"I can't help it," grumbled Jimmy, trying to maintain his composure with the sweet girl. *She can't even see me, and she knows what I'm doing.* "I'm a little agitated myself. You know what the first thing the board will ask when Rebecca and I are the only ones here, Alison?"

"They'll ask where we are." Alison's voice was humorous, but cold and dry. She was serious. "You'll tell them we had an important case pop up, and when they ask what's more important than doing our jobs at the conference, tell them that children's lives are more important. Tell them that's why the Red Sea Initiative exists in the first place. Tell them that's why they have the jobs they have."

"Yeah," scoffed Jimmy impatiently, "that sounds real non confrontational."

"Then rephrase it," chuckled Alison. "That's why you're there explaining it and not me. I am great at being confrontational. You are great at keeping your cool."

Jimmy rolled his eyes and groaned. "Alison, you have got to give me something to work with. I can't just jump around questions like I'm some greasy politician."

"Our case moved down the road," said Alison. "Since I am the only one with enough experience, I'm down here, and since the new guy needs training, and I'm training him, I have to bring him with me. Can you work with that?"

"I could use some extra details." He pressed the speakerphone button on his phone and held it out to Rebecca. "Rebecca and I need more to pacify the board of directors."

"We got the older sister," said Alison. "She says that the little girl is being chained to a Pack n' Play overnight. She's not being fed or allowed to go to the bathroom until she's been sold and does what she's told. She's only being bathed and such when she has a customer that wants her that way, except she's forced to call them friends, not customers. She's kept in a diaper the rest of the time with no other clothes. Sometimes the family forces her to do hard labor in the yard with no water or breaks. She's nine years old."

Jimmy froze in place and swallowed hard. "I can probably work with that."

Both the Swift sisters exchanged glances as they heard what Alison was saying. Walter stiffened just enough to be noticeable, and even Kitsen opened her eyes.

"That's more like it," sighed Alison over the phone. "I could hear you pacing over the phone. It was driving me up the wall."

Kitsen giggled, and Jimmy sighed deeply.
*And she says I'm the non confrontational one.*

"Paul Edwards is going with us," continued Alison. "He has connections with the circuit judge and the police department up there. We'll have this wrapped up by the end of the day tomorrow."

"I sure hope you do," grumbled Jimmy. "I am getting tired of all this malarkey. I wasn't kidding earlier. I know we're short handed, but I'll be the next one out the door if things don't improve."

# <u>38</u>

*Claremore, Oklahoma - Friday - 11:45 PM*
Mindy heard the door click and squeak open behind her in the kitchen. She froze in place. The running water pouring from faucet to sink basin rang out in the room. She heard nothing else. She held her breath, and tried not to let tears spill from her eyes. Her hands set a soapy plate into the sink to rinse it. She didn't want it to break in whatever was going to happen next.

"So she's just gone, huh?" Joseph's voice was soft with a hinting tone of anger. He sounded like he had a really bad cold with his smashed nose. It could have been comical in other circumstances. "You just let her go? Just like that? Well, she's your daughter. Did you talk to her? Where did she go?"

Mindy said nothing, still frozen like a statue. Did she think he was a T-rex? As if he couldn't see her if she stayed still? *Fight, flight, or freeze.* Here she was, frozen. Her eyes darted to her left to a lone kitchen knife lying on the drying rack next to the sink. A last resort, and possibly her only hope. *Fight.*

"I asked you a question." His voice was in her ear now. She glanced at the knife again, only moving her eyes. The pointed edge was directed behind her. Grab it and pull, and it would be over. A police report and a couple of days of cleaning. She wouldn't have to look. He was right behind her. It would save her life. It would save Abigail's life. It might save Olivia's life. They had barely survived the last fit of rage. If she disabled Joseph now…

His hands gripped her forearms from behind, squeezing the bones to the point of breaking. Her eyes filled with tears that seeped through squinted eyelids as she tensed and tried to remain still. *Freeze, bitch. That's all you're capable of. No fight left in you.*

"I. Asked. You. A. Question." Each word came out separately and pronounced clearly. Deep, growling words said through tightly clenched teeth. She closed her eyes completely now, pushing the tears out of her eyes and down her face.

"I…" she wanted to lie, but she knew what that would get her. Much worse than whatever she was already going to get. "I don't know. She didn't text or call. She didn't say anything to me. She just ran. I don't think she had a plan. She just had enough, and got out of here."

"You just let her go?" he grumbled. "No questions asked, no calls or texts?"

"Nothing," Mindy cried, as confidently as she could. "She didn't tell me anything, and I didn't ask. You know, just as well as I do, that she'll come back. She always comes back to you. We all come back to you, don't we?"

"You tried to run, too, huh?"

"No." Her blood ran cold. She felt the color leave her face.

"You grabbed Oliva and you tried to run. I stopped you."

"I'm sorry," she whispered, inhaling sharply. "It won't happen again. I don't know what I was thinking. I was just scared. Abigail scared me."

"It won't happen again?" asked Joseph, keeping the grip on her arms.

She shook her head. "It won't. I swear."

"I know it won't," he whispered back. "I'll make sure of it."

He yanked her arms behind her back, wrenching the muscles in her shoulders as he pulled her away from the sink and dragged her through the kitchen. She tripped going backwards, but Joseph held her upright by the arms, bending them behind her at a painful angle. Her feet dragged along the tile floor, her shoulders carrying all of her weight.

She was at the garage door before she got her footing back again. Joseph didn't let up. He dragged and he pulled, causing her feet to slip on the stairs going down into the concrete garage. She felt something in her left shoulder pop followed by an ache that crept down her arm. She cried out, only to be thrown forward against the garage wall, planting her face against the sheet metal with a loud gong sound. Her good arm was thrust up against her will, a strap of some sort wrapping itself around her wrist and holding the hand aimed at the ceiling.

Her other hand went upwards, finding its own bonds to keep it from pulling back to her body. The movement shot pain across the entire left side of her body, radiating up and down her neck, head, side, and leg. She felt a hand let go of her arm and heard footsteps on the concrete behind her. Snipping metal sounds came from behind her. A test of the garden shears.

Something pulled at her shirt, tugging at random. She heard the shears grinding together. She felt the cold metal and rough rubber of the shears as the tool made its way up her back. After a moment, she felt her shirt loosening around her. The collar of her shirt at the back of her neck fell away, and the flayed shirt hung limply at her sides, opened like a gutted animal. Fear shot through her body like a jolt of electricity.

More rattling from behind her. Clattering of metals. It was different from the metal sounds of the hand tools. This noise sounded… bigger. A deeper tone in the rattle. A lower pitch in the echo off of the sheet metal surroundings. A grunt like the call of a wild whitetail buck.

The grunt came again, short and sputtering. It came a third time, this time catching and sustaining indefinitely. A tinny growl filled the room. The growl sounded artificial and mechanical. She recognized it now. The rumble of a two stroke engine. She'd heard the sound while working in the yard hundreds of times.

The weed trimmer.

"Wait." It was all she could say. Her voice trembled and her body shook. She tried to pull at the straps holding her wrists, but her dislocated shoulder couldn't produce any strength. It only produced more pain. "Joseph. No."

"You shouldn't have tried to run." Joseph's voice behind her was low and soft, almost inaudible over the trimmer engine. The trimmer engine revved twice behind her. She tensed. Her eyes burned with tears every time she squeezed them shut. She whimpered.

The trimmer engine roared, maxing out its internal RPMs and spinning the trimmer wire as fast as it was able. She felt and heard nothing else for another few moments.

Then she felt the searing pain in the muscles on her back. She heard her own voice shrieking in agony as Joseph set the trimmer wire against her skin. The twin wires struck again and again, slicing deep into the muscle and fat of her shoulder blades. Joseph raked the trimmer back and forth across her upper back.

Mindy howled. Her head reared back, and her torso arched to get away from the torture. Her chest and stomach pressed against the garage wall, the trimmer string following her as she tried to escape. She moved to the left, scraping the trimmer string across her back by herself. She moved the right instinctively, and the trimmer string dragged back across.

Then Joseph dropped the trimmer down and tore into Mindy's lower back. She could feel the flesh of her love handles flaying open and spraying blood in all directions. Her arms naturally pulled her up to get away, and this time she didn't even notice the pain in her shoulder. The trimmer followed her up. It dragged side to side across her lumbar, shredding her body to pieces.

And just like that it was over. She never heard the engine die on the trimmer. She was still screaming. Her body couldn't relax. Her eyes wouldn't open. A hand grabbed her face from behind, and she quieted. Her wails became soft whimpers and sobs of pain. Her head was forced to turn to the side in a poor attempt to get her to look at Joseph.

"If you ever run again, I'll kill you. Slow. Painful. This will feel like a deep tissue massage at the parlor."

She believed him.

He pushed her face away, smacking her skull into the garage wall again. She cried again, and heard the clatter of metal on metal behind her. She heard the same footsteps she had heard before the torment behind her, moving from her right side to her left. The steps slowed, and then stopped. She turned her head to the left, seeing Joseph standing at the garage door, halfway through going into the house. He looked back at her.

"Just because I split the money with you," he said quietly, "does not make you someone important. It doesn't even mean the money is yours. It means you belong to me. You owe me."

Nothing he said mattered to Mindy. She was glad Abigail had gotten away; glad she had gotten away from this even if it was just for a few days. Mindy could suffer this. Abigail could go to the police, now. She could end all of this. Mindy could trust her daughter to handle the police, and Mindy wouldn't be implicated in any crimes as long as she cooperated when the time came. Especially not after this. Not with these injuries on her back. No one would convict her. She would take a plea deal, and escape. All she had to do was make it another couple of days. Then she would be free. She could start over with Abigail and Olivia. All she had to do was suffer through it.

She sniffed in, trying to hold eye contact with Joseph while he stared into her soul. She could feel the warmth of blood running down her back now, soaking her pants. Her legs gave out from underneath her, her shoulder throbbing as it held her weight. Tomorrow she would go see Abigail and get the plan together. She would leave. She might even take Olivia. She could hide from Joseph, too. She could kill Joseph while he wasn't looking, or just leave when he was distracted. Charles and the police would protect her. She blinked, and her eyelids sank over her eyes slowly as the world around her began to swirl. All she could see was Joseph's nasty smile aimed at her like a rifle.

"Goodnight, my love," said Joseph.

The lights in the garage clicked off, leaving Mindy in complete darkness.

# <u>39</u>

*Claremore, Oklahoma - Saturday - 10:00 AM*

"She wanted him in there with her," Alison told the police officer. "I think he's really struggling with all of this. So much has happened all at once."

"That's her boyfriend?" asked the police officer, staring at Charles through the glass door of the police station. It faced the parking lot, where Charles Langley stood, looking strangely focused on the pavement in front of him. "He seems a little… robotic. Inhuman, if you get what I mean."

"I do," replied Alison. "He's a little strange to begin with, but he's also dealing with a lot right now. I'm trying to train him, and normally we wouldn't put him in this situation, but our options are very limited."

"And this trafficker," said the police officer. "She says it's Joseph Smith? I know that guy. He doesn't have a kid. Just the wife and step daughter. It would be impossible to hide a child for nine years. Too many people come over, too many houses sit way too close next door. It's way too risky to try that."

"You don't know these kinds of people the way we know them," said Alison. "I've worked around them for ten years. They are resourceful. They get creative when they really want to make money."

"I have more experience with them than you might think," said the police officer. "Enough to know it's hard to give a statement about it to the police. That is what she's doing in there, right?"

"It is," replied Alison. "It'll be one of the hardest things she'll ever do. She's been so abused and manipulated over the years, she'll struggle just to let out the smallest bit of information."

"But she's going to get it all out?" asked the police officer.

"I hope so," sighed Alison. "She already gave it to Charles and I. The more we get from her, the faster we can wrap this up. The faster we can wrap this up, the safer everyone is with one more bad guy off of the street."

The police officer glanced through the glass window again. Alison followed his gaze, spotting Charles now sitting on the trunk of a police cruiser.

"Is he stable enough to work this case?" asked the police officer.

"I think he'll do fine," said Alison. "He's done very well so far. I'm a little worried about the girlfriend situation, but we're kind of on our last leg here."

"Anyways." The police officer shrugged. "I have to get back to work. What was your name?"

Alison smiled as the officer put out a hand. "Taylor."

The police officer shook Alison's hand and smiled back. "Nice to meet you, Taylor. I'm the

Police Chief here in Claremore. My name's Tom Leonard. I'll see if there's anything I can do to help Charles through what he's going through. I have experience with trauma."

"That would be nice," said Alison.

Tom Leonard made his way to the exit and walked through the glass doors, his gaze focused on Charles Langley. Abigail came out of the back room only a few seconds later. Her face was soaked with perspiration and flushed a bright pale color; her eyes were bloodshot, and wide.

"It's done," she told Alison. "What's next?"

"Go home," said Alison. "To Charles's apartment, that is. We'll have everyone brought in later today when the Judge signs the warrant. Tomorrow at the latest. Usually we would bring you in with everyone else, having you stay the night at his house. That would make Joseph think it wasn't you that turned on him. Unfortunately, since you fought your way out, there's no hiding it now. Once we get the raid going, we'll have your mom and Olivia released, and hopefully the three of you together can get into a recovery program for victims of trafficking."

Abigail nodded. "One more night of hiding, then total freedom."

Alison followed suit, and nodded slowly. "One more night of hiding. Then you'll be able to do whatever you want with your life."

"Is that what you did?" asked Abigail, looking in Alison's eyes. "You said you had been trafficked, too. I can see it in the way you act. Bulking up in weight so no man can overpower you, training in martial arts so you can fight back. You're very aggressive and combative. It's all very obvious where you came from. I tried to join the National Guard to learn how to fight men off, but…"

Alison nodded again. "Women in the military are never treated right. I've always said we shouldn't be allowed to enlist, just for our personal safety, but we do it anyway."

"I want to serve my country, too," said Abigail. "I want to make something meaningful out of my life. Just like Charles."

Abigail gulped, so hard her throat clicked.

Alison nodded, and put a hand on the girl's shoulder. "One more night, Abigail. Then you're free to live your life. Whatever you want to do."

"Meaningful," Abigail muttered. "Like what you guys do."

Abigail's phone rang, and she checked it, her eyes widening. "It's my mom. I haven't heard from her all day. What do you think she wants?"

"She's going to try to find out where you are," replied Alison. "Don't tell her. There's a chance Joseph can hire someone to track your phone signal, but it'll just place you here. Leave it somewhere else before going back to Charles's apartment before going there."

"Okay," said Abigail, "but I can answer it?"

Alison nodded, and Abigail answered the phone call, listening for several moments.

"Mom? Are you sure?" She was silent for a few more seconds before handing the phone over to Alison. "Believe it or not, she wants to talk to you."

# <u>40</u>

*Claremore, Oklahoma - Saturday - 10:15 AM*

"Okay," said Mindy, "Tonight, please. This afternoon. Right now, even. As soon as possible. I just want to get this done. I'll take care of the hotel, just let me know which one."

The sounds of muffled voices on the other end of the phone echoed in the bedroom, a woman's voice, and Mindy was silent for a few moments. There was a shuffling of paper, and the scribbling sound of a pen scratching the surface.

"Holiday Inn Express Suites here in Claremore? Tonight at nine? Okay, I'll be there. I'll get you the money back for the room. I promise. I really appreciate this. This whole thing has gone too far, and I really just need to get it out of my system. I'm sorry it took me so long."

More sounds of muffled voices on the phone. A woman's voice. No. Two women's voices. Mindy sighed softly. "What's my deal? What do I get?" She paused, and there was just the slightest sound of speaking over the other end of the phone. It was barely audible.

"Okay. I'll take that." Her voice almost sounded broken, like she was trying not to cry. "Thank you so much. I was going to go to you guys myself, but I wasn't sure what to do. Thank you."

There were a few soft sobs from her, a beeping sound from a cell phone, and the clatter of her phone on the bedside table.

Joseph Smith stepped away from the closed bedroom door and stood in the hallway to consider what he'd just heard. He had been in the bathroom for no longer than five minutes, and his wife had made a phone call in his absence.

So his wife was meeting someone at a hotel tonight right after dark. Who was it? What was it about? Nothing made sense anymore.

He reached down into his pocket and withdrew his pocket knife. He looked down at the small weapon that he was staring to twirl around in his hand.

Who was his wife talking to? She offered to pay for the hotel. She said she wanted to get it over with. She thanked whoever was on the other end of the line. She asked what was in it for her. She said something had gone too far, and that she had wanted to reach out in the first place.

*The police.* It had to be the police. There were no other options. *Abigail.* Abigail had escaped, and must have gone to the police. Now Mindy was going to them, also.

It might not matter. Two of his top customers still held all of the power here in

Claremore. They could shut a police investigation down pretty quickly.

There was only one way to find out for sure.

Joseph opened his bedroom door and joined his wife in bed. He heard her sigh. He looked down at the pocket knife in his hand again, wondering what else he could do today. He could find out who she was calling right here, and right now. Mindy was already in pain, and scared from last night. It wouldn't take much pressure to make her squeal. He could find out everything, or at least everything Mindy knew.

"What are you going to do when Abigail comes back?" asked Mindy, her voice just barely even a whisper. "Are you going to do to her what you've done to me?"

Joseph looked down and stared at her for a long time. He wasn't sure what to do. Today, with a knife in his hand, he could find out everything. He could put an end to that right now.

"No," he growled softly, turning back to his dresser. He wasn't sure if he was talking to Mindy, or himself. He set his knife on his own bedside table. He could find out everything today, but his mind was elsewhere. It was working overtime. If he tried now, he wasn't sure he could come up with a coherent thought. Something else might slip, something that really would get him in trouble. He was in control right now, he didn't want to lose that control. He was tired from all the thinking.

He had customers that could protect him. Very powerful people that did not want to go down with him. He was safe, for now. This could wait, for now. Just a few more hours. At least he had time to think about it. He had time to plan. Whatever it was, he would find out tonight at nine o'clock.

321

# <u>*41*</u>



*Claremore, Oklahoma - Saturday - 10:15 AM*

Charles leapt off of the trunk of the cruiser and sighed. Swinging his arms around in their joints, he tried to loosen up, his blood pressure feeling like it was about to burst his arteries. So many mixed emotions. Happiness that Abigail could help get this job done, and they could move on in life together. Anxiety on the safety of the little girl and Abigail. Grief for his father. Anger at the betrayal of Abigail from last week. Hatred for Joseph for doing this to these poor girls.

*Anger. So much anger. Welcome to the dark side of The Force.* He just needed a release. He needed *that* release, the one he couldn't get until he was back in his hotel room later tonight.

*Would it be too suspicious to just go take care of it in the bathroom real quick?*

His mind fluttered back to the restaurant, to the young girl. His brain conjured images of the two of them together, maybe in a hotel room. Then it wasn't the young girl at the restaurant.

It was Abigail's little sister.

He shook his head to clear those images. It wasn't him. That wasn't who he was. That was who he was fighting. That was Joseph.

An image of Alison was next, large and intimidating, standing in his living room towering over the puny and terrified Abigail. Abigail came last, worried, timid, and hurt. A tall girl with barely any weight behind her. A weak girl. Inferior.

*Stop it!* Voices in his head screamed at him. What was wrong with him? Abigail was beautiful, strong willed, and caring. She was just hurt and needed help. She wanted nothing more than to be with him, and she displayed that now by turning in her own family to the police. She wasn't tainted, it would be inhumane to call her that. Her past was not her fault. Her past was forced on her. She was growing out of that now. She was making her own future.

The front door to the police station squealed open and a large male police officer walked into the parking lot.

"Mr. Langley," said the man. "I'm Chief Leonard of the police department here in Claremore. I wanted to congratulate you on your success in this investigation."

"I wasn't aware I had made any success," replied Charles.

"Of course you have," said Chief Leonard. "Your girlfriend is in there giving a statement to the police, and your buddy is going to the judge, all on your progress in the investigation. I'd call that a win. You could have this wrapped up by the end of the day."

Charles shook his head. "We can only hope."

"One more thing," said Chief Leonard. "Just in case something happens, and I need to get a hold of you, where are you staying? Are you local?"

"Tulsa," said Charles. "I have an apartment out there in Broken Arrow."

"Okay." Chief Leonard nodded. "You have a phone I can reach you at?"

Charles hesitated. "I do not."

Something didn't feel right with Chief Leonard. Why was he so concerned with where Charles lived and how to get a hold of him? This officer had all the resources to find that out without asking. It didn't make sense. Did it?

He glared up at the police chief. "Leonard?"

"Yes," replied Chief Leonard. "Tom Leonard."

Charles leaned back against the police cruiser. "How long have you been police chief here?"

"Ten years or so," replied Tom Leonard. "I worked my way up through the years. Been in law enforcement nearly half my life."

"That's a long time as police chief," said Charles. "In most places the terms are about two or four years on average."

"The people like me here," said Tom Leonard. "I get the job done."

*Ten years.* Charles thought to himself. *Abigail would have known him back then.* He made a mental note to ask her about this guy. Ten years was a long time to be police chief, even for someone who'd been in police work that long. Most guys that lasted that long were usually part of some corruption scheme.

Or maybe Charles had just seen too many movies.

"What part of Broken Arrow can I find you at?" asked Tom Leonard.

Charles shook his head. *Abigail will be alone there. Do not let anyone find out where it's at. You have to protect her at all costs.*

He shrugged. "You have background checking software on your computer. Use it to look me up."

# *42*

*Claremore, Oklahoma - Saturday - 10:30 AM*

Paul Edwards opened the door to the Judge's office and stepped in. The smell of old tobacco and expensive Scotch touched his nose. *Perks of being the District Judge in the Midwest.* Walls decorated with newspaper headlines covered in cases with the Judge's name on them surrounded him. The Rogers County District Judge, Honorable Larry Bates, stood from his desk by the window and waved Paul away with lowered eyebrows and pursed lips.

"What do you think this is?" asked the Judge with a primal growl in his voice. "I get a request for a warrant to search the house of Joseph Smith based on nothing but hear say? An anonymous source tells you there's something going on, and you just jump right on it, yeah?"

"Your honor," Paul started softly. "It's the crime against a child that did it for me. I might not be the chief of police here in this city, but I wanted to put in words personally with an old friend who could help rescue a child. I was in this business for a long time before I became police chief in Tulsa. I wasn't certain it was true, but we need to be vigilant when it comes to the safety of those who cannot defend themselves."

"And how do you expect it looks when the man gets arrested for child abuse, when it isn't actually happening?" asked Judge Bates. "When he doesn't even have a child? Just the step daughter who's an adult? How does that look on a man's reputation?"

"I figured it can't hurt to try and quietly wrap things up," said Paul. "Someone goes out to the house in an unmarked car to check things out, maybe takes a couple of extra guys to handle the man if he happens to get out of control. It doesn't have to be showy or loud. You know that as well as I do. If we do it right, the journalists won't get a hold of it until we know it to be confirmed."

"And if you're wrong?" cried the Judge. "He will take this to social media. He will go to the local paper. If the journalists get a hold of a story that a man was falsely accused of not properly taking care of a child he doesn't have? How does that look for the department?"

"In my opinion, your honor," said Paul, "it makes it look like we want to double check things. If we're wrong, then he won't be arrested and we won't have to make it a big deal. It makes us seem at least a little competent that we can at least look into things when we're told about them."

"It makes us look like fools!" screamed the Judge. "We spend money and time paying reparations in lawsuits and apologizing for making accusations." He inhaled deeply, holding his breath for several seconds before letting it go. "I'm sorry. That was a little uncalled for."

"Emotions have been high all around lately," said Paul. "I don't take it personally. It's part of the job. I've been in this job long enough to know that."

He didn't exactly feel that way, but keeping the peace was necessary at times like this one.

"You want to know if Joseph Smith is doing what you say he's doing?" asked the Judge, lowering his voice and sitting back down at his desk. "I'll ask him tonight. I'll go to his house and ask him at dinner."

Paul's heart stopped. He sat up in his chair "Excuse me?"

"When I get there," said Judge Bates. "I will see, with my own two eyes, that he doesn't have a nine year old daughter. He has a wife, and he has a step daughter. Let me guess. It was her that gave you this information?"

Paul said nothing. He couldn't give away information like that. If the Judge knew Joseph, then anything Paul said to the man was likely to be relayed to Joseph. He'd already said too much. Now he had to be careful.

"Anonymous sources usually want their identity kept secret in order to protect themselves from someone they deem dangerous," he said carefully.

"An angry or upset step daughter of any age is a prime candidate for false accusations," growled Judge Bates. "Family relationships, with step children especially, are tense and strained. You can't take the word of a kid too seriously."

"She's in her mid twenties, your honor," said Paul. "I would hardly call her a kid."

"Did you make the best decisions in your twenties?" asked Larry Bates. "Were you the most emotionally steadfast person around? We all say things we don't mean to get others in trouble at some point in our lives. This generation in their twenties is the worst about false accusations, except these kinds of accusations are the most effective at ruining a man's life."

He sat down in his chair and took a deep breath, waving his hands out to the side to calm himself. "I'll tell you what. I'll go over there for dinner tonight, and when I'm there I'll double check and see if Joseph has any other children. I won't mention the warrant or anything. I'll just say something along the lines of rumors that he had a child from a past marriage are floating around, or something like that. I'll do it subtly, and I'll keep things on the downlow to protect the reputation of the police department, and maintain the security of the family relationship."

Paul sighed deeply. "Subtle is what we're going for. We're worried that if he's really dangerous, then he'll hurt, or even kill, the little girl."

"I'll keep it a secret," said the Judge, "but you listen to me. The Smiths are good people. Joseph has been here in Claremore most of our lives. His wife is a beautiful woman with a kind heart that we love to have in our hometown. We have drinks at the bar and have dinner together. If anything was going on there, I would likely know.

If I get a bad feeling tonight, though, I'll sign your warrant first thing in the morning and let you guys go at it."

Paul nodded. "Thank you, sir." He stood from the chair and turned to leave, opening the door and stepping out.

"Paul?" Paul turned back to look at the judge. "You really think he would kill a little girl if this was all true? You really think he's that kind of a man?"

"I don't know him, your honor," Paul replied. "Never judge what a man is capable of, even with proper knowledge and evaluation. The step daughter says he is, and she doesn't seem like she's doing a whole lot of acting. If she is, she's damn good at it. I'm just trying to be careful about this. My biggest concern is that no one gets hurt. It always is."

# *43*

*Tulsa, Oklahoma - Saturday - 5:00 PM*
The noises of the banquet irritated Jimmy Limone's already overstimulated brain. His face squeezed into a grimace, and his grip tightened on the dinner glass in his hand, and he hoped to God it didn't shatter from the force. He took several large gulps of water, trying his best not to slurp loudly, and slammed the glass back onto the table with a sigh. He glanced around, ignoring the impatient stares of Rebecca Swift from his left and looking for his real target: the board of directors.

He knew they would be coming to their table soon. There were three empty seats at their table where Walter, Katie, and Alison were supposed to be sitting, and Jimmy would have to defend their absences. He knew what to say, but saying it in a conversation was a whole other ball game. *Be the non confrontational one. Be the calm one.*

*If not me, then who?* Who had said that? That sounded like something a politician or someone in the Army would say, or maybe someone in his industry. Had he come up with it all by himself, or was it really something some old philosopher had said ages ago. *If not me, then who?*

Rebecca stared at him hopefully. She had no idea what to do; she was so full of rage at her sister's injuries, so she decided she would leave the talking to him. He didn't like it, but he was the best in the team at it. That's why he was usually the one in the field. *Not today. Today I'm here dealing with office politics. No human traffickers here, just a bunch of people that don't understand my...*

"Mister Limone," came a voice from behind him. Knowing who the voice belonged to, Jimmy stood and turned around to shake hands with the three people behind him.

"Misters and Misses board of directors," he greeted with a smile so false it hurt to put it on. It almost felt like a slap in the face to wear it. "Wonderful to greet you here. How goes the campaign for donations and awareness?"

"It would be a lot easier with our CEO here," said the man in the middle, glancing over to the empty chair at the table. He was a pudgy man in his sixties with a balding head and glasses thick enough to be considered telescopes. His eyes bulged in the lenses like what his glasses revealed to his eyes constantly astonished him.

"Yeah," grumbled Jimmy, "he's taking a sabbatical. Spending time with his kid. They recently had a family emergency that requires some distance from the job."

"So, where is Walter?" The man on the left, Jimmy's least favorite director of whatever on the board, was waving his hands like he was trying to get Jimmy's attention. This man was thin and frail, although much younger than the man in the middle.

He was probably in his forties and just not handling the aging process well. His hair thinned along the middle of his head and his dull, sunken eyes peeked through thick and heavy eyelids.

"He's up in the hotel room with Kitsen," said Jimmy, smiling to himself that they hadn't asked about Alison. "Like I said, they just had some issues the other day. He's a little jumpy about it. Katie is up there, too, recovering from her beating."

"Is that where Miss Rotskoya is at as well?" asked the man in the middle. "Seems like a poor decision to split your team up like that."

*They didn't even apologize for what happened, nor express any concern.* Jimmy tried to take a deep breath. *Non confrontational.*

"She is over in Claremore working a case," said Jimmy. "Training the new guy, too. One or two Undercovers, max. Plus, that leaves Rebecca and I here to help with public relations."

"Walter is up in the hotel room with that Katie girl," muttered the man on the left. "She must be a favorite of his."

*You son of a bitch, she got beat up! I'll beat you and see if you don't stay in a hotel room for a week!*

"She helps take care of his daughter," said Jimmy. "But, like I said a few seconds ago, very clearly I might add, she's currently recovering from a savage beating she received from the guy we're chasing several days ago."

"Yes," said the woman. "We are very distraught about that. It's hard to maintain a public image with your operators getting injured and the bad guys getting so close to home." Her eyes flickered down to Jimmy's arm, still resting in its sling.

*Forgetting that a child was almost taken, and a woman was beaten senseless, she focuses on my mistake.* Jimmy sighed deeply to calm himself. *Non confrontational, Jimmy boy.*

"Alison is leading the investigation in Claremore, then?" asked the man on the left.

"She's good at what she does," replied Jimmy. "No doubt about that."

"Still," sighed the man on the right again, "doesn't seem like a good idea to split the team up and essentially go rogue on a random operation with her little sidekick like that. All based on a minor tip."

*Call him a sidekick to his face,* thought Jimmy with a smile, remembering the prisoner in the hospital. *See how hard he actually kicks.*

"The new guy is a lot of things," he said out loud, "but he's not little. Alison is training and operating down there while Walter and Katie recover. One of our old operators is working with them. He has connections in that town. We already have someone inside the circle and are just waiting on warrants and police responses. I trust my team, and we're just as effective as anyone else even when we are split up like this. My gut feeling is that this will benefit us in the long run."

The man on the right laughed. "My apologies if it offends you, Mister Limone," he said, "but I'm not sure your gut feeling is the best compass to use."

*Non confrontational.*

"Look," Jimmy said with a low tone. He tried keeping his teeth from grinding together. Even human traffickers were easier to deal with than these idiots. "They had an important case pop up. One that has injured two of us, and left our main guy terrified of leaving his daughter anywhere. We have a new recruit we're training so that we're not short handed. We can't just drop all of this at the beck and call of some political funding operation. Let's be honest, according to our source, the girl's being trapped in a kiddie pen and made to wear diapers and whatnot. Beat with a belt and all that. Word is, though, we might even get a solid recruitment out of it."

"Walter knows how important this event is," sighed the woman on Jimmy's right. She was short and bony, with a dress that exposed far too much of her elderly flesh for Jimmy's taste. Her white hair was bobbed just below her earlobes with great curls at the ends. She was the only one not wearing glasses, but she was constantly squinting at him like she needed them. "This is a hub for exposition and fundraising. Without our CEO, we stand to lose support. This event is the most important event of the year for this organization. What is he thinking?"

*He's thinking of his family!*

"What's more important than doing our jobs at the conference?" Jimmy asked, his voice rising into a boom. "Children's lives are more important. That's what. Isn't that why the Red Sea Initiative was founded in the first place? Isn't that why you guys, and lady, have the jobs that you have? Plus, if it gets out that the only reason and time they ever skipped this fancy party was to delve again into that nasty underbelly of the society to rescue children, it tells the public that we are dedicated and we don't waste donations. These people know these events cost money, and they hate that we use their hard earned money for public image stuff like this. So if anyone asks where the big boss is, or his top investigator for that matter, you just go ahead and tell them that when given the choice between saving the lives of beautiful children in mortal danger, and hanging out with schmoozy business folks like you, a real hero would choose the former."

*Non confrontational?*

He took a deep breath at the end of his speech, his lungs exhausted. In fact, he took several deep breaths as the board of directors stared blankly at him in silence. Their faces, shocked and wide eyed, didn't seem to be able to comprehend his words. His insult seemed to linger in the air, the only remnant of his monologue that had stuck in their minds.

"Mister Limone," muttered the woman on Jimmy's right. "Speaking so passionately in a setting such as this is not necessary."

"I wouldn't even be here if it wasn't necessary," replied Jimmy. "If it were up to me, I'd be out helping Walter and Alison, but I have a broken arm, that I got in the course of investigating this very case, and Walter knew he needed someone to fight the three headed hydra that he knew would attack while he was out doing what we're supposed to be doing anyway."

*Confrontational.*

"This conference is necessary for funding and public relations," said the bony man.

"That is correct," said Jimmy. "Which is your job, not mine, or Katie's, or Rebecca's, or Alison's. Our jobs are to be out there fighting the evil of the world, not the evil in this organization."

*Confrontational!*

"We're evil?" asked the woman.

*CONFRONTATIONAL!*

"If you weren't, you wouldn't be questioning Walter's ability to make the right call. Right now there's a nine year old girl half an hour away that hasn't eaten in a week and only gets to shower when someone comes out to have his way with her. She spends most of her time tied up in a play pen, wearing nothing but a diaper, and being forced to both work in the backyard moving stuff too heavy for her or getting to have adult relations with her daddy's buddies, and maybe even her own daddy. So let our guys do their jobs of saving lives, and you focus on your job of cozying up to the big money for handouts."

Three red faces glared at Jimmy, who let out a sigh bigger than he thought human lungs were capable of holding.

"Lay off the man, okay?" he continued, his tone softening. "He has enough on his plate trying to make the world a better place and raising a child without you three breathing down his neck all the time. So forgive me if it offends you, Misters and Misses Board of Directors, but why don't you focus on funding and public relations instead of gossiping about my partner and my boss, and whoever the hell else it concerns, to bring the light of freedom into the deep dark underworld we call a home."

There were several moments of silence from everyone, and even some stares from some nearby tables. The bony man stepped forward towards Jimmy, his red face attempting to square off with Jimmy's blazing eyes. The passion he felt defending Walter and Alison, and keeping the secret of the new recruit that may or may not work out made Jimmy feel alive. He felt like he was on fire with all of that adrenaline coursing through his veins. He didn't want to quit anymore. He wanted to fight. He wanted back in the game. He was the last wall of defense between his guys and this monster of a bureaucracy.

*If not me, then who?*

The problem was, this walking skeleton was probably about to fire him on the spot.

"Your passion never fails to both impress and upset me," said the bony man with slitted eyelids. "Partially because you're so fiery, and partially because I always seem to be on the receiving end of it. Keep fighting for the right thing, Mister Limone."

Jimmy was glad the bony man did not insult him by trying to shake his hand. Instead, the three members of the board of directors turned, washed their faces of their frustration, and made their way to other tables to continue their bureaucratic scheme.

It was the age-old issue of business. Money made the world go around. Money was the reason things happened. Money was the necessary evil that fueled the machine. Then came the workers. The people on the ground making the operations happen. The ones putting their lives on the line for people they had never met. The business people had no idea what that was like, and never understood what it really took to make the decisions of ground operations.

But it went both ways. Ground operators didn't get to see behind the scenes of business. They didn't see the public relations or the imaging problems that caused tensions like this. There was war going on everywhere, fighting for freedom in the field, and fuel in the office. That's why the board was important at this event, and Jimmy's team was important in the field. Everyone had their jobs they were good at, and no one understood anything else.

Jimmy sat down at the table and drained the remnants of his water glass, glaring around for a waiter to refill it. His eyes settle on Rebecca Swift beside him. She had a hand over her mouth, tight cheeks with dimples, and wide, bright eyes. Her body lurched from stifled laughter.

"Wonderful speech, Jimmy," she giggled. "Way to be non confrontational."

# <u>44</u>

*Claremore, Oklahoma - Saturday - 5:30 PM*
"Your wife makes the best food. I swear." Larry Bates raised his right hand in the air and dropped his left on the table like it was a Bible. "The truth, the whole truth, and nothing but the truth. So help me, God."

"What is the truth, Larry?" asked Joseph, glancing up from the last scraps on his plate. Mindy had made this, however sour and slow she was doing so, and it was good. She always made good food for friends, but never just for them. "You want action, you come incognito in the middle of the night. You have information, you come to dinner as a friend."

"Why not both?" Judge Bates pulled a wad of cash out of his pants pocket and rolled it across the table to Joseph. "There's enough in there for a small tip on top, you know? For being such a good friend all these years."

"It's nice to have friends high up," replied Joseph, staring down at the roll of cash. "And it doesn't get any more powerful than you. Again, you don't bring cash and information all at once. What's going on, Larry?"

"It really doesn't get much more powerful than me," laughed Larry Bates, his ego exploding from him like an overinflated balloon. "Which is why I'm here to tell you the police are onto you. I denied a search warrant for this house this morning. Someone gave a very detailed statement at the police station this morning. I couldn't find out who the source of the tip the police got a hold of was, but you might check who's coming and going. You have a lot of customers, and the two people living here know quite a bit."

"Mindy wouldn't say anything," growled Joseph. "I handled that already."

"How about Abigail?" asked the Judge.

"Not for sale anymore," mumbled Joseph. "If there's a leak, it's probably coming from there. I'm still working on that right now. She's found some boy she used to know from her childhood. A boyfriend she's now moved in with. I've tried to keep her here, but she's adamant. I knew it was futile when she joined the National Guard. I handled that, though, too. Put in the word at the base that she was worth a few extra dollars and got some business out of that. Now this boyfriend is going to ruin that flow for me. He even beat me up in the hotel parking lot yesterday. I'm still sore because of that. Now Abigail's got that idea into her head that she can fight me, too. She finally had enough and fought her way out of here last night."

"Is that what happened to your face?" asked Larry Bates.

Joseph nodded with a somber look on his face.

"You don't think they're working together?" asked the Judge. "If the boy beat you up, he has experience fighting. How much do you know about him?"

"Everything," muttered Joseph, staring hard into the table. "He grew up in Kansas City, killed a guy and his sister, spent some time in jail, and he's been living here ever since. He's actually a decent guy, working at the factory up in Tulsa. Good job, decent income. In another life, he'd make a great husband, just not for Abigail. I need the income too."

"He killed two people?" asked Larry.

Joseph waved his hand. "The sister was accidental, but he killed the man that was on top of her on purpose."

Larry Bates pondered the thought. "A special hatred for men like us."

Joseph nodded. "And he knows it's me."

"Does he have police connections?" asked Larry Bates.

Joseph glanced up. "He's working with undercover operatives to investigate me. I didn't realize until yesterday that it was him, but we had a run in and met face to face. He's the one that put the police onto me here at home. He's the one that turned Abigail. He's the threat."

Joseph shook his head, and sat back in his chair. "He's bringing his war to my homefront. Anyways, I had one of my guys follow him around, but had to push the blame off on Abigail after he got caught and brought in to the police. I tried to frazzle the organization by taking one of their kids, but the new boy stopped me and really beat the hell out of me. He's being trained, I guess, by some woman."

"Another woman?" asked Judge Bates. "What kind of woman?"

Joseph shrugged. "Tall, kind of built, and older. Not my type. She looked like a bodybuilder, or a fighter."

"I don't mind a fighter," said the Judge, "but tall women aren't my favorite. Abigail would be the exception to that, though. She's still so young and thin."

Larry sighed watching Joseph's face as Joseph continually glanced down to the wash of cash on the table. "You let me know when Abigail is back on the market. I will be your first customer. Until then, where's our girl?"

Joseph grabbed the cash from the table and rolled it in his palm. "Bedroom upstairs. She's not been prepped. I didn't know she had a friend coming tonight."

"That doesn't bother me," said the Judge. "I'll just adapt and overcome like always."

The roll of money went flying through the air, landing back in the Judge's surprised hand. Bates looked up at Joseph, who was staring again, off into oblivion, his brain grinding through a thinking process equivalent to a professional chess player.

"This one's on the house, Larry," he said under his breath. Bates had to lean forward to hear him. "Thanks for the warning."

Judge Bates stood up, rolling the cash in his fingers. He smiled at Joseph one more time before turning to leave the room.

"I'm always willing to pay, my friend," he said, staring across the table. "I need you in business anyways. I know how this works. If you go down, so do I. On top of that, Olivia's just my favorite little girl. I couldn't stand to lose access. I'll keep your operation safe as much as I can. No police will raid this place."

Moving away from the kitchen table, The Judge reached the hallway and paused for a moment. Joseph looked up.

"Do you want me to pay Abigail a visit?" The Judge asked. "I can straighten her out very quickly before I leave."

Joseph sat back in his chair, hands flat on the table as he chewed on his tongue.

"Yes," he said softly with a slight nod of his head. "She's not here right now, but when I get her back here in this house, you show her what it means to be a part of this."

Larry Bates simply shrugged, a clear smirk streaking across his face, and turned to continue up the stairs to pay a visit to Olivia.

# <u>*45*</u>

*Claremore, Oklahoma - Saturday - 7:30 PM*
"This is the worst part of it all," said Alison. "Absolute torture, if you ask me."

"We're just writing reports," said Charles. "I do this every time I have to repair a piece of damaged equipment at work. It's easy."

"Not in these quantities, it's not," said Alison. "In all seriousness, we spend more time doing paperwork than we do actually being a part of investigations."

"At least it gives us something to do while we wait," said Charles. "I'm not sure I could get much sleep with everything going down tonight."

"It's horrific," said Alison. "I need action, not paperwork."

Charles smiled. "Like a regular Liam Neeson."

Alison laughed out loud. "If only people knew the amount of paperwork guys like Liam Neeson and Jason Bourne had to do, they wouldn't watch those movies."

"Oh yeah?" asked Charles.

"Think about the first Bourne movie," started Alison, dropping her pen and clasping her hands together. "It starts with an assassination attempt, right?"

"A good way to start a movie."

"Exactly," continued Alison. "What you don't see is all the setup that an assassination attempt like that takes. It takes months to get everything together. Bourne had to set up an LLC as a boating business or whatever he had. Then he had to build a reputation with the locals. He had to blend in and become indiscernible from the population. That's how he got so close to his target. He didn't stand out as suspicious. Months and months of paperwork, and living a normal life, all for one night of action. That is the side of this job no one likes to talk about, because it doesn't make a good movie."

"Same thing with Liam Neeson?" asked Charles.

"What's Bond's main thing?" asked Alison. "A license to kill. Still, as a highly trained operative, he has to make some sort of judgment call about it, which means filing reports with his supervisor about why he pulled the trigger." Her eyes squinted. "Or didn't pull the trigger. Like Ian Fleming says, a license to kill is also a license not to kill. That's where the judgment comes in. Judgement calls get passed up the chain of command, and that's why Bond gets his ass chewed when he does something reckless."

Charles sighed. "Okay, you got me. Being Liam Neeson or Jason Bourne isn't that exciting in real life. Tell me, though, if you need action, why do you deal with all the paperwork just for one night of action?"

"Having night after night of action means I would have to be in combat," replied Alison. "Although, even most soldiers and law enforcement don't live a life of constant tension. No, that would put me as some sort of criminal, bank robber, or otherwise law breaker."

Charles couldn't help but smile.

Alison sighed, and looked out of the window of the tiny hotel room. "The reality is, I know what it's like to be rescued."

Charles set his own pen on the table in front of him, glancing at the window. The curtain was drawn over the glass, the deep crimson color of the fabric staring back at him. Alison continued to stare as he looked back at her, his eyes drawn to the bright reflective hazel rings that shined like neon lights. She blinked, shook her head, and returned her attention to him.

"I know what it's like to be in that room," she continued. "To be tied up, or chained. To be told no one cares, or that no one is coming to help. To be…" She hesitated. "To be broken in ways no one else can understand. You can talk about it all you want, but no one around you will understand what you're even talking about. They want to. They feel like they should or that they do understand. They imagine themselves in those situations, and try to picture how they would feel, but all they know is that they wouldn't feel good. They don't truly understand the misery behind that, because they've never been put through that misery. It's the kind of thing that you just kind of have to accept that people can't understand, and you don't really want them to understand because it would put them through the worst torture they've ever been through. One of those things that you really have to be fucked in the head to understand."

She looked up at him, the face of the fierce woman softer now, changed, and looked more like the face of the little girl she had once been. The little girl she could have been, but wasn't allowed to be.

"On top of that," she continued. "You have to be able to accept that those people that can't understand will do anything to try to understand, will fall short, and will say and do the wrong things to make up for it."

Charles nodded. "That part I can relate to."

"It's a curse I wouldn't wish on anyone," Alison muttered. "It's a curse I can help people come out of because I'm one of the few that really does understand it. It's a curse that I can help people enter recovery from because I know what it's like to recover from it. Being able to do that gives me a good feeling. Beyond all the action and the violence, and the adrenaline rush from the risks we take, that feeling when I get to see those boys and girls walk away with the recovery team and taste freedom for the first time in most of their lives… That feeling makes all the tedious paperwork worth it."

She leaned across the table, putting one of her hands on top of his free hand. It sent a shiver up the rest of his arm and down his spine. He felt his eyes widen unwillingly at her warm touch. *Warm hands; warm heart.*

"I hope you get to feel that when this is over," she continued. "I hope you get to see the little girl recover. Once you feel that, you'll never leave this job. Not for money, or love, or anything else. That feeling saps all those emotions out of you and makes you want to keep moving on. It makes you want to fight."

Charles squeezed her hand gently, his face tightening as the question came to his mind. "Have you ever been able to love since you were rescued?"

She stared at him. The thought buzzed in his head like a lingering wasp. *Not for money, or love.* Could someone feel love after a life like that? Was it possible? Like Abigail's life. Could Abigail love him after all that, or was he just the escape she needed to get away? She had tried to escape with the National Guard, and now she was trying to escape with him. Did she really love him?

"Walter," said Alison. "But not romantically. I'm not sexually attracted to him. He's like the family I never had, the one that never would have abandoned me here in the states. No one else in my life has done anything to earn real romantic love from me, like in the movies. I'm not even sure that kind of love even exists."

He really didn't want to ask. It was one of those wrong things to say, but he had to know. *Abigail.* This was his only outlet to find out what she really felt. Was it all real for him, or was Abigail just trying to escape her old life?

"Are you sexually attracted to anyone? Are you able to feel that?" His mind trailed off to Abigail, her body against his, the feeling of being inside of her, the feeling of kissing her and touching her. Did his touch do nothing but remind her of past customers. Was he really the love of her life, or just another 'friend'?

"I don't know," she whispered, her fingers clenching on his hand. "Sometimes I wonder, when I see someone, if I find them attractive or not. I don't think about it very often, but sometimes I try to imagine what I would want to do with them. Most of the time I can't seem to figure anything out. It always ends in violence. It always ends with both of us getting hurt. I just can't seem to help it."

He wanted to help her. He wanted to hold her. Her eyes glistened, lines forming where tears flooded but refused to fall. Her lips trembled; her voice cracked. Her grip on his hands intensified.

"Charles," she whispered. "I wish it were easier for me. I really do. I just don't know how. I see the way Walter looks at Katie, and the way Katie looks back at him. I want that, but I'm just not sure how it works. It's so hard to trust after all that. You have no idea."

*I have an inkling.* But no, that would be the wrong thing to say, like one of those people that just had to understand.

All he wanted was to help, and there wasn't a way he could do it. She was older, much older, a half of a decade older than he was and twice as traumatized as he had been. He was small, weak, inexperienced in life. He had nothing to offer her.

No. He could do one thing. One thing that kept the bond between himself and Abigail, but created another different bond with Alison.

"Alison," he said gently, squeezing her hand back. "We're a team now. Whatever risks we'll be taking on, we'll take them on together. From here on out, we have to trust each other, no matter how difficult that is or how frustrated we get with each other. Our lives are going to be in each other's hands, and it's up to us to have each other's backs. We told each other our pasts, and we've done field work together. Moving forward, I will put my trust in you, if you'll put your trust in me."

*That was the right thing to say.*

Alison looked up, staring at him apprehensively. "So, we're married now?"

Charles sat back, shaking his head. At least he could say he tried. "I don't see a preacher anywhere. Maybe one of those 'get married quick' places will still be open."

Alison laughed. "You're a little young for me, aren't you? Besides, you don't have the patience for all this chaos that is Alison Rotskoya, and you already have a girlfriend. You are right, though. Going forward, we have to work together. That means we have to be able to count on each other to have our backs. That trust comes with the responsibility and accountability of having someone's life in your hands. I will put my trust in you. Until death do us part."

"Don't say it like that," said Charles, trying not to smile. "I thought you said I wasn't your type."

She smiled at him. "I don't even know if I have a type. Do you?"

Charles thought about what he would like to do with Alison if he were given the chance. Large, strong, tall. A powerful woman that wanted to be in control. A woman that didn't mind taking what she wanted, the type of woman that wasn't afraid of anything, and had that extra confidence. That could be his type.

Maybe tall, thin, and tight bodied. A meek and mild academic that could still hold her own in a fight, but loved with every ounce of her being. Abigail really was his type.

*Young.* The girl at the restaurant. He had known she was young, albeit without knowing she was underage. He knew she was too young for him, and he still had some form of hunger. The same hunger that he felt for the *Teen* category on the bookmarked website on his phone. That girl was fourteen. The ones online were only four or five years older than that, and he was in his mid twenties. *Young. Fresh.* Was that his type? Too young to play? His age? Older? All three? Was he concerned with age and looks, or was he so desperate for love and attention that he would take anything he could get? The fourteen year old girl, the girls in the videos, Abigail, Alison… Was there a type? The categories page of the adult website came to mind again, the endless list of types of women scrolling for what felt like an eternity. He'd been in every category over the years. He'd seen them all. Did he have a favorite?

Or had it grown into an addiction? Had he become a junkie that took whatever he could get at the time? Would he just take whatever it took to get a fix? Old or young. It didn't matter as long as they were willing.

Or was that even a requirement?

He shook his head, trying to clear his head. *No. Not true. You are not a monster.*

"I'm not sure I know what my type is, either."

"Your girlfriend," laughed Alison. "Tall and skinny."

Alison never seemed to consider herself in the list of attractive women. Charles wished he could change that. He wanted to show her that she was worthy of love. He wanted to show her that she was worth caring about. She deserved that much. She earned it after everything she had done.

He leaned forward in his chair. Alison matched his movement, coming closer. Their eyes met, and she froze in place. Her eyes flickered down to his lips, reminiscent of Abigail at his apartment. She inched backwards, her eyes widening just the slightest degree. *Fear.*

Images of a young Alison, restrained and beaten to a pulp, rose in his mind. The face of the little girl he was seeing now, scared and hopeless, etched itself in his mind. He sat back, and she did the same. Their hands separated and returned to their respective pen and paper.

"We have a lot of time together as partners," said Alison, clearing her throat. "Maybe we can help each other figure it out along the way." She smiled up at him. "Anyways, try not to sound like Liam Neeson when you fill out your reports. He's always too vague with his fancy one liners and mysterious quotes. I see it a lot in Jimmy's paperwork where he wants to sound as cool as possible. Just keep it simple and factual."

She was interrupted by a knock at the door. Both of them sat up straight, exchanging looks, wherein Alison pointed to him.

"It's your hotel room," she whispered. "You answer the door. If someone bursts in, I'll jump in once they've cleared the door."

"Short, simple, and factual," he whispered back with a smile. "Take up a spot in the bathroom. It'll give you the advantage. I'll let them push me in and back so we can attack from both sides."

Alison nodded. "Looks like you're no stranger to the action."

*Jump right to action.* There were only a handful of people that knew where Charles was staying, but neither of them wanted to take that chance. It almost made him smile. *We're just alike, the two of us. Always ready.*

She slipped into the bathroom with no hesitation, her feet never seeming to touch the ground and making absolutely no noise at all. Charles waited for her to vanish, and made his way to the door. He squinted through the peephole first, seeing a cloud of grey filled with pale flesh below it. He smiled, and cracked the door open.

"Paul Edwards?"

"I hadn't thought about setting up an identity challenge earlier," Paul said. "Do you know what that is?"

"Sexual deviants call them safe words," said Charles, opening the door for the old man.

Charles stepped away from the door, and Paul entered the room, stopping at the bathroom door to look in at Alison. He nodded at her. "Miss Rotskoya." He made his way into the miniature hotel room. Charles noticed Paul do a double take of the room, his eyes scanning the tiny Microtel with intense amazement.

It was the absolute bare minimum. A tiny, sub four hundred square foot studio room with a single queen bed against a dull wall, and a chair in front of a desk just barely big enough for a laptop. The window to the right of the bed was large and the colorful curtains kept the room contained and dark. There was a lamp on one side of the bed, and a phone on the other. There wasn't even a clock on the shelf next to the bed.

Paul Edwards turned to Charles with a perplexed look on his face.

Charles shrugged. "It was sixty five bucks after taxes and fees. I'm not complaining about a damn thing."

"I'm just wondering why you're here in Claremore and not at home in Tulsa," he said. "It's only a half hour drive to save yourself sixty bucks."

"We're all together here," said Charles. "No reason to split up the team. Plus I'd have to get up earlier to get here and meet with everyone. It's just quicker and easier to stay here. It's just one day."

Charles believed his own words, but he missed Abigail. At the most difficult point in her life, when she had to turn on her family and rely on others to save her sister, she was alone at the apartment. He couldn't help his desire to join her; to hold her.

*One more day.*

Paul jutted out his lips like a duck and nodded. "Okay. Now let's talk about why I'm here."

Alison came out of the bathroom, and the three of them gathered around the single queen bed.

"I'm assuming this means something didn't go as planned today?" she asked.

Paul shook his head. "Something like that. I visited the Judge to speed up the warrant process, and he lost his shit about this whole Joseph thing. He says the Smiths are and always have been good people. He went so far as to offer to ask over dinner at the Smiths's house tonight."

Charles sucked in air through his teeth. "So he's in on it, then?"

Paul blinked hard, and guffawed. "That's a hell of an assumption to make about a district judge."

Charles shrugged again. "Did he mention being friends since they were kids?"

Paul nodded.

"Then he's either biased toward Joseph, or he's in on it. Either way, we're not getting that warrant." Charles looked over at Alison. "Agreed?"

Alison nodded. "He sounds kind of crazy, but he's probably right. Judges don't just deny warrants like that with drastic statements and police reports like the one Abigail made today.”

“He said it was a stubborn and disagreeable step child looking to get her parents in trouble,” said Paul.

“Abigail is in her twenties,” said Charles. “She hardly counts as a child. That's a terrible argument.”

“That's what I thought,” said Paul. “Verbatim. He said women of all ages make false accusations all the time.”

Alison hissed. “But now we have a bigger problem. We have to assume he's going to dinner to warn Joseph.”

“That means we have to assume Joseph is going to hurt those women,” continued Charles.

“More likely he'll run,” said Alison. “If he does anything at all. He's probably certain that the Judge can block it, but if he's convinced that there's something coming, he'll clean the house like Charles said. He'll hide any trace that the girl is there. He'll stay up all night to take care of it.”

Paul shook his head. “Legally, there's nothing we can do about it. We risk way too much just barging in there to save them.” He glanced at Charles. “He has a judge on his side, and if we're sounding crazy, there's no reason to think there's not a police officer or two there, as well.”

Charles thought about the police chief that had spoken to him earlier that day. Tom Leonard. The man with all the questions. He thought about the ten year career the man had.

"Then we're stuck," Charles mumbled. "The police chief was asking me all sorts of questions today."

Alison turned to him. "Chief Leonard. He was bugging me, too."

"Leonard?" asked Paul, his face tilting in confusion. "He's been the Chief out here for more than a decade."

"That doesn't strike you as odd?" asked Charles.

Paul shrugged. "As far as I know, his record is clean. I've only been Chief of Tulsa for a few years, but I know Tom. He's cocky, but straight."

"He asked a lot about Abigail," said Alison. She looked at Charles. "He spoke to you."

"He wanted to know where I was staying," said Charles. "Where I lived, too."

"Did you tell him?" asked Paul.

Charles shook his head. "No. What is Joseph going to do with the girls?"

"Olivia, he'll keep," nodded Alison. "He needs that revenue. Does he know Abigail is the one that said something?"

Paul shook his head. "I dissuaded him from that, but it's not hard to sniff out. He only has two other people he can blame it on. His wife and his step daughter. Which one would you think of first?"

"The one that escaped," muttered Charles. "I sent Abigail back to my apartment, though. She'll be safe there, as long as no one figures out where I live."

"We have a meeting with the mom tonight at nine at the Hampton on the south end of town," muttered Abigail. "We get her confession, take her into protective custody in Tulsa so the dirty cops can't get her, and finish this. You can hide one testimony. It gets a whole lot harder to hide two of them."

"So what do we do?" asked Charles. "Wait until then? They're probably having dinner right now, and talking about us."

"What do you want to do?" asked Paul.

Charles thought about it. *Charge into the house, take out Joseph, and get the girls out of there.* Violent, but foolproof.

*How often do things go according to plan?* He thought of a car chase in Kansas City ten years ago. No. Things never went according to plan, because the plan never accounted for other people's decisions. Nothing was ever foolproof.

What if Joseph decided to kill everyone the second Charles kicked the door in? What if Charles never made it to the door? What if the crooked cops and Judge were waiting for him when he got there? There were just too many variables to account for.

"We have no choice but to wait," he sighed deeply, actually trying to convince himself. "It's too risky any other way, isn't it?"

Alison put a hand on his shoulder. "We aren't vigilantes. That's not what we do. I feel the same drive to be a superhero, but all it does is put everyone in more danger."

"It didn't work for me the last time I tried it," mumbled Charles. "Maybe it's best. Maybe he'll show mercy. They'll all recover from whatever he does, I guess, unless he kills them."

"He has a cop, and a Judge on his side," said Alison. "He's not killing anyone. Not yet."

Charles could say whatever he wanted to himself. It didn't change the fact that everyone in that household could die.

*He needs the income.* If Joseph killed anyone in that house, it would take away everything he worked for. It was too much work to kill them. Disposing of the bodies, and covering up? He could hurt them, but he couldn't kill them. Fear: the most powerful motivator. Pain: the most effective implementation of fear. *They'll recover from whatever he does to them.*

They would be safe for one more night.

"Just a couple more hours," said Alison. "If we don't hear from the mother by then, we have cause to do a wellness check on the house. We keep the chief and judge out of the loop until the job is done if we have to."

"I can handle the judge," said Paul. "I'll go again, first thing in the morning, to hold him off. With any luck, the police chief will be busy elsewhere, otherwise we'll have to get clever."

Alison's phone rang, and she answered it without looking, holding the phone out in front of her as she pressed the speaker button. "Walt?"

"You knew it was me?" Walter's voice echoed in the small hotel room on the speaker phone.

"There aren't many people that have my number," replied Alison. "One of them is in this room. How are things in Tulsa?"

"Jimmy had it out with the board," said Walter. "From what I hear, it was a big one. I really wish I was there to see it happen. We're under the microscope now. Where are you guys?"

"Claremore," replied Alison.

Walter took a moment, and sighed over the phone. "Where in Claremore? I know about as much as Jimmy and Rebecca do."

"The Microtel," she said without hesitation. "I'll give you the room number when you get here." She paused. "Are you coming, or staying in Tulsa?"

"I'm staying here in Tulsa," mumbled Walter. "I can't leave Katie and Kitsen. They aren't safe here. We have a new hotel room just in case, but… I'm just worried."

"We've got it handled down here, Walter," said Paul. "You don't have to worry about anything. Take care of your family."

"You guys are my family, too," muttered Walter.

Alison glanced at Charles. "We have everything tied up here. We're running into some obstacles, but we have contingencies in place to make up for it. It's all done tomorrow. We're just down to playing the waiting game overnight."

Charles dropped his eyes. *Waiting.* He stepped over to the window, flung the curtain open, and stared out into the sunset. "Now we just wait."

Walter had avoided speaking to or about Charles. He hadn't given out the new hotel number. He hadn't even mentioned Charles's name. Charles wasn't even sure if he was included when Walter had said they were his family as well. *Waiting. Waiting on everything.*

There were a few moments of silence, and Paul stepped up to the window next to Charles. "You know I worked for the Red Sea Initiative for a while before getting into police work?"

Charles nodded his head. "Early on, when it had just been founded."

"I was a police officer for fifteen years," said Paul. "Mostly undercover drug and prostitution stings. I took off early, and came to the Red Sea Initiative with an ex CIA guy named Walter Faucet who wanted to change the world."

"Walter was CIA?" asked Charles.

"Not necessarily," replied Paul. "He was Homeland Security."

Paul Edwards took a deep breath. "One of my first operations was in Matamoros, Mexico. It's down at the most southern part of Texas, right in the point. Across the border from Brownsville. Anyways, in order to get the information I needed, I had to pose as a 'John', the customer, and go see where the brothel was at and try to get a count of the children and the working conditions. Once we have that, then the police can move in and finish up. Everything went really well, including the fact that the girl I paid for just talked openly with me about her business. I got all the information I needed without really having to fake anything. In the end, we don't use children, obviously. I would normally just say that I was scared and couldn't go through with it, and put on this whole acting game. A 'you keep my secret and I'll keep yours' kind of thing.

Pay the girl for her trouble, maybe some extra for keeping my secret, and be on my way."

Paul let out a sigh. "Anyways, there's always this moment, while you're in that room, where you start to wonder. 'I could take her, right now, and leave. We could escape right now.' It's incessant. You plan your escape routes, you run through all of your hand to hand training, and you start to mentally prepare yourself for the fight. Then you stare at that child, and you think about the danger that puts her in, not to mention the others. You think about the stray bullets, or the violence that she has to witness to execute that plan. That's when you come to the realization."

Charles glanced over at Paul. "What realization?"

More silence. A dramatic effect of waiting done masterfully in storytelling.

"The realization that you have to leave her there," said Paul. "That you aren't Liam Neeson, or Liam Neeson, or whoever else. You're just you, and if you start a fight like that, more people are going to get hurt than necessary. So I looked down at that little girl in Matamoros, Mexico, and I thanked her for keeping my secret and apologized for being such a scaredy cat, and I did the hardest thing I've ever had to do in my life."

Charles nodded, the slow realization creeping up on him. "You let the next customer have his turn."

If Paul Edwards was breathing, Charles couldn't hear it. "He walked in as I walked out. I held the door for him and told him what a great time it was. I told him to enjoy it."

Paul's voice cracked, and he reached up and ran the heels of his palms across his eyes. "The point is, at some point, the hardest decision you have to make is the one that's going to save more lives. This is just how we do things. This is how the real world works."

Paul patted Charles on the back and stepped away from the window, leaving Charles to stew on his own thoughts. *Waiting. Waiting. Waiting.* His future depended on whether those girls survived. His future depended on Abigail.

He was stuck. Her family was in danger, and he was stuck. The instinct to protect them surged in him, and he thought of Emily. He thought about the gun in his hands; the bullet he'd fired. The single bullet that had taken everything from him. His life, his family, and his future. *Better off waiting.* The girls would be tortured, and he was stuck in a hotel.

*Torture.* Alison was wrong. Paperwork and reports were easy. *This* was the hardest and most torturous part of the job.

*Waiting...*

# <u>46</u>

*Claremore, Oklahoma - Saturday - 8:00 PM*

Quiet in the house. Silence. A wife that had betrayed him was now sleeping in their bed, a bed that he had bought and provided for her, and soiling it with the impurity of her choices. A step daughter, unstable and uncontrollable, violently escaping and leaving him literally flat faced and scarred. She had done that even after the life and home he had provided for her for ten years.

*Ungrateful bitches.* All three of them. They did nothing but complain, fight, and run, and yet he continued to provide for them. What did that say about him?

*A good husband. A good father.* He provided for them. He spent so much time finding customers just to pay the bills. It all had to be done incognito; it all had to be done under the radar. He spent so much time dealing with the problems that those girls caused. They had beds, they had a house to live in, and they had food. So they had to work for it? That was the price of the world. Everyone pulled their weight. Joseph kept the secrets, Joseph worked the public side, and Joseph was the base of the operation. What little work they did compared to him was nothing. They had nothing to complain about, yet they still did.

But they kept their mouths shut in public. They never said anything negative about their home life or anything else while around other people. Olivia had it the easiest; she was never allowed around other people in order to talk in the first place. The world didn't even know she existed. *That* was hard enough to manage. The other two kept quiet, like Mindy was currently doing, because they knew better.

The most powerful motivator in human history was always fear. Properly employed, ruthlessly employed, it was the best form of control.

*It is much safer to be feared than loved because love is preserved by the link of obligation which, owing to the baseness of men, is broken at every opportunity for their advantage; but fear preserves you by a dread of punishment which never fails.*

An old quote from an old book Joseph had memorized in grade school. Wise words that applied to his business. Running a kingdom; the subject of the book. That's all Joseph was doing, running a kingdom. Tonight, the kingdom was quiet.

Except for the world of chaos that was beginning to descend upon him.

That peace rudely got interrupted by knocking at the front door, then a return to silence. A visitor. *A Friend?* Customers were not often allowed at the house. Hotels only, but special treatment for those willing to pay the Hazard Fee that went with the risk of having work done here at home. The risk of exposure. The girls were already expensive enough, but that Hazard Fee…

*Charles motherfucking Langley.* It could be the boy coming to fight for the two left in the house. It could be rogue police officers not wanting to wait for a signed warrant to come through.

*It could be anyone.*

He rose from his chair in the living room and made his way to the front door. Larry's warning rang in Joseph's head. *The police are onto you. I stopped the warrant.* That didn't mean someone couldn't come snooping. That didn't mean that Charles didn't feel like being the hero. At this hour of night, it only meant trouble was standing on the other side of a three inch thick barrier.

A quick peek through the peephole gave him an idea of who it was. A tall, bulky man, broad in the chest and shoulders and with a fading buzz cut running up the sides of his head. A tight, short sleeve t-shirt that reminded Joseph of a college athlete showing off his physique.

Joseph opened the door and greeted the man. "It's strange seeing both you and the Judge at my house in the same night. I'm starting to wonder if I shouldn't go into hiding."

"Joseph?" asked Police Chief Tom Leonard, with more than a little distress in his voice. The big man smiled, knowing the process of what he was doing. Information in exchange for pleasure. "I have some information that you'll like to know about my girl."

"She gave a statement about me at the police station?" asked Joseph. "Larry told me he shut that warrant down."

"I'm sure he did," said Tom Leonard. "I have good news, though."

Joseph tilted his head to the side. "I could really use some good news."

Tom Leonard laughed. "The boyfriend wouldn't tell me his address, or where he was staying. I figure that means that she's there and he's protecting her. He told me I had all the things I needed to get his information without him."

Joseph cocked an eyebrow. "And?"

"So I used my resources," chuckled Tom Leonard. "I found out where he lives. I got his address in Tulsa. Wanna go scare the shit out of them?"

Joseph let out a sigh of relief. "I have to stay here and keep a close eye on the other two. You can handle her, can't you?"

Tom Leonard smirked. "I can handle both of them."

# <u>47</u>

*Tulsa, Oklahoma - Saturday - 8:00 PM*
Walter Faucet sat down at the table, setting a styrofoam container filled with fried chicken and waffles off to his left. Kitsen stared down at the plate, totally uninterested.

"Come on, Kitsen," said Walter. "You like chicken and waffles. What's the matter?"

Kitsen looked up at her father. "Daddy, who was the guy that saved me the other day?"

Walter sat back in his chair at the desk and stared at his daughter on the hotel bed. He'd been avoiding that conversation, that memory, for as long as he could. "Why?"

"I didn't ever get to say thank you. I was scared, and you were yelling. When I wasn't scared, he was already gone. I want to meet him again so I can thank him. Is he one of your Mega guys?"

Walter smiled at her mispronunciation of his undercover teams. His real baby didn't really know or care much about his other baby.

He had called his NGO The Red Sea Initiative because the Red Sea in the Bible was the only thing that stood in between the Egyptian slaves and their captors. It swept the brutal slave owners away, and that was what his organization did. He called his undercover operators Omega Team because they were the last thing that most human traffickers had to deal with before being captured. That, and it sounded cool when he talked about it for interviews and seminars.

*The conference.* He had forgotten the conference. He tried to picture Jimmy talking nicely to the board of directors, and could only come up with a mental image of how he felt every time he had to personally face the board. Jimmy Limone, wearing a roman belted tunic, holding a broadsword, and fighting a three headed hydra. He tried hard not to laugh at that one.

He knew Jimmy had it handled, though. If anyone could take on the hydra and win, it was that man. Walter just wished he had been there to see it happen.

And Walter was here in the hotel room, hiding from his responsibilities, and having breakfast with his daughter. *What have I become?*

"Daddy?" He shook his head and focused back on his daughter. "Can I meet him again? I want to say thank you. That other guy was hurting me, and your guy saved me."

Walter looked into Kitsen's sweet, baby blue eyes that sparkled, and sighed. He had not given much thought to Charles the last several days. He wanted to avoid thinking of what Charles had done to get Kitsen kidnapped. Charles handed his girlfriend all the information she needed to have her stepfather infiltrate the hotel and hurt Katie. To hurt Kitsen.

The other images followed. Charles, stepping into the hotel lobby, shaking off a fistfight like he'd just gone for a brisk walk, and carrying the six year old girl in his arms to her father. The good man, who hadn't meant to give that information away to the wrong people. The man who had done everything in his power, even risking his own life, to make it right.

If Charles survived this mission and training with Alison, then Walter didn't have much choice in the matter. Kitsen Faucet's word was law around here.

"Yes," he said. "You can meet him, and thank him."

Kitsen jumped with joy. "So he is a Mega Man?"

"Yes, Kitsen. He's one of my guys."

# <u>48</u>

*Tulsa, Oklahoma - Saturday - 8:00 PM*
*One more night.* She just had to survive one more night, and all this would be over. She could take Olivia, and maybe even her mother, and start a new life. Maybe she could start a life with Charles. Maybe she could work with him and Alison. Maybe she could do something to change the world. She could do whatever she wanted to.

All she had to do was make it one more night.

She kept a small journal, a new one that she had gotten today on the way here. It was a recommendation from a friend many years ago that had helped her through the major events of her life.

Two words so far. *Charles Langley.* The man she loved more than anything. No longer just a way to escape her past life, but a way to create a new future. A way to change her life for the better. A way to find love. Two words written in red ink like streaks of blood.

All she needed to do now was convince him to keep loving her. He cared, that much she knew, but his love for her felt ruined. She could see it in his eyes. That look of disdain, like her body had soiled what innocence he'd had left. Like she'd stolen something from him. She wanted to earn that back. She wanted to make things better. She wanted to say two words to make everything okay. Two words that she added to Charles's name in the journal.

*Marry me.* Words written over and over again on the page, words she hoped telepathically reached Charles's subconsciousness and influenced him via the power of manifestation. *Start a new life together and fight the evils of human trafficking side by side.*

*Adversity.* She and Charles just had to overcome that. There was no shortage of it between them, but that journey began tomorrow. All she had to do was wait for all that to begin.

The glass sliding door on her left shattered, the drawn curtain flowing outward as a shape blasted into the dim room. Abigail leapt to her feet and spun around, the pen and journal dropping onto the couch and bouncing on the cushions. She stared at the broken entry to the room, wide eyed and tense, her heart thumping loudly in her ears.

One man stood in the room with her, a man she knew all too well. A nightmare came true with a face curled into a scowl so horrible that he looked inhuman.

Chief of Police Tom Leonard stood behind Joseph in her doorway, a smile reaching across his face from ear to ear. Her first customer; her first Friend.

"Little girl!" boomed Tom Leonard from across the room. "You will never guess what brand new information I learned today. I'd like you to hear it as well, although you probably already know it."

Abigail gulped loudly. Her heart pounded in her chest, and sweat beads gathered all across her body. The nightmare…

Tom stepped into Charles's living room, leaving the curtain over the glass door billowing wide open behind him, but blocking her escape. That front door was locked, and Tom could clear the space between himself and her before she could get out. Abigail didn't dare look at the bedroom. A two story drop wouldn't feel too nice on her legs.

*It would feel nicer than whatever he's going to do to you.*

"Something came across my desk today," said Tom Leonard. "Something huge for the town of Claremore. I didn't realize we had a human trafficking network here in town. A whole report from the last several years. I didn't see my own name in it, though, which is both a good thing, and a bad thing. Come on, Abby, did I make such a fleeting expression on you? That's okay, though, because I'm not sure what happened to that report, but it never got filed. Doesn't even look like it made it to my desk."

Abigail's stomach dropped inside of her. The report went nowhere, and she was trapped in here with this monster. She was going to face her punishment all alone.

"The judge also came by your daddy's house today," sighed Tom loudly. "Had dinner there with an old friend. He says that the police department applied for a warrant to search his house. His house.

Can you imagine? The Judge denied the warrant. He told the police they were crazy for assuming we had anything illegal going on there in Claremore. Judge Bates is an old friend, you know, just like me."

Tom shuffled deeper into the room, and Abigail stepped to the side, closer to the bedroom. She hissed, realizing she'd cut herself off from the best exit out of fear. *No escape.*

"He and I do make pretty good friends, don't we?" laughed Tom. "Sad to say I missed him tonight. He and I could have had fun together with our girls. We could take turns or something like that. Maybe one at the same time. First Olivia, and then you. Have the two of you ever had that before?"

Abigail's breath caught in her throat. She leaned down as Tom came closer into the room with her, placing her hands on the kitchen counter in case she needed something to push off of. *The bedroom window. It's a double pane. Hard to break. No escape.*

"Probably not the little one," said Tom, coming closer. "You, though," he smacked his lips, "you've had it all. I bet Joseph has made so much money off of you. You're the one that's paid most of his bills and debt. Did you know that? I can't believe you want to leave us."

Abigail did not move. Could she break the glass in the bedroom window if she had to? Was it locked shut? She knew it was not easy to break window glass. They were flexible, built to withstand storm force winds. Not something that her bodyweight, maybe just over one hundred thirty or one hundred forty pounds, could force its way through.

Tom shook his head, his face saddening. "Abby, you don't want to leave me, do you?"

*Cornered. No escape.* She was trapped. A critter caught in a cage and brought home to slaughter. A critter facing certain doom. An animal with only one option left. *Fight. You have to fight.*

"You were asked a question," growled Tom. "Answer me. Do you really want me to leave, Abby? I thought we had something special."

"I…" Something burned deep within Abigail. The rules dictated that she accept Tom. Her past, the creature of habit inside of her, wanted to comply. *Inside of her.* The man wanted to be there, hurting her both inside and out.

Another man wanted to be there, too, a better man. A man that didn't want to hurt her at all. He didn't just want to be inside of her. He cared about her. She couldn't, she just couldn't, let Tom Leonard, or anyone else, have her anymore. It was unacceptable. She had to remain herself for Charles.

*Marry me.* Words on paper now murmured in her head. If she wanted that to happen, she had to keep herself persevered for him. She had to stop this here and now.

"I want you gone," she whispered. "Get out."

Tom hissed like a snake. "Abigail, you can't think this is going to work. You and Charles, just running off together. Leaving us? Leaving your mother? Leaving your little baby sister?"

"You don't control me anymore," Abigail said. "I am my own woman now. I am allowed to have a future."

"You have a future," said Tom. "At home with your family."

"No." Abigail stepped back away from him, into the kitchen, *a knife,* creating distance in case she needed the extra time. "My future is what I say it is. You don't get any control anymore."

"My girl is growing up," laughed Tom, coming deeper into the room and circling to the side of the bar like a shark.

Abigail took another step backwards, bumping into the stove against the wall and rattling everything on top. "Get away. This is my house now. You don't get to bark orders. You get to do what you're told, or you get to face the consequences."

She sucked air through her teeth, baring her well kept whites like an angry dog. *One option left.* Tom Leonard still moved to her right, creeping slowly like a hunting tiger. She took a step towards the bar to get away from him.

"You know," chuckled Tom, shaking his head. "It looks like the two of us are going to have to work this out ourselves. I'm tired. Exhausted, really. Let's just get this over with."

Tom shot her a wicked smile. He continued moving towards her, and she placed her hands on the stovetop and launched herself over the kitchen range and the bar. She came down on the tile opposite the kitchen, right next to the door. She has time. She could unlock it and run.

*No escape. It doesn't end if you run. He will catch you, just like he caught you tonight. Your only option is to fight.*

"Come on over here, little girl," teased Tom, coming back around into the front room.

A fire burned in her chest, the fire for Charles, and the fire for freedom. *I am not a little girl.* Something glittered in the low light from the couch cushion. Thin and round. *The ink pen.* Her beloved source of comfort, and the only voice she'd ever been able to have until now.

*I am a woman.* Power. She had power. She remembered the first time Tom Leonard had cornered her in her room, the puppy that had been stolen from her, and the happiness that had gone with it. Abigail fumed over the things that had been stolen from her; over the life that had been stolen from her; over the things her sister had gone through.

*No more.*

"Come here, girl," moaned Tom Leonard, stepping away from the wall and coming towards her. "I can't promise not to hurt you, but I'll promise you'll live through it."

She stepped towards him, maintaining eye contact with Tom and stepping away from the door. *There is no other way.* She circled around the room, Tom Leonard prowling in her direction until the backs of her legs bumped against the edge of the couch.

*No. I am not a little girl. I am a woman.* The life she'd lost in the past flashed before her eyes, long nights crying in her bed in that house and on her bunk at the National Guard bases. Multiple men a day. *Multiple men at a time.* Thousands of friends. Thousands of little cuts. Thousands of little bleeding orifices that opened up wide to allow the shedding of her old skin.

That little girl was dead.

*I am a woman.* She had everything she needed now. The power to control. The power to change things. The answer sat on a cushion behind her. For Olivia, for her mother, *for herself.* She didn't have time to wait until tomorrow for Charles to rescue her. She couldn't contact him. She was on her own; the animal that was backed into a corner.

*No. The Lioness.* No more little girls. No more games. No more playing. This was going to end right here.

Tom Leonard stepped forward again, his eyes locked with hers. "Look, Abby, my little three holed wonder, it all comes full circle. The spot you probably took that little boy's virginity, didn't you? Did you do it here? Did he fuck you on this couch? Was he as big as I am? Did he fill you up like I do?"

She stumbled back onto the couch, plopping down in the spot she hoped for. Her fist squeezed the pen. Her arms shook. She held the gaze, her lips puckering, her eyes filling with tears, her breath trembling. She inhaled.

*I am a woman, and this is a new beginning.*

"Just like the last time," growled Tom Leonard, his hands creeping up to Abigail's throat. His fingers dug deep into the flesh at her neck, ruining her future with Charles. She could feel his hot breath on her lips as his face inched closer to her. He was kneeling down to face her, staring into her eyes. "I'm going to choke you, and not with my hands. If you do it really well, and swallow everything like a good girl, I'll let you breathe. Do you like the sound of that challenge, Abby? If you survive that, I'm going to… what's the word for it?"

He squinted. His voice sounded like it was full of gravel. "Sodomize you. The best part is, there's no one here to save you."

Her arm shot up in a flash. Her hand turned over, aiming the tip of the pen and pressing on the back with her thumb. Tom Leonard's eyes grew to the size of dollar coins, his jugular vein opening up with the impact of the weapon.

"I don't need anyone to save me." The words left her throat in a guttural snarl. Her spare hand slid up his torso, where she placed a hand on his chest. "I'm not a little girl."

She pushed back with both of her hands, one shoving on his chest, the other dragging the tip of the pen along the inside of his neck and throwing him off balance. His hands released her neck, reaching for his own throat as Abigail yanked the pen from the side of his neck. She watched the color of Charles's walls change with the arterial spray jetting the contents of Tom Leonard's body in all directions. He choked, his fingers unable to provide enough pressure to staunch the massive flow of blood spilling out of him.

He stumbled towards her, dropping to his knees. One hand reached out, and she caught it, supporting him just enough to force him to maintain eye contact with her. His bloodied hand grasped for her clothes, still looking to tear them free of her one last time, and unable to gather the strength. She stood up and stared down at him, watching his eyes flicker, the rage turning to indecision, then to terror.

Abigail Smith looked down at Tom Leonard, standing over him for the first time in her life. Standing there with the power to control what happened to him. For the first time in recollection, she had the power to control her own life.

"Look at me," she growled like an angry leopard. She grabbed his face, drawing it up to where she could see his eyes. "You belong to me, now. I make the rules, and what I say goes."

He gagged on blood, coughing a mouthful into her face. She neither flinched, nor retreated. She dropped him, letting him fall to his back. He choked, spewing blood from his mouth like a geyser. His eyes flooded with tears, pleading with Abigail to help, to show mercy. She would do neither of those things. She would watch.

Then it happened. His face changed. His eyes became empty and glazed over like a camera that had been turned off. She had seen death in movies, and this was not it. Living human eyes couldn't help but fixate. These eyes were stuck in place; they followed nothing and saw nothing. The muscles in his face relaxed, a look of sheer indifference creeping over his countenance. Tom Leonard didn't care about anything anymore.

Tom Leonard was dead.

She glanced down at the pen in her hand, globs of crimson dripping from its end. Like a leaky faucet the pen shed the filthy remnants of her last encounter with a man she hated. She took a deep breath. Once, in a room far away, Tom Leonard had emptied his bodily fluids into her. He had done it again and again over the years. She had tasted it. She had felt its warmth and slimy texture covering every inch of her, inside and out. He had used it to ruin that bedroom for her.

Now she was soaked in it again, ruining this room in a world she wanted to keep separate, covered in bodily fluids and reeking of misdeeds. Now she could relish the feeling of release. She could enjoy the moments before everything fell apart. No more rooms would be ruined by this man.

She stepped over the leaking body that poured blood out onto the living room carpet now. Pouring out his bodily fluids like he did every time he came to see her.

Tom Leonard now released his bodily fluids on her for the final time.

# *49*

*Claremore, Oklahoma - Saturday - 8:15 PM*
Eight fifteen. She had forty five minutes to get to
the hotel and meet with Charles Langley. It would
only take about ten minutes to get there, assuming
she was able to control herself and not fly at the
speed of sound to get away from this place. She had
to remind herself to be calm. Her life depended on
it. Olivia's life depended on it. Abigail's life
depended on it.

Eight fifteen and ten minutes put her at the
hotel right around eight thirty. She might as well
start now. It could take a half an hour to get away
from Joseph.

"Honey," said Mindy, grabbing her purse
from the table and making her way to the living
room where Joseph was sitting in his chair. "I have
to get groceries. Do you need anything?"

Joseph grumbled slightly. "No." He didn't
even turn around to look at her. It made her hesitate.
That was too easy.

"I'll be right back."

All he did was grunt in return. That was
pretty typical, but she felt beads of sweat gather on
her forehead. A dull ache grew in her torn apart
back as she tensed. That had been way too easy.

Way too easy. She stopped at the door, watching him sit and stare at the TV like he didn't care where she was going. He always cared where she was going. That was part of his power trip. Why didn't he care now?

"Are you okay?" she asked him.

He grunted. She wasn't sure if it was a 'yes' grunt or a 'no' grunt, but she nodded to herself.

"You seem a bit off today. I'm just checking."

Silence from him. *What is going on?*

She had to get out of there. Once and for all. Images of the concrete wall of the garage, sprayed with blood filled her mind. She had to get to safety right now.

She made her way out the door and to her car, where she tried not to race away as fast as she could. Joseph's reaction had sent adrenaline coursing through her. Her pulse was racing, thumping in her ears. She had to maintain her calm, or Joseph would know something was wrong.

*If he didn't already know something was wrong!*

She took a deep breath as she pulled out of the driveway and down the street, allowing the car to propel itself and make a slow getaway. She had to stop torturing herself. The hotel was right across from the Walmart. All she had to do was make a quick trip to the grocery store to make her story believable, and then meet Charles at the hotel. She had a half an hour to get that done. After that, the whole thing wouldn't take more than a day. She didn't even have to come home tonight. She would stay in a different hotel. She would go to Tulsa, or somewhere in Missouri or Texas. She just had to wait this out. Then everything would change.

She just knew it. Her life would change forever.

* * *

Joseph waited until she had pulled out of the driveway, and looked up the location of the hotel he'd heard her talk about over the phone. The Holiday Inn Express, easy to find in a small town like this, sat across from the local Walmart. That was smart. A grocery trip made for a good excuse to get to that hotel. Either she was thinking deeply, or whoever she was meeting was a professional.

*The woman.* That tall, beefy woman that Abigail had described. She was older; she was a professional. She would have to be dealt with, too. One way, or the other, Joseph was going to have to take things very seriously moving forward.

He might have to put in some work and dispose of some bodies.

The Walmart was ten minutes from home, he knew that. The hotel was right across the street. A ten minute drive. He checked the clock. Eight thirty. She'd probably be at the Walmart right now, she would get groceries, and then meet whoever she was meeting. Another smart move on her part.

Charles and that bulky woman. It had to be their work. Mindy wasn't that smart.

It didn't matter who it was running things behind the scene. He knew where they'd be, and when they would be there. He stood up from his chair and grabbed the keys to his truck. He reached into his pocket and felt for his folding knife.

Tom Leonard had not come back last night. Not that he was supposed to, but he hadn't even sent a message or brought Abigail back. *He's soiling Charles's bed. He's soiling the apartment with her body.* It was enough to make him smile. Abigail would never leave home again. No one would. Joseph would be back in control.

Right now, though, he had to deal with Mindy, the betrayer of good husbands. She would be so surprised when he showed up to meet her at the hotel.

***

Mindy pulled into the hotel parking lot and exited the car. She hurried towards the lobby door as fast as she could, forgetting to check around her for followers. She hadn't seen Joseph's truck behind her on the way there, so she wasn't too worried about it. She did, however, want to get into the hotel and get this over with. If it took too long and she showed back up without groceries, Joseph would know she was sneaking around behind his back. Even if he didn't know she was talking to the police, Joseph was dangerous when provoked. He had abused both his daughter and hers throughout the past ten years she had been with him.

She stepped into the lobby of the hotel and checked in, taking a key card to her fourth floor room and trying to put as much distance between her and the ground as possible. This way, she could watch the window to see who was coming and have time to escape if Joseph showed up. She could relax if Charles and his friend came, and run if Joseph arrived. It was foolproof.

Up high in the room, she immediately pulled a chair over to the window and stared down into the parking lot, watching. She was so amped up, she could barely sit still at the window. Her hands fell to her lap, wringing together and straining the torn flesh and muscles in her back. This was it. She knew it.

Life was going to change forever.

***

Joseph jumped out of his truck and stared across the parking lot of the movie theatre, towards the Holiday Inn Express he had watched his wife enter. From this angle, he avoided being viewed from any of the windows on the front. Mindy would want a view of the hotel parking lot to watch for him or whoever she was meeting, so he would just stay to the side of the hotel to keep his advantage of surprise.

He moved casually, crossing the parking lot, the street, and the side lot to the hotel. He stepped onto the sidewalk and made his way around the wall to the front door, hugging the wall of the hotel. She would look further out, not this close to the building. She wouldn't be expecting him to come from the side.

He slipped in without ever being in view of any of the front windows, and approached the front desk. The clerk looked up at him and they exchanged friendly smiles.

"Hello," he said warmly, almost chuckling. "My wife checked in here just a little bit ago. She travels a lot for work and we don't get to see her very often. I thought I would surprise her. Her name is Mindy Smith."

His hand came forward with his driver's license, a twenty dollar bill tucked in his fingers behind it. "Here's my ID, so you know I'm actually her husband. Can you tell me what room she's in?"

***

Mindy took in every vehicle that passed by the building, whether it was on the road or in the parking lot. No Joseph. No red, square body, Chevy Silverado. She sighed, watching for Charles to come through the parking lot, not knowing if he was driving his own truck or the other woman's. She wondered if he would come through the parking lot at all. If he was trying to remain under the radar, he would probably sneak in a back door or a side door.

No, they would come along the back of the building, or the side, to avoid being seen.

That's exactly what she figured he'd done when she heard the knock at her hotel door. Her heart skipped a beat, and she leapt from her chair, barely noticing the two figures entering the parking lot from the far end outside of her window. She made her way to the door, coming to a strange realization as she reached for the handle.

If Charles could sneak around back unseen, why couldn't Joseph. Joseph drove the most memorable truck in history, one that stood out anywhere, but who's to say that he didn't just park in a different lot?

That was the moment she opened the door to let the boy in.

Except it was not the boy.

Standing at her hotel door, with a malicious smile on his face, was her husband, Joseph. Without waiting for an invitation, he pushed past her, stepped inside the room, and shut the door behind him. Her weak, fearful hands stripped away from the door handle with ease. She stepped back to get away from him, backing deep into the room and away from her only escape route left. Joseph followed right on her toes, reaching into his pocket as he faced her one last time.

"Hi, honey," he said softly. "We need to talk."

***

Charles crossed the road and entered the Holiday Inn parking lot, making his way to the front door from the back of the lot.

"I don't see him or the truck she described to us," said Alison. "That being said, I'll run a quick perimeter check and look for him around the sides and back. If I were him, I wouldn't park here in this lot. Too easy to be spotted."

"Copy that," said Charles as he filtered through the cars. "See you upstairs."

"Hey. If I'm not in the lobby when you go up to the room, don't answer the door for anyone. I'll text you when I have an all clear, and when I'm at the door. I won't knock."

"Okay," said Charles. "It'll take some time to set up the equipment. Do you want me to start the interview without you or…"

Something moved in front of Charles, and a loud crunch echoed in the parking lot. He stopped.

That noise, so real and juicy, made him look. He stared down at his feet, and at the thing lying there.

Trembling and twitching on the ground just a step further in front of him was the mangled body of Mindy Smith.

# **<u>50</u>**

*Tulsa, Oklahoma - Saturday - 8:30 PM*
*Shower, and a change of clothes.* That was all she needed to feel better. Wet hair draped over her bare back she slipped one of Charles's t-shirts over her head. His clothes felt fresh, good, and clean.

*Clean.* She was finally clean after all these years. Washing the blood of Tom Leonard off of herself for the final time.

She should have called the police. She should have taken care of the situation, but she didn't. A shower, and a change of clothes. It was amazing what something so simple could do for someone's sanity.

*Says the girl standing over a dead body right now.*

No, there was nothing sane about her right now. She should have called the cops. She should have gotten everything sorted out, but she didn't. She couldn't. She held that new power in her hands. She had killed the man that stole her innocence. She wanted to hold onto that.

She wanted to kill Joseph, too. Kill him, and rescue Olivia and her mother all at once. She wished she had a gun, but all Charles had was the knives in the kitchen.

*Gun. The safe.* That gun safe that Charles had. *He doesn't even like guns.*

She was in his closet before she knew what she was doing, sitting cross legged in the carpeted floor and staring strangely at the steel box standing above her. The towering menace stared back at her, taunting her with the numbers on the keypad.

*Try me.* It said to her in a voice that reminded her of Joseph, or Tom. *Try me, if you dare. Try me wrong enough times, and you'll never get in.*

Passwords could be anywhere between four and eight digits long for these things. A series of numbers between zero and nine, then hit the pound key.

Four to eight digits, and Charles was not a simple man.

He was still a man, though, and passwords came from deep within. A birthday? A phone number? His social security number?

What would she use if she was him?

She typed in zero-one-one-four. His birthday. Pound key; red light; three sharp beeps. Wrong code. Most locked items had three tries before locking for extended periods of time. Did she have the time to wait? Couldn't she just ask Charles? Tell him what happened, and help him— *help him*— for once instead of betraying him.

But he would tell her to call the police. He would give her the sane option, and she just couldn't do it. She was in trouble anyways, she might as well fight with the good guys to help her image. That was what Charles had done— tried to do— for Emily.

*Emily.* That was it. The birthday that Charles would use.

Zero-eight-two-two. Three sharp beeps, and that flashing red light again. Wrong answer again.

Then she sat up straight, the number blaring in her head like a neon sign. All the documents and news articles she had read about Charles ten years ago. His story. That night in Kansas City with his sister, and a pedophile. Why would he use it?

Because no one would suspect it.

Zero-six-one-four. The day that Charles had fought for– killed for– his beloved sister. The day his old life had ended, and his current path had opened to him.

Pound key. Two beeps. Green light. She reached up and turned the handle, and the door fell open almost by itself.

Her mouth gaped. Four stacks of hundred dollar bills, thick and barely held together with rubber bands, sat on the lowest shelf of the safe. Another small stack sat on top of one, only a few layers thick. Her best guess, with Charles as meticulous as he was? Just over forty thousand dollars in cash. Why did he have that much in cash? She knew he had other savings, but if he had this much just sitting here, how much did he have in other places?

The better question was, how had he gotten all of it in seven years?

Then her eye drifted up to the top shelf, where she saw the thin blue box that she recognized immediately.

A hard plastic pistol case.

She grabbed it, snapped open the latches, and lifted the top of the case. Inside, pressed deeply into thick, lumpy foam inserts, sat a shining, silver, wood gripped revolver. The engraving on the side said Smith and Wesson, .38 S&W SPL +P. She picked it up, and flipped it over. *Air weight.* Written on the side underneath the cylinder in cursive. Manufactured in Springfield, Massachusetts, Smith and Wesson USA.

*This is it.* She knew it now, her ticket to saving Olivia. Her solution to stopping Joseph once and for all. It didn't matter to her if Charles liked guns or not, she had everything she needed, including bail money if it came down to it.

It was foolproof. All she had to do was get down to Joseph's house, and take care of things. She had several hours to get it done. Her mom would be dealing with Charles and Alison. It would just be her, Olivia, and Joseph. After that, no one would convict her of anything.

She stood up, and removed the gun from the case, watching the small red tag dangle from the trigger guard. She hesitated, staring at the words written on the tag, and wondering why Charles would own *this* gun, much less any other gun.

**Evidence**
**Case number: 6021895**
**Item number: 3**
**Description of evidence: Smith and Wesson Model 642 .38 Special Revolver**
**Date: June 15, 2017**
**Agency: Kansas City Police Department**
**Type of Offense: Homicide**

# <u>*51*</u>

*Claremore, Oklahoma - Saturday - 9:00 PM*
Charles stumbled backwards several steps, dazed and disoriented by the sight in front of him. The silence around him was overpowering. There was nothing, not even crickets or birds. Nobody stood around them. He hesitated for a moment, and stepped forward again towards the body on the ground.

"Charles?" asked Alison in a quiet, horrified tone. Her voice quivered.

Charles took another step and looked down at Mindy's body. The fingers on her hands flickered and moved, but the rest of her body had given out. He knelt down next to her, and almost reached out to touch her. He stopped himself before he actually made physical contact, and withdrew his hand.

Mindy's eyes stared up at him, unchanged physically, but somehow void of life. It wasn't how people stared when they were alive. He wasn't sure what the change was in those eyes, but it was there. Emptiness.

"It's her," he muttered, his voice steady and soft. Alison grabbed his shoulder from behind and tried to pull him away. He didn't budge.

"Charles," she said quietly. "We need to call the police."

"I know," he said, unable to peel his eyes from the corpse in front of him. "Call them."

He heard Alison step away and begin a phone call, but he wasn't paying attention to her. He was focused on the body in front of him. Mindy.

She had a stab wound at the side of her neck. He could see the blood flowing from her throat, seeping steadily instead of pumping. *No heartbeat.* That was why she hadn't screamed on the way down. Whoever had killed her had disabled her voice. *Whoever had killed her.*

Who else would have killed her? There was only one person with means and motivation. Any way it happened, it was done. It could not be undone. Their second biggest lead has been taken out of the equation.

*Death.* He'd seen it before, caused it, even, but it made no difference. Seeing something horrible over and over again didn't make it easier to cope with. It just paralyzed the nervous system. It activated a survival mode without abstract thinking, and put the brain in focus on one thing only.

That one thing walked out of the hotel door and stopped dead in its tracks as Charles's brain zeroed in on it. Charles's back straightened, and his head perked up.

Joseph Smith stepped out of the hotel door and froze. He stared over at Charles with eyes that seemed to extend from their sockets, the eyelids peeling back as far as the muscles would allow them to. Charles remained knelt down beside Mindy's body.

"Charles," Alison's voice came from behind him. "We can't just leave a crime scene to chase him."

"He's going home to hurt the little girl." It was soft, barely audible, like the low growling of the stalking predator.

Joseph shrank at just the sound of it, the predator he had been just moments ago in the hotel room reverted to the terrified prey that he had chased over the years.

"I know," Alison said softly, sounding like she was trying to calm down a very angry tiger, "but we can't leave the crime scene. You know that. Don't worry about it. The police are on their way. They'll get him and the girl."

Charles did not move. Joseph did not move. Alison continued to talk to the police on the phone. Charles did not listen to Alison's conversation. All he cared about was protecting those that were still alive. *Olivia.* If she was still okay, Charles would be the only thing left to protect her. There was only one danger to her, and that man was standing right in front of Charles.

*The police won't get there in time. They never do. This time I will not fail. Protect the girls. Stop Joseph.*

If he acted fast enough, he wouldn't even have to leave the crime scene. There would be no collateral like last time.

All he had to do was act. *Act first. Act fast. Act fierce.*

*We aren't vigilantes.* Walter's voice, and Alison's voice, both saying the same thing. *That's not who we are.*

"Charles!" Alison called again, but it was too late. The tiger sprang.

Charles leapt to his feet, clearing Mindy's body and trying to close the space between himself and Joseph. Almost simultaneously, Joseph pushed from his legs and took off in the opposite direction towards the side of the hotel.

Alison screamed.

Charles wasted no time taking off after Joseph. Joseph sped along the sidewalk and around the corner of the hotel, toppling over two recycling bins to try and slow Charles down. Charles leapt over the bins, moments behind Joseph and already nearly within arms reach.

*I will not fail. Not this time.*

Charles's foot came down on a small pile of empty water bottles, and his confidence shook as his feet went out from under him. He tumbled to the ground, skidded a foot or so, and pushed up with his hands to regain his feet. His momentum and the burning sensation in his palms made him stumble, but his determination pushed him on anyway. He gathered his footing quickly as Joseph disappeared around the other corner of the building, moving at a surprising rate of speed for a man who could not have been in as good of shape as Charles.

Charles rounded the second corner to see an empty back lot. He looked behind the building into the weeds and saw no movement in the weeds, or swaying of the tall grass. He looked back at the building and saw a closing glass door along the back wall leading into the hotel. He made a run for it before it closed, and nearly smacked his face on the glass trying to beat it.

He wrenched the door open and sprinted inside. There were several people in the hall, mumbling and looking towards the front of the building, but Charles easily noticed the one that stood out. The only one running around a corner and into the front lobby like he was being chased.

Charles pushed through the crowd of people and followed Joseph around the hallway corner. Joseph was already heading out the front door again when Charles entered the lobby. He followed as quickly as he could, squeezing through the closing sliding doors before they could pick up that he was there to open again. He ignored another scream from Alison as he dashed into the parking lot and slipped through the parked cars. He could barely see Joseph's head above the stationary vehicles, but continued as fast as he could. Charles peeked over the top of a Honda sedan, and lost Joseph as he ducked behind a large pickup, moving to the left.

Charles dipped sideways in front of the pickup, and saw nothing on the other side of the truck. Charles dropped flat on the ground and looked under the vehicles, catching a quick glimpse of a pair of feet moving past the last parked car and exiting the parking lot to the side. He glanced in the direction of the movement. Joseph was headed towards the movie theatre across the street.

Of course he would have parked over there.

Charles climbed back to his feet just in time to see Joseph cross the street and into the movie theatre parking lot. Charles followed quickly, but hardly made it to the end of the hotel parking lot when he heard a truck engine roar to life.

He saw the truck fly through the exit of the theatre parking lot and race towards him. Straight towards him. The old square body Red Chevy Silverado that had haunted the streets of Claremore for so long was headed directly in Charles's direction.

Charles ducked back into the hotel parking lot as Joseph's truck hit the curb, bounced away from the grass, and skidded sideways back onto the pavement. The truck slowed for a split second, and Charles took the opportunity.

He jumped forward, reached up, and grabbed the bed of the truck at the corner of the tailgate. He swung himself up and into the truck bed just as Joseph hit the accelerator. The momentum of the truck lurching forward nearly yanked Charles's arms out of their sockets, but he had just enough time to push off the ground and cross the frame into the bed.

Charles tried to stand, but the truck swerved left and right violently. The motion tossed Charles back and forth and kept him from getting his feet under him. His head banged against a wheel well, filling his vision full of stars. He threw his arms up and curled them around his head to protect it from further impact.

He felt the truck accelerate, then brake hard. He was thrown towards the cab of the truck. His arms protected his head, but his unprotected arms felt like they shattered with the impact of the steel bed walls. The truck accelerated again, making a very hard left turn that threw Charles into a short barrel roll. He hit the steel side wall of the bed again, banging up his shoulder in the process. He groaned loudly with the impact.

*Enough of this. I'll die before we get to his house.*

The truck straightened out and began speeding down the road, the wind now roaring in Charles's ears. He tried to shake off the pain in his upper body and clear his head. If Joseph swerved again or hit a bump, the truck was moving fast enough to make Charles's evening a whole lot worse. He wasn't sure what the speed of the truck was, but he was definitely not comfortable being in the back of it like this.

He stood up and braced himself on the roof of the cab to break the glass with his knee, hoping he could get the job done without crippling himself.

Joseph hit the brakes, and made a sharp right turn.

With one foot off the bed of the truck, Charles was thrown off balance and went over the side of the bed. Soaring through the air for what felt like an eternity, he tumbled into the grass of someone's yard. The dirt and grass cushioned his fall, but the hedges he rolled into were not as kind to him. He struggled for much longer than he wanted to to get out of them, and moved back over to stand on the corner of the street. He saw the truck take off into the distance, and knew he'd lost the chase.

He let out a loud expletive. The thought of riding in the bed of the truck until Joseph parked it at the house and then beating Joseph up in his own driveway seemed somehow both satisfying and far too late of an idea. He might have been hurting or sore, but he would still be there. Olivia would have at least had a chance.

He remembered something. Something important. A series of numbers and a street name. *Joseph's address.* The one he'd gone to, and saved in his phone for future use. He started walking in the direction of the truck to save time, and drew his phone from his pocket, hoping it hadn't broken in his fall.

It hadn't, and opened his navigation app. He entered the address and hit the directions button. It brought up the route. He memorized the blocks and turns that were left on the route. It was only a mile and a half away. He sighed, rolled his eyes, and kicked out his legs a few times trying to catch his breath, shake off the pain, and warm up his legs.

**<u>52</u>**

*Claremore, Oklahoma - Saturday - 9:15 PM*
Abigail opened the door of the house and poked her head inside. Silence. The barrel of the revolver followed her head in, peeking around the corners just in case. She said nothing, and made no noise. All she did was listen.

There was nothing. The house was empty except for two people. Herself, and Olivia. *Foolproof. Get Olivia, and get out of here. Move!*

She glanced around, tip-toeing through the house to make sure it was empty. She kept the revolver close to her chest, and her finger on the trigger. She had to be ready for anything. It went into every room simultaneously with her head, and she checked every single room. The house was deserted. She was alone in the house with Olivia.

The thought came to her like a raging bull: Joseph followed Mindy to the hotel. He had to. The distraction of his wife sneaking around was the only thing that could have gotten him to leave the child at home. That meant Mindy was in danger. That meant Charles, and Alison, were in danger.

*Charles will protect her.* She thought. Even if that wasn't the case, this was Abigail's only chance. *Focus on Olivia, and get out of here.*

She rushed up the stairs and gave the locked bedroom door three of her hardest kicks to break it open.

*I have got to put on some weight. It worked for Alison.*

Inside, the little girl screamed and tried to leap up from the bed. Her left hand restrained her, the handcuffs attached to the bed frame holding her in place. Olivia looked up at Abigail as Abigail wasted no time running to the dresser, grabbing a set of clothes for the girl, and tossing them to Olivia. Abigail leapt over to the bed and grabbed the thin wooden pillar of the head board. Olivia stared up at Abigail, tears in her eyes and her mouth agape. Abigail made eye contact while placing a size nine combat boot against the pillar.

"We have to go, Sissy," she whispered down to the little girl. "We have to go somewhere safe. It's time. We have to hurry. Put those clothes on."

She pressed, snapping the tiny wooden stick with ease and freeing the little girl as well as she could. Olivia's hands fell free of the bed, the handcuffs hanging on to her wrist. Abigail slipped the revolver into the small of her back, and struggled to get the nasty diaper off of the little girl and slip the clean clothes over her body.

"I'm sorry, Olive," groaned Abigail as Olivia whimpered in pain with certain movements, the bruises and other unseen injuries restricting her movement. "We don't have time. We'll get you cleaned up at the police station."

"No!" cried Olivia. "Not the police!"

"The police will help," Abigail whispered. "They're going to protect you from Joseph. He'll never hurt you again."

Without another moment's hesitation Abigail wrapped her arms around Olivia's bone thin torso, and picked her up. Olivia squeezed Abigail's neck tightly, and Abigail felt her neck dampen.

"Thank you, Sissy," cried the little girl.

Abigail took one deep breath to keep herself from sobbing. *Stay strong, for her, and get out of here.* She spun around to leave.

That's when the front door came crashing open with a tremendous sound of splintering wood and fiberglass. She never saw anything, but she could hear it all.

"Abigail!" The primal scream came from the front of the house, and Abigail wasted no time. *Fight, flight, or freeze.* She couldn't fight with Olivia in her arms, and she couldn't afford to freeze.

She passed through the open bedroom door and across the hall into the bathroom before Joseph could make it to the stairs.

"Abigail! You little bitch! Where are you? I'll kill you! I'll kill both of you!"

She hid behind the door as Olivia squeezed her neck. She shushed the little girl as she heard footsteps stomping up the stairs.

"What are you doing?" Came the growl from the other side of the door. Abigail peeked through the crack in the door frame, seeing Joseph's outline storm through Olivia's bedroom door to find the empty room.

She yanked the bathroom door open and rushed out into the hallway. Joseph turned around to see her flying around the corner and starting down the stairs to the first floor.

In a rage, he let out one more terrifying scream and chased after her. Olivia screamed when she saw Joseph round the corner and start down the stairs towards them. Her grip tightened on Abigail's body. Abigail never turned around to look. She focused on her objective ahead of her. The kitchen, then to the left to the entryway and the front door.

The footsteps behind her were thumping louder and faster every moment as she made the left at the bottom of the stairs. She took two steps into the kitchen before she felt a sharp pain at the back of her head, a pain she'd felt so many times over the years from someone pulling her hair.

Her whole body lurched backwards as if she'd hit a wall. She felt Olivia fly from her grip as she fell backwards and landed flat on her back on the tile floor. She tried to look for Olivia, but found only a shaded mass that stood over her. Her head moved without her consent as the form moved around.

Joseph had a handful of her hair in one hand, the other tucked stealthily behind him, and stood over her. He knelt, revealing his opposite hand to her. It held his pocket knife.

"You should not have done that, Abigail," he growled, holding the knife to her face. "You shouldn't have run, and you shouldn't have fought. I'm going to make you regret it. No one will get here in time to save you."

*The gun!* She reached underneath herself, drawing the revolver and pulling the trigger the second the weapon came out of hiding. At this distance, it was too easy to fail.

She fired once, the shot flying wide of Joseph and up into the ceiling. A scream filled the kitchen as she fired again, her shot blocked by Joseph's elbow, which angled the gun away from himself. He swept along her arm as she pulled the trigger again, the third shot sending the gun off into the distance as his elbow knocked it out of her hand. She heard the rattle of the metal frame on the tile. Joseph reared upwards with the knife pointed down at her. She whimpered, trying to search for Olivia. Maybe she had gotten to safety. Her eyes glanced to her right to see the little girl cowering under the table. Abigail sobbed. She had to get the girl to run.

"Olivia." It was the only word that left her throat before Joseph's knife entered it.

# <u>53</u>

*Claremore, Oklahoma - Saturday - 9:30 PM*
Charles struggled to breathe as he came closer to the house. He ran every morning as a workout, but this had been on another level. This was more than a mile of sprinting. He slowed his pace as he approached the door, taking clear notice of the partially opened entrance and smashed frame of the door jam. He stepped up the driveway, watching the door and the windows for any movement.

He heard a scream from inside, the scream of a child in a state of sheer terror, and jumped for the door. He crossed the threshold and into the entryway, looking left and right for the source. The smell entered his nose before his eyes took in the scene. It was a smell he hadn't experienced in exactly a decade.

The mixture of gunpowder and blood.

To his left was the kitchen, and on the floor across from him was a body. Deep, black and red fluid puddled around the upper half of the body, and it twitched sporadically. He ran to the side of the body.

"Abigail," he muttered, finding the open wound on the girl's neck. It was a stab wound on the side that gushed blood. There was still the faint pump, meaning she had a heartbeat. What was he supposed to do now?

*Put pressure on the wound.*

He grabbed her throat, wrapping his fingers around the sides and pressing lightly on the injury. Was it enough? Neck injuries were touchy. Too much pressure would cut off circulation to the brain. Too little would cause her to bleed out. Finding that sweet spot was a chore, but all he needed to do was to keep her alive until help arrived.

Abigail's eyes met his eyes the second he knelt down beside her. Flooded and pouring tears, Abigail's eyes closed and she reached out with one hand to push him away. He reached down and took her hand in the hand that he wasn't using to keep her neck injury closed. She resisted for one single moment, then squeezed his hand back. It was a weak, dying squeeze.

"I'm sorry, Abigail," he whispered down to her. "I got here as fast as I could."

*I'm sorry, Emily. I didn't mean to.* The echo of his past filled the room, and brought a blurring coat of fluid to his vision.

She shook her head, unable to speak as she choked on her own blood.

A squeal came from the stairs to his right, and he turned to see Joseph standing at the base of the stairs with a young girl in his hand. The man halted as Charles shuffled his feet to spring up, and he stopped when he saw Joseph swing out a knife. The blade attached itself to the little girl's throat, where the sharp blade pressed lightly as a threat.

*You've done it. You've put them in more danger. This is your fault.*

The young girl was scrawny and pale. Her clothes, a crop top that barely covered her chest, and a pair of short shorts that looked more like spandex underwear, hung loosely on her body as she swung around in front of the man. Her eyes were wide, her chin high, and her body frozen with fear.

Joseph looked down at Charles, then to Abigail.

He smiled. "Well, look at that. I guess you've got a choice to make."

Charles felt Abigail's hand squeeze his again, but his eyes never left Joseph. He knew what she was doing. She was telling him silently to save Olivia. *That's what I would do. I'm dying, so save the girl and let me go. It's okay.*

*Abigail will die.* He couldn't let that happen either. Not one more person would die on his watch. Not today. Not in the name of Emily.

"I'm leaving," continued Joseph. "We're leaving. You can choose to try to follow us and save this little girl, or you can stay still and save your girlfriend. Oh, and you'll have to move quickly to get Olivia free, because the second you move, I'll kill her, too."

Joseph began to shuffle towards the door with Olivia in tow, and Charles stole a quick glance down at Abigail. What was he supposed to do? Kill the love of his life? *Kill her.* Not let her die. Removing his hand would be a choice, and that would make it murder, right? Should he let the little girl go and be in more danger?

Abigail's heartbeat was slowing down, and while Charles couldn't count the beats each second he was sure she didn't have long. He glanced at the knife in Joseph's hand. One wrong move, and Charles would be squeezing Olivia's throat to keep it from leaking as well, then fighting off a very angry, very desperate man.

Charles locked eyes with Joseph, causing the man to freeze in place again. Joseph had to know there wasn't much chance of saving Abigail, and knowing Charles was doing the math would keep him hesitating. If Charles could just stall for a little longer, the cops would show up. They had to. Alison had them on their way. All he had to do was say something, but what?

"Mr. Smith?" The voice came from the front door. A man's voice that gave Charles such a sense of relief that he resisted the urge to scream. His eyes stayed locked to Joseph, but Joseph turned to face the front door. The house fell silent except for the soft, weak choking sounds Abigail was still making.

Then, in the distance, Charles could hear the faint wails of police sirens. Backup had arrived, but there was still a knife against Olivia's throat, and his only living friend was bleeding out in his hands. That knife was still very skittish. One wrong move, and everything went wrong. One mishap, and the little girl they had worked so hard to save would be dead.

Charles was glad he wasn't the only one here, even if his backup was not the police.

***

Walter Faucet stepped into the kitchen, trying to take in as much information as he could as fast as he could. A man was standing on the right; a man he assumed was Joseph. Joseph had a little girl, most likely the trafficking victim by the looks of her, by the arm with a knife to her throat.

Joseph's eyes widened when he looked at Walter, understanding that his escape route had been blocked. He was a cornered rat in panic mode, claws ready to slice whatever they could get a hold of. *Desperate. Dangerous.*

On the left was Charles, kneeling in a growing pool of blood with a hand wrapped around another girl's neck. That had to be Abigail. The girlfriend. The one Walter had hated so much. Walter could see jets of dark fluid squeezing between Charles's clamped fingers. Her face puckered up in pain, her eyes alternating from squinting shut, to wide open.

He didn't hate her so much watching her die on the floor.

Charles's face was statuesque. He held a stare on Joseph with the look of an animal hunting his prey. His body stood frozen, his grip on Abigail tight, yet still ready to pounce if needed. Like a jaguar poised for the kill.

"Mr. Smith?" Walter asked again, returning his gaze to Joseph. "My name is Walter Faucet. I'm with the Red Sea Initiative. I'm just here to de-escalate before the authorities arrive, and everyone makes decisions that we all regret. I just need you to listen for a few minutes."

"I'm leaving," grumbled Joseph, looking around towards the back of the house. His exit was still mostly blocked by Walter standing in the entryway, the only access to the back hallway, but he looked nonetheless.

"Not yet," returned Walter. "Listen. The police are on their way. Do you hear the sirens? They're going to be here in just a few minutes. There is absolutely nothing you can do to escape them. The only two things you can do now are make things better, or make them worse, for yourself. If you kill that girl, it's straight to death row for you. If you let her go, you might get away with just a life sentence. If you cooperate, you might get less than that."

The last part was a lie, but he needed to get that knife away from the girl's throat and out of Joseph's hand. He needed to get Olivia and Joseph separated and detained.

"Double murder," muttered Joseph, looking down at Abigail. "Neglect and abuse? Trafficking? Bribery? I know what I've done, and I know what I can go to jail for. You're lying. There is nothing for me short of execution."

"That girl isn't dead yet," said Walter, glancing over at Charles. "My guy is keeping her alive. Then the EMTs will keep her alive also. Let's make things better, not worse."

Walter knew it was all a lie. Neck wounds didn't just go away, even with medical technology as advanced as it was. Joseph would likely get a life sentence at the very least. He glanced down at Charles and the now silent girl on the floor.

*Silent.* That meant dead, didn't it? Charles' expression hadn't changed, though. If the girl he loved was dead, he wasn't showing it to Joseph. He was still ready to attack at any moment, and now the police were on their way. The second that girl died, Charles Langley would be on Joseph to hurt or kill him. He had to stop that before it happened.

He turned back to Joseph. "What do you say, Joseph? Can we put that knife down?"

***

Abigail's pulse was weak, and definitely below thirty beats per minute. He didn't have to count to know that. Charles wasn't sure what to do. Walter was talking to Joseph and trying to get him to put down the knife, but Charles knew he still needed to be ready. If Joseph cut Olivia's throat, there would be just enough manpower to save her and restrain Joseph. Charles wasn't sure which he wanted more, to save the little girl, or to kill the man holding her.

The knife moved away from Olivia's throat, the hand holding it relaxed its grip, and Joseph's hand fell down to his side. The police sirens were getting louder. The loud wee-woos opened up from their muffled, distant cries to open shrieks. Charles watched the knife closely, just in case, his eyes switching from knife to Joseph's eyes and back constantly.

One heart beat thumped against his fingers, and he waited for the following beat. It didn't come. He couldn't tear his eyes away from Joseph's hand. He couldn't look down to see Abigail's eyes. The one thing he wanted to see. *Abigail.* He couldn't save her anymore. The only thing he could do now was save Olivia, but if he moved too soon, he could cause more harm than good. He'd already done so much of that.

Tires screeched to a halt outside. Sirens blared to an earsplitting volume. Flashes of red and blue shone through the windows on the front of the house.

"Sissy?" Olivia stared at Abigail's body.

*She called her Sissy. Emily.* Now Abigail was dead, and Olivia knew it. *One more life to save. I will not fail.*

But he had failed. Abigail had no pulse. Joseph looked down at Charles, and Charles kept his fingers pressed on Abigail's neck. Walter had said something about Abigail surviving. Joseph had to believe Abigail was still alive.

Car doors slammed shut outside as the sirens went quiet. The sounds of men shouting and boots stomping across the yard penetrated the quiet house. Shadows danced on the walls across from the windows, playing in the patriotic red and blue light show.

Charles looked up to Joseph's eyes again, and he saw Joseph staring at Abigail's face. Joseph's eyes widened again.

*He knows!* Charles looked back down at the knife just in time to see the fist gradually clench down on the grip again. The boots outside drew nearer to the front door. The crunching of dirt and grass changed to rubber soles on wood and tile.

"Police!" The boots hit the floor of the house as the cops rolled in. Joseph screamed in terror, and the knife reached up into the air. Walter shouted. The police officers shouted. Charles's feet propelled him into the air; his arms outstretched towards Joseph as the knife came down.

Charles felt a sharp pain in his left palm as his right hand connected to Joseph's face, a palm strike right under the nose. It knocked Olivia free of Joseph's grip, and dropped Joseph on his back. A shout came from behind Charles, and then a loud, popping noise. Charles felt a hot, searing pain in the back of his right calf. He screamed as he fell to the floor on top of Joseph and rolled to the side, the knife now sticking out of his left hand.

In another moment Walter was by his side, his hands on Charles's leg and asking questions that Charles couldn't understand. Charles saw the police move in on Joseph, shouting and manhandling him all over the floor as he writhed to get away. Blood flowed from a crooked nose, bent for the second time it seemed, and wild, animal eyes jumped around the room.

Then those eyes locked onto Charles, and the two of them held eye contact. A mean, enraged stare met Charles' view, teeth bared in a predatory snarl. Charles saw Joseph's lips move.

"I'll kill you." Everyone glanced between the two men, watching for a reaction from Charles.

Charles just shrugged. "Not from your current position, you won't."

# <u>*54*</u>

*Claremore, Oklahoma - 10:00 PM*
Outside of the house, Charles was laid on a gurney, and the EMTs worked on him. His leg and hand were packed and wrapped to the best of the poor EMT's experience because Charles refused to go to the hospital for actual surgery. He wanted to remain at the scene with Walter and Alison. He wanted to be a part of the action.

*All that waiting, and here we are.*

"The abuse of children will never be tolerated or go unpunished." Paul Edwards was telling a reporter who had shown up on the scene. "The years of abuse the victim suffered at the hands of those she should have been able to trust is both heartbreaking and unconscionable. My office in Tulsa and our law enforcement partners here in Claremore are committed to prosecuting perpetrators of child abuse."

Walter wrapped up a phone call, walked up to the gurney that Charles was laid out on, and put his phone back in his pocket. He was shaking his head. Alison joined them from Charles's left, placing a hand on the gurney to hold herself up. Charles almost flinched, expecting a punch that could knock an elephant on its ass.

"She weighs forty one pounds," Walter sighed to Charles. "They're going to hospitalize her to treat malnutrition and several infections from open wounds. I'll let your imagination run on where those wounds are."

"What about Joseph?" asked Alison.

"He won't shut up," replied Walter. "He just keeps confessing to things. Wants to get the plea deal to avoid the death sentence. Supposedly, he and his wife routinely denied the girl food and access to the bathroom, handcuffed her to a pack n' play, and beat her with a belt and a livestock whip. He also forced her to work outside moving rocks and dirt with her hands, pulling weeds, and picking up sticks for several hours at a time before selling her for sex. Ask me why she was handcuffed to the pack n' play."

"Why was she handcuffed to the pack n play?" asked Charles, unsure if he really wanted to know the answer.

"From her own mouth," started Walter. "She was hungry and used to sneak out for food in the middle of the night. She got caught, and they handcuffed her. Stripped her of her clothes, and put a diaper on her."

"Doesn't get much worse than that," mumbled Charles, thinking of sitting in that tiny hotel room and waiting for an interview that never happened.

Walter stared at Charles. "He also says he sent that police chief, Tom Leonard, out to your apartment last night to take care of Abigail. I had my guys run out there and check, and they found him in your living room with a stab wound in his neck big enough to stuff a whole beach towel in. Looks like he broke in through the sliding glass door, then she took him out, and came here to finish things out in style."

"The sliding door?" asked Charles. "I live on the second floor."

"You've never climbed the railings at an apartment complex?" asked Paul Edwards.

"I can't say that I have," replied Charles. "What about the Judge?"

"He's confessing as we speak," replied Alison. "Joseph gave us enough to bring him in, and he's ratting everyone out just trying to get a plea deal."

Charles glanced back at the house. Coroners were wheeling out another gurney with a body bag on it.

*Abigail.*

"You aren't going to believe this," said Paul Edwards, approaching the three of them. "Joseph gave up the guy that broke Jimmy's arm. Jackie Brannigan. Mid thirties, average height, average build, dark haired?"

"That's the guy," said Walter.

"That's also half the guys in the United States," said Alison.

"Joseph said he's laid low outside of town," continued Paul. "He's been hiding in an RV in a campsite on the north shoreline of Oologah Lake. Joseph says he had the guy break Jimmy's arm to shut down our operation and allow them all to escape."

"Chief!" called a police officer, walking up to Paul Edwards. "Check this out."

He held out a plastic bag with a shining object in it. Charles saw the red tag attached to it, and his breath caught in his throat.

*She always asked about the gun safe. How did she get the passcode?*

"What is it?" asked Paul Edwards.

"It's mine." Charles tried to sit up, and Alison put a hand on his shoulder to press him down. "She must have taken it from my apartment."

"This tag is way outdated," said Paul. "This thing is from ten years ago. It's a homicide tag. Where did you get it?"

"It's mine. It's from my case in Kansas City."

"Why do you have it?" asked Alison. "You don't like guns, and I can't imagine you like that one any better."

Charles sat quietly for a moment. "I'm not sure. It was a daily reminder of my failure, and a motivator to do better moving forward. It was the only thing I had left of Emily, so I kept it even though the memory was negative."

Paul looked at him. "We have to keep it. It's now evidence in this crime."

Charles stared at the revolver, thinking about Abigail rampaging into the house with it and attacking Joseph.

*I missed her by so little a margin. I could have saved her. Why didn't I just make the drive back to Tulsa? It's only a half of an hour. I could have been there to back her up, and get this settled before the meeting at the hotel. I could have…*

Charles shook his head. "No. Keep it. It's caused me too much trouble."

The gurney with the body bag rolled by him, and he stared at it. *Abigail.* She was there, just out of view, hidden in the place she could never come back from.

"We shouldn't have waited."

"Why not?" asked Walter.

"Two of the people we wanted to protect are dead," replied Charles. "One more is dead, even though he was the bad guy. We waited so that we could save everyone's lives. We should have just kicked in the door and taken him this morning."

"Hindsight is generally better than foresight," said Walter. "Besides, it's always better to take precautions."

"It usually takes a day or two to get a warrant," said Alison. She rolled her eyes. "Government efficiency."

"Waiting." Charles thought about the night Emily had been taken. Waiting would have hurt her, also. There was just no way to win. "All it's ever gotten me is death and pain."

Walter almost chuckled. "'The jackal was born in August, the rains came in September. He said a more dreadful flood, I surely cannot remember.'"

"What?" Charles looked up confused.

"*The Jungle Book*," said Walter. "Rudyard Kipling. There's a story about a crocodile that says good things come to those that wait. An annoying jackal responds that all waiting does is get him punishment. The crocodile responds with that little rhyme."

"Thanks for calling me annoying," sighed Charles.

"What I mean," continued Walter as Alison stifled a small giggle, "is that you've not been around the block long enough. Paul knows the value of waiting, Alison knows the value of waiting, and so do I. You will, too, if you stick around long enough. We've been doing this for more than ten years now. Trust us, and trust the process. Speaking in general terms, our process works. We'll get you healed up and put together in a team. Once everything settles, you'll be killing it like Alison here."

Alison glared, and Charles stared at the ground.

"How did you know to come?" asked Charles.

"Alison called," said Walter. "The second you took off after Joseph, she got a hold of me and got me down here. I turned my hazard lights on and made record time."

Charles sighed and glanced over at the police car with Joseph in it. The man was twitching like a crackhead and talking rapidly. One thing didn't make sense. He thought about the young girl at the restaurant. He thought about that change in himself, the move from those older women, the MILF category, to the young girls. The real girls, the fresh girls. *Why?*

"Why did he switch?" asked Charles, looking up at Walter and Alison.

"Switch?" asked Walter.

"To sex? She was working in the yard, and he switched to prostitution instead. Why?"

"Money," said Alison. "Why else?"

"I think everyone is more concerned about the what than the why," said Walter.

Charles held out a hand. "Take me to him. I'll ask."

"You're going to stay right there," laughed Alison. "Let the cops do their job."

"I will," said Charles. "Help me over there so I can ask him myself. I want to know how these people think."

Alison waited a moment, exchanging glances with Walter before spinning the gurney around and wheeling it towards the police car where Joseph was being held. The police officer put out a hand to stop them, but Charles interrupted him.

"I would like to ask him a question. Just one. No other issues."

The police officer looked back at Paul Edwards, who was taking down statements on a notepad. Paul looked up at Charles and shrugged his shoulders.

"The kid's put in more effort and taken more damage than any of us," he said, stepping back. "Let him ask."

The police officer stepped aside and Alison wheeled Charles over to the open door where Joseph was sitting in the back seat. His hands were cuffed behind his back, and his face had gone from rageful to defeated. He turned his head to look at Charles, and sighed with a loud and exhausted groan. He looked back into the cabin of the police car, avoiding eye contact with Charles.

"What do *you* want?" he grumbled, emphasizing the word you.

"I have to know something," said Charles, leaning forward on the gurney to get closer. A sharp burn in his leg only allowed him so much room to move.

"What?" Joseph sighed.

"Why?"

"Why what?"

"Why did you get into underage sex?" asked Charles.

Joseph looked back to Charles, raising one eyebrow. "That's your question?"

Charles nodded, the movement barely noticeable even to himself. "It is."

"It started back when I was twelve years old," said Joseph, shaking his head again. He turned his body to hang his legs out of the patrol car, and when Paul Edwards and his officers tried to stop him Charles held out a hand for him to continue. "I remember picking up a playboy magazine. I was with my mom at a hardware store or something, and she was busy doing something else, so I went to look at the nudie magazines. Those women lit my insides on fire, as well as my outsides. That was when I discovered what pleasure was. Then came the Internet. I remember the old photoshopped photos of my favorite celebrities. After a while, the effect wore off. I couldn't get my fix anymore. I had to have the motion and the sound, so I switched to videos. After a while, that got old. Two adults weren't enough. I got into the more exotic stuff. Threesomes, orgies, and anal. After a while, I couldn't get off anymore. I went through every category I could find. Asian, Black, MILF, Specialty. None of it kept me hooked for long. That was my problem, though. When I started, every girl was well over my age. So I was hooked in the MILF category forever. All of my girls were older."

*When I started, every girl was well over my age. I was hooked on the MILF category.* He watched himself, sitting in a jail cell, conjuring images of his own older women.

Joseph's eyes shifted back and forth from Charles to the others, and then to the ground. "After a while, I couldn't get off to the older women. I searched, and searched. Finally, I found myself buried in the 'barely legal' category. That was before all of this political correctness started going around. Now they just call it the 'teen' category."

Charles's eyes widened. The bookmarked tab on his phone. The category was so good he had deleted all the other bookmarks. He had started in the MILF category, and gone to the Teen category. The first night Abigail had teased him and ran off. Alone in the shower, hiding from the pain of the memory of Emily.

"After a while even that didn't get me off," continued Joseph. "I dug deeper into the Internet, the dark web, and I found my fix in sixteen year old girls. After a while it was fourteen year olds, then twelve."

*Fourteen.* That girl at the restaurant. *No.* It was too similar. Charles could feel his hands trembling.

"Soon, the videos quit working for me. I had to get a real fix. I just had to have the real thing. Then I realized that there was a six year old in my house, and she resembled her mother very closely. So I had my fix."

Charles's stomach was in knots. Visions of the beautiful fourteen year old girl entered his mind, the burning sensation becoming a confused battle of desire and rage. *It's like looking in a mirror.*

"Then I realized that I wasn't the only person that needed a fix," continued Joseph, "and a lot of guys would pay for her if I wanted to make money. I joined an underground community of guys that would like a turn with her, and started to sell her services to them."

Charles reached back and patted Alison's hand. His own hands trembled. "I'm done, take me away."

She did. Joseph furrowed his eyebrows and continued his story to the police. Alison rolled Charles quickly back to the ambulance, where another EMT took his vitals to make sure he was still okay. Charles tried to wave him off, but the man was persistent.

*BP = 175/100*
*BPM = 125*
*BO = 94%*

*Have I become my father?* He asked himself, watching the numbers jump like they had a week ago at the hospital. *Or have I become Joseph?*

"It's an addiction, Charles," said Alison. "They all say the same thing, and just like all addictions, it just gets worse as time passes. You get numb and need more, and it escalates."

She tilted her head, looking into his eyes. "Are you good? You look a little spooked. I know it's kind of disturbing the first time you hear it."

What would happen to him if he continued doing what he was doing? What if he kept slipping down the same path that Joseph had started down? Those young girls on his phone would turn into younger, and real teenage girls. Where would he end up? Especially if he was working with these kinds of people all the time, exposed to evil. Would it tempt him? Would he be able to resist?

He looked up at Alison. She was staring at him. That little girl inside of her, the one that still survived through all the pain and trauma, stared back at him. He knew the look. He'd seen it growing up. *Emily.* When was the last time someone had cared for him? His father making up for lost time? Abigail trying to make things right? His mother? Hadn't they all been doing things for him to satisfy their own guilt? What had anyone really done for him?

Alison was all he had left. He had a problem. He needed help.

"I have that addiction," started Charles. "I need help with it."

"What kind of addiction?" asked Alison, almost as if she hadn't quite understood. "Drugs? Alcohol?"

He took a deep breath, and let it out slowly. "Jail doesn't allow much opportunity for a guy to pursue his hobbies. There's only a couple of things to do there. You can read, which I did plenty of, and you can…"

Alison nodded. "What guys do when they're alone and bored?"

"And depressed," added Charles, looking up. "It makes a good substitute when you don't have access to drugs and alcohol."

"It's a problem?" asked Alison.

"I started in the MILF category," said Charles. "Then, just a couple of days ago, that wasn't doing anything for me. I found myself in the Teen category. It's all legal girls, but they looked young. Then, the other day at the restaurant, you were listening in on the conversation of the teenage girl. Before you mentioned it, I was starting to feel… I felt different after you mentioned her age, but it was still there. It was still prevalent. When Joseph told his story, it resonated with me. I saw my escapism and my… addiction. I saw that I was just doing it because I was bored, or I needed to get away from what was bothering me. I was using it like a drug."

He shook his head, sighing deeply again before looking back up at her.

"I don't want to follow that path," he muttered, choking back a tear. "I want to be the good guy, not the villain. I need help."

Alison put an arm around his shoulder and pulled him close. His head fell softly against her ribs as she rubbed his arm up and down, holding him closely. He felt her warmth, he felt her affectionate touch; he felt *Her.* The real her. The one that wanted to love, care, and nurture, but couldn't figure out how.

She was figuring it out now.

"You're one of us," she said as she stepped back. "Walter will get the funding to get you help, and you'll get better. I promise. I know what recovery is like. I'll be here, by your side, to help you the whole way."

# *<u>Epilogue</u>*

*Dallas, Texas - Friday - 9:45 AM*
The headquarters building for The Red Sea Initiative was not a large building. With three board members, most doubling as other officers of the NGO, a fourth that was the President, and a single secretary, there were less than ten offices and one conference room.

Walter knew the building like the back of his hand. The glass door in front opened into the lobby, where Stella Martinez, the clerk and secretary, always waved and asked him how his day was going. Today, his response was no different than all the other times he had to come in.

"It'll be better after this." He was only ever here to deal with the board of directors, so his days here at the office weren't often positive.

The door to the right of the clerk's desk opened up to a thin hallway barely large enough for two people to pass through simultaneously, where the offices lined the walls. Walter counted them. Four on each side. His office was the first on the left, but he was not going in there. He would be lucky if he wouldn't be cleaning it out and going home permanently. He was here to go into the conference room at the end of the hallway, and have a meeting with the three members of the board of directors.

The door to the conference room was the fanciest door in the building. A set of glass french doors that opened up into the large room, where Walter found the three board members sitting at the end of a small meeting table to his left. All three of them met his eyes when he walked in, staring up at him through thick lenses and all three of them missing the typical smug looks they usually had on their faces. Instead, they looked content, or even happy.

"You wanted to see me?" he asked, standing at the end of the table opposite from them. None of them spoke for a while. They all exchanged quick glances.

*Here it comes,* he thought to himself.

"The three of us have come to a decision," said Mark Atwell, whom Jimmy Limone always described as The Bony Man. Walter, again, had to resist the urge to roll his eyes. *Just stay calm.*

"You are reckless," said Tony Mullarky, the shorter chubby man across the table from Mark. "You are impulsive, and you are quick to jump the gun."

"I haven't fired a gun in a long time," retorted Walter with a smile. That smile vanished as he thought of Charles Langley keeping that revolver, only having fired it once in his life. *The only time he ever fired a gun in his life.*

Walter looked to the head of the table, where the old woman was sitting and staring at him.

"Marie, I see you finally got the glasses you needed."

"My son can be quite convincing," said Marie Edwards, smiling over at him. "Which is why we've decided to keep you on with the Red Sea Initiative. Paul came down for a visit and told me all about the way you and the new boy handled things up in Claremore. I have to say, for a man with no experience, I'm rather impressed with his performance."

"I am, too," started Walter. "That's why I brought him in in the first place. He needs guidance, but he seems to think he has no other purpose in life. He seems to think that we are his home, and that this is his calling. He's passionate, and dedicated. Most importantly he's motivated to do the right thing. I think he'll make a great operator."

"Your judgment is a little weird," said Tony, "but it never seems to be wrong. You always end up on the right side of things."

"As always," said Marie, "we're glad you're a part of this organization. Without you, our reputation would be synonymous with Congress."

Walter shook his head. "God forbid."

"There are a lot of organizations that do what we do," said Mark. "We're the highest in donation income because of news stories like this one."

"And our marketing team," interrupted Walter. "You can't forget about that."

"Yes," chuckled Tony. "Miss Martinez is wonderful at everything she does for us here in the US."

"You should give her a raise." Walter turned to look back through the glass and down the hallway, unable to see Stella.

"We haven't met him yet," said Mark. "The new kid. Are you hiding him from us?"

*Why, yes I am.*

"He's requested some assistance while we train him," said Walter. "On top of the standard psychological assessment program we do, we'll also be providing one on one therapy sessions to handle some trauma, and an addiction he's struggling with."

"What addiction is that?" asked Marie.

"Does it matter?" asked Walter. "It's an addiction, and we'll get it treated. He'll get better, we'll put him through training, and we'll get him out in the field. Six months, tops."

"You said we're providing extra therapy," said Tony. "Is that the organization providing funds for it?"

"I didn't think you guys would pass the resolution," replied Walter. "So I've provided it through private parties."

"You're paying for it yourself?" asked Marie.

"We held our own fundraiser," said Walter with a malicious smile. "I was there personally. We raised enough to provide six months of treatment. You were right. I am key in those events."

***

The facility here in Dallas, was one of the few places in the United States that focused on treating sex addiction, whether it was a simple porn addiction or a full blown couple's affair with marriage counseling. Walter had arranged for Charles's treatment, keeping the pressure off of Charles and allowing Charles to start clearing his mind.

Eight days. He'd gone eight days without visiting a website. He was eight days from finding one of those young girls on the internet to… satisfy himself to. He was fidgety, and a little agitated, but he felt better overall. He felt clean.

Alison drove him here. She hadn't said much the whole time, but it had still been nice to have the company. Someone he trusted. Someone he was starting to care about. Someone he knew, especially now, cared about him. A new family. Not an escape, but a refuge. *Support.*

When the car pulled up to the front of the facility for Charles's first counseling appointment, he smiled at the people waiting in the parking lot for him. Walter, and his daughter. A new family. *Support.*

Charles exited the car and began his approach to the awaiting friends, but was quickly cut short by a missile. It was an eight year old missile that caught him completely off guard and showed no concern for the limp in his leg. She moved so fast he never saw her coming. She jumped onto him, all the way up to his neck and shoulders, and he did his best to grab her in his arms and hold her up. She was heavy, or he wasn't as strong as he thought he was. Either way his leg wouldn't support the action, and he was forced to drop to one knee.

"Thank you," she whispered in his ear. "Thank you for saving me."

"You're welcome." He laughed, trying to put her down. She wrapped her arms around his neck and held on tight.

"Can I call you Charlie?" she asked, finally backing off. A moment of pain lurched in his stomach as he thought of Emily. The only person allowed to call him that. Not just the name, though. It was the girl that made him think of her.

Because it was Emily standing in front of him.

This little girl, Walter Faucet's daughter, resembled Emily in every single sense. The soft, smooth blonde hair, the hypnotizing blue eyes, the beaming smile that could infect others and lift their spirits.

He nodded. This girl was extra special, just like Emily. She was Emily.

"You can, but you're the only one who can. What can I call you?"

The little girl looked back up at her dad with a smug look, and returned her attention to Charles with bright eyes. "Kitty."

Charles saw Walter shake his head with a silent chuckle. Charles stood up from the little girl, shaking hands with Walter, who looked sternly into Charles's eyes.

"Charles," he said firmly. "I want you to know that when you get done with your treatment, you have a spot waiting for you with the Red Sea Initiative."

Charles nodded.

"Until we can put you in the field," Walter continued, "you can help us with some basic fundraising and get back to your training. You can take part in some of the big educational events, and do some educating yourself. You can even tell a personal story relating to how you feel about your own problem. Then there's one more thing."

Walter raised his chin, using it to point over Charles's shoulder. Charles turned to see a Transit Van in a parking spot near Alison's car open its doors. Four people got out. Jimmy, his arm sling shed and his demeanor pleasant, both of the Swift sisters, bright eyed and bushy tailed, and a little girl.

But it wasn't just any little girl.

It was *the* little girl. Olivia.

She was being pushed in a wheelchair by one of the women. She was barely recognizable from a week ago. She had been cleaned up and had gained a little bit of weight. Her eyes weren't as sunken into her face. The expression on her face had gone from defeated and depressed, to joyous and excited. She didn't look scared anymore. Without her tormentor, or a knife held to her throat, she seemed somehow free. She didn't exactly look happy, but she did look happy to see Charles.

Charles nodded at each of them as they all smiled at him, but his concern was with the little girl. *The* little girl. The only remnant of the events of Claremore. The only one of the Smith's left alive and free. Olivia.

She was smiling. Really smiling. A smile that a child should have. A happy smile. A genuine smile, and it was directed at him. Behind those eyes was pain and terror, but it was tucked away for another time; for therapy; for recovery. It was enough to know he had been a part of that.

She stood up from her wheelchair, wobbling at the knees. Kitty ran over and grabbed Olivia, supporting her under the shoulder and helping her walk over to Charles. Charles glanced over at Walter, who nodded back at him with tears in his eyes. Raising good children was the best way to build a good world, and through all the turmoil, Walter was doing a decent job of it.

*Thank God for Katie Swift.*

This missile did not impact as hard with him physically, but he felt it on a deeper level than just the surface. He felt the weakness in her arms strain for grip on him. He felt her skeletal frame, still malnourished almost a week later. More importantly, however, what he felt was relief. He felt her let out a deep and satisfied sigh when she grabbed him. He felt the tension leave her body. He saw her shoulders drop. He felt wetness on his shirt.

He wrapped his arms around her. Gently; tenderly. She was still fragile, but he held her. He supported her. He made her feel safe. He fought through the pain in his leg to hold her up. It was the least he could do in her current situation.

"Thank you." It was barely a whisper, but he heard it. It made him smile. He ran a hand up and down her back to comfort her, unable to come up with the words to respond. He couldn't seem to get sound past the large lump in his throat.

"She tried to protect me," whispered Olivia. "Sissy. She did everything she could. She even shot a gun at him."

The little girl was crying now. She was sniffling and poofing with her breath. "Joseph said she had tried to send me to jail. He said she tried to betray me, but she was saving me when he…"

"I know," Charles whispered back, "she wanted nothing more than to save you. It's all she talked about when she escaped. She got all of us involved. She got you out of there."

*She gave her life for this.* Abigail, the one that had suffered for years, at home and on a military base, tortured by everyone around her. Abigail, the one who was okay now. She didn't have to feel, she didn't have to worry.

He thought about the words Alison had spoken to him a week ago. *I hope you get to feel that when this is over. I hope you get to see the little girl recover. Once you feel that, you'll never leave this job. Not for money, or love, or anything else. That feeling saps all those negative emotions out of you and makes you want to keep moving on.*

Kitty helped Olivia back to her wheelchair, and Alison stepped up in front of him.

"I want you on my team," she said. "You did good. It got out of hand, and you handled yourself and got the job done. Those that aren't alive, were completely out of your control. You did everything you could do given the circumstances. You work with us, and we'll make you unstoppable, and you won't be the only man on the team if Jimmy sticks around."

Jimmy threw up a hand. "If not me, then who?"

"Did you come up with that yourself?" asked Walter.

"Travis Manion," replied Alison. "Marine corps lieutenant."

"I thought it sounded very like a military quote," chuckled Jimmy.

Charles made eye contact with Alison, noticing the glint of hope in the deep brown irises. "If not us, then who?"

She pulled him in and hugged him. Tightly. Tighter than anyone had hugged him before. He could feel the muscle definition in her arms pull him close, squeezing the life out of him. He felt warmth seep from her body to his, and he felt a sense of caring beyond that of anyone.

"You have a place here," she whispered to him. "You have a home here. You have a family here."

*I just don't know how.* Now he had helped her learn to love. Love like she loved Walter, or Kitty, or the rest of the team. Not just an escape. Not just a distraction. A home. A family. *Support.*

*I will not cry. I will not cry. I will not cry.* The mantra repeated itself in his head over and over again.

It did not work. The other female voice in his head made it impossible. The image of a sister that stood in front of him, young and fresh, alive and well.

*You did good, bubba. I'm proud of you.*

At least one tear made it out of each of his eyes. He backed up from Alison, who patted him on the shoulder and let him turn to walk away. He saw Walter, wide eyed and staring at Alison.

"He gets hugs?" Walter asked, his mind apparently blown.

Alison winked at Charles. "He's my favorite."

*I did what I wanted to.* He thought to himself. *I helped her know how to love.*

Charles had to look away. He focused on the gates ahead. He focused on the task at hand. The future would come soon enough, more missions, and more children, but in order for him to get there, he had to get through this. He had to get better. He had to get right. He would not allow himself to fall down the path that Joseph had gone. The path that so many other monsters were going down.

*People.* They were people, not monsters. He knew that now. They were hurting, they were lonely, or they were trying to cope. They came from horrible backgrounds full of bad things and trauma. They came from addictive personalities, and they came from everywhere else.

They were people. That was all. They were sick, just like he was, but they were still people. All they had to do was follow the path he was on. Regular people, coming from all sorts of lives and backgrounds, tormented by whatever ailed them. All they had to do was get better. There were places like this to get help. It was always there. There was always someone to talk to.

*He* would get better. *He* would get right. He was lost, he had been lost for a long time, but that was okay. He would be found again. Without Emily, or anyone else, to help him. He had found a place. He had found a purpose.

He was lost, but he would find himself.